WAIT FOR THE WHISTLE

Hywel Lewis
MBE

WAIT FOR
THE WHISTLE

HYWEL LEWIS

Matador
9 Priory Business Park
Kibworth Beauchamp
Leicestershire LE8 0RX, UK
Tel: (+44) 116 279 2299
Email: books@troubador.co.uk
Web: www.troubador.co.uk/matador

ISBN 978 1784622 602

British Library Cataloguing in Publication Data.
A catalogue record for this book is available from the British Library.

Printed and bound in the UK by TJ International, Padstow, Cornwall
Typeset in Garamond by Troubador Publishing Ltd

Matador is an imprint of Troubador Publishing Ltd

In remembrance of 1996 Private John Robert 'Taff' Nicholls, 11th Infantry Battalion Australian Imperial Force, whose portrait used to hang on the wall over the dining table in my grandma's house and now hangs above my desk. Great Uncle John gave his life for his comrades and his adopted homeland on 21st August 1916 during an attack on Mouquet Farm, Pozières, Somme. He is commemorated on the memorial wall at Villers-Bretonneux with those who have no known resting place.

CHAPTER ONE

April 1914

Bryn lay still, his eyes closed. The grunting, heaving and moaning had been obliterated. He breathed in hard and a thin trail of liquid seeped between his lips and trickled into his nose. His face was pressed deep into the quagmire. He felt a sudden surge of panic. *I could drown here*, he thought as the malevolent mud slowly enveloped his body and he was pressed deeper into the earth. He was powerless to move, weighed down by the bodies that lay on top of him. They were his friends; they meant him no harm.

He was sodden; the glutinous mud had penetrated every fibre of his torn kit, which barely clothed his bruised and bloodied body. His relief was the warmth of the bodies that lay heaped across his back. At least they had blotted out the freezing rain that had been driving into his face since the shrill of the whistle.

The ground that had once been luscious green meadow, that had been painstakingly mowed and tended by a local farmer, was now a patchwork of brown and green. The pitted surface was like a saturated sponge, swollen with water and mud from the recent rain. Dotted around the quagmire were islands of green grass that lay untouched by the carnage that had unfolded across the area.

Bryn was a young man; his life had been short but he had maturity well beyond his years. He was not the sentimental sort but he knew that what he had achieved would become folklore. He felt elation, not just for himself – his friends had given their all in equal measure. He was happy to savour the silence but hands were already grabbing him, pulling and tugging, yanking him off the ground. He looked down to be sure that there was a white line.

It was indistinguishable in the mud but he knew that it was there. Bryn Tallent had crossed the line, the ball clutched to his chest – a try, a winning try!

As he trotted back towards the centre line Bryn allowed himself a wry smile. He was almost embarrassed, but equally as happy to accept a few pats on the back from his teammates. As he did so, Davies the Fly Half dug his heel into the mud to form a small kicking mound. It was a bit of a formality as there was no time to restart the match, but fair play meant that an attempt at the conversion had to be made.

He stepped back from the ball, inhaled deeply and settled his breathing. The Fly Half rocked on his heels and traced the line of the kick towards the crossbar with his eyes. He took just two short paces forward and struck the ball squarely, allowing his right leg to follow through. The ball lifted directly towards the posts. It sailed high over the bar and through the uprights. The roar from the right-hand side of the pitch could be heard throughout the village. Gwersyllt's miners and the other supporters, who were stood three-deep in places, raised their arms aloft to the new champions of the North Wales Colliery Cup.

CHAPTER TWO

The steam had long since evaporated and cold condensation ran down the creamy white tiled walls of the colliery bathhouse. Water sloshed around the floor, mixing mud and grass and creating a brown concoction of cold slimy muck. There was almost as much water on the floor as in the giant bath. The surface of the bath was a crust of dirt and grime; the tepid water below smelt of eau de beer and the odd sneaky piss. There was no possibility of getting clean, let alone warm, but the young Gwersyllt lads didn't care.

They slid their battered and bloodied bodies over the side and into the water, breaking the thin crust and releasing the last vestiges of warmth. They wrestled to get in and out but mainly with each other. Chorus after chorus of *Mae Hen Wlad fy Nhadau* rang out as the beer and water flowed in equal measure.

The warm water stung their frozen bodies as they lowered themselves into the bath and gradually their numbness began to ease. As normal feeling returned so too did the realisation of how hard the game had been. Cuts, swelling and bruises soon became apparent but copious quantities of beer would replace the cold to numb the body and keep the aches and pains away for the night. For the moment, none of that mattered.

'I reckon I set that try nicely for you Bryn,' Huan shouted above another chorus of the Welsh national anthem.

Bryn looked up at a rather tubby lad standing over the bath with a beer in one hand, scratching his scrotum with the other. 'Set it up? How do you reckon you did that then? The last time I saw you, you were twenty yards back throwing your guts up.'

Huan slid his legs over the side of the bath and eased himself gently into the water opposite his friend. He winced as the water passed over his cuts and bruises. 'Well that's nice I must say. If it wasn't for Rhys and me you wouldn't be taking all the glory. That's bloody gratitude for you, isn't it boyo?' he said, looking to his partner for support.

Rhys took a gulp of beer and shook his head. 'Don't ask me, I was busy ripping some bloke's ear off. I dunno where you were but if Bryn says that you were a bit slow getting about, then—'

'Slow my arse! There was nowhere you were that I wasn't.'

Rhys and Bryn looked at each other. Bryn shook his head and downed a mouthful of beer.

'I didn't say you weren't, but if Bryn says you were…'

'Oh, I see. What Bryn says is important now, is it? Well, if I was slow, which I wasn't, then it was only to let you catch up. Which, when I think about it, I spent a great deal of time doing, only I'm too polite to say anything.'

Rhys raised his eyebrows and plonked his beer on the side of the bath. 'Right,' he cried and launched himself across the bath. A great cheer rose from the rest of the team. Huan and Rhys disappeared momentarily beneath the slimy surface before erupting through the froth like two frenzied crocodiles. Huan was spitting water and rubbing grass from his face. Rhys made a dart for the opposite side of the bath towards his beer, but Huan was down on him in an instant. The rest of the team roared them on with cheers and laughter.

'Are you going to stop them?' Bryn shouted to a lad who was having a piss in the urinal. The young lad looked around and shrugged. His head, arms and legs were caked in mud and streaks of blood. They were a stark contrast to his pasty white torso that was slowly turning pink with the warmth.

John Roberts shook his cock and hung his towel on a peg. For eighteen years of age he was a solid mass of muscle. His arms were as round as the metal pit props that he beat into shape as he pulled them from the roaring furnace of the blacksmith shop. For a big lad he had exceptional speed around the park and his tackling was ferocious. There were few on the team as proud of their places as John the Hooker. He had been the first choice No. 2 at all levels since he started at the colliery club as an under-twelve-year-old. Not only was he physically strong, he could read the game better than most forwards. Scouts had been watching John in particular from a young age, which should have opened the way to rugby greatness but lads from North Wales were never going to break into the big teams from the south.

'Do I look stupid?' John said as he lowered himself into the bath, savouring the tingling warmth as it seeped over his body.

'Of course you're stupid,' Bryn said. 'All hookers are stupid.'

'Maybe, but we're also stronger than fat flankers,' John shouted as he lunged for Bryn's head. Bryn twisted his body as John crashed down on top of him. The bath became an explosion of water as the players pounced on one another in uncontrollable ducking and drowning.

'Oi, oi you buggers!' the sergeant major cried as he rounded the cubicle wall. 'I've got to clean this lot up after you've finished messing about like a bunch of schoolgirls.'

There was a spontaneous lull followed by a torrent of water aimed in his direction. He might have been on the wrong side of fifty-five but he was nimble enough to take cover behind the wall, which took the impact of the torrent of water that followed in his direction. He chuckled to himself. He was desperately proud of his lads even if he did have to spend an hour cleaning up after them. Still, he had spent a lifetime looking after others; another hour wouldn't hurt.

'You'll be lucky if Mr Owen ever lets us use this place again,' he cried from behind the wall. 'Water isn't cheap you know. When I was in India—'

Another wall of water coupled with cheers and beer cut him short. The boys had heard his stories before.

The communal bath was rarely used these days. In fact, it had hardly been used at all since it was first built. It was warm and clean for the first few miners who got in but the rest of the shift came out dirtier than they went in. More than one accident had resulted from the scramble for the bath. New individual cubicles had been built with overhead showers, and clean and dirty changing areas meant the miners could leave their kit at work and go home clean; the days of the tin bath in front of the fire at home were passing. There were still a few old boys who preferred the old ways but on the whole the pressure from 'the missus' meant that coming home clean prevented domestic disagreements.

Huan and Rhys had finally given up trying to drown each other and were now conducting a choir of naked men singing *Men of Harlech* between gulps of beer.

'I reckon we had it sown up by halftime,' Rhys said as he plonked himself down on the side of the bath.

'At halftime we was eight points down you idiot. How does that make it "sown up"?' Huan replied.

'I knew they was beat. You could tell by the fear in their eyes.'

'I don't think so boyo, they was tears they were, not fear.'

'Yeah, they was pissing themselves laughing at you wobbling around the park,' John interjected.

'Oh and I suppose you rucked them out singlehandedly, did you?' Rhys asked.

'Someone had to while the rest of us waited for you two lardy arses to catch up.'

Bryn sat on the side, listening to the banter with a smug look of self-satisfaction on his face as Huan and Rhys slid back into the water. At six feet two inches tall, muscular, fast around the field and with just the right knack of being in the right place at the right time, no one else had a chance of taking the No. 7 jersey off his back. He had worn it since he was thirteen years old. He not only led the pack, he drove them, cajoled them and inspired them to give every ounce of effort, and then a little bit more. Now at eighteen years old and in his prime he was never short of admirers.

He was a good-looking lad, not that he ever thought about it. Rugby was his only passion. Girls and all that stuff could wait.

Bryn was lost in his own thoughts as John sidled up to him, half-swimming and half-dragging himself across the bath. 'You still thinking about that try?' he asked as he wiped the water from his face.

'No, I was just thinking whether or not we will be here again next year,' Bryn replied. He paused and looked at John.

'What do you mean? Where else are we going to be?'

'Nothing really. Just, well, you know.'

'Not really, no.'

Bryn looked around and leaned in towards his friend. 'I was thinking of moving.'

John looked puzzled. 'What are you on about, moving? Moving where?'

'I thought we might go down south. See if we can pick up some work down there in a mine and get a game with one of the bigger clubs.'

'What are you on about? Why would you want to leave here?'

'I just thought that you and me and Huan and Rhys could move down there and try to get a better game, that's all.'

'You're fucking serious aren't you? Hey,' he called over his shoulder to Huan and Rhys. 'Bryn wants us to go down south and play rugby for some club down there.'

'Oi, keep it down,' Bryn hissed. The splashing and squabbling subsided. Bryn put his hands to his head and gave a slight groan.

'If we go down south how are we going to play up here?' Rhys said.

'We're not, you idiot. Bryn wants us to play down there,' John said. Rhys looked at Huan and shrugged his shoulders.

'I'm game if you are?' his friend replied.

'I didn't say I wanted to go, did I?'

'No but—'

'No but nothing. I just shrugged didn't I? That doesn't mean anything.'

'Well, what does it mean then?'

'I dunno.'

'Well I don't want to go then. I like it here.'

'Me too.' Rhys looked at Bryn, who was still sat with his head in his hands. 'Bryn, you go on your own if you want.'

Bryn sagged. 'I didn't say I wanted to go. I just thought.'

'Thinking now, are you? Now there's a first. A moment ago you were dragging us off to some foreign place without even asking,' John said.

'South Wales isn't a foreign place!'

'Well, I've never been there,' Huan shouted, 'so that makes it foreign doesn't it?'

'No,' John replied, shaking his head in despair. He looked back at Bryn. '"I want to play for a better team," you said.'

'No I never!' Bryn claimed as the rest of the team were starting to draw closer. 'Now hang on. That's not what I said. I'm very happy here in this team.' The team were closing in. 'Now hang on,' he cried as hands dragged him into the centre of the bath. He took a deep breath as he got the feeling that he was going to be under the water for some time.

CHAPTER THREE

Charles Symonds woke with a start. His eyes were wide open but his brain failed to make any sense of the brown-stained ceiling above his head. The throbbing started at the back of his skull; pulsed through his brain to the back of his eyes. The pain confirmed that he was still alive.

He turned his head towards the light from the window but still nothing registered. Slowly, as if he was afraid of what he might see, he turned the other way. There was a young woman lying with her back to him. Her breathing was slow and shallow. He lay his head back down on the pillow.

'Shit,' Charles said, the words little more than a hiss of air.

He tried to gather his thoughts. He looked across at her again. He was sure that he didn't know her. She stirred at his movement and as she opened her eyes she glanced over her shoulder and gave him a faint smile.

'You're awake early,' she said as she rolled over. 'I thought that you would be asleep for hours yet, after last night.'

He stared at her voluptuous breasts as they emerged from beneath the covers. He couldn't remember her name. He felt his stomach churn and sweat began to trickle from his brow. He knew the feeling well – he was going to vomit. He rolled off the bed and placed his hands on the wall to steady himself. He could feel the bile rising in his throat. The walls felt sticky. He took a couple of big breaths. 'Toilet?' he managed to blurt out as he pushed his way around the bed, one hand on the wall and the other covering his mouth.

'Outside,' the woman said as she turned to follow him round the room and through the door.

Outside? Symonds was sure that he had used it last night. Perhaps he hadn't. He'd been far too drunk to know for sure. He tried the only other door on the landing but was faced with an ottoman piled up with spare clothing that stank of urine. Perhaps he had.

'Shit,' he said to himself as he hurtled down the stairs. There was only one way out and that was through the parlour and into the kitchen. He lurched for the door but it was bolted. He was out of time. Unable to hold the contents of his stomach down any longer, he grasped the cold edge of the kitchen sink. His body heaved as he repeatedly retched. He could barely hold himself up against the stone sink, his body shaking and breaking into a cold sweat. As the retching subsided he sank to his knees and placed his forehead on the cold stone. He wiped his mouth with the back of his hand. He breathed heavily, but the relief was short-lived as the throbbing returned to his temples. He pulled himself up, realising for the first time that he was naked. He cupped his hands under the tap and allowed the water to flow into his mouth and over his face and head.

'Oh that's great, that is. Thanks very much.' The woman's voice startled him but his head stayed facing the bottom of the sink. 'You could have made it to the privy,' she said as she grabbed a towel off the oven plate. He breathed again and slowly turned towards the woman. 'Come on, move out the way. I'll sort it,' she said.

Despite the oversized dressing gown that she had pulled around her he could tell that she was still naked beneath it. She was a shapely woman, not plump but she clearly wasn't on the poverty line. She had let her hair down and it fell loosely around her shoulders. She wasn't unattractive but that did nothing to diminish his contempt. *I must have been pissed to go to bed with her*, he thought unkindly. He couldn't remember where he had met her and didn't much care.

He was trying his best to piece together the previous evening. He had been out with some friends. They had dined at the Penrhyn

Park hotel; lamb cutlets. He remembered the dinner and the waitress who had served them – *oh shit, the waitress.* It was starting to come back to him. She had been flirting with them all evening until his friend, Edward, had felt her bottom. The woman feigned offence but it had been obvious she was enjoying the attention. He remembered the maître d' who had seen what was happening and had come across with all his best bull and bluster. He dismissed the waitress and proceeded to scold the men as if they were naughty schoolboys. Someone told the pompous arse to go to hell. It wasn't the first time that Charles and his friends had been asked to leave a restaurant. Not that he cared. The food was pretty poor and certainly overpriced. *Overpriced? Shit, my wallet,* he thought. *Where's my jacket?* He patted his chest as if he was wearing his jacket.

The woman was filling the kettle and taking a drag on a cigarette. He glanced at her hand – a wedding ring; the large dressing gown. *God, she's married.* Another wave of nausea rose in his throat but he swallowed it back down. He just looked at her and let out a heavy sigh. He had to get out. He gave a grunt as he pushed past her and ran back up the stairs, grappling with the banister for support.

'Do you want a cup of tea or not?' she called after him as he climbed the stairs. He found his dinner jacket and trousers crumpled in a heap next to the bed where they had fallen. His socks – *where the fuck are my socks?* – he found under the bed next to his shoes. As he struggled into his clothes the room started to sway and he sat down on the bed to regain his balance.

They had gone to a gentleman's club further along the road but were refused entry. He remembered seeing the waitress across the street smoking a cigarette. He had gone across to her, while his friends tried to persuade the doorman to let them into the club. She said she had wanted to make sure their reputation had not been sullied by what had happened. He assured her that their reputation was beyond redemption. She had laughed at his jokes. She said that the manager had sacked her, 'which was only right

11

and proper'. Symonds remembered looking at her and thinking of her vulnerability.

'Don't you worry about that old idiot,' he said as he placed his arm around her shoulders. 'I'll pop by tomorrow and make sure that he understands things my way. I'll get you your job back.'

'That's very kind of you, sir. If there's anything I can do to repay you?'

'Well, perhaps a drink then?'

'Well I wouldn't normally, sir, but seeing as how you're with your gentlemen friends I'm sure it will be alright.'

He needed some fresh air. He needed to be out of this room. He looked around. It was barely big enough to swing a cat. The whitewashed walls were a dull grey, except around the cold grate where they had been blackened by the coal smoke. The bed had a thin mattress and a crocheted bedspread over a thick, coarse woollen blanket. He daren't lift the bedspread to look at the sheet. A chest of drawers stood against the wall opposite the bed, with a mirror on the wall behind it. He resisted the urge to look at himself. As he pulled up his trousers and tucked in last night's shirt he pinched the edge of the curtain with his thumb and forefinger and sneaked a look outside. He was in a terraced street of small red-bricked cottages.

'Do you want a cuppa, love?' the woman called again. 'Kettle's boiled.'

He released the curtains and grabbed his jacket. He checked the inside pocket of his jacket for his wallet. *At least she hasn't robbed me,* he thought. As he walked around the bed he saw the money lying on the bedside table. He looked down at the coins and scooped them up. He had no intention of paying someone he didn't know or couldn't remember. *If I can't remember what happened, she clearly wasn't worth it so I'm damned sure I'm not paying for it.* He pocketed the money and hurried from the room. The woman was cleaning up the remnants of his vomit as he brushed past her.

'I take it that you don't want any tea then?' she said.

Symonds didn't speak. He didn't even look at her. The woman shrugged and turned back to the sink.

As he stepped into the street the cold blast caught his breath. It had been a chilly night but it was a bit too early in the year for a frost. He quickly glanced along the narrow cobbled street, trying to get his bearings. The pithead gave it away. He turned and looked at the house. *How did I end up here?* he thought, and cursed himself under his breath. He put his hands to his head to massage his throbbing temples. *I need a drink.*

He pulled his collar up and drew his dinner jacket across his chest against the biting wind. As he walked he kept his head low and furtively scanned the street. His pace quickened as he strode away from the house. The once red brick terraces, now dark and coated in soot, ran on and on from one street to another; long rows of factory cottages; homes to men and families who did his bidding.

As Symonds rounded the corner a man was standing in his doorway three doors up. His cottage door opened directly onto the pavement. The man was wearing his Sunday best and smoking a pipe. The man said nothing as Symonds passed him. He heard the cough as he passed, and then the spit.

CHAPTER FOUR

July 1914

Bryn lay on the wispy coarse grass staring up at the deep blue sky streaked with hair-like filaments of cirrus cloud. Beads of sweat had formed in the wrinkles above his eyes as he squinted to block out the sun. The boys were stretched out on a grassy mound, bare-chested, enjoying the midsummer sun.

Bryn always enjoyed the summer. Each day he would look forward to coming up the pithead shaft in the cage and feeling the sun's rays dance on his face. The air always felt warm, clean and fresh. They would come out of the mine into the early evening sun, grab a quick wash and then down a pint at The Grapes before heading off home.

He had put his shirt across a boulder to dry. As the coarse cotton dried in the sun, a white patch of sweaty salt hardened around the armpits. It was Sunday; he would have a clean shirt tomorrow. The walk from Gwersyllt had been pleasant enough; the trees provided plenty of welcome shade from the heat of the sun but the race up the hill had broken the dam and sweat poured from all of them as they crowned the hill. It didn't matter what they were doing, it always ended up in a competition. Breathless and sweaty, they had collapsed at the foundations of the ancient castle's wall.

Huan was chewing on a blade of grass as he gazed into the sky. 'Do you reckon there'll be a war then?' Huan asked no one in particular.

'I reckon so,' Bryn said without glancing across. His eyes were fixed on a circling hawk as it spied its prey.

Rhys propped himself up against the cool stone, which had done little in the past to repel any invaders but did at least provide some welcome shade. Caergwrle Castle had sat on top of the mound since 1277, in the days when the English and Welsh fought each other to the death. Nowadays the rivalry was fought out on the pitch. The rivalry was no less intense and the combat just as fierce but once the final whistle was blown there were handshakes and a few shared pints. The onetime bastion of great kings now lay in ruins on top of a small hill on the outskirts of Wrexham, explored mostly by children who re-enacted the great battles of bygone years. The boys had been coming up to the castle since they were ten years old to re-enact a great but fictitious battle. Now they came up on a Sunday afternoon to get away from the grime that enveloped the village.

'I don't reckon the Germans are that stupid, do you?' Rhys said, looking across at Bryn.

'I dunno,' Bryn said, 'they've been shouting the odds loud enough.'

'Hey, don't forget they are foreigners. No telling what they are up to,' John added for good measure. 'Funny lot if you ask me.'

'I don't reckon that they've got the stomach for a decent fight. There might be a bit of sabre-rattling but I don't think that they'll fight,' Rhys said.

'They don't seem very happy about that prince chap being shot the other day,' Huan said as he propped himself up on one shoulder.

'Archduke. Don't you know anything?' John chided.

'Well, whoever he was, they seem pretty upset.'

'It's the Austro-Hungarians who are getting upset, not the Germans.'

'Same thing isn't it?'

'No, it's a different country. Didn't you learn anything at school?'

'Not really, did you?'

'More than you, obviously.'

'Well they're all friends over there. Same difference.'

'That's where you're wrong, boyo,' Rhys said. 'France are friends with Russia, Russia is friends with Serbia and Germany is friends with the Austro-Hungarians. And England hasn't got any friends because nobody likes them.'

'They must have some friends,' John said.

'Why?'

'Erm… fair point I suppose.'

'Well if there is a war, who do you reckon is going to be in it?' Huan asked.

'If it happens, I reckon France and Germany,' Bryn said.

'Which side do we play for then?' Huan asked.

'Well it's not going to be Germany is it, you donkey?'

'But I don't want to play for France either. The beer tastes like piss and they eat snails.'

'How do you know? You've never been further than Chester and there aren't any Frenchies there,' Rhys said.

'I read it in the paper,' Huan retorted to his friend. 'Oh sorry, I forgot that you can't read.'

'I read better than you, boyo.'

'Oh, is that right? I seem to remember being in the same class as you at school and you were always having extra reading with Miss Brown.'

'Actually I think you'll find that she just fancied me,' Rhys replied, which brought laughter from his friends.

'I suppose we had better help the French then; they'll never manage it on their own,' John said.

'Do you reckon we can get a game if there is a war? You know, sign up and all that,' Huan asked.

'The army's big enough, I expect, without us,' John replied.

'I don't think so. I think they'll need a few more to see them off.'

'Why are you so keen to join up anyway? You could get shot. Then you wouldn't be so keen.'

'It wouldn't come to that. We could join up, have a scrap, get a couple of medals and still be home in time for next season.'

'There might not be a next season if there's a war,' Bryn said, bringing the chatter to a sudden end. They sat in quiet contemplation for a few moments.

'If you joined up you would have to stay for good,' Bryn said. 'I can't see Mr Cunliffe giving you your job back at the mine, and then you'd end up like the sergeant major.'

Rhys and John looked at each other and laughed. 'Have I told you about when I was in the army...?' they said in unison.

'What do you want to get out of the mine for anyway?' Bryn asked Huan. 'I thought you liked it down there?'

'Who said I wanted to leave? I just think that it would be fun to get out for a while. You know, see the world a bit.'

'I don't think joining the army is the same as seeing the world,' John said. 'Anyway, what's wrong with seeing Wales?'

'It's not exactly abroad is it? And if we join up the army will pay for the trip. Win-win is how I see it.'

'Why do we want to go abroad?' John asked. 'What's wrong with Barmouth or Rhyl?'

'Well the girls are bit different for a start, aren't they?' Huan replied, lowering his voice and looking around at invisible crowds.

'What do you mean, "different"?' Bryn asked.

'Well you know, they're just different.'

'I heard they eat snails,' Rhys said.

'Who cares what they eat? It's the other bits that make them different.'

'What bits?'

'Oh for goodness' sake. Girl bits.'

'You reckon that they've got different bits?' John teased.

'No you mutton head, the bits are the same, it's just that they put them about a bit more.'

There was a long pause as the other three looked at each other, shook their heads and shrugged.

'You know?' Huan persisted. 'Do I have to spell it out? We can get ourselves a girl!' The others burst out laughing.

'The closest you've ever got to a girl was sheared in the spring,' Bryn managed to say as he lay on his back, laughing hysterically.

'Oh is that right, Casanova? And I suppose you're God's gift to women are you? Swooning down the High Street are they?'

'Well I reckon that I am pretty good-looking, as it happens.' Bryn was a good-looking lad: tall, lean, muscular with dark wavy hair and a glint of mischief in his eyes. He had never had a girlfriend. He had always assumed that it would happen one day but he had never given it too much thought. His mam kept telling him that he needed to find a girl but he reckoned that she was trying to marry him off just to get him out of the house. He always told her that the right one would be waiting for him in the clubhouse one day.

Huan, John and Rhys had been together as the front row for six years; they were Gwersyllt's answer to the Three Musketeers. They knew each other better than anyone knew their own mother. They gave each other a knowing smile. John nodded and they scrambled to their feet and dived on Bryn. They rolled across the grass, laughing and groaning as Bryn erupted from beneath them and then took his revenge on each in turn. After a few minutes they lay panting, sweating and laughing.

As John rolled onto his stomach he froze. Three young ladies were staring back at him. They had come over the hill from the far side; only their heads were visible above his horizon. They were staring at him, all smiles. The girl in the centre muttered a few words to her friends and they all giggled.

'Hey boys,' John called over his shoulder, 'we've got company.' The others turned and glanced in his direction. There was a sudden scramble as they dived around for their shirts.

'Hang on,' Bryn called, 'we need to put our shirts on.'

'Don't mind us,' one of the young ladies replied. 'We'll turn our backs until you are ready.' The boys exchanged glances with raised eyebrows as they struggled quickly into their shirts.

'We're decent,' Huan said, tucking the last of his shirt into his trousers.

'So you are,' a pretty red-haired girl said, as she turned around. 'I'm sorry; we didn't mean to spoil your fun. We only heard you as we came around the back of the ruins.' The boys stood staring at the three women.

'We thought you were a gang of little boys playing soldiers,' a taller dark-haired girl said.

The boys looked at each other. 'Oh no,' she blurted. 'I'm sorry, that came out slightly wrong. I didn't mean you were little boys. You're not little at all…I mean…oh it doesn't matter.' She covered her face with her hands to hide her embarrassment. Her companions laughed.

'Don't apologise please,' John replied. 'We were just messing about really. Letting off a bit of steam, you know. It's good training. Keeps us fit.' He gave a short cough to clear his throat.

'Well you all look pretty fit to me,' the dark-haired girl said. 'Oh, I don't mean – I'm sorry again. I don't know what I'm saying.' An embarrassed silence descended.

Huan and John looked at Rhys, who looked at Bryn, who was looking at the floor. Bryn stifled a laugh, which broke into a cough and broke the ice. They all started laughing. Rhys was the first to hold out his hand.

'Hello, I'm Rhys,' he said, introducing himself to the red-haired girl.

'Hello, I'm Mary and this is Bronwyn or Bron for short,' she said, introducing a tall dark-haired girl on her right arm, 'and this is Cerys.'

'Hello, I'm Huan and this is John and Bryn,' Huan said, pushing himself forward and pointing to each of his friends in turn.

'Well, it's nice to meet you all but perhaps we had better be getting down and leave you to your training,' Mary said with a slight hint of mischief in her voice.

'No, don't go,' Rhys said, quicker than he had intended to. 'Why don't you sit down in the shade for a bit? You must be warm after that climb.'

Mary looked at her friends, who smiled and shrugged. 'Well it is a bit warm. Perhaps we could, just for a few minutes.' The girls moved into the shade of the wall and sat on the grass. The boys stood in front of them, unsure for once what to say.

Rhys was staring at Mary. She was the most beautiful girl that he had ever seen. Her hair tumbled over her slender shoulders. The tight belt around her skirt accentuated her narrow waist. The white blouse highlighted the colour of her hair, which glistened in the sun. 'Do you come here often?'

Mary smiled. 'No, not really but it was such a lovely day that we thought a walk would be nice.'

'Where have you come from?' Huan asked.

'Hope village,' Cerys replied.

'*Duw*, that's a good walk,' he replied.

'Don't worry, we took our time.'

'Oh, I wasn't meaning to suggest that it was too far for a woman.'

'I should hope not,' Bronwyn said.

'Crikey, no. My mam often walks further than that into town and back.' The boys looked at their friend.

Bryn was starring at Cerys. He had never seen such natural beauty. Her short, dark brown hair accentuated her green eyes. He had never seen a girl with short hair before; all the girls he knew had long hair tied up in a bun or something like that. This girl was different but he didn't know why. She was sitting bolt upright, back straight with her head held high. Her legs were tucked back under her thighs. She wore a straight, plain cotton skirt down to her ankles with laced-up boots that went up below the hemline. Her white blouse was cut into her slim figure. He could see her chest rising and falling as she breathed. He knew he was staring. Cerys also knew he was staring and was trying hard to concentrate on the banter between the others, until she could no longer resist returning his gaze. She turned to face Bryn, who was brought back from his trance. She looked at him and smiled, a genuine smile that showed gentleness and sincerity. Bryn grinned back and blushed, not knowing what on earth he was meant to say.

'Well,' Mary said at length, looking at Bryn and Cerys, 'it's probably time we made our way home.' Her two companions smiled and scrambled to their feet.

'Right. Well, we'll walk down with you if you like?' Rhys said.

Bryn stepped forward and offered Cerys his hand. 'Would you like a hand?' She looked up at him and smiled as he helped her up. Cerys toppled forward. Bryn put his other arm out to catch her and felt his arm sweep around her waist. Cerys grabbed his arm and steadied herself.

'Sorry,' Bryn said. 'I don't know my own strength sometimes.'

'It's alright,' Cerys replied as she slowly released his arm. 'I don't break that easily.'

'Hark at you two,' Rhys said. 'Is that brute trying to kill you?'

'No, he's just being polite,' Cerys replied as she smiled at Bryn.

'Well that'll be a first,' he said and laughed. Bryn gave Rhys a hard stare.

'I'm sure it's not,' Cerys replied.

John led off down the hill, followed by Mary who had Rhys almost stumbling alongside her. Huan walked a few paces behind, in animated conversation with Bronwyn about rugby. Cerys and Bryn brought up the rear.

'What do you do when you are not up here then?' Cerys asked as she watched the ground to maintain her footing.

'I'm a miner,' Bryn replied.

'Gosh, I'm not sure I could go underground. It doesn't seem natural somehow. Do you like it?'

'I suppose I do. My da was a miner and so was his da before him. So I suppose it had always expected that I'd follow them. We

21

all work together. Except John that is; he works with his da in the smithy. He's still at the mine but he sees a bit more daylight than we do. We're more like moles.'

Cerys laughed. 'Does that mean that you only come up at night in people's gardens?'

'It feels like it sometimes. You know, you go down the pit in morning while it is still dark and it's dark again when you come out in the evening. But at least no one's banging me on the head with a spade as I come up!' They both laughed. 'Sometimes I only see daylight on a Sunday, although it's alright at this time of year with it staying light in the evenings.' They reached a steep section of path and Cerys hesitated as she checked her footing. Bryn held out his hand. 'You can hang onto my arm if you like.'

'Thank you.'

'What do you do then?'

'I work in Simpsons' in Wrexham.'

Bryn shook his head. 'I don't think I know it. Should I?'

'I suppose there's no reason why you should know it. It's a milliner's shop on the corner of the High Street.'

'Ah! Sorry, I... I'm not sure I'm too familiar with it.'

'There's no reason why you should be. I don't think ladies' hats are the latest miners' fashion.'

'Oh, I knew what it was, it's just that I wasn't familiar with that particular shop, you see.'

As they looked at each other she raised her eyebrows at Bryn and smiled. Bryn coughed and laughed. Cerys laughed again. Her smile was captivating.

*

The boys watched in silence as the girls walked off down the road, arm-in-arm. They turned and waved as they neared the corner. The boys waved back and waited until they had rounded the corner and were out of sight.

'What about that then?' Rhys said, rubbing his hands. 'I reckon I'm in there, boys.'

'Only if she's desperate,' John said as he turned and walked towards home.

'Desperate? She couldn't get enough of me.'

'You couldn't have given her any more of you if you tried.'

'Is that a bit of jealously there, boyo?'

'No. I'm just saying how it is. She's probably laughing about it right now.'

'Laughing about what? If it wasn't for me you three would've let them walk away without so much as a word.'

'We couldn't get a word in edgeways anyway.'

'I don't see those two complaining,' Rhys said as he pointed to Huan and Bryn, who were walking behind them.

'That's because Huan finally found someone new to listen to him rambling on about how great he is and Bryn couldn't take his eyes off that other girl's tits.'

'Hey! Don't be rude. I wasn't looking at her tits,' Bryn protested.

'Why not?' John said. 'Great tits. The rest of her wasn't bad either.'

'Hey, there's no need to be coarse about it. I thought that she was pretty nice actually.'

'Oh no, that's all we need, Bryn's in love.'

'I didn't say I was in love, did I? I just thought that she was very nice that's all.'

CHAPTER FIVE

September 1914

'What have you got?' a voice echoed out of the gloom.

'Ham. What have you got?' another voice responded from the other side of the small, dark gallery.

The two lads were only a few feet apart but the darkness enveloped each man within the confines of his own breath and thoughts. The recent installation of electricity to the mine was great for the men back in the headings and passages, but up at the face the grafters still relied on candles and the safety lamp. The candle was the miner's sun that provided a thin, flickering ray of late autumn light that danced around the coalface as he hacked away at the lumps of black gold. Although they were working cheek by jowl, shrouded in dust and noise, it was easy to be isolated within the confines of the glow of the candle. Lunchtime was always a welcome break. Once the dust settled and the candles were extinguished all that was left was the faint glow of the safety lamp and the hammerings of men in the other galleries and faces. Despite the inky blackness they were experts at eating in the dark.

'I've got cheese,' Rhys piped up.

'Oh for goodness' sake,' came another voice from further along the gallery. 'It's the same every bloody day. Who cares what you got? Just eat it why don't you?'

'Well it's nice to know what you're eating. It's sometimes difficult to tell with my mam's sandwiches. Anyway, I might want to swap it,' Rhys said.

'If your mam heard you talking like that about her sandwiches she would clip your ear. She only ever uses the best Caerphilly.'

'How is it that you're allowed to moan about her cooking and I'm not?

'Because I'm married to her, that's why!' the voice roared. The boys laughed. It was a bit of an old routine but Albert fell for it every time.

Bryn, Rhys and Huan had been assigned to work with Rhys' da from their first day in the mine almost three years ago now. It was common practice to assign new miners to old hands, particularly if they were related, which was pretty common in Gwersyllt. Sons were expected to follow their fathers, as they had invariably followed theirs.

Albert Taylor was in his thirty-first year as a miner. He was a veteran of the mine who had seen, heard and experienced it all. He started as a boy at the age of fourteen, a little bit younger than Bryn, Huan and Rhys, as he constantly reminded them. He liked to think that times had moved on – 'It was never this easy in my day,' he recited on almost a daily basis. But in truth he was right. Albert's early days had been fraught with danger; backbreaking work in appalling conditions. On more than one occasion he had been sent ahead of a mine crew to ensure that the coalface was stable enough to work safely, or to retrieve unexploded charges.

Albert was a traditional miner but had the intelligence to see that new inventions and better working practices were in his best interests, so long as the mine continued to be productive. He particularly enjoyed teaching the young lads, taking pride in his knowledge and enjoying the success of seeing his son and the other young boys like him who he had trained pass though their apprenticeships. Perhaps, he thought, he might apply for one of the teaching posts on the surface once he had got rid of these three monkeys. Thirty-one years was a long time and he wasn't getting any younger.

'I need a cup of tea,' Albert said as soon as the laughing died down.

'Aye, and me,' another voice said.

'And me.'

'Me too,' came two other responses in quick succession.

'Bryn, you were last,' Albert judged.

'How do you know that I was last? You can't see from over there.'

'Believe it or not lad I've got bloody good hearing and premonition and if I'm right, I'm about to hear some cock-and-bull story about how the tunnel distorts sound and how it couldn't possibly have been you. Well let me save you the trouble and tell you it's poppycock. So go and get the tea.'

Huan and Rhys cheered while Bryn huffed. 'That may be lad, but you need the practice. It was like cat's piss yesterday.'

'That's because yours was cat's piss,' Bryn said as he got to his feet.

'Well if that's the case, ask the cat to put sugar in it this time and tell him to make it a bit hotter,' Albert called after him. Rhys and Huan laughed as they shoved the remainder of their sandwiches into their mouths and gathered their kit together.

Bryn hated having to go and make the tea. Along with electric lamps, they also had a water boiler at the bottom of the main down shaft, but it still meant a walk of about a quarter of a mile. He sighed as he walked, stooped low in the gallery – at least he would be able to stand upright for a while and it was better than no tea at all.

'Right then you two, let's get back to it. You can have some tea when the big lad gets back,' Albert instructed.

'Can't we just wait here till he gets back?' Huan asked.

'No you can't, you lazy scamp,' Albert replied. 'You know the sooner you three get qualified, the sooner I can get some decent lads working for me.'

'You'll miss us when we're gone,' Huan said.

'No I won't,' Albert replied as he stood to release the cramp that had been building in his legs. The coal seam was quite shallow and at his age the strain from stooping all day was taking its toll.

Not that he was a big man; he was barely an inch taller than Rhys, although he was twice as round. His own rugby days had long since passed and his wife's cooking wasn't nearly as bad as his son made out. The cramp reminded him that Mrs Taylor would be nagging him again before long to get a job on the surface. Perhaps he would once these three had moved on.

*

'Albert, are you joining up?' Bryn asked as they took a ten-minute break.

'Of course I'm bloody well not, you lunatic! I'm hardly likely to go fighting Germans at my age, am I? I might do myself a mischief and then who would put the bread on the table, eh? Anyway, someone's got to keep the mine going.' Albert paused for a moment, drawing his sleeve across his blackened brow. 'And you needn't think that you lot are going either. Your apprenticeships are due up in a few months and you don't want to be throwing them away, do you? Anyway they are only taking grown men, not young lads, so don't let me catch you wandering along Regent Street.'

'But the war will be over by the time we get our apprenticeships,' Bryn replied.

Albert sighed. 'Well let's hope so,' he said as he lit his candle, causing a pool of creamy light to fall upon his charges. 'You mark my words, boys. This will be a bloody war, of that I have no doubt. You don't want to be throwing yourselves away just now.' He let his words sink in, but he knew that he was losing the battle. 'Right, let's be getting back to it. Coal waits for no man.'

'They reckon it will be over by Christmas,' Rhys said.

'Well, that's as maybe but your tea break is over now so let's get on with you,' Albert said.

'But what if it isn't?' Huan asked. 'Field Marshal Kitchener wouldn't have asked for all those men if he thought that it would be over by Christmas, would he?'

Albert sighed and put down his pick. He knew there would be no stopping the questions; it was all anyone was talking about since Mr Asquith's government had declared war on Germany a couple of weeks earlier. 'He wants all those men because he doesn't trust that ragtag militia bunch we've got here, that's why. That lot couldn't save us from ourselves, let alone the Germans. No, he wants proper men from hardworking backgrounds.'

'Men like us,' Huan stated.

'Exactly,' Arthur said. 'Oh, no you don't. I see what you did there. No, no, no. He wants normal people, those that don't have proper jobs. You need to stay here to bring out the coal. We're important, see! Anyway if you go wandering off there will be no guarantee of a job when you get back. Then where will you be? Jobless, homeless and starving, that's where.'

*

The boys picked their way back to the coalface, sixty-five feet underground with several thousand tons of Welsh earth above them. As senior apprentices they had, to all intents and purposes, finished their training. They had shown such promise under Albert's expert tuition that they were being groomed as team leaders. Their final few months would be spent on supervised mining tasks. They were mining a shallow seam, no more than ten or twelve hands high. Albert watched as they undercut the seam propping up the ceiling with wooden posts. Once they had cut far enough into the seam they would pull the posts away and hope that gravity would bring down the roof. It was hard work in the final stages and the new jackhammer was too difficult to manoeuvre in the tight space between the roof and the seam floor. It was back to basics, hacking out the face with picks. Lying on their sides and swinging a pick with the wrists and elbows without moving their shoulders was second nature; a skill long since learnt after two years in the mine.

'Tea up!' a voice shouted in the dark.

'*Duw!*' Albert shouted, as he nearly jumped out of his skin. As he turned to where the voice had come from, John's face was lit up like a ghoul with a candle beneath his chin. John was laughing so hard he smacked his head on the roof of the seam and dropped a couple of thermos flasks on the ground.

'I thought you lot were hard men down here? You look like you've just seen Daffyd's ghost.'

'You'll be a bloody ghost once I've killed you,' Albert shouted as he reached to smack John round the head. Bryn, Rhys and Huan lay on their backs laughing.

'What brings you down here then? Not lost again are you?' Huan asked.

'Ha, ha. Very funny,' John said. 'I've just come down to shoe a couple of the ponies.'

'And you thought that you'd come and see where the work's being done, did you?' Rhys replied.

'Well if I did, I wouldn't have come here would I? Call that work? Lying on your back all day? You lot wouldn't know hard work if it bit you on the behind. A few hours in front of a furnace would sort you lot out. They're calling a meeting at the end of the shift.'

'Who is?' Rhys asked.

'Mr Hulbert. For the whole mine,' John replied.

'What's it about then, *bach*?' Rhys asked.

'What do you think it's about, you great lump of coal? It's the war isn't it?'

Huan scrambled from beneath the seam. 'What about it?'

'Well, rumour has it that there is going to be a recruiting office set up in the Old Police Station.'

The boys gave a collective groan. 'Is that all you can come up with?' Bryn said. 'We've known about that for days'.

'No you haven't,' John said. 'You never mentioned it last night.'

'Well we don't tell you everything, do we?' Huan retorted. 'Don't want to overload your brain.'

John paused as he peered into the dark. One of the benefits of working above ground was that John generally knew more about what was going on than his friends did. They couldn't see the triumphant grin on his face. 'Well, if that's the case you won't want to hear the rest of it will you? I'll be off then.'

'Hold your horses boyo, no need to be hasty. You might as well tell us now you're here. However, if it's not very interesting you will never see the light of day again.' Rhys threatened his front row partner.

John paused for effect and said in a rather superior tone, 'As you put it like that, it seems that Mr Lloyd George is going to raise a Welsh army and *we* are going to be in it.'

The boys looked at him agog. 'How do you work that out then?' Bryn asked.

'Mr Hulbert has agreed to release fifty men from the mine to make up a company of Welsh Fusiliers. We are going to be like them soldiers that General Kitchener said: work together, train together and fight together.' He pinched his shirt as if he was wearing braces and spoke in a rather superior grown-up tone. 'Anyway Mr Hulbert has called a meeting at the end of the shift.'

CHAPTER SIX

The silence was deafening; the only sounds were the metronomic tick of the longcase clock that had stood in the corner of the room since 1851 and the scraping of cutlery on the china plates. The clock, a burr walnut veneered arched brass dial clock of slim proportions, was almost eighty years old when the late Edward Symonds had bought it from a prominent businessman and Member of Parliament. The importance of the clock had nothing to do with the accuracy of the timepiece or the craftsmanship of the casing.

Edward had bought the clock, for the sum of one pound, following the acrimonious takeover of his first coalmine, his first major capital investment. The clock had stood in the director's office when he had moved in and the outgoing owner told him rather petulantly that he could smash it into firewood for all he cared. Instead, Edward sent him a pound note to rub salt into his wounds for having lost the mine. To Edward it was a sign of his success, a sign that he had achieved status and respectability. Unfortunately he died at a relatively young age but was able to pass on his success and business prowess to his son Donald.

Donald Symonds now owned a string of collieries across North Wales and down through Staffordshire. He had inherited sufficient wealth from his father to be comfortable but Donald knew and appreciated that his wealth had been bought through hard labour, ambition and enthusiasm; qualities that he now possessed in even greater store. The boom of the late 1800s had allowed him to expand his father's mining business; fuel for the ever-expanding economy and the Empire.

31

Donald sat at the end of a large mahogany table that was more than capable of seating ten guests. He ate in silence, the anger burning deep within him with every mouthful that he ate. Donald and Margaret, his wife of twenty-five years, had enjoyed a modest social life, never extravagant but guests were always warmly welcomed and their hospitality was gracious. Margaret sat at the opposite end of the table, trying in vain to engage her son, in desultory conversation. What responses she did get were laced with sarcasm, which she neither understood nor liked. Donald Symonds fought to control his anger as he gazed across at his son, though he rarely referred to him as such.

Charles drained his glass and placed it heavily on the polished mahogany. As the glass toppled, John the butler, who stood impassively by the dresser throughout the dinner, seemingly detached from the events, sprang forward to catch the glass. Charles grabbed and steadied it, sneering as he did at the butler, who stepped back into his position of invisibility. As the senior member of the household staff it was John's responsibility to maintain order, discipline and standards amongst the rest of the small staff. He was averse to gossip but he would share this little display with Cook and the head gardener later in the afternoon as they ate their own dinner in the kitchen. Charles reached across the table for the decanter.

'Haven't you had enough?' his father rasped without looking up from his plate.

Charles paused and smiled to himself. He turned his head slowly towards his father; any quicker brought about another searing pain behind his temples. 'Not nearly enough,' he replied.

Donald Symonds slammed his knife and fork onto the table, causing Margaret to choke on an already cold roast potato swathed in congealed gravy that she had chased around her plate for the best part of ten minutes.

'That's enough,' his father shouted. 'You go out drunk; you come home drunk. Look at the state of you, you're not fit to be fed on the step with the dogs and you stink of brothels—'

Margaret raised her hand to interrupt.

'No Margaret, enough is enough,' Donald cried. 'He's a disgrace. Anyone else of his age would be in France by now.'

'Oh God, here we go again,' Charles sighed as he grabbed at the wine decanter, pouring himself a large glass of rather good Châteauneuf-du-Pape that he allowed to dribble over the rim onto his father's beloved table. 'What is it you want from me, Father, my blood as well as Harry's? Is that what you want? Will that make you happy? Wasting my life for pointless Belgians who couldn't even fight for a few days? What will that achieve? What did Harry achieve? Absolutely bloody nothing!'

'Don't you dare talk about my son like that. At least he knew his duty. At least he had honour and pride.'

'Yes, and where is he now? He's dead. Does that make you happy?'

Harry's war had been short. He was one of the four hundred and sixty-eight men who didn't answer their names when the battalion formed up on the outskirts of Mons as evening drew to a close on the first day of war with Germany.

Margaret gasped and placed her hand over her mouth. She flushed as tears welled up at the corners of her eyes. Her anguish and sadness were overwhelming. She took a lace handkerchief from her sleeve and gently dabbed her eyes but she couldn't stem the flow of tears as she sat in silence.

'Don't you dare talk about your brother in that tone.' Donald had risen from his chair and pointed an accusing finger at Charles. 'At least he did what was right, what was honourable by his men. At least he knew what honour meant, what responsibility meant. All you do is drink and whore. Well, I won't have it; do you hear me? I have had enough.' Spittle spurted from his mouth as he rasped out his words. 'I want you out of this house, today,' Donald roared. 'If you have no intention of honouring this family then you will no longer be part of it.' He threw his serviette onto the table and shoved his chair back. As he stormed across the room Charles clapped.

'Bravo, Father. Fine words but who exactly will run your precious mines? You can't go on forever you know. Harry's gone. Well it wasn't my fault, was it? He was the one who wanted to run away to war and look where it's got him and us. Maybe now you can spend a little bit of time wondering about me. It's clearly never entered your mind before, has it? Oh no, poor Charles – the second son. I might as well not have existed as far as you are concerned. Well maybe now you'll have to think about it: who else are you going to hand over your pits to? You have never asked me what I wanted to do, whether I was interested in running the mine. Oh no. It was Harry, always Harry. Well I'm sorry he's dead but perhaps now you will give me some consideration.'

Donald placed his hands on the Chesterfield chair that stood empty next to Margaret, who was sobbing quietly. He turned and faced his son.

'If you had bothered to stay sober long enough to open your eyes and look around, you would have seen that there are no longer any Symonds mines.' He let the news sink in for a moment. Then he saw his son's cynical smile slacken at the edges, just very slightly. 'Yes, that's right. Whilst you have been out playing the damned fool I've sold them.' Donald let the words hang in the air.

'What? You have sold the mines?' Charles said as if he had misheard. 'Who to?'

'Robert Marsden,' Donald said, looking directly at Charles.

'Who the bloody hell is Robert Marsden?'

'Quite!' Donald said. 'If you had ever bothered to learn anything these past few years instead of gallivanting and whoring you would have realised that Marsden's have been steadily buying mines for the past ten years, taking the less profitable mines and turning them around. They have ambition, they have experience, they care about the industry and more importantly they care about their workers.' Donald paused and was about to turn away, but stopped and turned back. He pointed his finger directly at this son. 'I want you out of this house by tonight.'

'You can't do this,' Charles shouted after his father. 'Those pits are mine; my life, my inheritance.' He caught his father in the hallway and grabbed him by the arm, spinning him around. 'You can't do this, do you hear me?'

Donald looked into his son's eyes.

'I can and I have,' he replied. 'I have had Fotheringtons amend my will. It makes ample provision for your mother. As far as I am concerned and as far as my solicitor has been informed, I no longer have any other dependants. In the event of my death your mother will be cared for appropriately. As for any residual inheritance it will be invested and an allowance given to the miners' welfare fund.'

'How am I meant to live?' Charles shouted. Spittle was spurting from his mouth as his rage grew.

'I suggest that you join the army,' Donald said. 'Perhaps there you will learn some humility and perhaps, in time, you might recover your inheritance.'

CHAPTER SEVEN

The news of the meeting had spread like wildfire throughout the mine and into the village. The oncoming and offgoing shifts were assembled around the pithead as there were no buildings big enough to take them all. The men gathered in groups; some dirty from the day's work, others less so. Most were clad in thick, filthy moleskin trousers and collarless shirts with scarfs tightly wrapped around their necks to keep the dust off their chests. The oncoming shift were sparklingly clean in comparison but wore the same rough woollen clothing. The older men chatted quietly in small tightknit groups. The younger men were more animated, sensing that something dramatic was about to take place.

The younger men pushed their way to the front, intent on having a good view. The very young boys tried to push around the legs of the older men. Most got a clip around the ear for their troubles but they pushed and barged all the same until they reached the small stage that had been set up.

Bryn, Rhys and Huan stepped out of the lift cage and found John leaning on the winding gear frame.

'Is this is it? We haven't missed it have we?' Rhys said.

'No, nothing's happened yet,' John replied. 'I reckon this is serious you know. Look see,' he said as they wandered out into the late summer evening. The air was still warm and fresh. 'Everyone's here. Mr Hulbert is going to stand on the platform over there, look.'

'Right,' Bryn said. 'We need to get to the front. Come on.'

It was never going to be a struggle. It was just like being back on the park. Rhys, Huan and John naturally bonded into their front row positions and Bryn guided them forward from the back as the sea of bodies parted for them. The boys were well liked at the mine and the crowd parted with good humour as they drove through the throng, getting plenty of slaps as they barged their way through their workmates. When they finally made it to the front they acknowledged the cheers, jeers and good-natured abuse from the crowd.

Mr Hulbert emerged from the colliery offices, flanked on his right by Gethin Roberts the miners' representative, and Mr Owen the mine manager on his left. As they made their way towards the platform, the crowd parted as if Moses had parted the waves. As they did so the wild chatter gradually abated. There was an audible hush around the mine as Mr Hulbert led the small contingent to the platform. He purposefully climbed up the steps onto the scaffold, looking every bit like a condemned man on his way to the noose. The mine was still; nothing was moving. Even the winding gear was silent except for the hum of the engine.

Mr Hulbert had a determined, serious, look about him. Gethin Roberts nodded to Mr Owen, who responded with a purposeful nod. He turned to Mr Hulbert. In his hands he turned his bowler hat round and round. He stepped forward and took a sheet of paper from his jacket breast pocket. He opened the letter and stared at it for a moment, then refolded the paper and looked out across the faces. He knew them all by name. He had mined with some of the older ones, taught most of the older men and employed all of the young lads.

'Gentlemen. Good afternoon. I would like to thank you for coming to this meeting.' He paused. He drew breath and spoke. 'As many of you will know by now, Mr Lloyd George, Chancellor of the Exchequer, Member of Parliament for Caernarfon Boroughs, gave a speech yesterday at the Queen's Hall during which he proposed the formation of a Welsh Army Corps. Up and down our principality our brothers and our countrymen are delivering on this promise. I have agreed with Mr Roberts and Mr

37

Owen that we should release one hundred and fifty men from the mine to Mr Lloyd George on the promise that your jobs will be here when you get back.'

There was a huge cheer across the mine as Mr Hulbert made his announcement. He let the cheering continue for a moment before holding up his hands for quiet.

'Wales will do its duty and we have been given the opportunity to be part of this great sacrifice. For sacrifice it will be; a sacrifice for those who go, those who leave their families, friends and colleagues behind and those of us who unfortunately have to stay to carry on the work. Let me be quite frank with you: war is an ugly, unpleasant business. I hope and pray that it won't be so but some men may have to pay the ultimate sacrifice. But it is a sacrifice that we must be prepared to make if we are to honour our commitments to Belgium, a defenceless country already ravaged by war and our commitment to our own way of life and freedom. Wales will do its duty and we, our mine, will be part of that duty.'

He paused to let his words reach the back of the large gathering.

'It's not just personal pride and national honour, but also an honour for the mine. Those of you who are brave enough to join up will carry that honour on all our behalf. It is my greatest regret that we cannot all go. I know that you will all, young and old, want to play your part and you will, but we cannot all go. If it wasn't for the ravages of time I would myself be part of this great expedition.'

The crowd gave a great cheer. He paused and raised his hands to dampen the applause. His rhetoric had broken the silence. He gave a short cough to clear his throat and to let his miners know that there was more.

'Those of us who cannot go will stay behind and continue our work diminished by your absence. Be in no doubt, our work is war-winning work and our production must and will increase to support our army, our nation and our men. Without coal there will be no power to generate the huge war industry that will be crucial to rid us of our enemy. I know that you will not disappoint me. Just as we have all stood here today, united, we will stay united in purpose, sacrifice and fortitude, be it on the battlefield or at the coalface for as long as it takes. We will all do our duty. I cannot express in words how proud I am to stand here in front of you, knowing that to a man, you will want to go. We are proud to be miners, we are proud to be Welsh and we are proud of our young men. I know that you will do your duty. Our country needs you now more than the mine needs you. God bless every one of you who does this selfless thing.' Mr Hulbert raised his hat. 'God save the King.'

The crowd erupted. Men and boys tore the caps from their heads and raised them heavenward. 'God save the King!' came the reply, followed by a great cheer and a rousing rendition of *Ma Hen Wald*.

Mr Hulbert had tears running down his cheeks. As he descended the steps a group of miners grabbed him by his arms and legs and hoisted him into the air. He sat upon their shoulders as his men surrounded him in full song. They needed no persuading, no direction and no instructions as they began to walk towards the entrance of the mine. One of the miners' representatives called the young lads to the front and got them into three ranks. The older men drifted towards the rear, cheering the young lads as they jostled for places at the head of the column.

Having forced their way to the front of the crowd to hear Mr Hulbert, Bryn, Rhys, John and Huan now found themselves at the back of the crowd as it headed out onto the Mold Road towards Wrexham.

'Come on,' Bryn shouted to the others although he could barely be heard above the cheering and singing. 'We need to get to the front before they run out of spaces.'

'We'll not get through this lot,' Huan shouted as he tried to crane his head between the bobbing mass.

They were out on the road now, passing the cottages that had once been red brick but which were now as black as the mine, along with every building in the village. Mothers, sisters and daughters, many holding babies, had come out to see the commotion. They too cheered as their men, their husbands and sons, passed by.

Bryn and his friends continued to fight their way to the front. Young men who found their way towards the rear were cajoled by the older men to make their way up to the front. The mine boys ran alongside, marching with the young men. Two groups were formed, those who were going to enlist were in the front group and those who were going to support them stood to the rear. Mr Hulbert was keeping a close eye on who was in which group. In spite of his patriotism and excitement he wanted to make sure that not too many men were in the front group; he still had a mine to run.

Gethin Roberts believed that it was his duty as the miners' senior representative to lead the young men along the road. They marched in step with a swagger that would delight any seasoned professional soldier. As he glanced behind, Mr Roberts couldn't help but smile at the front rank. Jones, Roberts and Taylor, the Gwersyllt front row, were beaming from ear to ear and singing proudly. Tucked in behind was Bryn's head, bobbing; always on the lookout for a quick move. Mr Roberts looked forward and joined in the chorus with his deep baritone voice. *With men like these, the war will be over by Christmas*, he thought to himself.

CHAPTER EIGHT

The Royal Welsh Fusiliers Band had been playing outside the County Hall as the miners appeared over the railway bridge. The band sergeant major stepped off the band and marched them towards the miners, who cheered even louder. The band countermarched in front of the miners and led them into the centre of Wrexham. The large crowd of men, women, wives, girlfriends and children had gathered outside the Imperial Hotel and cheered as the miners marched along to *Men of Harlech*.

'Halt!' Mr Roberts yelled.

The miners stopped outside the County Building. The young men who formed the three ranks stood ramrod straight and bustled with pride. The older miners gathered around the fringes, eager to see their youth enlisted into the army to defeat the King's enemies. They might have been too old to fight but nothing was going to stop them cajoling others to stand in their place. If their mine was going to war with their sons and colleagues, there would have to be a celebration and the pubs were doing a roaring trade.

'Right turn,' Mr Roberts called as if he was already a sergeant major.

The order and the movement were a little too complicated for most of the men; what should have been a sharp drill movement was more of a shuffle. The miners relaxed a little and chatted as they waited for the next instruction. The County Building had once been the yeomanry barracks, and more recently the police station and county court. More than one of the men now facing the building had been inside for one reason or another.

An old corporal who had watched them arrive shouted into

the Recruiting Office to warn the staff to make ready to receive the next batch of volunteers. He marched forward and stopped in front of the miners. He had three medals dangling from his tunic.

'Here we go then boys,' Bryn said, as he struggled to contain his excitement. 'I reckon that we will have a few of those medals by this time next year.'

'A Victoria Cross for me,' Huan said.

'More like a wooden cross,' John quipped.

'Not likely boyo, no German is going to get me.'

'Is that right? With an arse as fat as yours they can hardly miss.'

The corporal took his place in the centre of the line. 'Gentlemen,' he cried in a voice that carried across the length and breadth of the column. 'Your attention.' The chatter died away instantly. 'It might take a little while to process you all through the attestation so I would ask you to be patient. There are plenty of spaces for everyone so there is no need to panic; you will all get in.'

A loud cheer resounded as the men raised their hats in the air.

'Once you are called forward, you will go to the clerk in the main hall who will help you fill in a few forms. The doctor will then see you and if you are certified fit you will be moved into the officer's room where you will swear your allegiance to His Majesty. From there you will be given a shilling and told to parade outside over there.' He pointed towards the wall that surrounded St. Mary's Church. 'Look over there now so you know where I am pointing. That way you won't get lost with your shilling.' The young men turned their heads in the direction that he was pointing. 'Then you will be given further orders. Right, stand easy,' he cried. 'Starting from the left, I want you to file into the hall.' The corporal pointed to his right, the men's left, so there was no confusion. Even so, one or two men from the opposite end started to move. One look from the corporal stopped them in their tracks. He shook his head in despair.

Rhys looked along the line. 'Bugger. We're at the wrong end.'

Bryn shook his head and gave his friend a push. 'Get a move on, you idiot. You're at the right end.'

Rhys stepped off and looked behind to make sure that his friends were coming with him. As they reached the entrance a young man barged past them as he left the building. He was swearing and cursing to himself, tears starting to well in his eyes as he made off down King Street.

'What's up with him?' Rhys asked over his shoulder.

'How do I know?' John replied.

'Huan, what's up with him?'

'How should I know?' Huan looked around at Bryn. 'Hey Bryn—'

'No, I don't know. Rhys is bloody closer than me, ask him.'

The corporal marched towards the door. 'Nothing to worry about, lads. The sergeant major just thought he was a bit too young. Perhaps he'll come back next week,' he said. 'He's just a bit upset now but he'll be fine.' There was a murmur of sympathy.

'How old do you have to be then?' Bryn asked the corporal.

'Nineteen.'

Bryn gave a glance at his three friends. 'Oh that's alright then,' he lied. 'Who's the sergeant major then, boyo?' Bryn asked the corporal. The corporal turned slowly to the voice that had obviously been addressing him.

'If that comment was aimed at me then I suggest that you try again and address me using my rank and my name.'

Bryn pause and thought a moment. 'Oh, right. Sorry. What's your name then?'

The corporal waited until the laughter had subsided. His faced flushed as red as his best tunic. 'My name is Corporal Jones of the 3rd Battalion, the Royal Welsh Fusiliers. You can call me Corporal Jones.'

'Well then Corporal Jones, do you know who the sergeant major is or not?'

The corporal was trying desperately hard to control his temper. 'Sergeant Major Rolland is your recruiting sergeant major. He is a distinguished soldier, formerly of the 2nd Battalion, the Royal Welsh

Fusiliers and now on extended service with the 3rd Battalion, the Royal Welsh Fusiliers. Now might I suggest that you either go in or *fuck off*?!'

'Blimey, I was only asking his name.' The boys looked at each other. Bryn gave Huan a push, which rippled forward into Rhys, who tripped in the doorstep. Corporal Jones was gripping his pace stick so hard it almost snapped.

'Get up you maggot before I ram this stick so far up your arse you'll be spitting woodchip for a month. Now get yourselves inside before I get someone else who can.'

The entrance led into a large waiting room with row upon row of benches. The boys sat themselves down and looked around at the other men who were waiting to be called forward. Most were chatting nervously but the excitement was palpable.

Huan was looking puzzled. 'How did Mr Rolland get to be a sergeant major so quickly? I thought he left the army years ago?'

'Well they obviously wanted him back, didn't they, stupid?' Rhys replied.

'Don't call me stupid. You're stupid.'

'Why am I stupid? You're the one who asked.'

'It's good, isn't it? One day he's our coach and the next he's our sergeant major; marvellous,' John suggested.

Bryn had his head in his hands. 'No it's not, you idiot. He knows how old we are, doesn't he?'

'Bugger,' Huan said quietly as the situation dawned on him.

'What are we going to do?' John asked. 'He's bound to see us.'

'He might not,' Bryn suggested.

'I am not walking out of here without my shilling,' Rhys said.

'He won't say anything,' Bryn protested.

'But what if he does?' Rhys replied.

'What did Bryn just say? He won't stop us,' Huan said.

'Since when did he become the expert?' Rhys chided.

'Since he was three feet bigger than you! Just stay calm, will you; he'll let us in. You'll see.'

'There has to be more than one recruiter,' Bryn said, trying to sound upbeat. 'He'll be proud as punch of us, you'll see.'

A lance corporal was watching the desks. 'Next three step forward,' he growled. The boys stood up and walked to the front. The corporal stared at them for a moment. 'There are four of you,' he said. 'I said the next three. Having difficulty counting, are you?'

'Of course we can count... and read,' Bryn said as he towered from the back of his friends, 'but we want to go in together if we can.'

'Oh you do, do you? Friends are you?'

They all nodded. The lance corporal shook his head and pushed the door ajar. 'I hope you'll all be very happy,' he said. His cynicism was wasted. 'In you go then... friends.'

The boys filled in the forms and had a cursory inspection by the doctor. They dressed and moved through another door into an office. A corporal was sat at an overly large oak desk in the centre of the room that had once been the police inspector's office. On the front edge of the desk were three Bibles. The boys' metal-studded boots scraped on the wooden floor as they shuffled to the front of the desk. It was windowless and airless. The wood panelled walls added to the mustiness. A single low-wattage light bulb hung above the corporal, who didn't even bother to look up.

'Hold the Bible in your right hand and repeat after me. I, state your name, do solemnly swear to serve His Majesty the King, his heirs and succ—' He was cut short.

'What's going on here then, Corporal?' came a soft, low voice from behind the boys.

The corporal, momentarily startled from his repetitive trance, sprang to attention and looked directly at the sergeant major.

'Attestation, sir!'

'I can see that, Corporal. Where's the officer?'

'Just popped out, sir. Call of nature. Asked me to carry on sir, given the amount of men that we have.'

The boys stood rock-steady, still not daring to turn around.

'Who are they?'

The corporal was starting to look a little nervous. He checked his list.

'Mr Jones, Mr Roberts, Mr Taylor and Mr Tallent, sir!'

'Jolly good. How old are they, Corporal?

The corporal gathered the papers and glanced through them, 'Erm… Nineteen, sir!'

'Well here's a funny thing, Corporal. You see, I have got a Jones, Roberts, Taylor and Tallent in my rugby team but they can't be the same ones because they would be too young to join.'

The clock on the wall ticked but time had stopped; everything had stopped. The boys had stopped breathing; Bryn slowly closed his eyes and prayed. He couldn't do this to them, he couldn't. The corporal looked at the sergeant major, who was staring at the backs of the boys. The sergeant major sighed.

'My mistake,' he said. 'It must be a coincidence. Carry on, Corporal.'

CHAPTER NINE

'Left, dight, left, dight, left, dight. Platoon 'alt'.'

The drill sergeant had been relentlessly bellowing orders for the past hour. Up and down the race course squads of men dressed in their best suits were dripping in sweat. They had eventually been allowed to dispense with their jackets, ties and hats but their thick woollen serge blue suit trousers were like lagging on hot pipes. The heavy material was like sandpaper on the inside of their thighs, many of which were now red-raw.

'Right, when I give you the word of command "fall out", you will turn to the right, bend and drive your right leg into the ground and step off for three paces before breaking off. You can have a ten-minute break before we move on to saluting. Right, listen in... platoon... fall out.'

The men called out the timing, one-two-three, one-two-three, left-right-left, and broke off.

The boys had been split up when they had been sized for the platoon. The shortest man was in the middle, rising in height to the tallest on both ends. John was in the very centre, flanked by Huan and Rhys, just like on the pitch but the wrong way around. They had swapped around to their normal playing positions when the sergeant wasn't watching. There was no breaking up the front row. Bryn took his place on the very left on account of his height.

'What do you reckon then?' Huan asked as Bryn approached.

'I reckon I'll be cooked by lunchtime, that's what,' Bryn replied as he wiped the sweat from his brow.

'Good training though,' John said as he sat down on the grass.

'Training for what? I can already walk in a straight line; I don't need training in that. We should be shooting and doing army stuff.'

'I'm sure we will in good time,' John replied as he flopped onto his back.

'By the time the war's over at this rate.'

'Don't you worry, Bryn *bach*,' Rhys said. 'I reckon there will be plenty of Germans left for us to get our teeth into. They wouldn't have taken us on otherwise would they?'

'I still can't believe that we are here. When Uncle Bob turned up I nearly died.'

'I knew he would let us in,' John said as he gazed up into the cloudless sky.

'Oh really? Well it's the first time I'd heard you praying for a long time,' Huan quipped.

'Rubbish, I didn't want you three to be left out. I was praying that even the Royal Welsh Fusiliers would find it in their hearts to take grotty, filthy miners like you as well as highly skilled artisans like myself.'

'Oh is that right?' Huan said, raising his head from the grass to look across at John. 'Well if you are so blinking highly skilled and intelligent why do you keep turning right when the sergeant shouts left?'

The boys laughed.

'Right, fall in,' the drill sergeant cried.

'Fall in? I've just fallen out and will probably fall over if this goes on much longer,' Rhys groaned.

'Come on lardy arse, I'll give you a hand up,' Bryn said as he jumped to his feet. 'By the end of the week you'll be as fit as me.'

'Fitter I might be but I still won't be as ugly as you,' Rhys retorted.

The boys moved back into their assigned positions. Despite the banter they were happy. Although the men had been split up, miners dominated the platoon and most of the other platoons that were marching and countermarching around the field.

There must have been sixteen platoons moving in every direction. How they avoided crashing into each other was a secret known only to drill sergeants. The rest of the boys' platoon was made up of working men from just about every trade and industry of Wrexham's business community: tailors, tanners, butchers, gardeners, brewers, bankers and clerks. Everyone wanted to be in at the start.

The officers, drawn from the upper echelons of society, were being drilled separately, distinguished by the fact that they were still wearing their ties and jackets rather than their ability to do drill any better than their men. Officers or not, the drill sergeant still screamed at them but he liked to add 'sir' at the end of his endless barrage of sarcasm to give his orders a degree of polite correctness.

*

The mess tent was overflowing with men by the time the boys arrived. Several large marquees had been put up on the old racecourse that was now the home ground of Wrexham Football Club. Unlike the officers' and senior non-commissioned officers' tents that were pitched at a discreet distance away from the recruits' tent, there were no tables and chairs and no mess staff to serve refreshments. Men were sprawled on the grass in the welcome shade with bowls of steaming food and chunks of bread.

John brought up the rear, very much in disgrace. He knew his left and right well enough but he just couldn't get the hang of marching and turning. The drill sergeant had been as patient as a drill sergeant could be but finally he had had enough. Despite John's protestations that he wasn't doing it on purpose he had incurred the instructor's wrath.

'You will live, work and if necessary die together,' he had screamed at John, their faces less than an inch apart. The sergeant's spittle had peppered John's eyes, nose and cheeks. 'And by God, you will march together.' Marching, he explained, is the basis of good soldiering. It had clearly been a well-rehearsed script. The whole squad suffered for an extra thirty minutes.

'Well, we'll not get any lunch now will we?' Rhys said whilst looking at John.

'Come on, it's not his fault that he's too clever for the simple things in life. It's not like he has to know the difference between right and left when he's shoeing a horse, is it? They're all the same bloomin' shape,' Huan said.

'I do know my right and left, it's just that he makes me nervous,' John said.

Bryn came to his friend's rescue. 'Come on, stop moaning you two. I'm sure that they will have made enough for everyone.'

'That's as maybe but not everyone needs it as much as I do,' Rhys moaned.

'Well, that's for sure. So why don't you stop moaning and get in the queue?'

Rhys looked around. '*Duw* Bryn, this is the queue.' They gave a collective groan. The extra drill had meant half an hour less for lunch. They were famished but then they always were. There was silence and hope as the queue edged forward slowly. Bryn had a peek around the flap of the marquee and calculated that they would miss their dinner by about five minutes at this rate.

'We need a plan,' John said.

'Well then, best you think of one, seeing as how you got us into this mess,' Huan said.

Bryn sighed. 'Look, just shut up and think.'

'I can't think on an empty stomach.'

'Nor an empty head,' Rhys quipped.

'Right, that's it. I'm going to give you such a bashing.'

'What's going on here then?' came a voice from behind them, a voice that they had got to know all too well over the course of the morning. Sergeant Smith had been screaming at them all morning. He was a squat bull of a man with a huge barrel chest that gave him his baritone voice. The boys couldn't decide if his face was red from all the shouting or just naturally crimson. Rhys thought that he would have been a cracking tight head prop in his younger days. 'Dissension in the ranks is it?'

'No, Sergeant,' Bryn said quickly with an innocent smile. 'We were just talking about how much we are enjoying being soldiers. Although we were wondering when we might be doing some tactics and stuff. You know, how best to clobber the Germans and all that.'

'Thank you, Private…?

'Tallent, Sergeant.'

'Well Tallent, you will be pleased to know that I am well aware of what tactics are and what they are not. You let the officers worry about the tactics because they know what they are doing and you don't. That way we will win this war. The only tactic you need to understand is do whatever you are fucking told when you are told to do it. That is a tactic young man that will win this war. Got it?'

'Yes, Sergeant,' Bryn replied.

'It's a shame you were not discussing your drill. That way we might finish today instead of tomorrow.'

'When do we get to kill someone, Sergeant?' Huan asked.

'Kill someone?' The sergeant almost screamed. 'My God lad, you lot couldn't kill a pint of beer let alone a German. Drill is the only way to win this war and by my hand you will be good at it.'

As the sergeant wandered over to the senior non-commissioned officers' mess tent Bryn had an idea. 'Right you three, form up as if we were marching.'

'What?!' Rhys cried.

'Just shut up and do what you're told if you want some food. Now we are going round to the kitchen; just follow my lead. By the left, or is it right? I dunno… whatever – quick march that way,' he said, pointing towards the rear of the mess tent.

The boys stepped off in quick time around the corner to the entrance of the kitchen.

'Squad 'alt," Bryn screamed. He turned smartly to the right and halted in front of the chefs who had gathered for a smoke at the rear of the kitchen.

'What 'ave we got 'ere then?' the master chef asked.

'Private Tallent, No. 3 Platoon, sir.'

'Sir!' The master chef screamed. 'Do I look like a sir to you, Private? Would I be serving grub to pond life like you if I was a sir?'

Bryn looked at the stripes on the chef's arm. 'No, Sergeant. And jolly fine food it was too if I may say so.' The compliment took the wind out of the master chef's sails and he grunted.

'Well then, Private,' the chef asked, looking Bryn up and down. 'What do you want?'

'Sergeant, we have been sent to pick up four plates of food for our instructors, who have been unexpectedly detained by an officer.'

The master chef looked aghast. 'What? Is this a blooming café now? Do I look like I do packed meals?'

'No, Sergeant.'

'Bloody right "No, Sergeant"!' Who are your instructors?'

Bryn took a moment to look confused. 'I don't know their names, Sergeant, on account as we have only been here for half a day. Sergeant.'

The master chef stared at Bryn. 'What rank are these instructors?'

Bryn paused. 'I'm not too sure of the ranks but they must be important as they had big badges on their arms and carried big sticks.'

The master chef hesitated. He continued to stare at Bryn. 'Gone to a meeting with an officer, have they?'

'Yes, Sergeant. The officer didn't seem very happy and said he didn't care if they missed lunch. One of them told us to fetch some lunch for them.'

The sergeant's stare bore into Bryn. 'Oh, the officer didn't care, did he? Well I'm sure that he had probably had his lunch. You say that you've eaten?'

'Oh yes Sergeant. Very nice. Thank you. Almost as good as my mam's.'

'Takes four of you to pick up four plates, does it?'

'Well no, not really, but we were sat together when the instructor asked us to pick up some food so we marched down for the practice. Shall I go and tell him that he can't have any?'

'No. Go on in and get four plates but I want the plates back, do you hear?'

'Yes, Sergeant. Squad fall out.'

The boys ran into the kitchen, filled up four plates and fell in again outside. As soon as they were ready Bryn stepped them off as the sergeant stared after them.

'Is he still watching?' Rhys asked, barely able to control himself.

'Shut up and keep walking or we won't be getting any lunch ever again.' As they rounded the marquee the boys broke into fits of laughter as they joined the rest of the men who were sitting on the grass, enjoying lunch in the afternoon sun.

'Do you reckon he'd give us a cup of tea if we went back?' Rhys asked.

*

The men fell in. Rhys looked around the football field at the other platoons. Young men just like him jostled to get into position as sergeants buzzed around, waving their pace sticks in the air, shouting and screaming at anyone who seemed to lack the right amount of enthusiasm. He counted nearly twelve platoons the same size as his own. He grinned at the spectacle as another platoon passed in front of their own. Rhys saw Daffyd, Jonesy and Geraint and some other friends from the mine. He waved across to grab their attention.

'Hey, how you doing?' he cried.

Geraint raised a hand as if to wave back, but brought it down suddenly.

Rhys cried over to the other platoon again, 'This is better than being down the pit isn't it?' Geraint nodded across and there was a shuffling of feet and few nudges into Rhys' ribs.

'Watch out boyo,' he said turning to the man behind him. 'There's plenty of room.'

Huan stifled a laugh.

Rhys looked to his left. 'What are you laughing at boyo?'

Huan nodded his head towards the end of the front rank. Rhys turned to look. There stood a giant of a man. Sergeant Major Flint, 'Tiny' to his friends although there weren't many of them who knew him well enough to call him that glared at Rhys. At six feet and five inches tall he towered over the miners, immaculately dressed, pace stick tucked under his arm, his cap peak slashed and re-stitched so that it dropped down to the bridge of his nose. He walked slowly but purposefully along the front rank of the platoon, his eyes boring down on Rhys. Each man held his breath as the man-mountain walked past them. He stopped in front of Rhys. He looked down.

'Hello Private,' he said in a rather mild manner.

'How do?' Rhys said back with a nod.

'And what is your name?'

'Rhys... Rhys Taylor.'

'Well Private Rhys Taylor, my name is Sergeant Major Flint,' he said keeping his voice calm and level. 'I am here to see how you are getting on. So, how are you getting on?'

'Oh, lovely thanks, although I am not sure we should be spending so much time walking up and down. I think perhaps we should be doing some more military things. You know, things that will help us kill the Germans.'

'Oh, quite right.'

Huan sniggered.

Sergeant Major Flint turned his head. 'And what might your name be then, Private?'

'Huan Jones... sir,' he added after a short pause, looking into Sergeant Major Flint's eyes.

'Well it seems to me, lads, that you two are getting along quicker than I expected, so what I would like you to do is to go and pick up those artillery shells that are outside the front of the Sergeants' Mess and bring them over here.'

Rhys and Huan looked at each other, broke ranks as they had been taught that morning and trotted over to the shells. Two large brass artillery shells were stood on end either side of the front entrance to the Sergeants' Mess tent.

'What are we going to do with these?' Huan asked as he picked up a shell. 'By heck it's heavy. You wouldn't want this falling on your head would you?'

'I reckon he's going to teach us about artillery,' Rhys said.

He grunted as he heaved the shell onto his shoulder. They walked back as quickly as they could to the platoon. Not one of the other men looked across as the boys returned; they were all standing stock-still as the sergeant major walked through the ranks. He stopped at the end of the rear rank.

'Listen to me, all of you, and listen very carefully.' His voice was still quiet but somehow threatening. Rhys and Huan gave each other a glance. 'I have been in the army for nineteen years and I have seen better men than you blown to smithereens; men whose bodies have been blasted to the heavens. Not a trace of them left to put into a paper bag, not a scrap of personal possessions left to send home to their families. They have just vanished. I have seen men with bullet holes clean through their skulls right between the eyes, shot by an unseen sniper. One minute alive, the next minute dead. They were the lucky ones, the ones who didn't have their arms or legs ripped from their sockets or their bellies spilled onto the dirt beside them. So I will decide what kind of training you do, how you do it and how long you do it for.' His voice was rising steadily and then it started to tremble. 'You lot have got a lot to learn and you will start NOW. This is not a game, it is not a laugh or a joke, it is serious and you will take it seriously. Do I make myself clear?'

'Yes Sergeant Major,' came a rather feeble response.

'I said, DO I MAKE MYSELF CLEAR?' he roared.

'YES SERGEANT MAJOR,' came a loud and emphatic reply from the platoon.

'You two,' he screamed, turning his attention back to Rhys and Huan, who had by now grasped that they were in trouble, 'if you want to do military training, you can blooming well start now. Pick up those shells and start running and don't stop until I tell you to.' Spittle was flying from his mouth, such was his rage. 'Get away with you, you horrible little urchins.'

Rhys and Huan hoisted the shells onto their shoulders and doubled off around the perimeter of the racecourse.

'Sergeant Smith,' Flint screamed at their drill sergeant, who had been stood at the rear of the platoon. 'Get these men off my parade ground. They are not fit or worthy to be here.'

'Yes, sir. Right, listen to me. Right turn,' he screamed. By the left, double march, left, dight, left, dight.' The men had to run to keep the step. 'Mark time. Keep the step!' The pace was relentless. Every time the pace slackened Sergeant Smith screamed out the timing.

'Halt!' he cried. The platoon stood still, panting and sweating profusely although not as much as Rhys and Huan, who were dragging themselves and their shells towards the platoon. 'Right, you two horrible little men, fall in.' They dropped the shells. 'I didn't say put the shells down, did I? Pick 'em up.'

Rhys and Huan took their positions in the squad, barely able to stand with the weight on their shoulders.

'Right, we are going to go for a little walk and these shells are coming with us. And like it or not, you will be happy. Do I make myself perfectly clear?'

'*YES*, Sergeant.'

'By the left, quick march!'

The platoon marched out of the gate onto the Mold Road. A crowd of young boys and girls had gathered by the gate to watch the men training. As the platoon passed through the gate they gave a cheer. With the children running alongside the platoon the men got into the step and started to swagger. All except Rhys and Huan, who staggered, trotted and marched the best they could.

'Come here you dollop,' John said as he grasped the shell from Rhys. 'Have a breather for a few minutes.'

'Thanks,' was all he could manage to get out. The relief was immeasurable.

Bryn shouted from the back of the platoon, 'Hey, pass that other shell here.'

Another man grabbed the shell from Huan and sat it on his shoulder. 'You're alright, I've got it for a moment.'

The drill sergeant kept the timing going as he watched the shell pass from pillar to post.

CHAPTER TEN

Bryn looked at himself in the mirror as he combed back his dark brown hair and adjusted his tie. His collar felt a little tight and he ran his finger around the rim – perhaps he'd put a bit of weight on, he thought. He adjusted his suit jacket. His mam had said that he should wear his best suit, seeing as it was a special occasion. He wasn't fond of wearing a tie and much less so having to cram his feet into polished shoes. He'd had them for a few years now and they pinched his toes as he walked down the stairs. He would treat himself to a new pair when he got back from the war, he told himself.

Sergeant Evans had broken the news to the platoon the previous day. They were to take the day off to sort out their personal affairs and report as detailed to the station. They were going to a new training camp, probably in Salisbury but they should remain flexible. The men grinned; the word 'flexible' was becoming the byword for being messed about.

His mam and da were stood in the parlour. His mam, Edith, was wringing her hands as Bryn entered the room.

'By heck lad,' she said. 'You seem to have grown. Doesn't he seem to have grown, Da?' Harold looked at his wife and smiled.

'Well he's not a little boy anymore Eddie, if that's what you were thinking.'

'I wasn't thinking that at all. I was just thinking how swanky he looks. He'll have all them French girls swooning after him.'

Bryn had never thought of himself as handsome; in fact he had never really thought about girls at all. Bryn had never had a girlfriend, although he had never been short of offers. Girls saw him but he never saw them. Rugby and his pals were all he had ever needed. Girls, he thought, were something that would just happened later in life. That was until he met Cerys. He had seen her a few times since they had met at the top of Caergwrle Castle, although she was usually with Mary or Bronwyn or both as a chaperone. Rhys had taken a fancy to Mary so the four of them had started walking out together. They usually went for a walk but once they had gone into town to the cinema to see the new Charlie Chaplin film. It wasn't to Bryn's taste, but it wasn't the film that he was particularly interested in. It was only lately that he had found himself thinking of Cerys more and more. As he lay in bed listening to the rhythmic breathing of his younger brother sleeping next to him he allowed his thoughts to drift. He could picture her face. It was always her smile that he saw first. It was an infectious and kind smile that lit up the room when she entered. She had the type of smile that instantly made you happy and smile in return. Only then did he see how pretty she was; her green eyes shone like emeralds, although he had told her that they shone like cat's eyes. She had playfully scolded him for referring to her as a cat so he went to the library to look up green precious stones.

He rolled his shoulders back and grew an inch as he braced up in front of his parents – *shoulders back, chest out* was all he had heard for the past week or so.

'Well lad, let's not stand here while there's ale to be drunk.'

*

A loud cheer rose the moment Harold and Bryn entered The Grapes. The small bar was crammed with miners, many on their way home. It was a bit grimy inside but then so were most places in the village. The years of coal dust had impregnated every joint and seam, and painted every piece of masonry a dull grey, which matched the equally grey landscape. Thin shafts of light penetrated the small panes of thick rolled glass and cut through the hazy wall of smoke. Opposite the door was a solid oak bar across which beer had passed for more than a century. The publican, Robert the Grapes, was busy pulling pints as men waited two-deep to be served. Bryn was rather taken aback but his father clapped him on the shoulder and shoved him towards the bar. John was already supping a pint with his da, Ted the Smith.

'Here's another one,' Ted shouted across the bar, but Robert the Grapes was already one step ahead of him.

'Here you go lad,' he said passing a beer across the head of a local man to Bryn. 'This one's on the house.'

'Thanks very much,' Bryn said, shaking the landlord's hand as he took the pint in his other hand. He raised his glass to his da and friends. 'Cheers.' Another cheer rose as Huan and Rhys pushed through the door.

'Room for two more?' Rhys cried as they battled towards the bar. More beer was passed across the heads of others.

The fathers retreated home after a couple of pints. This wasn't their night and although none of them would admit it they were needed at home where the boys' mothers would be anxious.

The boys planned to move into town after a couple of pints but they never made it out of the village. Neither did they have to put a hand in their pockets. It was as if the beer tap was stuck open. Every time they sank a jar another would appear as if by magic. It had been a long time since the village had seen this kind of send-off. No one was complaining, least of all the landlords of the public houses. There was enough beer downed to keep them in profit for the rest of the year. If this was war, they would be happy for it to continue for a long while yet!

*

The station was thronged with wives, girlfriends and well-wishers. Bryn wasn't sure that he had even seen a crowd this big at a football match. Excited children were everywhere, darting in and out of the adults, banging into people and getting a thick ear off one or two men. Beyond the waiting area a large green locomotive of the Great Western Railway was panting gently, waiting to release its power to the pistons the moment the driver got the signal. The driver was leaning on the side of the engine cab, his face streaked with black. Behind him the fireman shovelled another load of coal into the furnace to keep the heat building. As the wind gently blew across the line the steam enveloped the platform. Young men took the opportunity of the brief shroud to steal a kiss. Some of the older men hugged their children and gave the wife a peck on the cheek. Young boys were entrusted to be the man of the house and with a tussle of their hair fathers started to clamber into the brown and cream coaches that were more used to taking holidaymakers along the coast to Rhyl or Llandudno. The boys made for a tea stall that had been set up by the ladies of the church.

'I needed that,' Bryn said as he took a mouthful of steaming tea.

'Well I guess this is it then. No turning back,' John said to no one in particular as he looked around at the mass of people. Most of the crowd were in good spirits – more than a few of them were still full of the previous night's spirits, which reminded John that his head still hurt. Here and there a few women were crying.

'Why would we want to go back?' Rhys replied. 'I'm looking forward to seeing Salisbury.'

'Shut up, idiot. It's just a saying isn't it?'

'I can't wait. All that fresh air.'

'And more blooming drill, no doubt,' Bryn added.

'Crikey, I hope not,' Rhys said as he strained his neck, looking around.

'You lost someone, boyo?' Huan asked.

'No, not really. I was just looking that's all.'

'Oh, I thought perhaps you were looking for Mary.'

'Oh no. I'm sure she's busy.'

'That wouldn't be her over there then?' Huan said, pointing towards the ticket barrier.

Rhys looked across and saw Mary craning her head, looking across the sea of faces. The boys laughed.

'Go on boyo, we'll save you a seat.'

As they watched Rhys push his way through the crowd Bryn looked across to see if there was anyone else with Mary. Huan looked at his friend and smiled. 'Sorry Bryn but I think she's on her own.'

Bryn shrugged. 'She said she had to work but I thought… you know… she might if she could… but never mind.' Bryn and Cerys had said their goodbyes the day before, but not before they had promised to write to each other. It wasn't an engagement or anything like that but she had said that she would wait for him to return. That was good enough for Bryn.

'Come on, let's get on so that we can get a window seat. I promised Hugh and Enid that I would give them a wave when the train pulls out,' John said.

His brother and sister had joined the rest of the children who now lined the top of the embankment on the edge of the station, waiting to wave the men off to war.

The locomotive whistle gave a long shrill blast and the guards moved around the platform, calling for anyone leaving to get on board and close the doors. Rhys managed to squeeze through the packed corridors to the carriage that his friends had secured. Every man on board had his head through a window. The crowd cheered as the engine took the strain and edged the train forward inch-by-inch, gathering momentum as it pulled along the platform. The band played *It's a Long Way to Tipperary* and the crowds cheered and shouted. Even girlfriends and wives who moments ago had had tears in their eyes were now waving with excitement. As the train cut through the embankment a hundred or so children waved their Welsh flags and cheered. John spotted his brother and sister and gave a cheery wave back. 'See you at Christmas,' he shouted.

*

The shrill of the engine's whistle cut through Huan's head like a stabbing bayonet. He held his head in his hands, trying to cradle himself against the buffeting of the carriage. Rhys was moaning gently to himself as he sat propped up against an equally ashen-faced John. Only Bryn was watching through the window as the landscape began to slow. Houses emerged through the smoke as the engine crept gently forward towards Salisbury railway station. There was a buzz of excitement starting to build as the platform came into view. In contrast to the station in Wrexham, Salisbury station was empty save for a few soldiers. The boys stirred as the brakes squealed and the carriages juddered as they ran into each other. Bryn pulled down the window, engulfing the carriage with a cloud of thickened smoke.

'Are we here?' Rhys said as he ruffled his hands through his hair and stretched his arms towards the ceiling before collapsing down again on the bench. Bryn nodded and grunted.

John moaned. 'That's it, I'm not drinking again until Berlin.' He had turned a very pale green colour.

'They reckon that French wine stuff is pretty good,' Huan said without moving.

'I don't care what they say; I'm not drinking ever again.'

'I'm not sure I am up for any of that fancy stuff. It's for the toffs isn't it, like the officers? I'll stick to beer,' Rhys replied as he poked his head out of the window. 'I can't see any wagons lined up for us.'

'You're in the army now boyo,' Bryn mocked. 'You have to march here, there and every-blasted-where now.'

Soldiers were lining the platform at regular intervals along the length of the train. As soon as the doors of the Great Western Railway locomotive shuddered to a halt a rather vociferous and vocal sergeant major began bellowing orders to the troops on board.

'Grab all of your kit and fall in in three ranks on the platform. Come on, get a move on.'

The soldiers started to scream and shout the orders all along the length of the platform. The men danced around each other in their efforts to grab their kit and get off the train.

'Come on. We haven't got all day, there's a bloody war going on and you lot are going to miss it at this rate,' the sergeant major shouted as he stood in the centre of the platform, rigidly to attention with his pace stick clenched under his left arm.

Men tumbled from the carriages glad to be out in the open air, blessed with a clear day and warm sunshine. The boys grabbed their cases from the racks above their heads and waited patiently as lines of men shuffled towards the carriage doors. The journey had taken far longer than expected, having been delayed and shunted into sidings on several occasions due to higher priority trains, many of them carrying regular troops south towards the ports and others carrying wounded north to hospitals in Liverpool and Manchester.

'Crikey, what's the matter with him?' Huan said, referring to the sergeant major who had by now worked himself up into a rage.

'I reckon he's probably missed his lunch,' Rhys replied.

'Too much fresh air I expect,' John said as he grabbed his spare clothes and washing kit wrapped in a newspaper bundle.

'Well there is no point in making life any worse,' Bryn said. 'We've been in enough trouble lately without getting into any more. What we need is a fresh start and this is going to be it; come on.'

*

Charles Symonds had taken the same journey from Wrexham to Salisbury in a slightly more comfortable carriage reserved for officers. As he climbed down from the carriage he looked along the platform at the men as they assembled in three ranks. It had been a boorish journey during which he had been forced to share a cabin with three second lieutenants, all of whom were far too young and enthusiastic for their own good. They had introduced themselves as Smyth, Cruickshank and Gibbons. They had talked incessantly for the whole journey.

Symonds had learned that they had each been destined for university but had chosen to join up instead. *Idiots*, he thought to himself. Their universities had agreed to delay the start of their courses until they returned. Symonds found their enthusiasm nauseating and their company despairing.

He had grown bored of their immaturity very quickly and sought solace in his hip flask. They all looked slightly shocked as he took a long swig of a very fine malt whiskey. The animated chatter stopped and he saw them staring at him. Lowering the flask from his lips, he smiled and asked them if they would like a tot. They declined politely. He didn't think so. They should be at home, still being wet-nursed. He had eventually dropped into an alcohol-induced sleep. The screech of the engine as it pulled into Salisbury had awoken him with a start. His three young companions were already on their feet and pulling kit from the racks above their heads. They passed their bags down to a couple of soldiers who were waiting on the platform to receive them. The soldiers placed the bags on a hand-pulled cart and directed the officers to a waiting car.

One of the soldiers looked up at Symonds as he descended from the carriage. 'Good afternoon, sir. Got any bags 'ave you?' Symonds looked at the man who was smiling back at him.

'In the carriage,' he instructed. 'I take it that car is going to the camp?' The soldier's smile drained. The soldier was a professional and had been for many years. He wasn't particularly ambitious and had never sought promotion; he was happy being a private. He had seen many good officers come and go over the years, and a few not-so-good ones. He wasn't normally quick to judge but he knew straight away that this one was a bad 'un, and instinctively knew how to handle him.

'Indeed it is, sir. If you would like to take a seat, sir, with the other gentlemen, I will grab your belongings and then we will be on our way sir.' Saluting smartly, he waited for Symonds to descend the steps and then he hopped on board to grab the bags from the train, noting the name on the labels as he did so.

As Symonds made his way towards the car a man fell from one of the carriages, followed by another man who fell on top of him. Symonds had to stop as the men sprawled in front of him. 'God save us from idiots,' he said to himself as walked around the prostrate men.

*

Bryn was at the bottom of the heap thinking it was just like being back on the rugby pitch. His foot had slipped on the carriage step. As he started to fall he turned and grabbed hold of John who was right behind him but he only succeeded in pulling his friend on top of him. Huan managed to stop briefly in the doorway before Rhys bumped into him, sending him spiralling out of the door to add to the heap of bodies. Rhys roared with laughter from the carriage door. Hearing a commotion the sergeant major walked along the platform.

'What are you lot doing?' he screamed. 'Get up and get fell in. This is not a girl guide camp, you 'orrible Welsh things!'

The boys scrambled to their feet and grabbed what little kit they had with them. 'What are your names?' the sergeant major screamed in a heavy Liverpudlian accent.

'Tallent, sir.'

'Roberts, sir.'

'Jones, sir.'

'Taylor, sir,' Rhys said as he got down from the carriage.

The sergeant major's pace stick was almost rammed up Rhys' nose. 'When I tell you to get off a train, Taylor, I do not expect to see you and your chums larking about like a group of schoolboys. I expect you to get off the train and fall in like proper soldiers. Do I make myself perfectly clear?'

'Yes, sir.'

'I will be watching you four. Now get fell in with the rest of them.'

'Yes sir,' the boys cried in unison and ran to the end of the rear rank.

The sergeant major shouted a few words that most of the men couldn't hear. The soldiers who were dotted along the line repeated his words of command. The men came to attention and turned to the right.

'Bloody brilliant start that was,' Bryn said as they stepped off from the platform and onto the road that led away from the station.

'Well you were the one that fell over,' John replied.

'You didn't have to fall on top of me, did you?!'

'Well how was I to know that you were going to fall over?'

'Why didn't you look?'

'Why don't you two just shut up instead of arguing?' a man in the centre rank said.

Bryn and John looked at each other, shrugged and then looked at the man.

'Why don't you mind you own business?' Rhys butted in before the others could say anything.

'I wasn't talking to you was I?' the man said.

'Quiet in the ranks,' a corporal screamed as he marched alongside the squad.

*

The training camp was not too dissimilar to the racecourse ground. There were several fields with platoons of soldiers doing various lessons in drill, musketry, bayonet fighting and physical training. They entered through a gate that had two sentries, both of whom were carrying rifles. The hedgerows formed a natural boundary that had once kept the cattle and sheep in and now served to keep the children at bay.

The training camp had become more of an attraction than a travelling circus and it was free to watch. As soon as school was over hundreds of children descended on the camp to see what was going on. Gangs of boys copied the men by marching up and down along the lane, calling out the time and shouting orders. Many of them held sticks that they pretended were rifles and played war games in the adjacent field.

'Halt,' the sergeant major cried. 'Right turn, look sharp now,' he added for good measure. 'Right, first things first. We need to get you lot looking like proper soldiers.' An audible murmur started throughout the ranks. 'Alright, alright, calm down. It's only a bloody uniform not the crown jewels. When I give you the word of command I want the rear rank to form an orderly queue outside that tent,' he said, pointing to a large white marquee to his right. 'I want the middle rank to line up over by that tent over there,' he pointed to his left, 'where you will be issued with instructions for your accommodation. Some of you will be sleeping here and some of you will be billeted with some of the local folk who have very kindly given up a spare room or two to house you lucky men. The front rank are to move to the large tent behind me where you will get your dinner and the rest of your meals whilst you are here. Once you finished in each tent you will move in a clockwise direction,' he explained by pointing his pace stick in a wide arc. 'When you have done all three tasks, and not until you have done all three tasks, get yourselves sorted out and be back on parade at seven o'clock sharp tomorrow morning, wearing your uniform in a soldierly manner. Is that clear?'

'Yes sir,' came an enthusiastic and emphatic response.

'Right then, fall out.'

The boys were in the rear rank and followed the crowd of men towards the clothing tent. There was no clamour, the men were orderly but there was an air of excitement with the expectancy of getting a new uniform.

'Shame we aren't in the front rank,' Rhys said, 'I'm blooming hungry.'

'You're always hungry,' Huan replied before the other two could say it.

'At least we get a uniform,' Bryn said as they joined the end of the queue.

'What size do you think I should ask for?' Rhys asked.

'Extra wide,' Huan said.

'From what I've heard they only come in two sizes,' Bryn suggested as he strained his head to look at the first recipients as they trailed out of the tent. 'Large and extra large. So you three will have to cut the bottoms off your trousers.' Bryn laughed at his own joke while the other three stared at him, which made him laugh even harder. 'Calm down boys, calm down,' he said, mimicking the sergeant major and laughing even more at his impression. His friends looked back at him blankly. Bryn stopped laughing and looked at his friends, who were still staring at him. Bryn grimaced.

'Finished laughing have you, Private? Something funny you want to share with the rest of the platoon is there?' Bryn could feel the sergeant major's face inching closer to the back of his neck. He could feel his breath rushing down his collar. 'Well? Are you a fucking comedian? Do you have a joke to tell the rest of us? I'm sure that we all have a sense of humour.'

'No, sir,' Bryn said.

'No, sir! I didn't bloody well think so.' The sergeant major screamed so hard that Bryn could feel his spittle trickling down his neck. 'Do you know what I find funny? I find men marching around the square until I get too tired to watch them funny. Do you understand what I find funny?'

'No, sir.'

'No, sir? Well let me show you. Get going then you 'orrible little man.'

Bryn ran as fast as he could to the edge of the parade area and started marching in quickstep. The sergeant major stared at Rhys,

John and Huan, who hadn't dared to breathe. 'That's twice already today. I'm watching you boys. Do you understand?'

'Yes sir,' they cried in unison.

*

Bryn was the last to collect his uniform. As he stepped out of the marquee and strode towards the accommodation allocations tent he saw his friends sitting on the ground. He was covered in sweat from two hours of marching.

'Where are we staying?' he said.

'Well,' John said, 'the good news is that we are staying in a house near the town. The bad news is that you are sleeping here.'

'What? Didn't you tell them that we were together?'

'We did but we were the last ones to be allocated accommodation on account of you messing about and all they had was three spaces in the house.'

'Well where am I staying then?'

'Here, apparently. The sergeant major said it would be good for you.'

'What, and I have to stay here in those tents?'

'Sorry boyo,' Huan added.'

Bryn looked at his friends as they gathered up their new kit. He was too tired to argue. All he wanted was a warm bath and to change out of his sodden clothes. 'Right then, I'll see you in the morning I guess.'

The boys nodded. Rhys patted Bryn on the shoulder as he brushed past him and walked towards the camp gates.

'Do you think that we should've told him?' Rhys asked as they walked away.

'Nah,' John replied. 'Serves him right for being an idiot. Anyway, he'll see the funny side of it tomorrow. And we'll get first dibs on the beds.'

*

'Mr Symonds, sir?' a wiry old lance corporal asked as the officer approached the entrance to the officers' mess. He was an old soldier resplendent in his service dress, his chest adorned with medals that were testament to his service.

'Yes that's me,' Symonds replied.

'Your accommodation is ready, sir. If you would like to follow me.'

'Follow you where?'

'Over this way, sir,' he said pointing towards a row of immaculately spaced and fronted tents.

'Those are tents. You want me to live in a tent?'

'Yes, sir. It's the colonel's idea, sir. He wants all of his young officers to show willing, sir. It's to show the men that the officers are not afraid to rough it.'

Symonds gave the lance corporal a disdainful look. 'Really? Well you had better show me to my tent then.'

Symonds strode off with the old lance corporal in tow. As he walked he trashed the longer blades of grass with his crop.

'Come far 'ave you, sir?' the lance corporal asked.

'Far enough,' Symonds replied.

'I'm not from round here either, sir. Settled just outside Wrexham after I was demobbed a couple of years ago. We bought a little cottage up near Cefn Mawr. It's near my sister's place. I don't suppose you know it, sir. It's very nice but it's not the same as being in the regiment, you know.'

'No, I don't know. And I can't say that I particularly want to know either. Which is my tent?'

The lance corporal smiled to himself. 'This one here, sir. I'm sure that you'll find it quite comfortable, sir. Dinner in the mess is at nineteen hundred hours. The colonel doesn't like to be kept waiting, if you get my meaning sir.' The lance corporal saluted, received nothing in return except a look of disinterest, turned about and marched away.

'Lance Corporal!' came a cry before he had got more than ten paces away. 'There is already an officer in this tent.'

71

The lance corporal tried to stifle a smile as he stopped and turned. 'Oh yes, sir, that will be Mr Gibbons, sir. I believe you met him on the train?'

'Maybe so but what is he doing in my tent?'

'Sharing, sir. Two officers in a tent, sir. Is that all, sir?'

Salisbury Plain Training Camp
September 1914

Dear Cerys,

Just a line to let you know that we have arrived safely at camp. I know that you couldn't get to the station but I was sorry not to see you there. I know you would have been there if you could – work still has to go on I suppose. The train journey was fine, if a little long. The boys were pretty full of themselves although Rhys and Huan slept most of the way and snored very loudly!

We are in a camp just outside Salisbury, which seems a pretty nice place. It is just a couple of miles out of town. It's a good walk into the camp in the morning. Everywhere is so green and colourful and the air is very different – almost sweet, like. We've been billeted with Mrs Quigley. She seems very nice and happy to have us and before you ask we are on our best behaviour! We haven't been into town yet on account of the training. We have only had a couple of days but it is mainly marching and physical jerks. Some of the boys aren't too fit but we're absolutely fine – good training for next season! At least they are feeding us well. We are having meat every day and plenty of jam and bread. I need all the marching to keep me slim!

Well, look after yourself.
Best wishes,
Bryn

CHAPTER ELEVEN

November 1914

'Chop, chop, my lads or you'll be late and then the good Sergeant Major Ashton will be getting onto me.'

'There's nothing "good" about him, Mrs Quigley,' John assured her. 'We'll sort him out if he comes around here.'

'I think, my lad, that you should save your sorting out for the Germans and I'm more than capable of sorting out a sergeant major.'

Of that, the boys had no doubt. Despite her sixty-eight years Mrs Quigley was a formidable and spritely woman who would give any sergeant major a run for his money. Not that there would be any need. Despite their infamous start the boys had finally ingratiated themselves with the sergeant major by doing what they did best: playing rugby. The sergeant major's ferocity was only exceeded by his passion for 'the great game', as he called it. Ever since C Company had beaten A Company in the Battalion rugby competition his attitude towards the boys had changed. So too had their attitude towards him and towards being soldiers. His encouragement had brought out the best in them and they quickly learned the art of rifle drill, bayonet drill and fieldcraft. They took pride in being the best.

'Come on, come on, he'll be picking on me if you don't get gone. Go on, shoo, the lot of you.'

'Thanks for breakfast, Mrs Q,' Huan and Rhys called from the front door as they made their way out.

'Not so fast you two. I haven't had a look at you yet.'

'Oh come on Mrs Quigley none of the other men get

inspected before they leave their quarters. We're big enough to dress ourselves you know,' Huan wailed like a five-year-old.

'No you're not and I don't care what the other ladies do but I'm not having my boys going out looking like they've been sleeping in a hedge. Now let's have a look at you.'

She made the boys stand in line and gave them the once-over. They knew there was no getting round Mrs Quigley. She had inspected the boys every morning for the past ten weeks and she wasn't about to stop just yet. Her eyes hovered on their boots and slowly worked their way up their right-hand sides, over their heads, down the left-hand side then once more up and down the centre, as quickly and as efficiently as any troop sergeant.

'Well go on then. Don't just stand there.'

'Thanks Mrs Quigley,' Bryn said and gave her a wink as he passed her.

She sighed and then allowed herself a little chuckle as soon as the boys were out of the front gate. Her house and her life had been empty since the death of her husband a few years earlier. Having the boys billeted with her had given her a new lease of life. At first she had thought she would just be doing her bit for the war effort, but as the weeks passed she had grown fond of the boys. Now she didn't know how she was going to let them go. She knew she would have to cross that bridge when she came to it. Until then she promised herself that she would do her very best for them.

The boys quickly fell in as a foursome as if it was the most natural thing in the world to do, and stepped off. Rhys called out the step. As they marched the mile and a half to the camp other small groups of soldiers joined them and they were soon twenty strong. It was an easy march along the lanes that were lined with skeletal hawthorn bushes now that winter had set in. The overnight frost had given way to a crystal clear morning as the watery sun edged its way into the sky.

'Car!' came a cry from a soldier at the back of the squad. It was unusual for there to be a car on the roads at this time of the morning. The platoon of men moved in unison to the side of the road.

'Christ!' the rear man managed to shout as a black 1913 Crossley Shelsley hurtled around the corner. The driver, a fancy-looking woman, was glancing across at her passenger, laughing at some joke or other. As she rounded the corner her face turned to panic, when all she could see was a wall of men thirty yards in front of the bonnet. She slammed on the brakes, locking the rear wheels. The frost had all but disappeared except for the edges where the sun had not yet warmed the road. The car slid from one side to the other as she fought with the wheel. The men dived for the hedgerow as the car passed through the middle of them almost sideways on. The lady in the driving seat looked terrified; her eyes bulged from the effort of pressing the brakes, fighting the wheel, and from the certainty that they were going to crash. The car came to a crunching stop twenty yards in front the platoon.

The men picked themselves out of the hedgerow and started to run towards the car. The lady sat staring ahead, still clutching the wheel. Charles Symonds blinked a few times, then realised he wasn't hurt. He turned to the men running towards him. He clambered to his feet. 'You stupid idiots,' he cried. 'We could have been killed. What are you doing in the middle of the road?'

The men came to an abrupt halt just yards from the car. Symonds lent over the front seat and grabbed his cap and stick from the back seat before turning to the woman in the driving seat. 'Are you alright?' he asked. The lady nodded. Symonds looked back to the men. 'It's lucky that these bloody idiots didn't wreck the car. Don't you worry, if there is any damage I'll make them pay for it.'

His lady companion had still not moved. Her hands were locked to the wheel and she was still staring straight ahead in a state of shock. She nodded her head but her eyes remain transfixed.

'Listen, I've got to go otherwise there will be hell to pay. I'll… erm… I'll get this lot to sort the car out.' Symonds got out of the car, put on his cap and straightened his service dress. 'Right, seeing as you lot caused this accident you can sort it out, and you can think yourselves lucky there isn't any serious damage otherwise you would be paying for the repairs.'

The men stood dumfounded.

'Actually, sir, you were going rather fast.'

Symonds' head snapped round. 'Who said that?'

Bryn stepped forward. Symonds stared at him in disbelief. 'What did you say?'

'Well, sir, I don't know a lot about cars but it seemed to me you were probably going a little bit too fast.'

Symonds took a few paces forward before he realised that Bryn was a good six inches taller than himself. He poked his cane into Bryn's chest. 'Don't you dare speak to me you insolent buffoon. I'll decide how fast I go, not some filthy valley boy who has probably never been in a car in his life. Do you understand?'

Bryn lowered his head to the point of the cane and then looked into Symonds' eyes. They held each other's gaze for a second. 'Yes, sir,' he replied.

'Good. Now get this car out of the hedge and back on the road. Do you think that you can manage that?'

Bryn looked at Symonds and held his gaze. Symonds' rage was about to vent when he suddenly became aware of a slight movement of feet behind Bryn. He flashed a look at the men. One or two were covered in superficial scratches from the bushes and the rest had grass stains on their trousers and mud covering their boots. Symonds paused, read the situation and turned towards the car. The lady was still sat in the driving seat. Symonds turned and strode off towards the camp without another word to anyone.

The men quickly surrounded the car.

'Are you alright, miss?' Rhys asked.

She turned and looked at Rhys and then at the other men. 'Yes, yes, I'm fine thank you,' she replied. 'Just a little shaken I think. I'm so sorry.'

'Not to worry, miss. No harm done. We'll have this back on the road in a jiffy. I don't think that there is any real damage to the car.'

'No, no I'm sure there isn't. It doesn't matter anyway; it was entirely my fault. I'm really sorry.'

For twenty strong young men the car proved no difficulty and it was back on the road in no time at all. They fussed over the lady for a couple of minutes, more out of curiosity than concern, but they made sure that she was safe to drive and then saw her off. Huan, Rhys and John crowded around Bryn, who had the look of the devil about him.

'Who on earth did he think he was?' Huan asked.

'If I'm not mistaken, that's Lieutenant Symonds,' Bryn said as he wiped a bit of mud from his trouser legs.

'So that's the arrogant little bastard that everyone's talking about is it? Bit of a twerp if you ask me.'

'That he might be but don't let the instructors hear you call him that. I heard the other day that one or two of the corporals are on the make with him.'

*

Symonds burst through the tent flap just as Gibbons was buckling his sword to his Sam Browne belt. There was barely space between the two sleeping cots for two officers to stand at the same time. Simon stumbled forward and sat on the bed.

'Steady on old chap. Bull in a china shop and all that,' Gibbons said as he gathered up his hat. 'Bit of a late one last night was it?'

'Shut up Gibbons,' Charles replied. 'None of your business really, is it?'

'No it's not but you might be interested to know that the old man was wondering last night why you hadn't been to dinner for a few days.'

'Was he now? And what did you tell our dear commanding officer?'

'Well, if you must know I told him you were in town making the rounds of the billets. Making sure that the men were behaving and being properly looked after.'

Charles stared at his tent companion. 'Err... *thanks*,' he said.

'No need to thank me, old boy. I wouldn't want you to come unstuck would I?' he replied as he turned and slipped through the tent flap. 'Sword drill in ten minutes. Don't be late; the adjutant is taking the lesson.'

*

Sergeant Major Ashton was inspecting the company when he saw Lieutenant Symonds storm through the gates past the guard without bothering to return the customary salutations. Sergeant Major Ashton was old school. He had spent twenty-two years in the army serving under many good officers, and some not so good. He always believed that with a little bit of education and nurturing the less promising officers usually proved themselves to be among the bravest when it mattered. But Lieutenant Symonds worried him. He had gained a reputation for being arrogant and worse still, an ignorant officer. Stories of his indiscretions had quickly filtered down to the Warrant Officers' Mess. Symonds' activities in and out of the Officers' Mess had already cost the junior officer several extra duties and an interview with the commanding officer. Youthful exuberance was to be tolerated but reports of his indiscretions were less exuberance and more intolerance. Exuberance could be tamed, but intolerance was usually a block to military progress and that concerned the sergeant major. Symonds, he thought, did not share the enthusiasm of his fellow officers and that was surprising.

Bryn and the rest of the boys double marched onto parade ten minutes late. They were noticeably in rag order; it was going to be a bad day of drill bashing around the square. Sergeant Major Ashton told them to wait at the side of the parade square as he finished the inspection and detailed off the platoons to their training activities. As the company dispersed he marched over to the twenty men who had arrived late. He stood in front of the platoon and asked for an explanation. Bryn stepped forward and gave him an account of how a car had careered into them and how they had helped to right the car on the road. He made no mention of Symonds but the sergeant major had already guessed what had happened and was more impressed that the lads hadn't dropped the officer in it.

'Alright lad, fall in,' was all he said. He inspected the platoon in his customary fashion but without the shouting, cursing or jailing anyone. He moved quietly along the lines, pausing only once to tell a soldier to break ranks and dab the blood that was trickling down his cheek from a small cut under his eye. He handed over the platoon to Sergeant Murphy with instructions to despatch the troops to their training activities and quietly walked away.

'Well I'll be bowled over,' Sergeant Murphy said to himself. 'It must be a leap year or something.'

*

'STOP!' The platoon sergeant let out an elongated cry to make sure that no one missed his command. 'Has anyone not finished firing?'

The troops lay in the prone position and looked left and right. The three hundred yard rifle range had been built at the very far end of the training camp, facing a small hill that provided a natural butt area. Twenty men at a time fired their weapons from the one hundred, two hundred and three hundred yard markers. Sergeants and corporals passed left and right along the line, checking that the recruits had carried out their drills correctly.

'Okay, stand up and port arms.'

The soldiers scrambled to their feet, pulled back the bolts of their Lee Enfield Mk III rifles and held them at shoulder level facing down the range as the rifle instructor rushed along the line to make sure no one had any bullets left in the firing chamber.

'Don't want any of you silly buggers killing each other, or me for that matter. And remember, when you have finished firing at the bloody Hun I'm not going to be there so you will need to make sure the chambers are empty before waving them about at your own bloody side.'

He paused as the men on the firing line dressed back a few yards.

'Right. Next detail. Prone position. Down. When I blow my whistle I want you to fire five rounds at the target to your front. For those of you who have an imagination the big sack hanging in front of you is the Hun. Try to hit him or at least scare the shit out of him. When you have fired your five rounds I will blow my whistle and you will stand up and fix bayonets. When I blow my whistle a second time you are to charge at the enemy and stick it in him as you have been taught and then move on to the next target. Does everyone understand?'

'Yes Sergeant,' came the collective response from the firing detail.

'I repeat, do not charge at the target until I blow my whistle for the second time. We don't want any of you little Taffies having more than one hole in your arse now do we?'

The men laughed… anything to keep the instructors happy.

*

Stew had become a staple diet. Not that anyone was complaining. It was hot and filling. There might not have been a great deal of meat but there were enough potatoes, carrots and parsnips to fill a hungry man's stomach. The boys had never been so well fed or as fit. The mine had been hard work but this was different. The boys had always prided themselves on their fitness but the fresh air, marching, physical training and rifle drill, coupled with plenty of wholesome food, had toned their muscles and improved their endurance. They had never felt better.

Huan plonked himself down next to Rhys, spilling a bit of stew on the table. 'Oops, waste not want not,' he said as he scooped up a piece of potato and stuffed it into his mouth, followed quickly by another mouthful. The boys watched as he scooped spoonful after spoonful into his mouth without pause. He didn't speak until he had mopped up the last bit of juice with a piece of bread, at which point he leaned back and sighed. 'That was pretty good, that was.'

'How would you know?' Bryn asked. 'It went down so fast that you couldn't have tasted any of it.'

'Well you've got to eat fast round here in case there are any seconds. Cook won't let you have any more unless you've finished the first lot.'

'You can't possibly eat any more, boyo. You'll burst.'

'Oh, I dunno. That'll just keep me going until we get home and then Mrs Quigley might have got us a nice piece of brisket or some liver and onions followed by a rhubarb pie. I love her rhubarb pie.'

'Is that all you think about?' John asked.

'No. I'm also thinking about this here piece of paper,' he said, tapping a piece of paper that was wedged under his plate.

'What's that then, your Will?' Rhys asked. 'I hope you've left me your rugby boots, boyo. I remember you promised them to me some time ago.'

'No I didn't, but yes you can have them. They are a size too small for you, mind. No, this piece of paper is our ticket out of here,' he said, holding it up for them all to see.

The boys looked at the paper. 'Is that our orders?' Rhys asked in slightly higher pitch than he intended. 'Where are we going?'

'More importantly when do we get to see those French girls?' John asked.

Huan looked at them with a quizzical expression. 'What are

you two going on about? This is the regimental team sheet for the match against some team in Aldershot, next weekend.'

The disappointment was obvious to everyone except Huan, who still had the look of an excited schoolboy who had been given the first pick of the teams in the playground. 'This is a match against... well... it's against an English team. Next weekend. All weekend. Oh blimey, what's the matter with you? We're staying there. We get the weekend off. How good is that?'

'Are we all in the team then?' Bryn asked with a little more enthusiasm as he tried to snatch the list from Huan's hand.

'Well, not quite.'

'Well who's in then?'

'Me, Rhys and John.'

Bryn looked at his friend. 'Don't be daft. I've got to be in the team. I'm the best flanker in the regiment, let alone the whole battalion.'

'You're on the bench.'

'What?!' Bryn cried again, and grabbed the piece of paper. He read down the list. 'It says here that I'm in the starting XV.'

'My mistake,' Huan said as he chuckled.

'You can be a stupid bastard sometimes and you're not at all funny you know,' Bryn said as he tried to push Huan off the bench.

'You seem pretty happy, lads,' the sergeant major's voice boomed from behind them, killing the laughter. They scrambled to attention. 'Got too much time on your hands have you?'

'No, sir,' Bryn said. 'We were just looking at the team list for the match against the English team in Aldershot, sir.'

'I think you'll find, Tallent, that we are all in the British Army. We are all on the same side: English and Welsh – even the Scottish and the Irish. However, just for this little game I will presume that we are going to beat the English. Is that not so?'

'Oh yes, sir. No doubt about it, sir. We'll have it wrapped up by half-time...' John stopped as the sergeant major stared at him.

'If I had wanted a performing monkey I would have gone to

the zoo, Roberts. I do not want performing monkeys, although in your case it would be difficult to tell the difference. What I want are rugby players who can win, who want to win, who will win. You have been chosen because someone thinks that you can win. I hope you are not going to take this game for granted. I would hate to think that you were taking anything for granted, such as being late for my parade this morning.'

The boys couldn't breathe. *Here we go,* Bryn thought, *marching all afternoon and no trip to Aldershot. That bastard officer has sorted us good and proper.*

'Well?' the sergeant asked in a drawn voice. They looked at each other for an answer.

'Sir, we wouldn't dream of taking anything for granted, especially your parade,' Bryn replied.

'And definitely not a rugby match!' John added.

The sergeant major ignored Roberts moved his head closer to Bryn. 'I thought not, lad.' The words were left hanging in the air for a moment. 'And whilst you're about it, your performing monkey here could probably do with some additional training. Get the team together tomorrow afternoon for a practice. Do you think that you can manage that or shall I find someone else?'

Bryn looked at the sergeant major, whose stone-set face gave nothing away. 'Yes, sir,' was all Bryn could say.

'Good. Now get out of my sight and get on with your training. There is a war going on in case you hadn't noticed and some unfortunate regiment is going to have you four posted to it. God help them,' he screamed as he wandered away.

Salisbury Plain Training Camp
November 1914

Dear Cerys,

Just a line or two to let you know that I am still alive and
kicking despite all the attempts of the instructors to finish
us off before we get to France! The training is going well and
we are kept busy from breakfast to teatime, as you would
expect. It has got a bit colder here but it's not too bad. They
have run out of rooms in the town so most of the boys are
sleeping in tents in the camp. I think that we were lucky
getting a billet with Mrs Quigley. At least it is near the town
when we have the odd moment or two. It's not a bad little
town, probably the same size as Wrexham but there is plenty
of countryside, which seems to make it much bigger. Thanks
for the parcel; especially the sweets. They are great as thirst-
quenchers when we go on a march and I share them with the
lads - I hope you don't mind?

The big news is that we were selected to play rugby for
the regiment against another regiment in Aldershot. We were
allowed to stay there for the weekend. I reckon that hundreds
of blokes turned up to watch the match. It was a cracking
game. We won of course but it wasn't an easy game. They
were pretty fired up but the pack wasn't quick enough
around the park so they kept losing the ball. They were big
lads and pushed us off most of the set pieces, which earned
Rhys, John and Huan a bit of a ribbing but at the end of
the day they were too slow. The sergeant major was very
pleased, which should make our lives all the better.

I don't know when we are moving on but I don't think
that it will be for a while. There is talk of a bit of leave over

Christmas but I suppose it depends on how things are going over in France. This place thrives on rumour – it's worse than the mine!

Best wishes,
Bryn

CHAPTER TWELVE

The train juddered to a halt at Wrexham Junction. Smoke from the engine billowed around the carriage, obliterating the view. A little dusting of snow lay on the higher ground as the train left Salisbury. It had petered out into a light drizzle as they sat in the sidings looking out at the grey industrial Midlands, waiting for higher priority trains, and then slowly the sun broke through the low-hung clouds and shone on the low valleys as they made their way slowly towards home.

Bryn sat looking through the smoke as his friends and companions eagerly grabbed their kit that had been stuffed on the rails above the seats. There was no ceremony as they barged each other out of the way to get out of the door.

John turned and looked at Bryn, who was still staring through the window. 'Hey boyo, are you coming or are you staying on the train till next Christmas?'

Startled from his trance, Bryn smiled. 'No, I'm coming. I was just thinking about the last time we were here. You know, everyone waving and that.'

'Blooming heck, what were you expecting, the colliery band? Come on, let's get to the pub.'

'How about we go home first and then we'll see how it goes?'

John stared at him. Rhys stopped halfway through the door, wedged in and unable to turn. 'Eh?' he cried.

Bryn sighed. 'Just joking. Come on, let's line them up.'

'You had me worried for a minute there, boy. I thought you'd gone soft! We've got three days and I don't intend to remember any of them!' John said as Rhys and Huan scrambled onto the platform in front of him.

Looking around, even John could sense the stark contrast from when they were last here. A few other men were shouldering their kit and making their way out of the station, leaving the boys to share the platform with the stationmaster.

'Not to worry boys,' John said cheerily. 'At least it will be a surprise when we get home.'

Rhys sighed. 'Yeah, but it would have been nice to have had a bit more notice. They must have known we were going to get some leave.'

'I'm not at all sure they know anything,' Huan replied. 'I'm sure they make it up as they go along.'

What are you worried about anyway? Frightened your mam has let your room?' Bryn said as he poked his friend in the arm. 'Come on, we've got some leave, let's just get home and enjoy it.' They gave each other a knowing look and shrugged.

'Doesn't change much, does it? Huan said as they walked along the road to Gwersyllt. Rhys started to laugh and then Bryn.

'We've only been gone a couple of months you idiot,' John replied as he shouldered his kit. 'Come on, let's get gone.'

Dusk was approaching as the boys came to the edge of Gwersyllt. The temperature was dropping fast now that the last of the winter sun's warmth had faded. There would be a frost tonight. Chances were, it would be a white Christmas. The boys could see the smoke rising from the village long before they could see the houses. It hung over the village as a protective haze like an umbrella to ward off the bad weather. Women all over the village would be busy stoking the fire for water to bathe and to warm the house. Bryn looked at his watch. The mine would be changing shifts in another hour and hungry men would be coming home for a bath and good hot dinner. Bryn shivered. *At least it was warm down the mine*, he thought. He remembered how he used to look forward to seeing what the weather was like when he came out of the cage. He found himself smiling at the thought. *Perhaps I missed the mine after all*, he thought.

'Blimey!' Rhys said. 'Can you smell that?'

Thick greasy coal smoke seeped up their nostrils and clung to their throats as it sank down into their lungs.

'Smell it? I can taste it, boyo,' Huan replied. 'It's not like this in Salisbury is it?'

'No,' John replied. 'But then Salisbury's not home, is it?'

'I've missed that smell,' Bryn said, breathing in a lungful for added effect. As soon as the smoke hit Bryn's chest he started an involuntary coughing fit. 'Blimey, that is a bit much isn't it?!'

'You bloomin' great girl,' John said. 'You've become soft in all that fresh air. A bit of coal smoke will do you good.'

'Crikey, this is worse than smoking woodbines.'

'Oh, come on you lot I want to get home and see me mam,' Rhys said.

'I thought we were going to the pub?' Huan asked.

'We'll do that later,' Bryn replied. 'I think I'd rather go home first as well.' Rhys and Bryn strode on, leaving Huan and John a few paces behind.

'Are you still up for a pint?' John said, looking across at Huan.

'Of course I am. It's just that if Rhys goes home and my mam finds out that I'm home but not home on account of me being in the pub, you see, then when I get home I'll be in trouble. And if I'm in trouble then the news will surely find its way to your mam and da and then you'll be in trouble. So it's probably best if I go with Rhys.'

*

'Evening Mr Jones,' Huan called as they passed the grocer's shop. Jones the Shop, as he was known, looked up from the box of chestnuts he was sorting through.

'Oh it's you lot is it? Alright are you, boys? Home on leave, are you now?'

'Just a couple of days,' Huan called back.

'Killed any of those filthy Germans yet?'

'No Mr Jones, we have been in Salisbury.'

Jones the Shop stopped what he was doing and stared at Bryn. 'What you doing there? There aren't any Germans there, lad. They've put you in the wrong place; you need to speak to someone high up and get yourselves put in the right place.'

Huan sniggered. 'No they haven't Mr Jones,' he tried to explain. 'We're still training. We haven't been sent to France yet.'

'Haven't gone? Blimey lad, you've been gone for ages. The war will be over in a couple of days. Evans the Mayor told me, in strictest confidence mind, that it would be all over by Christmas. You need to get your skates on if you are going to kill any of them.'

'I think that it will last a bit longer than Christmas Mr Jones, even if the mayor said so. There will still be plenty of Germans out there for us to sort out in the New Year,' Huan said.

'Well, mind that you give them something to think about. I don't want any Germans coming around my shop. I don't want to have to get any of that foreign food in, you know,' Mr Jones called as Huan trotted away to catch up with the others.

'Right you are then Mr Jones; bye now and happy Christmas.'

'Some things around here never change,' Bryn said as Huan caught up with his friends. 'He's still as mad as ever.'

*

Bryn pushed open the back gate to a small two up, two down Victorian terrace. It was a miner's cottage, owned by the mine company for the use of the miners. It had been his home for the past eighteen and a half years. He had never really stopped and looked at the house before. He had just gone in and out and in and out.

It seemed smaller than he remembered it. He stood in the cobbled yard and looked up at the back bedroom he shared with his younger brother. He used to have the room to himself while his brother and sister shared a room but when Violet got a bit older his brother moved in with him. He knew his brother and sister would be sitting by the hearth reading a book while they waited patiently for their tea. It was something that his mam had always insisted on: 'Learning will get you to places that you can only dream of,' she used to say.

He felt the sudden chill in the wind. The back door was ajar and the smell of fresh pie seeped through the gap into the yard. *Rhubarb*, Bryn thought. It suddenly struck him how much he had missed his mam's cooking. He gently pushed open the door and saw his mam bending over the oven, testing the top of the pie with her finger. She put the pie back in the oven and shut the door. As she turned to face Bryn she gave a little jump in fright.

He stood in the familiar doorway, feeling like a stranger and not really knowing what to say. 'Hello Mam.'

'Oh, Bryn you gave me a fright creeping up on me like, you big lump. What are you doing here? You haven't run away, have you lad?'

'Of course not. I've got a few days' leave.'

'Well why didn't you write and let me know you were coming? I would have got some more food in.'

'We didn't know ourselves until yesterday. It's a bit of a Christmas treat.'

'So you will be home for Christmas then. Well that's nice. Your da will be pleased, not to mention your brother and sister. And by the way you need to talk to Geraint; he won't stop going on about you winning the war single-handed.' She paused and looked at her son. 'By gum lad, you look swanky in your uniform. Just wait till your da gets home, he'll be proud to see you all dressed up like that.'

Bryn smiled.

'Well don't just stand there making the place untidy, come and sit down and have a cup of tea.'

Bryn propped his kit behind the door and bent down to untie his boots.

'Oh don't worry about that, *cariad*. You can leave them on just this once, at least until your da gets home to see you in all your glory.'

Bryn smiled again and sat down at the kitchen table.

Edie put the kettle on the stove and took a cup and saucer from the cupboard. 'Well, you look as if they have been feeding you well enough. You haven't starved have you?'

'They look after us well enough and Mrs Quigley puts on a pretty good tea every night.'

'She seems nice from your letters. I'm sure she does her best for you. It's nice of her. Perhaps she can afford to.'

'Oh she looks after us well enough. You know, with what the army gives her and all that, but her cooking isn't up to your standard. I don't think she has had as much practice as you.'

'You think flattery will get you extra tonight, do you? Well you'll get no more and no less than the rest of us.'

Bryn knew that wasn't true either. His mam often took a smaller portion to make sure that his da got enough to keep him going. He had never really noticed until he had started down the mine. His mother's portion had become so meagre that he had asked his da about it one day. His da had said that he wasn't to worry. His mam, he explained, was like a sparrow and nibbled throughout the day while they were at work. Even so, they must have talked about it as his mam's portion increased slightly over the next few days.

'Well, you're not wrong; looking after you lot is a challenge. It might not be swanky food you get in those top restaurants in Salisbury, my lad, but it is well cooked and enough to fill you up. I've got a pot of stew in the oven. If I'd known that you were coming I would have made a bit more but there should be enough. I'll give the young ones a chunk of bread to fill them up.'

'I'm sure that there will be plenty, Mam. Don't worry about me.'

Edie poured the tea and sat opposite him. They both sat watching the steam rising from the cup. Bryn dropped a spoon of sugar into his tea and was about to reach for another but stopped. His mam looked at him and smiled. She pushed the sugar bowl closer to him. 'Go on, it's nearly Christmas.'

Bryn smiled and helped himself. They sat for a moment, aimlessly stirring their tea.

'And what happens after Christmas then?' Edie asked.

'Back to Salisbury I suppose.'

Edie sipped her tea. 'Better there than being in France, that's if the news is to be believed. The papers say that we have stopped them but you don't know how much of it is true do you?' she said and sipped her tea again.

'I reckon that we might be there for a while yet.'

'You know that Mrs Roberts' lad, Dai, was killed the other week?'

'No, I hadn't heard. I'm sorry to hear that.'

'Somewhere in France apparently. I don't know where. It's a big place I suppose. You don't really like to ask do you?'

'No, I suppose not.'

'There are a few others around here who have been injured. Mrs Evans' lad. I don't suppose you remember her. They live over the way towards Gresford.'

'I don't think so – should I?' Bryn asked.

'No, not really.' Edie paused for a few minutes as if she was gathering her thoughts. 'There have been quite a few in the paper. I kept the clippings for you.'

They sat for a moment, the only noise coming from the world outside the kitchen.

'Well,' Edie said at last, breaking the silence, 'at least you are home for Christmas. Da will be so pleased. Are the others home as well?'

'Yes, we all managed to get the time off together, which is great. They've gone home but we agreed that we would meet up again later for a pint or tomorrow after chapel.'

The kitchen door burst open and Geraint threw himself at his older brother. Violet stood in the doorway with a book in her hand. Her hair had been plaited, not the two pigtails that she used to have but one long tail that Bryn thought made her look much older than her twelve years.

'Bryn!' Geraint cried as hung onto his brother's neck.

'Oh no, I'm under attack,' Bryn shouted 'Stand to!' For an eight-year-old Geraint was a big lad. If he carried on at this rate he would be bigger than his brother but he was still small enough for Bryn to pick up under his arm and spin him around. Geraint roared even loader.

'Oi, oi, mind my kitchen; if you want to play that nonsense go outside' Eddie shouted. She grabbed her tea towel and started playfully smacking their bottoms as they span around.

'Right, outside it is then,' Bryn cried. 'Mam, get the door!'

'No!' Geraint screamed. Bryn conceded. 'Alright, but calm down or there will be no tea!'

Geraint caught his breath. 'Did you bring me a gun home?'

'No I haven't.' Bryn replied. His brother looked crestfallen. 'But I might have a few sweets for you.' Geraint shrieked and put his hand out in anticipation. 'What are all those bruises on your knees?'

'What do you think? their mam said. 'He's following in your footsteps. They are a result of a match last week against that club over near Holt, of all places. The ground was far too hard to be playing, but nobody asked me so that's what happens.'

Bryn smiled at his brother. 'Did you win?'

Geraint nodded.

'Good lad. Here you go. There's a quarter ounce but not until after your tea.'

Bryn looked at his sister who was still stood in the doorway. The simple white pinafore dress that was obviously fresh on; he knew his mam would have spent an hour scrubbing it to get it that clean. Geraint was expected to get dirty but Violet was becoming a young woman and young women were expected to be neat. 'Well, are you too old to give your brother a hug?' Violet smiled and let herself sink into Bryn's chest. He squeezed her gently. 'And I suppose you are too old for sweets as well?

Violet smiled up at him. 'Not just yet.'

'I thought not. And make sure you hide them from Geraint or there will be none left for Christmas.'

*

Bryn had missed the smell of the coal hissing and cracking in the grate. His da sat on one side next to the candle reading the *Wrexham Advertiser*. His pipe was clamped between his teeth. Opposite his da his mother sat in a straight-backed chair darning a pair of socks. Bryn was sandwiched between them, facing the fire. His mam said that he had grown so much he would block the heat getting into the room. Edie had been wittering on since they had sat down, never once taking her eyes off the needle and thread. Harold just muttered as always to give the appearance that he was listening.

Bryn smiled when he thought about his da coming home earlier. Bryn, Geraint and Violet had shut themselves in the parlour. When Da arrived his mam had told Harold to take his boots off, as she did every day without fail. Bryn heard her say that someone had called to see him and they were in the parlour. Harold had pushed open the door and saw Bryn standing in front of the fire with his brother and sister. Bryn looked at his da and smiled. He thought for a moment that his da was going to burst into tears, but he simply coughed and said, 'Well Edie, look what the cat's dragged in.' It was enough for Bryn to know that his da was happy.

'Geraint and Violet were pleased to see you Bryn; you know you have made their Christmas,' Edie was saying.

Bryn was shaken from his thoughts. 'They've certainly been pretty excited this evening. I hope they sleep alright.'

Harold folded his paper and sighed. 'They'll sleep alright.

Luckily for them they are too young to understand what's going on in the world.'

'Oh Harold, not now. I'm sure Bryn knows only too well what's going on. Can we just have Christmas without all this talk of war?'

Harold looked across at Bryn and raised his eyebrows. Bryn smiled. 'Well can we talk about rugby then?'

'No, I've had enough rugby talk to last me a lifetime. I probably know more about the game from listening to you two than either one of you.'

'How's things down the mine, Da?'

'A bit too busy to be honest; productivity targets have been raised to support the war effort and without the younger lads it's quite tough. But we'll muddle through I'm sure.'

Bryn thought that he looked older somehow. He was struck by a sudden pang of guilt for not missing the mine.

'Bryn doesn't want to know about your problems, Da. Give him a rest,' Edie chided.

'Well what are we meant to talk about?'

'Bryn can tell us what he has been up to.'

'We know what he's been up to. He's been training hasn't he? I don't suppose he's allowed to talk about it, are you lad?

Bryn shrugged. He wasn't about to get drawn into this argument.

'Exactly, so we'll go to The Grapes.'

'No you won't Harold, you sit there. Bryn can go to the pub but I'm not having you coming home smelling of beer and keeping me awake all night. I'm sure Bryn will be meeting the others and they won't want you hanging about, moaning about the mine.'

Harold knew there was no point in arguing so he picked up his paper and huffed.

'Go on *cariad*, you don't want to be sitting here with us all night.'

*

It had started to snow when Bryn left The Grapes. The night was as black as coal but the brilliance of the snow seemed to illuminate and accentuate the size of the slag heaps as he made his way home. Coal smoke lingered over the village; the acrid taste of tar caught the back of his throat. At least they would never be short of coal for the fires, he thought. The pub had been packed with men home on leave and it soon filled with some of the older men who were eager for news. He had sunk quite a few beers but he had been careful not to overdo things. He wanted to enjoy Christmas with a clear head.

He undressed as quietly as he could and slid into bed. He lay in his bed listening to Geraint breathing heavily in the bed next to him. It didn't matter that his own bed was a bit small; it was his bed and he was glad to be home. Bryn chanced a quick glimpse out of the window. Even at his age he was excited at the prospect of a white Christmas. He couldn't help wondering whether it was white in France, or what the soldiers in the trenches were doing tonight. He imagined them having a midnight service and a few beers and hopefully a good night's sleep. It slowly dawned on him as he lay in his bed, warm and snug, that he actually had no idea what they would be doing – whether they would be fighting and missing Christmas altogether or what?

As he drifted towards oblivion an image of Dai Roberts came into his mind. *Poor Dai*, he thought, *he must have been unlucky.*

CHAPTER THIRTEEN

The changing room was unusually subdued; there was none of the normal pre-match banter. The air was thick with the stench of rotting farts, liniment and beer. Only the occasional groan belied the lifeless forms curled up on the bench or slumped forward with their head in their hands.

'I'm not sure that I can do this,' Rhys said as he held his head in his hands. 'You'll have to go on without me.'

'Of course you can do it,' Huan replied. 'You've got to, the honour of the mine is at stake.'

'But we don't work here anymore. Why do we have to play?'

'First of all, there isn't anyone else to play, and secondly, this is still our mine, even if we don't work here anymore. So stop your moaning and get your kit on.'

'I don't want to play either,' Bryn said from the corner of the room.

He had pressed his six-foot frame into the corner so that he was propped up by two sides of the wall. A loud retching sound came from the toilet, followed by a groan and the sound of someone slumping to the floor. Huan picked his way across the debris of bodies and looked around the toilet door.

John was slumped on his knees with his head hanging over the bowl, which was lined with vomit. Huan stepped to the side of John and pulled the chain. Water splashed over John's face. Huan grunted.

'My sainted aunt,' Sergeant Major Rolland said as he entered the dressing room. 'You can smell this place before you can see it. Look at the state of you.' There was a collective groan from the team.

'I told them several times,' Huan said as he emerged from the toilet.

'Really? Well it didn't have much effect, did it? Come on you lot, get a grip. We've got a game to play and as God is my witness, we will win.'

Rhys groaned again. 'Oh give it a rest. We're not well.'

Sergeant Major Rolland turned towards the blob on the bench that had dared to speak. His face began to contort and change colour a to a bright crimson. 'Don't you dare sit there you useless lump of lard and tell me that you're not well. If I wanted to hear your voice I would have put my ear to the ground to listen to the worm that you are. Half a pint of a man's drink and you've got a fucking hangover. Well let me tell you boy, you'll have more than a sore head if you don't get that shirt on and run around that pitch until you spew up your guts, because that's exactly what you'll be doing when you get to the trenches. I can't believe I recruited a boy into my regiment to do a man's job. In fact, I think I should go outside and give myself a good talking-to for being so stupid and then perhaps I'll take myself along to the Regimental Headquarters throw in my badge and tell them I let a minor, an underaged, not-old-enough BOY into my regiment. Is that what you would like me to do? Well then, shall I tell them that I made a mistake, shall I tell them that the boy I thought was a man is actually a boy after all?'

Rhys looked up. He looked around the silent changing room. Everyone was looking at the floor. 'No, Sergeant Major,' he said, 'you didn't make a mistake.' Rhys pulled on his shirt. 'I won't let you down.'

'Right then, the rest of you can get out there and do what you're here to do.' As he turned to leave the changing room, Bryn started to chuckle. Bob Rolland snapped round in Bryn's direction. 'I don't know what you're laughing at, big lad. I heard you pissed the bed last night.' Bryn stopped laughing and looked around.

'I didn't,' he protested. Everyone started laughing. 'I didn't, honest, you ask my mam.' Shirts started to fly at him from every direction.

'That's enough,' shouted the sergeant major. 'Now we have established you are all alive, how about getting your kit on and getting out there to entertain the masses?'

Huan pointed to the toilet. 'Actually, I'm not sure John's alive.'

'Really?' the sergeant major said. 'We'll soon see about that.'

Bob Rolland stormed out of the changing rooms and was back a minute later with a bucketful of water and snow. The rest of the team looked and saw the inevitable. The scream was audible from the other side of the village. John was sat with his back to the toilet, dripping wet and gasping for breath. His mouth was moving but nothing was coming out.

'Seems to be alive now,' the sergeant major said as he walked away. 'Five minutes, boys.'

*

Gresford and Gwersyllt traditionally played a friendly on Boxing Day, followed by a buffet tea for the players and plenty of beer provided by the two mine managers. It had always been a hard but reasonably good-natured affair, but this was the first meeting since Gresford had lost to Gwersyllt earlier in the year. Most of the Gwersyllt team had signed up for the war a few months back and were fielding a young side with a few players who, like the boys, had managed to get Christmas leave. Gresford had retained most of their older players and bar a couple of key first team players they were fielding a full team. They meant business.

The first half was a bad-tempered affair. John caught the ball from the kickoff, which was the full extent of his contribution to the game. He was helped from the field, barely able to breathe. He couldn't work out if the pain was from the almighty crack he heard when the Gresford front row hit him or the remnants of his hangover. By half time they were twenty-six points to nil down and feeling pretty battered and bruised.

As the Gwersyllt team stood huddled together sucking in the icy air Bob Rolland sighed. 'Listen, I know it's Christmas and I understand that you lot want to be charitable but twenty-six points is quite enough now. This lot obviously mean business so let's take it to them.' Rhys moved aside and vomited into the snow. '*That's better,*' Rolland said to no one in particular. 'Now you've got last night out of your bellies let's entertain these people. Don't take them on up front, let's move the ball around, use a bit of speed and if you are inclined, try a bit of your rugby skills; they might work.' Everyone nodded. 'And don't forget, you're here to enjoy yourselves so make sure you do.'

'Hey Bryn,' Huan said as they trotted back to the halfway line ready for the second half. 'Isn't that Cerys over there with Mary?'

Bryn looked across the pitch to where two girls were standing. Cerys and Mary were huddled together, rubbing their gloved hands. Bryn smiled and looked across at Rhys. 'Hey, fat lad. Best you put in a bit of effort. You've got a fan club.'

Rhys looked across and waved. 'Oh heck, best we get down to business then.'

The second half defied the first. Rhys smashed his way through every rook and maul, gathering the ball and driving forward or taking the man and creating space. Huan ran around at his shoulder all the way, chuckling at his friend. Bryn was eagerly on hand to pick up the loose ball and to drive off the side of the mauls and scrums. Pressure turned to points and as four became five and five became ten the old hands that formed the Gresford pack dug deep and the lighthearted Boxing Day friendly became decidedly unfriendly.

For the first time in living memory the referee had no option but to send off a Gresford man for persistent infringements and fighting. Even down to fourteen men Gresford held out to the final whistle. Gwersyllt had managed to claw back twenty points to no further loss. The Gresford men squatted on their haunches in utter exhaustion as the whistle signalled full time.

*

Bryn looked over the top of his beer glass as he took a sip. It wasn't going down as quickly as normal. Rhys was making a show of how they had practised storming an enemy trench. Bryn had lost the thread of the conversation some moments earlier as he gazed across at Cerys, who was listening intently to his friend.

Bryn couldn't avert his gaze and was caught by a slight movement of her eyes. He was rewarded with a smile so subtle that only Bryn could see it as she politely re-engaged with Rhys' conversation. Bryn had said little since they had arrived in the clubhouse. He had been so pleased to see her but couldn't find the words that seemed to come so easily to his friend. Huan and John kept ducking and diving into the conversation but instinctively knew that their company would be more appreciated if they were elsewhere. A burst of laughter caught Bryn off guard.

'What do you think, Bryn?' Cerys asked. Bryn paused. He had no idea what the conversation had been about. Cerys stood and looked at him, her eyes fixed on his. Her smile had a mischievous lilt. She raised an eyebrow discreetly but it was obvious that she was playing with him. Mary and Rhys were looking at him.

'Well...' he stammered 'It's like Rhys said, really.' He took a sip of beer, wishing away the moment.

'*Exactly*,' his friend agreed. 'Right, who's for another drink? Mary? Cerys?'

'I shouldn't really but as it's Christmas, I'll have a small sherry please,' Mary replied, holding out her glass.

'Oh, I'm not sure that I should,' Cerys said. 'I've had two already. I'll be getting tipsy.'

'Oh don't worry. Bryn will hold you up, won't you?' Bryn

looked shocked at the thought. Cerys smiled at his discomfort. 'And as Mary said, it's Christmas. Who knows where we will be this time next year?' The comment fell on stony ground. 'Well, you know what I mean. Back here obviously... I'll get the drinks.'

'I'll give you a hand,' Mary offered and chanced a smile at her friend.

Bryn shifted his feet. Cerys politely held her glass and looked around the room. 'How's the hat business then?' he blurted out.

Cerys managed to stifle a laugh. 'Well, it seems to be alright. So you are going back tomorrow then?'

'Sadly. Well, not sadly exactly, in that I don't mind going. It's just that it's gone a bit too quickly really. Hardly seems five minutes since we got back. Especially with yesterday being Christmas. It's all been a rush.'

'I expect Geraint and Violet were excited weren't they?'

'Crikey, I don't know what excited them most, the snow, the presents or the goose. They were on the go all day. I got Geraint a toy gun that one of the blokes made, it's really good, and I got Violet a book, although I think she would have preferred the gun.' They both laughed. Bryn looked furtively to see who was around. He fished in his jacket pocket and brought out a small package. 'I wasn't sure if I would get to see you but obviously I'm really glad I did. I bought you a small present, which I hope you will accept. It's not much but I hope you like it.'

Cerys touched his hands as she took the present.

'Thank you. It's wonderful.'

'You haven't opened it yet.'

'It doesn't matter. It will be wonderful,' Cerys replied as she gazed at the present. 'Do you mind if I open it when you have gone? It will give me something to make me smile.'

'Of course not, you open it when you like.'

Rhys and Mary returned with the drinks. They were both smiling like Cheshire cats.

'What have you two been talking about then? And if you tell

me that he mentioned rugby I will take him out for a good talking-to,' Rhys said.

'Oh Rhys Taylor, you can be so insensitive sometimes,' Mary chided.

'What? What have I said now?'

*

It hadn't snowed again but the clouds looked threatening and the frost made the fallen snow crunch underfoot. Mary had suggested that they should go home just in case the snow came. They walked slowly through the snow, but not slowly enough for Bryn. Cerys had her arm through his, just in case she slipped on the snow, she had said. Bryn didn't care why she had taken his arm. He was just sorry that it was dark and cold so no one was around to see them.

'Have you ever been to Salisbury? Bryn asked. Cerys shook her head as she continued to hug Bryn's arm. 'It's not like here, you know. There's no grime; everything is brighter and cleaner. Even the air tastes different.'

'How can the air taste different?'

'I dunno, but really, it does. It tastes cleaner and fresher somehow. You should come down and see.'

'Well I'm not sure about that, Bryn Tallent,' Cerys said.

'Oh I didn't mean that,' Bryn replied in haste.

'Oh you don't want me to come?' Cerys said with a slight purse of her bottom lip as if she was sulking. 'I know what you mean. I'm sorry. I'm teasing you. It would be nice to get out of Wrexham for a few days.'

Bryn smiled. 'Perhaps I could write to you and let you know what we are up to. Just in case we are busy?'

Cerys smiled. 'I'd like that.'

Salisbury Plain Training Camp
December 1914

Dear Cerys,

I hope this letter finds you well. Despite the snow we managed to get back in one piece. Salisbury Plain is pretty unforgiving at this time of year but if we run around enough we manage to stay warm. There is always plenty of tea to keep us going and Mrs Quigley still manages to pull out the stops every night – I really don't know how she does it. Thank you for coming to the station to see us off. It was really lovely to see you and I did like your hat – very pretty. The toffee went down very well and kept us quiet for a long time, which doesn't happen very often!

It was really good of you and Mary to come to the rugby on Boxing Day. It wasn't the best game I've ever played but the afternoon was most enjoyable. Not a great deal has changed here; there is still no news of when we will be moving on. We have been told that we will be having a special visitor to review our training in a couple of weeks so we are busy doing more drill! We are not even getting New Year's Day off. My mam knitted me some socks for Christmas, which are keeping my feet warm although she must have thought I had grown since I left home as they are a bit big – still, it's better than being too small.

Well I must close now, not that I want to but it's getting quiet late and Mrs Quigley is very generous with her candles but I don't like to abuse her hospitality.

I wish you a very happy New Year and hope that it will bring us all peace and happiness.

My very best wishes,
Bryn

CHAPTER FOURTEEN

January 1915

The sitting room was usually reserved for visitors but the parlour wasn't big enough for the four boys and Mrs Quigley, so she allowed them into the sitting room as long as they took their boots off and their uniforms were clean. Mrs Quigley had bought a rocking chair soon after the boys had taken up residence so that they could all sit down at the same time. She had arranged the chairs in a semi-circle facing the fire with the rocking chair next to a small oval Westminster table. The delicate walnut table was adorned with various bits of pottery and a silver-framed photograph of Mr and Mrs Quigley on their wedding day. The boys knew better than to steal her spot, so they crammed themselves onto the settee and the two armchairs.

Rhys tore at the envelope that Mrs Quigley had left on the mantelpiece above the fire. The now-familiar writing and soft scent of perfume betrayed the author of the letter before he had even picked it up.

'Oh no, not another blooming letter,' Huan said as he flopped into the armchair closest to the fire that was roaring in the grate. 'Hasn't that girl got anything better to do?'

'Language, young man,' Mrs Quigley said as she walked through the door with a large pot of steaming tea. She placed it down on the hearth to brew for a few minutes and wiped her hands on her apron. Having the boys in the house had given new purpose to her life.

'Sorry Mrs Quigley, but it does get a bit boring don't you think?'

'No I don't, and one day you'll be doing the very same thing so stop going on.' She pulled the cake stand away from the corner of the room and put a large Victoria sandwich cake on the top. Huan pursed his lips in anticipation. 'I think it's rather sweet and you could do worse than spending a bit more time finding yourself a girl instead of poking fun at Rhys. You should be very happy for him. I'm sure she is a lovely girl. Now mind your big feet so I can put this cake stand over here out of your reach.'

'Why would I want a girl when I'm about to go to war?'

'So that you have someone to love and care for. Even a great lump like you needs a bit of comfort every now and again. That's why! You can't spend the rest of your life with these hooligans,' she said, pointing to Bryn and John as they came through the door.

John saw the letter in Rhys' hand and smirked. 'Oh crikey, not Mary, again?' he said.

'And you can sit down young man and take note as well. None of you are getting any younger,' Mrs Quigley continued as she wagged her finger at Bryn and John. The boys just stood looking bemused as she bustled her way out of the door.

'What was all that about?' John asked.

'Don't worry about it,' Huan said. 'Mrs Quigley thinks we should all have girlfriends instead of playing rugby and drinking beer.'

John gave Huan and Bryn a quizzical look. 'Why? I'm very happy playing rugby and drinking beer, thanks very much.'

'If it means that we all end up like this cloth head I'd definitely rather stay single,' Huan said, throwing his cushion at Rhys to attract his attention.

'Oi, get off, I'm reading.'

'You can't be reading, there's no pictures,' John said as he looked for cups and saucers to pour the tea. Seeing none had arrived, he made a grab for a piece of cake just as Mrs Quigley returned with the cups and plates. A large cake knife smacked down on his hand.

'You'll spoil your dinner lad, if you keep eating. Where are your manners? I'm sure that your mother didn't bring you up like that.'

'Sorry Mrs Quigley but it looks rather nice.'

'And it probably is rather nice but you are only having a small piece.' Huan couldn't help laughing out loud and got a rather stern stare for his trouble. 'And that goes for the rest of you too. It's not as easy to buy groceries as it used to be so there will have to be a few cutbacks. It won't do any of you any harm.'

The boys looked at each other. Bryn felt his waist. Mrs Quigley was probably right. Despite the regular training, three square meals a day, four if you included afternoon tea when they got home, meant that he was piling on the pounds. 'Not to worry Mrs Quigley, we won't starve and we are very grateful for everything you have done for us.'

Mrs Quigley blushed and fussed over the cake. 'Well just as long as you have enough. I wouldn't want you to starve,' she said as she handed Bryn the first piece, which was no smaller than normal.

'Hey listen,' Rhys said, looking up from his letter. 'Mary is coming down here to see me.'

'Hey, there's lovely boyo. At least if you take her out it will give us some peace for a few hours,' John said as he crammed a large piece of cake into his mouth.

'Going to treat her, are you Rhys? Three pints in the Four Feathers followed by fish and chips down by the river? She's a lucky girl,' Bryn said.

'That's where you are wrong, boy,' Rhys said, folding the letter. 'It'll be dancing, dinner and who knows what for my girl.'

'Oh how lovely, dear. I look forward to meeting her,' Mrs Quigley added.

'You can't dance,' Bryn scoffed.

'I'm sure Mrs Quigley will teach us, won't you Mrs Quigley?'

'Of course I will my dear. I love a little foxtrot. I've got some records somewhere.'

Bryn laughed. 'There is no "us" in "you", boyo. You're on your own with this one. I'm not gallivanting around the room for you.'

'Well my friend. That's a shame isn't it? You won't be able to get to grips with the lovely Cerys then, will you?'

Bryn's mouth stopped moving.

John hooted with laughter. 'Oh, this I've got to see,' he roared. Bryn still hadn't let the penny drop.

The mention of Cerys took him back to their farewell at the station. He had taken her hand and shaken it gently. Her other hand had enclosed his. There had been so many things that he had wanted to say but they had stuck in his throat. In the end the shrill of the whistle made them both jump. They laughed and parted. He turned as he reached the carriage to give her a wave. Her hand held a small handkerchief. He wasn't sure that she wasn't crying but she had smiled and waved back.

'Oi Bryn, close your mouth. The flies will have that cake out of there before you can swallow it,' John said. All eyes were looking at Bryn, who was still looking confused. 'Blimey, are you daft or what? She's coming here isn't she… with Mary! By heck, you can be stupid sometimes.'

The laughter broke the spell and Bryn coughed before he choked on his cake.

'How lovely! I take it that means you want dancing lessons as well then, Bryn?' Mrs Quigley asked as she clapped her hands with glee. 'It will be just like old times with Mr Quigley. He was such a lovely dancer. We used to go to the Imperial every week, have a few dances and a cup of tea, lemonade in the summer, and then have a halfpenny' worth of chips on the way home.'

'He sounds a bit of a smooth one, Mrs Quigley,' Huan said. 'But I'm sure you will have your work cut out with these two.'

'I'm not sure that I can go,' Bryn said.

The boys looked at each other for a moment; then burst out laughing. 'Got a prior engagement have you? Of course you're going, boyo. Come on, you haven't stopped thinking about her since we got back from leave. It's flipping obvious,' John said.

'What's obvious?' Bryn asked.

'You and Cerys, you mutton head.'

'No it's not.'

'Well, I think it's wonderful,' Mrs Quigley said. 'I'll go and put the dinner on and then we can start practising. We'll need a few weeks I think. When is she coming, Rhys?'

Rhys fumbled with the letter and scanned down the page. 'Oh brilliant – next weekend. Will that give us enough time to learn a few steps?'

'I'm sure we can sort out one or two dances,' Mrs Quigley said as she got up and left the room to get the dinner.

'How about it then Bryn?' Rhys asked, looking at his erstwhile friend.

'I'm not sure about the dancing but it would be nice to see Cerys and Mary obviously.'

'Right, that's a plan then,' Rhys said with a beaming smile.

'I think you two are forgetting something,' John said as he put down his cup of tea and looked at each of them. 'Next Saturday. Ring any bells?'

'What about it?' Rhys said.

'We're on duty.'

'Oh shit,' Bryn said, much louder than he had intended.

*

'Guard. Guard shun!' the orderly sergeant screamed.

It was five minutes to the hour and the orderly officer would be approaching in a few minutes. Timing was everything: too early and the men would start to fidget; too late and the tried and tested procedure would be thrown into chaos. The orderly sergeant had already inspected the guard and made sure that they were all present and correct. It was bad luck if the officer picked up a soldier for cleanliness – some officers felt it their duty to pick up one or two men just to emphasise to the sergeant and the men who was in charge, but if someone wasn't present then he would be the only one to blame.

'Stand at ease. Stand easy. Don't fidget, you 'orrible little Welshman. I said stand at ease, not do a fucking jig on the spot.'

Standing in front of the guard, the orderly sergeant turned to his right, raising himself a full two inches before bending and driving his left heel into the ground. He stepped off to the right, coming to a halt at the right-hand marker of the guard to await the orderly officer.

'I hope he's not going to be long,' Rhys whispered to Huan, who was stood on his left.

'Oh stop gabbing boy, you've got plenty of time.'

'I'm pretty excited you know.'

'Yes I know, you haven't shut up about it all week.'

'Do you reckon she loves me?'

'Oh please, you're making me feel sick and shut up for goodness' sake or we'll all end up in the back of the guardroom.'

Their conversation was stopped by the cautionary word of command, 'Guard. Guard 'shun.' The orderly officer approached guard and walked towards Sergeant Brown.

'Oh shit, not him for goodness' sake,' Rhys growled.

'Sssh… It'll be fine.'

Sergeant Brown took a pace forward as the orderly officer approached.

'Sir, I 'ave sixteen men of the guard, in the open order, awaiting your inspection. May I 'ave your permission to stand the centre and rear ranks at ease, sir, please?'

Lieutenant Symonds looked along the front rank of the guard.

'No you may not.'

'Thank you, sir. Centre and rear–'

Symonds cut the orderly sergeant short. 'I said no, or are you hard of hearing, Sergeant?'

Sergeant Brown was momentarily lost. 'No, sir. As you wish, sir.'

111

Symonds walked slowly along the front rank, looking with complete disinterest at the soldiers in front of him. He stopped at the end of the front rank, taking in the last man. 'What's your name?' he asked.

'Private Tallent, sir.'

'Where do I know you from, Tallent?'

Bryn looked ahead, over the head of the officer he was addressing. 'No idea, sir. Perhaps from playing rugby?' Bryn tried.

'No, I don't think so Tallent. I find rugby rather vulgar. I remember you. You were the clown who fell off the train when we arrived in this Godforsaken place and the idiot who nearly wrecked my car in the lane, are you not?'

'Yes, sir.'

Symonds looked him up and down. 'Clearly Tallent by name only.' He grimaced at his own humour. 'Those boots are a disgrace. Take his name, Sergeant.'

Sergeant Brown looked down at Bryn's gleaming boots. 'Sorry, sir?' he said.

'That's the second time you haven't listened to what I have said, Sergeant Brown. Would you like to take your own name as well as Tallent's?'

Sergeant Brown looked Symonds in the eye. 'No, sir,' he said.

'Good, then take his name.'

'Yes, sir.'

*

Having dismissed the parade, Symonds strode off towards the Officers' Mess. Sergeant Brown walked over to Bryn.

'Sorry lad, there was nothing I could do.'

'That's alright Sergeant, I think he just had it in for me.'

'Well I'll see what I can do. I'll have to put it in the book but I'll have a word with the sergeant major in the morning. Truth be told, I don't think there is any love lost between the sergeant major and him. Not that I said that of course. I'll tell him your boots were spotless.'

'Thanks Sergeant, I appreciate that.'

*

'I've sorted the roster,' Rhys said as he emerged triumphantly from the guardroom. 'Huan and John are on opposite shifts to you and me, Bryn, so they can cover our guard duty for a couple of hours. Problem sorted, we meet the girls, the guard is covered, everyone's happy and we'll be back well before midnight.'

'Yeah, as long as nobody finds out. I'm not sure that going is a good idea,' Bryn said as Rhys was having a final word with Huan and John. 'That little bastard is bound to come around and find us missing and then we'll cop it.'

'No he won't,' Rhys said. 'I've just been having a chat to the provost corporal who said he stays in the mess until midnight and then does a quick once-round before going off to bed. They don't want him around any more than he wants to be, so they put entries into the logbook to show that he inspects frequently throughout the night. That way the adjutant won't give him any more extra duties. Everyone's happy, see. We'll be back in plenty of time.'

'I dunno. I've got a bad feeling about this.'

'And just think about how bad the girls will be feeling if we don't turn up!' Rhys was starting to lose his patience. Bryn sighed and shook his head 'I can't believe you don't want to go. We can't stand them up now, how would that look?'

'I do want to go but I just know there's going to be trouble.'

'Listen boyo, who knows when you will next get to see her?' John said. 'We'll keep the coast clear at this end. Sergeant Brown is no problem and Symonds is too bloody lazy to come out on a night like this. Go and have a good time but make sure that you're back before midnight.'

Bryn looked at John. Of his three best friends John was by far the most sensible. He looked at Rhys, who was nodding anxiously. 'Come on then, what have we got to lose?'

'Nothing except your virginity,' Huan roared, which broke the gloom.

'Ha bloody ha. You're such an idiot. Come on then, let's get it over with,' Bryn said.

'Blimey, it's not a trial you know. You can have fun,' Rhys said.

'Go on then boys, give 'em both a kiss from me will you?' Huan said. Rhys and Bryn gave him a raised eyebrow and turned away.

'Fair enough then. Their loss I suppose,' Huan called after them as John clipped him around the head.

*

Rhys knocked on the door of a pretty Victorian terrace that ran perpendicular to the high street. The red brick was largely covered in ivy that had clawed its way up towards the roof. Bryn and Rhys looked at each and blew out their cheeks. Bryn rubbed his boots on the back of his trousers. A burly-looking woman in a striped pinafore apron that covered a light blue floral dress opened the door.

'Yes?' she said tersely.

Rhys took off his cap. 'We've come to pick up Mary and Cerys.'

'Have you, by gum? And what are you expecting to do once you have picked them up?'

Rhys looked across at Bryn. 'Well, er… we erm… well, we're going dancing and then we're planning to have a spot of supper.'

The landlady stood as still and rigid as a guardsman on parade. She held onto the door. 'I expect them to be back by ten o'clock at the very latest and I don't allow visitors. Do I make myself perfectly clear?' Rhys and Bryn looked at each and nodded. 'I expect the young ladies will be ready shortly.' She paused for a minute. 'You can wait in the hall until they come down.' She opened the door to allow them in. 'And wipe your feet on the mat. I don't want your mud all over the place.'

The hallway was barely wide enough for more than one person, with the stairs on the right leading directly up from the front door. The landlady stood at the bottom of the stairs, looking the boys up and down. No one spoke. Rhys fiddled with his cap between his fingers, wondering where to look. Bryn gave their host a smile and got a scowl for his trouble.

There was excited chattering at the top of the stairs. The boys looked up as Mary came down, straightening her skirt as she took each stair carefully so as not to fall. She smiled at Rhys and then at Bryn. She paused a moment on the stair. 'Hello,' she said.

'Hello,' Rhys replied, almost too tongue-tied to speak. He held her gaze as she made her way down the stairs. Bryn nudged him in the ribs and coughed to break the silence. 'You look lovely,' Rhys said.

'Thank you. You look very smart yourself. You both do,' she added.

'It's a bit drab but I suppose it has to be.'

More feet were on the stairs. Bryn couldn't see her at first until her head came below the level of the ceiling. She paused and looked first at Bryn and then at the others. 'Oh,' she said. 'Sorry, are you waiting for me?'

Bryn saw her mouth move but heard none of the words. Her hair had grown and hung in light curls around her collar. It glistened like a thousand diamonds against her neck. Her smile was warm and her eyes sparkled. He was sure that she looked older – not older; more mature, more grown-up.

'Well as we're all here, shall we go? Rhys asked.

'That would be lovely. Where are we going?' Mary asked.

'Dancing apparently,' the landlady replied, looking to all as if she would be glad to get rid of them. 'Although why you would want to be dancing when there is a war on I don't know.' She reached for the door to let them out. 'And make sure that you are back by ten o'clock sharp. I won't be opening the door after that.' The door closed heavily behind them. They looked at each other and burst out laughing.

'How did you manage to end up there?' Rhys asked.

'Apparently my Aunty Sissy stayed there a few years ago and thought that it was lovely,' Mary replied.

'She's worse than our sergeant major,' Bryn said.

Cerys paused as she reached the gate at the end of the garden path. 'I was beginning to think you had lost your tongue, Bryn Tallent.' She smiled.

Bryn blushed. 'I'm sorry, shall we start again?'

'Well you can start by giving me your arm if you like.'

'Of course,' he said, extending his left arm. Cerys nodded and placed her hand gently on his.

'Thank you,' she said.

'Oh, come on you two or we'll be stood here all night,' Rhys called as he and Mary made their way towards the town. Bryn looked at Cerys and they both laughed.

*

A thin early evening mist swirled around the entrance to the Regency Royal Hotel as Rhys and Mary stumbled out of the revolving door. Mary had insisted they do it together. The doorman offered Bryn and Cerys the normal door, which they felt obliged to take although Bryn would rather have squeezed into the revolving door with his guest. They all felt a little giddy from the dancing and the laughter.

'It has been a wonderful evening,' Cerys said as she felt the cold night air on her cheeks. 'Thank you, Bryn.'

'I'm not so sure about the music; it was dreary. I thought the chap on the double bass was going to nod off at one point.'

Cerys laughed.

'Oh, who cares about the music?' Mary said. 'The crowd was merry and it seems that you two dark horses can actually dance.'

'Of course we can dance,' Rhys replied. 'We do it all the time down the mine.'

Bryn hadn't been given any option other than to dance. Mary led the way to the floor as soon as they arrived. Bryn and Cerys followed suit. The lessons with Mrs Quigley paid off handsomely. She had proven to be an excellent teacher and rather than tripping over his own feet, he found himself leading Cerys with ease.

The first dance had broken the ice and they found themselves talking all evening on just about every subject. Bryn found himself enthralled as he listened to Cerys. She was intriguing and confident – 'cocky', she said her da called her. They agreed at the start of the evening not to talk about the war. Bryn said that only left him rugby and mining to talk about, which she might find a bit boring, but he was amazed by her knowledge of things he barely understood himself. He found himself agreeing with arguments that he would previously have dismissed. She guided his thoughts in a fluid, logical manner that made sense. He felt stimulated, not challenged in any way. As the only girl in the family with four older brothers she was used to debating male issues and clearly getting her own way. Cerys' father owned a small foundry over towards Chester. She had grown up in the country and could ride a horse and shoot. Having four brothers had made her pretty tough and she could even ride a motorbike, as long as her mother didn't find out! As far as Bryn was concerned she could do anything.

The high street was dark and deserted except for a few other couples making their way home. As they strolled along as slowly as they dared to make the evening last, Bryn felt Cerys' arm wrap tighter round his own. His heart sang. He would never be as happy in his life as he was right now, he thought. Rhys and Mary were a few steps ahead of them, giggling like little children. Rhys stopped and turned back towards Bryn and Cerys. He nodded to the side of the hotel. 'Listen boyo, we're just going down here for a few minutes, privacy like, you know. Are you going to hang on here?' Rhys said with a mischievous glint in his eye.

'Go on then but don't be long; it's freezing and we need to be back in half an hour otherwise we'll have to smuggle the girls into our camp for the night.'

*

Rhys grabbed Mary's hand and disappeared down the alley of the hotel. In the shadows Rhys wrapped his arms around his girl and kissed her full on the lips. She didn't resist.

'Well now Rhys Taylor, what would your mother say?'

'Good luck, I hope,' he said and kissed her again.

'You'll have to marry me now.'

'What! I only kissed you,' he said. Panic was etched onto his face.

'I'm only joking, silly. You can kiss me again if you want to.'

He leaned forward, more slowly this time. His right hand was on Mary's waist, the other in the small of her back. As their lips touched he drew her forward a little more and pressed his body against hers. The kiss this time was slower and more deliberate. He felt himself move.

*

'Well, they didn't waste much time did they?' Cerys said as Rhys and Mary disappeared down the alley.

'No, I guess not but he is pretty keen on Mary you know. Talks about nothing else really, except the war.'

'Yes, except the war,' Cerys said to herself. She looked up at Bryn. They were on the main street and people were passing by.

'Are you cold?' Bryn asked. 'I can't give you a coat, otherwise I would. They haven't got around to giving us coats yet.' They both laughed.

'No, I'm fine thank you.'

'I should go and get them. It's not fair, you standing here in the cold.'

'No, leave them be,' she said, grasping his arm. 'It's nice for them to have a few moments on their own. And who knows when they will see each other again?'

'And us for that matter. As long as you would like to, of course?'

'Of course I would. I can't think of anything that I'd rather do.'

Bryn looked up and down the road. It was now deserted. He coughed and moved slightly closer. He took Cerys' hand and looked at her in the light of the hotel.

'I think you are the most beautiful woman I have ever met.'

Cerys brought her other hand up to his face and gently brought it towards her own. She paused to look into his eyes and then drew him closer until their lips met. Bryn felt the softness of her lips and tasted the sweet lingering residue of the punch. It was such a gentle kiss that Bryn could barely feel any pressure; it was like kissing the flesh of a ripe peach.

*

Mary giggled. 'You cheeky devil you. What kind of girl do you think I am, Rhys Taylor? Anyway it is far too cold in this alley, and dark.' A door banged, which startled the smooching couple. A light went on in the room above.

'Ssh…' Rhys said as he pulled Mary under the window. Two men were talking loudly above them. He pulled Mary a little closer without any resistance.

She whispered in his ear. 'Is this just another excuse to get a little closer?'

'Ssh… They'll hear us.'

'So? We're not doing anything.'

'I'm protecting your reputation.'

'What's wrong with my reputation?'

'Nothing at the moment and it's best if it stays that way… for now at least.' Mary buried her head in Rhys' chest and stifled a laugh. The voices were getting louder. One was clearly agitated; the other was more menacing. 'Hang on, I know that voice.'

'How can you know that voice? It could be anyone.'

'No, hang on.' Rhys moved his head slightly so that he could hear better. There were two voices.

'It's quite simple,' said a man in a calm but threatening voice. 'You borrowed £200 and now I want it back. Now, I'm sure that's not difficult for a gentleman such as yourself to understand, is it?'

'Don't be so condescending. Of course it's not difficult to understand. But you can't have what I don't have. I'm sure that you understand that, don't you?'

'I'm sure I understand that this is a matter of some embarrassment to you. After all, I offered to loan you the money, in perfectly good faith, one gentleman to another. Now you tell me that you cannot repay me as we agreed. I'm actually embarrassed for you, particularly a gentleman in your position. However, these are difficult times so I'll tell you what I'll do. You let me have £250 by the end of the week and we'll not say anything else about this little matter. How does that suit you?'

'Are you mad – £250? I borrowed £200.'

'Quite so, and you have failed to pay me back. So to compensate me for your ingratitude and to assure you of my continued generosity I would like £250 in return, by Wednesday.'

'But I can't get that kind of money together in a few days.'

'Well I suggest you try.'

'I've told you I can't give you what I don't have. You will have to be patient. You know that I am good for the money. I just need a few days to get it together. I'm sure you understand.'

'Oh, I understand entirely but Mr Bellows here doesn't. You see, unlike you and me, he was dragged up from the gutter and doesn't understand why his wages are short when I haven't got any money to pay him. As you can imagine that makes him rather cross so I have to explain to him that because people like you haven't paid their debts I can't pay him. So he then understands that his cash flow problems are in fact caused by your cash flow problems. It's surprising really how fast he catches on. So unless you would like to be better acquainted with Mr Bellows then I suggest that you come up with the money.'

'It will take me more than a few days; I need to go to Chester but I can't get away from the camp. I can get it to you by the end of the week.'

'Mr Bellows, can you wait till the end of the week?' the gentleman asked. There was a moment of silence. 'No, I didn't think so.'

Mary grabbed Rhys. 'We should go,' she whispered.

'No, wait a minute,' Rhys said. 'I know that voice, I'm pretty sure that it's one of our blokes.'

'Well you're not going in there to give him a hand, that's for sure.'

'Shh…'

'Do you get my drift, old chap? I want the money by Wednesday or Mr Bellows is going to get very upset. Did I mention that he was a prizefighter? Unfortunately banned due to his lust for biting the ears off his opponents.'

'Look, there is no need for this to get out of hand—'

'You are right about that at least.'

'I can get some of it by Wednesday. Not all of it, but some of it. There is a fund the soldiers pay into at the camp. It pays for entertainment and things. I can get some tomorrow when I'm on duty. It will only be half but I can get the rest by next week. I promise.'

'Well so long as you promise I suppose that's alright. What do you think Mr Bellows? I'm sure a gentleman would never break a promise, would he? Well I'm glad that's settled. I will see you on Wednesday. Mr Bellows will collect you. And perhaps Mr Bellows will see you out. Goodnight Lieutenant Symonds.'

'Shit, come on, we need to get out of here now.' Rhys grabbed Mary, almost pulling her along the alley.

'Hang on, I can't run in these heels.'

'Come on, we need to get away from here.'

'Why?'

'Just – aaargh!' Rhys cried as he slipped on a piece of food that had been left outside the kitchen. The cats had been busy spreading their meagre rations across the floor. The war was difficult even for the feline community.

'Ouch, you bugger!' Rhys cried as he rolled over a bin and caught his shoulder on the side of the fire escape as he toppled forward. His shoulder smacked the upright hard. He regained his balance and grabbed Mary's hand.

'Are you alright?'

'No lasting damage. Come on.'

A window was pushed up. 'What the hell's going on out there?' shouted a dapper man in evening dress. Mr Bellows go, and take a look.'

A small wiry man in a cheap ill-fitting brown suit opened the kitchen door and stepped out. He put his hand on the railing and looked towards the window where he had been stood a few moments before. He glanced right and saw the upturned bin.

'Fucking cats,' he said to himself. He trotted down the few steps into the alley. He picked up a badge off the floor. He looked at the badge in the palm of his hand – *RWF*.

*

Bryn and Cerys were standing where they had left them at the corner of the hotel. They were laughing and holding hands.

'Come on you two, we've got to get out of here now.' Rhys and Mary were already twenty yards ahead of them. Bryn looked at Cerys and shrugged.

'Come on then.' He grabbed her hand and they ran down the street after Rhys and Mary. They stopped at the next corner and ducked behind a small wall.

'What's going on? Big rats down that alley were there?' Bryn sniggered. He looked at Cerys, who was finding it difficult to keep a straight face.

'Shh...' Rhys said. 'Worse than rats. Have a look over the wall. Carefully, mind.'

'What am I looking for?'

'To see who comes out of the hotel.'

All four of them peered over the wall and looked towards the brightly lit entrance of the hotel. A doorman stood in the centre of the doorway, rocking on his heels and rubbing his hands behind his back.

'There's no one there. Who am I looking for?'

'Wait a minute.' Just as he spoke the doorman turned as the door behind him was thrust open. An officer brushed past the doorman, placed his hat on his head, looked both ways and walked away.

'Is that who I think it is? Bryn asked.

'Oh yes,' Rhys replied.

'Well, who is it?' Mary asked.

'His name is Lieutenant Symonds and he's not meant to be here,' Rhys replied.

'Where's he meant to be then?'

'He's meant to be on duty, same as we are.'

'Oh no,' Bryn said. 'Do you think that he was looking for us?'

'No, I think we're probably the last thing on his mind right now. That's not the half of our problems.' Rhys looked at the girls, who were wide-eyed with bewilderment. 'It's ten minutes to ten!'

CHAPTER FIFTEEN

It was still dark outside as the early risers were starting to drift into the cookhouse. The boys were sat in an area that was reserved for the guard, who were required to sit together so that the duty officer knew where to find his men in an emergency. Being allowed to go to the front of the queue was about the only perk of being on guard duty. The chefs regularly gave the men a bit extra as long as the master chef wasn't watching.

'So, let's get this right. You were in the alley, groping Mary,' Huan said through a mouthful of stodgy porridge.

'I wasn't groping.'

'Well, whatever it was you was doing.'

'Look it doesn't matter what he was doing,' Bryn said. 'What matters now is what are we going to do about Symonds?'

'What do you mean "*we*"? In case you've forgotten, "*we*" were left here to cover your arses, which I might point out is going to cost you a few bottles of beer. Particularly as we had to buy off Sergeant Brown.'

'What do you mean buy him off?'

'Well, you were meant to be back by midnight and when you didn't turn up John and I had to stand guard again, which became a bit obvious even to Sergeant Brown.'

'Oh well, that's bloody marvellous that is.'

'It was lucky that you got back in time for parade otherwise you would have really copped it. I couldn't believe it when Symonds turned up with a fat lip and a shiner. Funniest thing I've seen in ages. I'd like to have seen the bloke smash him!'

'Well it isn't so funny now is it?'

'I reckon that the best thing to do is to tell the sergeant major,' John suggested.

'Great idea, professor. Then he'll want to know how we know and then he'll know that we weren't on duty and then we're in the shit as well,' Rhys replied as he sat staring at his congealed porridge.

'He's got a point you know,' Huan agreed. 'There will be some pretty miffed blokes here if there is no happy hour on Friday. Sixpence off one man is only a little thing but sixpence off five hundred men is a big thing.'

John put his spoon down and looked at his friend. 'What are you talking about?'

'I was just saying—'

'Well don't. It makes people realise that you are as stupid as you look.'

Rhys snorted his tea and spilt the rest down his tunic.

Bryn pushed his chair back abruptly and stood up. 'I don't believe you three. Am I the only one who realises how serious this is?'

'Oh come on Bryn, it's not that bad,' Rhys said as he dabbed his tunic with his handkerchief.

'No, bugger off,' Bryn said. 'I told you this would end in trouble. If you hadn't gone down that alley in the first place we wouldn't have been in this mess.'

*

'I see,' the regimental sergeant major said at length. 'If what you say is true, then this is all rather disturbing. Where exactly did you hear this conversation?' He was sat bolt upright behind his desk. Opposite stood Bryn and Rhys. He had not allowed them to stand at ease and both were starting to sweat. The regimental sergeant major wasn't sure if he was being spun a yarn or not.

'We were in town the other day, sir. On the way back to our accommodation,' Rhys said.

'You were on duty last night, weren't you.' It was a statement rather than a question. 'Why didn't you inform the duty officer last night or this morning?'

Bryn and Rhys looked at each other. 'It was a Sunday, sir, and we didn't think that you would like to be disturbed.'

The regimental sergeant major eyed them suspiciously. Company Sergeant Major Ashton would have briefed him prior to their arrival so he knew there must be some threads of truth in their story. Why else would they risk his wrath? Still, something was nagging him, something wasn't quite adding up. 'So you decided to wait until today to tell me. Is that right?'

'Yes, sir,' they both said.

'And you don't know who this person is?

'No, sir.'

'This is very disturbing news. I'm sure you understand how important this is. Thank you for bringing it to my attention. Dismissed.'

*

Lieutenant Symonds was stood in front of the adjutant, who was finding it difficult to hide his contempt for the officer who stood before him. He wasn't sure what it was that riled him so much about the man, other than his persistent misdemeanours. *No*, he thought, *the man is just arrogant.* The adjutant was shaken from his thoughts at the mention of the soldiers' fund.

'I'm sorry, say that again would you?'

Charles paused and gave the adjutant a wry smile. *That got your attention least*, he thought. 'I have written a statement if you prefer?'

The adjutant took the sheet of paper. 'Thank you. Please go on – you were saying?'

'Yes, sir. As I was saying, whilst carrying out a check of the regiment's accounts as directed by yourself, I found, somewhat alarmingly, that the soldiers' fund was not where it should have been.' Symonds hadn't been able to believe his luck when the adjutant had told him, earlier in the morning, to check the account. He hadn't even needed to find an excuse to open the safe, and it couldn't have been easier for him to take the money. Life was dealing him a bit of luck for once. 'I did of course ask the regimental accountant where the money was and he assured me that it should have been in the safe. It is all in my statement.'

The adjutant looked at the piece of paper while he considered what to do. 'Stay there for a moment, will you?' The adjutant's office had a connecting door through to the commanding officer's office. He knocked gently on the door and walked in. Symonds was working the situation through his mind. He had every reason to be in the safe, no one had seen him remove the satchel and he had reported the loss straight away. There was nothing to link him to the theft. The adjoining door opened sharply and the adjutant told Symonds to march into the commanding officer's office. The colonel was behind a large office table that would have been a welcome addition to any gentleman's study. He grunted as Symonds halted and saluted but didn't look up from the statement that he held in his hands. The adjutant stood silently by the door. The colonel placed the statement on the table.

'Bit of a rum situation this, Symonds.'

'Indeed so, sir. Criminal, sir, if you ask me.'

'I wasn't. Any idea who might have taken the money?'

'No, sir.'

'Bit of a nerve coming into a guarded camp. Must have been an inside job. What do you say?'

'Y-yes, sir. Whilst I find it difficult to believe, sir, perhaps it might have been one of the men. After all, they all knew about the fund and… well, let's be honest, sir, many of them are from, shall we say, dubious backgrounds.'

'Indeed. Very sad when a man steals from his comrades.'

'Might I suggest, sir, that last night's guard would have had easy access to the offices?'

'Every possibility of course. We do, however, need to keep an open mind and I am sure that the adjutant will welcome your suggestion whilst he conducts an investigation.'

Symonds half-turned to look at the adjutant, who was writing intently in his notebook. 'Yes, sir.'

'Seems to me that you have done quite a few duties recently, Symonds. Perhaps all of your extra duties have paid off in this case?'

'I would like to hope so, sir, but regrettably we have still lost the money.'

'Ah well, that's where you're wrong,' the colonel said with a little chuckle. 'I'll let you into a little secret. All the blaggards have got is a bag full of paper.'

Symonds' eyes grew wide. 'I'm s-sorry, sir, I'm not with you?'

'Of course you're not Symonds, why would you be? We had a tip-off that something was afoot. It seems that a couple of our sparky young men overheard the thief plotting his dirty deed the other night. They informed the regimental sergeant major, who alerted the adjutant here, who swapped the bag of money for a bag of old paper. We were hoping to catch the blighter in the act but it seems that he managed to get in before you checked the cash and found it missing. Damned shame. I would have enjoyed seeing the men's faces when we caught him. I'm sure they would like to have had a few minutes with him.'

Salisbury Plain Training Camp
February 1915

My Dearest Cerys,

I hope this letter finds you as well as I am. Thank you for your letter and the parcel. It arrived yesterday but I didn't have a chance to write to you last night as we had a night manoeuvre exercise. It was quite amusing really although it was desperately cold. I can't say too much but suffice to say that we spent quite a few hours digging a trench and several more sitting in it freezing half to death, only to find that the enemy had got lost in the mist and attacked the wrong place. It was a real hoot but I suspect that we will have to do it again soon. Anyway, the toffees and the humbugs are going down really well. I have shared them all with the boys, although I am careful to keep them away from Rhys or he would have the lot! The socks are fantastic – and the right size. It must have taken you an age to knit them. Thank you very much.

There is a bit of bother at the moment as enteric fever have broken out. We're alright but some bloke died last night. Mind you, they said that he wasn't well to start with. I don't know why he was in the army if he wasn't well. Anyway we have to gargle some medicine every morning. It sounds like a right racket when we all get going. I reckon we probably drink enough to fill a public bath between us.

There is talk of us moving to a place called Blackdown soon but we don't know when. I don't think that it is far from here. It can't be any worse but I don't suppose we will get a nice cushy billet again. There's even talk of us being thrown out to make room for the officers but Mrs Quigley said that she would rather have us than some toff.

Not much else going on here. We still haven't heard anything about what happened that night but I think it is done and dusted now. How are things at home?

My very best wishes,
Bryn

CHAPTER SIXTEEN

February 1915

The sergeant major dragged Bryn to one side. His face was so close that Bryn leaned back so that their noses weren't touching. 'This is your chance to shine, my lad,' the sergeant major was saying with all seriousness as they stood face-to-face. 'These men need leadership, discipline and a fine example to follow. You are that man. I have faith in you, lad. Show them what you are made of and they will follow you to the end of the earth. Got it?'

Bryn looked at his mates. They were stood tall and lean, and even Huan looked like he had lost a few pounds and grown several inches. The past twelve weeks had been a gruelling trial of military exercises. They had attacked imaginary Germans up and down Salisbury Plain, day after day. They had dug in and waited for the whistle to assault the enemy trenches. They stood in lines along the trench that no one had shelled. They had taken their turn as a sentry, watching the front for any sign of movement that never came. The platoon officer would check his watch, blow his whistle and lead his men over the top. The men clambered up the ladders and walked across the open ground to the opposing trenches. No one knew what would happen after that, as they never practised anything else. The men assumed that they would just occupy the German trench and then start again the next day just as they had been doing day after day for the past few weeks.

Bryn stared back at the sergeant major. 'Yes, sir,' he said.

'I'm counting on you lad, and so is the regiment. I picked you as the No. 8 so you have more control of the game. Show them what Welshmen are made of. Make them wish they had stayed at home.'

Bryn nodded and turned back towards his team. All fourteen of them were looking at him. There was no need for words; actions meant more than a few well-chosen phrases. He just jogged through the middle of them and led them onto the field. The referee raised his arm.

'Captains ready?' Bryn raised his arm to signify that they were ready.

The fly half lofted the ball high towards the opposition.

Bryn led the charge, keeping one eye on the ball and the other on the receiver. As he charged forward the same thought always came to mind. *Hit 'em hard once and they will remember, hit 'em hard twice and they will never forget.* Bryn hit the Hampshire second row like a train hitting a hay cart that had been caught on a crossing. The Hampshire lad wasn't small but the air was driven from his lungs and without any support he crumpled onto the floor, spilling the ball backwards. The roar along the touchline added to the pain of the six foot four inch young man who lay motionless on the ground as a maul formed over him. The referee blew his whistle for a scrum. He looked down at the second row, who was trying to raise himself from the ground.

'Are you alright lad?' the referee asked. He looked at Bryn, who just stared back at the man on the floor.

Bryn gathered his pack together. Rhys, Huan and John instinctually stood next to each other. He looked at each of them. 'I want the front row to drive in straight and hard, no turning, no wheeling – straight and hard, got it? Let them know who you are. I want a quick ball straight through the tunnel,' he said, looking at the scrum half. 'We'll peel off left. The winger doesn't look up to much. Break quickly and if we have to go into contact, stay on your feet and we'll drive forward. If it goes to ground then let's get it out quickly.'

Rhys, John and Huan bound themselves together as they had done a thousand times before.

'Let's do it then,' Rhys said through gritted teeth.

Bryn took a quick look at the backs that were lined up deep, ready to charge onto the ball if it passed along the line. When the scrum came together, the hit was massive. Bryn felt it shudder through his body. He often wondered how the front row took such a hit time after time. *No sense, no feeling*, he always told himself.

The scrum half watched for the sign and rolled the ball into the tunnel. John hooked it back as the drive from the pack thrust him forward. It was short but brutal. The Hampshires gave two yards in an instant. The ball passed through the channel that had been created by the second row. The Hampshire scrum half was standing too far back and the back row were trying to shore up the failing scrum.

Bryn picked up the ball and exploded off the back of the scrum, taking his own flanker with him. As he expected, the winger took one look at the speed, size and strength of Bryn and made a halfhearted tackle, which was brushed aside. The Hampshire fullback darted across to cover the gap but Bryn took the tackle and popped the ball up to his flanker, who had less than six yards left to cross the line. The crowd of Welshmen on the right-hand side of the pitch roared at the Englishmen on the opposite side.

*

'Not a bad opening – five minutes for a bunch of amateurs!' someone on the touchline uttered. Sergeant Major Ashton turned and was about to bellow out an insubordinate ranker. He turned and caught himself. His thoughts were drawn back several years.

'Well I'll be bowled over,' he said. 'Bob Rolland! I thought that you were long since buried. I haven't seen you for... blimey, let's see... oh, far too many years for me to remember.' The two sergeant majors shook hands. 'And look at you in uniform as well! They've never got you signed up at your age?'

'As I recall we're the same age so you can cut that out you cheeky sod!' They both laughed.

'What brings you down then? I hear they've got you doing the recruiting job back home.'

'That's right. I'm bugger all use to the rest of the army apparently so the least I can do is to make sure that the regiment gets the best.'

'Amen to that, Bob. I've certainly got no complaints; we've got some good lads here at the moment.'

Bob stared across the pitch as the Hampshire centre tried to smother the ball.

'Well I'm delighted to hear that. We do try you know but it's bloody difficult trying to weed out the chaff. There are so many of the silly buggers trying to join up it's nigh on impossible to stop the dud ones.'

The Welshmen turned over the centre with ease and left him writhing on the ground. The forwards took the ball and once again went crashing to the ground. More forwards drove into the rock.

'They're knocking hell out of each other,' Bob said. His friend grinned. 'You'd think it was an international.'

'It might as well be; I hear that there might not be a game next year.'

'Well now, I haven't heard that but it makes sense I suppose. What we need to do is get these lads over to France, sort out the Germans and then back in time for the Five Nations. Three years on the trot now they've beaten us. That has to stop.'

'*Duw*, I can't believe how close it was last year,' Ashton said.

'Close isn't good enough though, is it? One point is one point and they had it, not us.'

'I tell you what, Bob. Look at young Tallent out there. He's the big lad driving into the maul now. See him.'

'Aye, I know him.'

'Who does he remind you of, then?'

'Me?' Bob replied with a hopeful smile.

'Get away with you. No, look at him. Spitting image of David

Watts, he is. You know, the lock that they brought in this year. Had a couple of very good games. I reckon Tallent could give him a run for his money.'

'I heard he'd joined the light infantry.'

'Who?'

'Watts the Lock!'

'Ah well, there you go. The whole team will have joined up soon so that will be the end of that. Definitely no games next year.'

There was a loud roar but this time from the opposite side of the pitch. The Hampshires had turned over the ball. The Welsh back line had been sucked into the maul and a large gap had appeared on the left.

'Shift left,' Bob Rolland shouted.

'Hey, I do the shouting round here.'

Bob patted his friend on the shoulder and mouthed an apology.

'Shift left,' the sergeant major screamed, and looked across at his friend and smiled.

The advantage was short-lived as the play broke down into another maul. Hands wrenched for the ball. The Welshmen won the ball back with comparative ease. The scrum half spun it to the standoff, who popped it up for the centre, who took the ball at pace into the contact. The forwards went into another maul and again the ball came out quickly. The scrum half passed the ball to his right.

'Straighten up, take the contact,' the sergeant major shouted.

The ball reached the winger, who fumbled and dropped it. The referee saw the knock-on, checked his watch and blew for half-time.

Sergeant Major Ashton blew out his cheeks. 'Five points isn't a lot to show for all that pressure is it?'

'Maybe not but I see young Tallent is giving his lads a good talking-to. He'll sort them out.'

Sergeant Major Ashton looked across the field to the huddle of Welshmen who were being berated by their captain.

'How do you know him then?'

Bob gave a little laugh. 'I've coached him and the terrible trio that you have got in the front row since they were boys.'

'I might have known,' Ashton said with a little chuckle. 'Your lads, hey? Well you've done a good job with them Bob, I'll give you that.' Sergeant Major Ashton looked across the pitch as his team moved into position to receive the kickoff at the start of the second half. He looked at his friend and smiled. 'Despite their terrible upbringing by you they are four fine young men and excellent soldiers. They will do the regiment proud, you mark my words.'

*

The sergeants and colour sergeants were becoming quite vocal around the mess bar. The banter between the Welshmen and the Hampshire senior non-commissioned officers was good-natured. The more senior warrant officers were expected to take a seat in the anteroom where the mess stewards would bring their beer to them. Bob looked around for any other friendly faces.

'There's no one else Bob. They're all young lads these days.'

'That's a shame, it would have been nice to catch up with some of the old lads.'

Ashton laughed. 'You daft idiot, we are the old lads!' They both burst into laughter, which drew a few stares from some of the younger members of the mess. 'So come on then. Are you going to tell me or do I have to guess? You didn't come all this way just to watch us win a rugby match.'

Bob put his beer on the side table. 'The match was an added bonus but we have a slight problem that we need to sort out so the recruiting major asked me to come down to see what's what.'

'And what might this problem be then?'

'It's like I said earlier; we can't stop recruiting. The powers that be have said that we have to keep taking them in but we've nowhere to put them. We've got no uniforms, no instructors and no space. So I've come to see if you can free up a bit more space.

'You've seen this place Bob, it's crammed as it is. There are plans to build another camp over the way but that's a few months off yet. Even then we'll have the same problem with instructors, not to mention uniforms and other supplies. To be honest they are probably better off where they are at the moment.'

'Have you been given any indication of when this lot will be moving out?'

'No. And to be honest with you they're not ready yet. You know how when we joined, everyone but us knew what was going on and we just fitted in? It was easy. Well, it is totally different here because everyone is new and there's no one to follow. If we could merge them piecemeal into the regiment it wouldn't be so bad but with this many men it's all about discipline and training. The last thing we need is for them to think for themselves. They need to be taught by the book.'

'You need to kick a few of them off to France,' Bob suggested with a wry smile.

'I wouldn't trust half of this lot to face the right way!'

'The depot has been sending the reserves forward as quickly as they can get them sorted and shipped out but they're drying up. On one hand I've got the battalions screaming for replacements, on the other I've the depot telling me to recruit for all I'm worth and on my third hand we've got the top brass who won't let your new blokes go. It's madness, it is.'

'I take it you have heard how the regiment are getting on?'

'The odd snippet here and there but not much makes it out this far. You?'

'I believe the First and the Second Battalions lost a few good men during the retreat from Mons but I haven't heard much recently. I know that Skinny Jones was killed. You remember him; he was always the right marker?

'Oh aye, I remember him, nice lad. Should have kept his head down. Mind you it would have been bloody difficult with his height.'

'I think both battalions have moved up north somewhere. Last I heard the Second Battalion were in some place called Fromelles, somewhere in Belgium or France; I don't know which it is. I haven't heard from the First Battalion recently but I know they were somewhere around Wipers.'

They sat in silence, sipping at their beers. The mess tent had been furnished with as much regimental memorabilia as possible but it was still a marquee at the end of the day. It reminded Bob of his time in Africa but without the sweltering heat. *Good days*, he thought.

'It's going to be a pretty rough do, isn't it?' Bob said.

'It will be very different to anything we were in, that's for sure.'

'What do you think about all these young lads then? Do you reckon they'll be good enough?'

Sergeant Major Ashton twisted the pewter mug in his hands and looked at the pale brown liquid. 'Well if they're not then we're in trouble, aren't we? So they're going to have to be good enough. It's going to be hard for them though.'

'It was hard for us too if you remember, and we didn't turn out so bad did we?'

'More luck than anything, Bob,' Aston said with a smile. They sat for a moment, still staring at his beer. 'You know I said that these lads won't be ready for ages?' he said without raising his eyes from his beer. Bob nodded. 'Well, that's not quite true. There are one or two who could go now and not get themselves into too much trouble. The problem is that unless the Regimental Headquarters calls them forward they won't be going anywhere.'

'That might be so but I've been in the game as long as you have and there are ways and means. I tell you for free, I could get your boys out there and get them replaced here with some new lads in the blink of an eye without anyone knowing. Win-win, as I see it.'

Sergeant Major Ashton looked at his old friend for a moment as thoughts raced through his mind. He leaned forward although there was no prospect of them being overheard. The other mess members were giving them plenty of space. 'Actually Bob, you might be able to help me out.'

*

'I can't believe it.' Huan was the first to speak. The four boys had just marched out of the Sergeant Major's office. 'We're actually going.'

'Better than that boyo, we're actually going to the Second Battalion,' John said.

Salisbury Plain Training Camp
March 1915

My Dearest Cerys,

I can't believe our luck (although I don't suppose you will call it luck). On today of all days (St. David's Day - a good omen) the sergeant major had us in his office and told us that we are going. He said that we were ready and that we are to pack our bags. Not only that but we're going to the Second Battalion - that's brilliant. I can't wait to get out there. The best bit is that we are all going - Rhys, John and Huan as well. The sergeant major said that it would be better if we all went so that he could get rid of his rot all in one go but he was only joking... or at least I think he was. Unfortunately they need us out there pretty fast so we won't get the chance to get home before we go, which is a real shame as I would like to have said cheerio properly but I'm pretty sure that we won't be out there for long. Things will start to happen when the weather gets a bit warmer and we will be back before you know it.

I've packed up my stuff and sent a parcel back to my mam's with a few personal things that I can't carry and Mrs Quigley is making us a special dinner. I think she's pretty sad to see us go - she has been so good to us. We bought her some flowers to cheer her up. She said that the last time she had some flowers was at her husband's funeral but I think she liked them just the same.

We're leaving early tomorrow morning so I will say cheerio for now. Please don't worry about us; we'll be fine. You just take care of yourself and we'll be back before you know it - I promise.

My very best wishes and happy St. David's Day,
Bryn

CHAPTER SEVENTEEN

The train rumbled slowly through the night, the hypnotic rhythm, as it passed over the tracks, rocking the passengers into oblivion. For most of the men oblivion had come from another source; several pints in the Queen Anne before boarding the train. The air was rank from the inebriated bodies that littered the floor and the corridors. The men had lain down cheek by jowl wherever they could find a flat surface, or they had slumped against the wall before slowly sliding down into a crumpled heap. Most were still dozing; those who were awake were lost in their thoughts as they stared out of the windows watching the landscape rattle by.

The train had pulled away from Salisbury station at midnight, shortly after last orders had been called in the pubs. The men downed their final pints, took the handshakes that were offered and made their way to the station for the Southampton-bound train. More than a few of them had sunk more beer than they could hold and had to be held up by their comrades. The train warrant officer, who had been a stationmaster with the Great Western Railway Company before the war, cared little about their state as long as they made it onto the train.

The station had been crammed when the boys got there. Wives, girlfriends, parents and well-wishers had stayed up late to see the men off. In amongst the party atmosphere the women held their children close, as fathers stooped to playfully tweak a young son's cheek or to kiss a shy daughter. There was a quick peck on the cheek for the missus before they turned to the train and then they were off again to the colours. The younger soldiers were neither shy nor sober: women were kissed by more men than they knew and were happy to oblige.

The carnival finally managed to make it onto the trains before the doors were slammed and the engine shunted forward to wild cheering from the men who were hanging out of every window. The older men settled into the seats and smiled as the younger men cheered and waved.

The boys knew no one in Salisbury except Mrs Quigley who had insisted on going to the station. They had tried to dissuade her but she was adamant. 'I'm coming to make sure that you four get on the right train. I know what you're all like. You'll end up in Bognor Regis,' she had said. She had put on a brave face when the boys had broken the news to her that they were going that evening. The sudden decision had caught her off guard and she could not disguise her sadness. She had made them a special dinner and then saw that they had everything before she shooed them off to the pub, 'like real men,' she had said. She told them that she would be able to tidy up the house with them out of the way, and that she would bring anything that they had left behind to the station to see them off. She had hugged each of them in turn before waving them towards the train. Before they could turn around to give her a wave she had disappeared into the crowd.

*

'Anyone fancy a cuppa?' Huan asked.

A large mound covered in an overcoat moved. Rhys emerged from beneath the khaki coat. He rubbed his hand over the window and peered into the grey gloom of the coming day. He looked across at Huan, who was stretching like a bear who had just woken from a long winter's hibernation.

'Where are we?'

'How the heck should I know?'

'Well you're awake aren't you?'

142

'That doesn't mean that I know where we are, does it?'

'Probably not but you can find out whilst you get the sodding tea.'

Rhys pulled his coat back over his head and turned his body back towards the window. Huan looked around at the other bodies that still lay in a comatose state. He shrugged and sighed. He peeled away his own coat and got up. His head started to spin with the sudden movement and he grabbed for the luggage rack, narrowly preventing a fall onto John, who was somewhere under the bundle of coats opposite him. He gathered himself together and stepped as deftly as a prop forward can over the slumbering mounds.

The window had steamed up again by the time Huan got back to the carriage. As he opened the carriage door the smell hit him like a brick wall. He gasped and turned his head away as if that would somehow make things better. He took a couple of quick breaths before he slid the door open again with his foot. The smell hadn't gone.

'Tea's up boys,' Huan cried as he pushed his way into the carriage. In his hands were four steaming mugs of tea. He tottered from side to side as he tried to avoid spilling the steaming contents of his mugs. 'Come on, let's be 'avin you. There's a war on you know.' Three slumbering mounds stirred beneath their overcoats.

'Sod off.'

'Now then there's no need for that kind of language, particularly as I might have four bacon rolls here as well.' Three heads appeared from under the coats. Huan looked at them and gave them a childish grin. 'Or then again, maybe I don't.'

'You are going to be the first person I kill,' John promised as he raised himself off the floor and ruffled his hair through his hands.

'He'll be dead before you get to him,' Rhys added as he took a steaming mug from Huan. 'That's going to be my guilty pleasure.'

'Hey Bryn, *bach*, do you want this tea or not? Only it's starting to burn my flipping hand.'

Bryn poked his head out from underneath his coat and gave Huan a long look before he held out his hand and took the mug.

'Why are you so happy this morning?' Bryn asked as he blew over the rim of his cup to cool the tea that was so hot it would have scolded the devil himself. 'Why isn't your head hurting like mine?'

'Well, you know the saying; the early bird catches the worm and all that.' Huan paused and gave them one of his best grins. 'Well this little birdie managed to find more than just a worm.' From under his tunic he produced four bacon sandwiches, to the delight of his friends.

*

It was almost midday before the train finally ground to a halt at Southampton docks. The final mile seemed to take an age but people everywhere waved back at the boys as they leaned out of the window shouting at everyone they could see.

As they drew into the station the boys could see other soldiers moving in every direction as if in an uncontrollable frenzy. Beyond the platform the boys could just make out ranks of men lined up, waiting to be counted. It was organised pandemonium. As the train screeched to a halt the doors flew open and men clambered stiffly from the carriages. Before the steam and smoke from the train had a chance to lift there were corporals scurrying from every direction, barking orders and calling men together. Their volume and pitch increased with every soldier who disembarked from a carriage.

Huan paused in the doorway to the carriage and looked behind to his friends. 'Let's see if we can get off this train with a bit more dignity and professionalism than last time eh?'

'You! You idle soldier,' a sergeant screamed as he stepped in front of the door and pointed his pace stick at Huan. 'There's a war going on if you'd like to join it? If not then you can fuck off back to where you came from. Get over there you 'orrible little man!'

Bryn stood behind Huan and towered over the sergeant. The sergeant looked back, checked the size of Bryn and quickly strode off along the platform, bellowing for all he was worth.

*

The sky was clearing as the squads of men entered the dockyard. A fresh inland breeze was blowing across the Solent, which put a bit of a chill on the day but the march to the port had kept them warm enough. Marching through the dockyard gates was like entering another world; every inch of ground was covered in bales and boxes stacked as high as any building the boys had ever seen. Men were everywhere, moving stores on carts or their backs. Giant cranes rotated above them, their loads swinging precariously in the breeze as gangs of men were roping and lashing loads together ready for the next lift.

The men halted on the quay alongside three ships where sailors were busy humping coal up the gangplanks and into the bowels of the ships.

'That's hard graft, that it is,' John said.

'Just as long as they don't expect me to do it, I don't mind,' Huan replied. 'I've had my fill of humping coal for a while.'

A sergeant called out the names and the men were detailed off to a ship. They broke ranks and reformed into three long ranks in front of each of their allocated ships.

'We can't be going to war in that thing, surely?' John said as they took their places in the ranks.

'What's the matter with it?' Rhys asked.

'Well it's not dignified is it?'

'It's hardly a warship is it?' Huan noted.

'They're not going to waste a good ship on us, are they?' Bryn suggested. 'Anyway it doesn't matter as long as it gets us there in one piece.'

It was dusk when the ship finally let go from her berth and the steamer started to edge away from the dock. It had been a long day for the men who had spent six hours hauling ropes, carrying sacks or passing goods from hand to hand from the quay up the gangplank and into the hold of the ship. All manner of war stores had been loaded, from boxes of bully beef to rolls of wire and cavalry horses.

A cheer rose from the men who lined the decks as they waved to the crowd, who were on the dock and had stayed to wave them off. The boys had no one to wave to, but waved as enthusiastically to anyone who looked as if they would wave back. The euphoria remained as the ship made its way out of Southampton waters and into the Solent. Then the party came to an abrupt halt as the ship reached the open sea and began to pitch and roll. The railings were soon full of pale-looking men, whose stomachs lurched in time to the rocking motion of the ship. Groans and heaving were very soon the only sounds that could be heard around the ship. The boys were happy enough. With so many men opting to stay outside in the night air there was plenty of room inside, and more importantly, more food for those with stronger constitutions.

*

'There it is!' John cried. 'Land ho.'

'You're not a pirate,' Bryn berated him from beneath his greatcoat. His hand appeared first as he pulled down the heavy material.

It had been a cold and damp night. Sea mist had enveloped them like a magician's cloak soon after leaving Southampton. 'That's a good sign,' one of the sailors had said, 'it'll stop the submarines seeing us.' After which Huan had stubbornly refused to go below deck in case they were hit and couldn't get out. So they had sat on deck all night talking about the war, wondering when they would get into action. It had been in the early hours before they had curled up under their coats to grab a few hours' sleep.

Bryn stood up, put his coat on and flapped his arms around his body to generate a bit of warmth.

'How long have you been up?' Bryn asked.

'Long enough to hear those two snoring,' John replied, pointing at two mounds huddled together. 'Considering he was so frightened of the submarines, he slept well enough.'

'Those two could sleep for Wales.' Bryn leaned on the railings and looked out across the sea. 'Where is it then?'

John pointed towards the bow of the ship. 'Just over there, look. The mist will part in a minute. It seems to be lifting quite quickly now. Should be a good day.'

Bryn had to wait a minute before the coastline breached the mist. 'Blimey, it's closer than I thought. It can't be much longer now.'

'I can't say that I will be sorry to put my feet on solid ground again.'

John was looking down into the sea. 'Me neither. I can't understand why anyone would want to join the navy.' John watched the motion of the great wheel as it churned slowly through the green sea. 'What do you reckon will happen when we get there, Bryn?'

Bryn thought for a moment. 'I dunno, John. I heard some blokes saying that there was a camp just outside the town, where they do a bit of front line training and sort us out before we go forward.'

'Sooner the better I hope. I'm getting tired of waiting.'

'You and me both, boyo. Get it over with and get home.'

'Blinking heck Bryn, we haven't even got there yet and you want to go home. Not homesick already are you?'

'No, I'm just saying that I want to get there so that we can get back and get on with things,' Bryn said.

'Well if you're not homesick then you must be lovesick. "Oh Cerys, my love, come to me,"' he said as he held out his arms to embrace his friend.

'No I'm not, you stupid ass, all I said was–'

'You don't have to explain Bryn. You could have stayed at home with her. We wouldn't have thought any less of you. We could have managed without you.'

'That's not what I said.'

'Well what are you saying? You don't want to be with your mates anymore? You'd rather be cuddling up with the love of your life?'

'I didn't say I was in love and you know it.'

'Well we need to know, Bryn. That's all. We can't have you gallivanting all over the battlefield, love-struck and all that. You'll be all over the place; we need to know if we can depend on you.'

'I'm going to land you one in a minute, boy. And then we'll see who wants to go home.'

'Will you two keep the noise down? We're trying to sleep,' a muffled voice said from beneath the mound of coats. 'Oh and for what it's worth Bryn, there's nothing wrong with being in love.'

'Enough now. See what you've done,' Bryn said as he stabbed his finger into John's chest. 'There'll be no peace now,' he called over his shoulder as he strode off along the deck. Rhys and Huan emerged from beneath their coats. John was laughing to himself.

'Bit cruel, that,' Rhys said.

John looked down at his friend. 'Worth it though, wasn't it?'

'Right, where's this land of yours?' Huan asked.

'Sod the land,' Rhys replied before John could point out the direction of France. 'There's breakfast to be had.'

*

Bryn, Rhys and John watched in fascination at the scene on the dock below them. Men from the Service Corps were everywhere, moving and stacking every conceivable type of war store. There were mountains of boxes, sacks, vehicles, horses and material. The Service Corps men moved about like a nest of ants. As they watched the scene below them other men were being discharged off the ship to waiting sergeants, who were screaming orders and getting them into lines and columns.

'I can't believe that there is so much stuff coming over here,' Rhys said as he gazed at the scene below him.

'It's not all coming this way,' John replied. 'Look over there.' He pointed towards the end of the dock where the train had stopped. Medical orderlies were busy transferring stretchers from the train straight into a waiting ship. The boys stared for a while.

Huan found them still staring at the long lines of injured being carried from the train. 'Come on you lot, we need to get a move on.'

'Where've you been, boyo? I was starting to think that you had jumped ship,' Rhys said.

'Not likely,' Huan replied as he looked over the handrail. 'I can't swim. More importantly, I've been downstairs talking to a bunch of First Battalion boys. They reckon that they're going straight to the front line. Apparently that training camp thing is bollocks. It's called the Bullring, which even sounds like a load of bollocks. All they do is march you about a bit and piss you off. The First Battalion boys are all ex-regulars so they are going straight to the front. I reckon if we tag along with them we can get up to the front a bit quicker.'

'But we're not going to the First Battalion are we?' Rhys asked.

'I know that you cloth head but they can't be far away from each other, can they? All we've got to do is say we made an honest mistake and make our way over to the Second Battalion.'

'Oh yes, they're going to be very impressed with that aren't they? John said. 'We're going to spend the first six months of the war in jail.'

'Their officer is meant to be good bloke. He used to be a second lieutenant before he left and got a job somewhere else and he's from our neck of the woods.'

'Whereabouts?' Bryn asked.

'The posh bit round Acton Park. The blokes said he'd be fine. Come on, he's not going to shop us, is he? We're almost neighbours for goodness' sake.'

'Oh and I bet we probably went to the same school as him as well?'

'*Duw*, you've got the grumps this morning haven't you? Do you want to spend the next few weeks being messed around by a bunch of tick-tocks or do you want to get to the front?'

Rhys grabbed his kit. 'Well I'm with you, boyo.'

'Me too,' John said. They all looked at Bryn, who shook his head and sighed.

'And I suppose that's me as well then?'

'Of course it is. Come on,' Huan urged. 'We need to meet up with them before they disembark.'

The fusiliers were easy to spot in the crowd with their white hackle sticking out of their headdress. They were waiting on the lower deck to be called forward.

'Wait here,' Huan said as he pushed himself forward through the throng. A few minutes later he returned with a short man who looked like he should be at home or sitting in the corner of a pub with a pipe clamped between his teeth rather than standing on a ship waiting to go forward to meet the enemy.

'This is Corporal Williams; he's from our neck of the woods. Says he can sort us out.'

Corporal Williams gave the boys a glance and nodded his head.

'Are you boys sure that you want to go forward just now? There will be plenty of time to kill the Germans; you mark my words. Soldiers should not be in a rush to go to the front.'

The boys looked at each other but it was Bryn who spoke for them all. 'If it's alright with you, Corporal, we'd rather go to the front with you lot. As long as we're not going to get you into trouble,' he added.

'Trouble?' Corporal Williams chuckled. 'There's not a lot they can do to me that they haven't done before, my lad.' He looked at the boys for a moment and sighed. 'Be it on your own heads then, boys. I'm sure the Second Battalion will be glad to see you. Now if for any reason you get found out then I don't know you and you just tagged along, right? I don't mind helping you but I'm getting a bit too old to cop a field punishment. Got it?' The boys grinned and nodded. 'Right, fall in with the rest of the lads when we get off.'

*

'How long have we been in here now?' Huan asked.

'Too bloody long, that's how long,' Rhys replied, although it was so dark in the carriage that no one could see each other.

'I don't believe that I'm sitting here in this—'

'Will you stop bloody moaning and just be grateful that we're not stuck in a camp somewhere doing bloody fatigues? Which is where we will probably end up when we're court-martialled anyway,' Bryn replied.

'I reckon we could have walked faster than this bloomin' train,' John said.

He had been up and down like a yo-yo, trying to stretch his legs. The cattle truck was crammed with forty men and their kit. The train had barely moved faster than walking pace and had stopped every six hours or so when the doors were slid open and the troops spilled onto the platform for a bit of fresh air. Once or twice some Royal Army Service Corps soldiers had arrived with urns of steaming liquid of dubious origins.

The boys had been on the move for nearly twenty-four hours. They shunted forward in short stretches at a snail's pace and then moved to a sideline and waited for an eternity before moving off again.

'Do you hear that?' John asked.

'What is it?' Bryn replied as he lifted his head off his pack.

'What do you reckon, thunder?'

'*Duw*,' said a voice of experience, 'I don't know where they're getting you boys from these days. Thunder my arse! What do you think it is? It's the guns firing, isn't it?! Best you get to know the difference pretty quickly otherwise you'll end up taking cover from a storm and getting soaked from a drumming!' The other men in the carriage laughed. The carriage shuddered to a halt. Outside there were already corporals screaming commands to get fell in. The boys grabbed their kit and waited for the doors to open.

'Out you get, Taffies. Get fell in on the road. Three ranks facing that pile of bricks what used to be a row of houses,' a blustery old corporal roared. 'An' we ain't got all day.'

The boys dropped from the carriage and surveyed the scene. Gone were the pretty French cottages that had surrounded the railway stations along the route. Gone too were the cheering children, the old ladies waving handkerchiefs and the occasional young mademoiselle who was happy to give up a kiss for a few centimes.

Beyond the railway platform was a deeply rutted track with potholes full of gravy-coloured water that belied their depth. A string of wagons was being hurriedly driven forward. Drivers were eagerly encouraging the horses to prevent them from becoming sucked into the mud-filled ruts. The filthy state of some of the drivers told a tale. Beyond the road lay a wasteland littered with detritus. As they stared at the scarred landscape they could see that it wasn't a wasteland at all; there was movement everywhere and the ground seemed to be alive. Men who looked like soldiers moved in and out of the rubble that had once been a small village. They seemed to appear from holes and moved steadily through the rubble before disappearing down another whole.

'*Duw*,' Rhys said at last, 'Where the hell are we?'

'Exactly there,' Bryn replied. 'Hell.'

'Come on you lot. We ain't got all day. Get fell in unless you want to spend the rest of the night hangin' around here.'

Huan blew out his cheeks. 'Well, here we go.'

The corporal had already completed the count twice and was busy looking at the papers in his hand as a captain approached. Seeing the officer, he brought the squad of men up to attention. He turned and saluted the officer. His age and confidence immediately suggested that the captain was a regular officer. His uniform was clean but it had a lived-in look that betrayed the service and action that he had seen since he arrived in France in August 1914. He was unlike any of the officers that the boys had seen before, and he was wearing one of the new steel helmets that they had recently been issued with.

'Corporal Higgs, why are all these men standing around in straight lines looking ominously like new arrivals?' the captain asked as he took in the rows of men standing before him. 'It's likely to rain soon and we don't want them getting wet do we? At least not on their first day.'

Corporal Higgs grinned as he spied some of the men looking up at the clear sky. 'No, sir.'

'Well then, let's get them away.'

'Yes sir, but I seem to have too many, sir.'

The captain looked at the corporal. 'Well, that makes a nice change. Obviously eager to join us. How many too many?'

'Four, sir.'

The captain looked puzzled. 'One easy way to sort this out, Corporal.' He turned his attention to the men in front of him. 'When I say fall out, all of you who are destined and fortunate enough to be here to join the First Battalion, the Royal Welsh Fusiliers, form three ranks on my left and the remainder stay where you are. Good. Right then, here we go. Fall out.'

The men turned to the right and took three paces before breaking ranks and reformed on the captain's left. The captain looked at Corporal Higgs for a moment.

'Well, there you have it Corporal Higgs. Get the men away and get those four fellows over to the Command Post so we can find out who they are.'

Corporal Higgs looked at the four young soldiers who hadn't moved, shook his head and sighed. 'Come on then, you lot.'

*

The boys entered Command Post through the front door of a bombed-out house. Remarkably the doorframe was still intact although most of the walls were long since destroyed. The boys followed the corporal along what would have been the hallway of a fairly modest house until they reached a pile of rubble. In amongst the rubble was an opening that had been covered with cloth sacking.

'Down you go then, and don't forget to salute the adjutant when you get down there. He is a very nice gentleman but the Regimental Sergeant Major isn't and he eats young lads like you for breakfast.' Corporal Higgs held the sacking aside and motioned the boys down the stairs into a dimly lit cellar.

'Privates Tallent, Jones, Taylor and Roberts, sir,' Corporal Higgs said, reading from his notebook. 'Seems they were meant to be going to the Second Battalion, sir, but got... confused,' he added.

The adjutant looked up from his desk. 'Second Battalion eh? Well, you young fellows are a long way from home aren't you? Where have you come from?'

The boys looked at each other, unsure of what to say.

'One of you silly fuckers needs to answer the officer,' the regimental sergeant major said quietly as he turned in his chair to face the boys.

'Sir,' Bryn said, 'we are from Salisbury, sir. Well actually we are all from Wrexham originally and then we joined the army.'

Corporal Higgs was at Bryn's ear in a second. 'Shut up, you idiot. The officer wants to know why you are here, not your bloody life history.'

'Sorry, sir. Er, well you see sir, we have just finished our training and we were posted to the Second Battalion, sir.'

'I can well believe that, Private, but how did you end up here?'

'To cut a long story short, sir, I think perhaps we joined the wrong group of fusiliers. No one on the ship seemed to be going to the same place as us and nobody knew where the Second Battalion is so we thought we had to find our own way and we ended up here.'

'So let me get this right,' he said, sitting back in his chair. 'You took it upon yourselves to get to the front line because nobody told you what to do?'

'Yes, sir.'

'How long have you been in the army?'

'Since last August, sir.'

'And during that time have you ever done anything without being told?'

'Yes, sir, all the time. There was this one time—'

'Shut up, you maggot!' The regimental sergeant major screamed as he rose from his chair.

The adjutant was struggling to suppress a laugh. He wasn't sure if it was naiveté or stupidity but it was the best story he had heard for a long time, and even longer since he had lasted laughed. He looked across at the regimental sergeant major, who was almost frothing at the mouth with rage. 'Well, Regimental Sergeant Major, what do you make of that? Four highly motivated and freshly trained young fit men who have used their initiative to serve their country. I don't care if they are Second Battalion, I think we should keep them.'

'We could, sir,' he said without taking his eyes off the boys, 'or we could just arrest them for talking an absolute load of bollocks and send them back to the base where they belong.'

'Of course you are right Regimental Sergeant Major, what would I do without your insightful knowledge and experience? What do you think, Private?' The adjutant switched his gaze to

Rhys, who shuffled slightly and coughed. Rhys turned slightly to catch Bryn's eye but he was looking straight ahead. 'Well?' the adjutant asked again. 'Should I let the regimental sergeant major jail you for the deserters that perhaps you are, or should I let you go to your battalion?'

'Oh no sir, you've got it all wrong, sir. We're not deserters. We just wanted to get to the front as quick as we could. We thought that this would be the quickest way. We would never desert; we've only just got here.'

The adjutant looked at each of the young men in front of him. 'You say you're from Wrexham?'

'Yes, sir. Gwersyllt actually, sir. All of us, sir. Born and brought up together, sir,' Bryn replied.

'And what do or did you do in Gwersyllt before all this came along?'

'We're miners, sir. Except Private Roberts, sir. He's a blacksmith but we all work in the mine together.'

'And we play rugby together too, sir,' Huan said.

The regimental sergeant major gave a sort of snorting noise from where he was still standing.

'Rugby? Really? Regimental Sergeant Major, I'm sure you have told me on several occasions that men in North Wales can't play rugby'

'They can't, sir,' he said, his Welsh accent seeming to deepen. The boys turned as one to look at him. He looked back at the boys and snarled at them. 'What are you lookin' at? Look to your front when the officer is speaking to you.'

The adjutant was trying very hard to stifle a smile. 'Are you any good?' he asked, leaning forward across his desk.

'Yes sir, I believe we are, sir,' Bryn replied.

'Well, Regimental Sergeant Major, it does seem as if we have a little problem. Here we have four of North Wales' finest young men, not to mention four fine rugby players, and as you know we are short of a few good men. Perhaps we should keep them to bolster our own team, should we ever be in a position to play a game.'

'With all due respect, sir, I prefer my original idea. I could get the provost corporal to take them away now, sir, if you would like. You'll not regret it, sir.'

'As usual the regimental sergeant major is right,' the adjutant said, looking directly at the boys. 'However, on this occasion I'm going to give you boys the benefit of the doubt. Lance Corporal Jones!'

There was a moment of silence before the regimental clerk poked his head through a canvas divide.

'Yes, sir?'

'Find out where the Second Battalion are and get me some movement papers.' He looked at the boys who were still looking straight at the wall above his head. 'Now you four men listen to me very carefully. War is a bastard thing. It is ugly, boring, frightening and very bad for your health. Any sane man would do well to stay out of it for as long as possible but it seems that you are intent on doing the opposite. So, I am going to let you find the Second Battalion. But if you want to be good soldiers then I suggest that following orders will save you a whole heap of trouble. Dismissed.'

The boys saluted and turned about. As they reached the bottom of the steps the adjutant called out behind them, 'Oh, and by the way, if we ever get to play the Second Battalion at rugby you four had better not be playing. Agreed?'

Bryn turned to the adjutant, who had slumped back into his chair. 'Absolutely, sir. Thank you, sir.'

'That is the last time you will ever thank someone for sending you to the front, Private.'

France
March 1915

My Dearest Cerys,

I hope this letter finds you well. We are all fine and dandy. So much seems to have happened that I don't know where to begin. The crossing was pretty uneventful although we had to spend the night on the deck as Huan was scared that we were going to be sunk by a torpedo. Still, at least it was calm and not too cold. We managed to catch a lift on a train up to the front but ended up with the other battalion, not the one we are meant to be with but they were very understanding and said that we could get our heads down here for tonight and they gave us a spot of dinner so we are doing alright.

We haven't really seen much of France as we were stuck in a cattle truck for most of the time but it's alright as they moved the cattle out of it before we got in (and cleaned it). I expect that you are pretty busy at work but if you get the chance to write it would be lovely to hear from you. Of course, you don't know where to send the letters to at the moment but I will let you know as soon as we get to where we are going. It's pretty late and we have got a long day tomorrow as we don't really know where we are going. I'm sure that we will find where we're meant to be at some point. At least it's not raining!

Yours as ever,
Bryn

CHAPTER EIGHTEEN

It was a bright morning and a light frost had hardened the mud on the roads. The boys marched in step two abreast, except when a truck or cart came past them. Once they had cleared the immediate battle area the land turned green. Most of the fields had been left fallow and untended. Birds flew between the trees as they marched along in silence.

'How far do you reckon we've gone then?' Huan asked.

'Couple of miles I suppose,' Bryn replied.

'Is that all? I'm starving.'

'You're always starving so that's no indication of distance is it?'

'Hark at you, know-it-all! If you're so clever what's that village up there?' Huan was pointing to the outskirts of a small town.

'I dunno but by my reckoning we should be in the right place. Come on.' The boys cracked on through the outskirts, past houses that had either been boarded up by their owners or taken up by the army. It didn't take long to reach the edge of the square. The centre of the town was a large cobbled square surrounded by elegant, ornate buildings. The boys had never seen such pretty buildings. The square was a hive of activity; there were soldiers everywhere, either milling about in small groups or piling into motorbuses. Horses drawing carts were slowly moving in every direction, just as the provost corporal had told them they would be.

'Hey look boys, that's got to be a regiment of cavalry over there,' Rhys said, pointing to the far end of the square where horses were tied to ropes strung across the cobbles from one side to the other. "Look smart, don't they? Perhaps we should have joined the cavalry. At least we wouldn't have to walk everywhere.'

'Good point that, Rhys,' Huan replied.

'Can either of you ride? John asked.

'No,' Rhys said.

'Well you'd still be doing an awful lot of walking then, wouldn't you?!'

'Come on you lot, let's get this sorted,' Bryn said. 'We need to find the Provost Office.'

The Provost Office wasn't difficult to find. They had set themselves up in an office next to the Marie, which dominated the town square. Bryn presented their movement orders and a note from the battalion's provost corporal to a sergeant who was busy supervising the loading of stores onto a horse-drawn wagon. He took the note and read it. He looked about and called a young private over and told him to put the lads on a motor wagon that was packed and ready to leave. There was barely space to move in the back but the soldier told the boys to make themselves comfortable. There was no explanation or instructions, so the boys made themselves comfortable and waited.

*

It was early evening when the wagon finally stopped at Armentières. The driver told the lads that this was the end of the line for them and set them off on foot in the right direction with instructions to ask for new directions frequently or they would end up at the front before they knew where they were.

'Right, who've we got here then?' the orderly room clerk asked without even glancing at the boys as he entered the room.

The boys jumped to their feet, having only just sat down. The sentry had told them that he had woken the duty clerk and they were settling down for a long wait, particularly as it was the middle of the night. The sudden appearance of the clerk surprised them; more so by the fact that he was fully dressed. He was a gaunt, scruffy-looking man who desperately looked like he could have done with a few more hours of sleep, a good hot bath and a shave.

'Sorry to wake you,' Bryn said. 'We were told to report to you as soon as we got here, just in case we were needed.'

The clerk stared at the four young men in front of him as if he was trying to work out what they were doing in his office. 'Needed for what?'

'The war of course,' Huan replied.

The clerk stared at them even more intently and shook his head as if in a daze. A moment or two passed in silence.

'Urm… we can come back in the morning if you like?' Bryn ventured.

The clerk broke from his thoughts. 'No you're alright, best we do this now just in case you are needed,' he said.

He pulled the chair from under the table and sat down, turning up the paraffin lamp as he did so. He opened a book that lay on the desk and grabbed a pencil that stood upright in the little pot in front of him.

'Right, well, you're here now and I'm awake so why don't you tell me who you are and where you've come from? And then,' he added, 'I can go back to sleep with a clear conscience that if you are killed in the night, in our hour of need, at least I will be able to report you as being dead. I don't suppose that I will care very much that you are dead but at least I will be able to report your untimely demise correctly. And then you can fuck off and leave me in peace!'

'Well, we've come from Gwersyllt but then we went to a training camp in Salisbury, which was actually quiet nice–' Bryn said, looking at the others who were nodding.

'Shut up or I'm going to save the Germans the time and effort of having to kill you. Just tell me who you are,' the clerk shouted.

'Oh, right then. Jones 325, Roberts, Tallent and Taylor, due to report on 25th March 1915.'

'You're early. Which means that you are too keen or too stupid.

161

I suppose you'll want to take a few days off, seeing as how you're early?' he said in jest.

The boys looked at each other and shrugged.

'Well, if it's all the same to you we'd rather just get started,' Bryn replied.

'Well that's jolly decent of you,' the clerk replied without looking up. 'I'm sure the men will be glad of your help. In fact, I'm not sure how they have managed without you to be honest.'

He shut the book and removed the thin wiry spectacles that he had been wearing. He looked at the boys for the first time and shook his head.

'Right then, that's done – you're officially here and my conscience is clear. Now fuck off and come back in the morning.'

'Where to?' John asked.

'Where to what?'

'Where do we fuck off to?

'I don't know and I don't care. Just go away.'

*

The following morning the boys returned to the Orderly Room straight after they had eaten a breakfast of a couple of rashers of bacon, bread and plenty of jam washed down with steaming tea. They presented themselves to a young-looking clerk who looked up and read their names from a piece of paper that had been left on his desk.

'So you're the boys who arrived last night are you?' he said with a wry smile. 'Eager to get to the front I hear.'

'We might seem eager but we just want to do our bit, you know,' Huan replied.

The clerk couldn't believe his ears. He thought his colleague had been joking. 'Well now, this is how it is: the battalion went back into the front last night so you are to report to the transport platoon and they will make sure that you get yourselves up to the front at the earliest opportunity. Do you reckon you can manage that?' Without waiting for a reply, the clerk went back to the paperwork on his desk.

*

'Do you reckon this it?' John asked.

The transport platoon was in a shabby-looking farm complex on the edge of the village. A few soldiers were busy around the yard, packing horse-drawn wagons with rolls of wire, pickets, sandbags and wooden braces. In the corner was a row of stables where six horses were being groomed.

'Oi!' came a sharp cry from the doorway to the farmhouse. 'What are you lot up to? Either get working, get over 'ere or get lost. I don't mind which but stop hanging around my yard.'

The boys doubled over to the sergeant.

'Jones, Roberts, Tallent and Taylor, Sergeant,' Bryn stated as they drew themselves to attention. 'We're new and the clerk told us to report to you so that we can go to the front.'

'New are you? Well I'd never have guessed it in a million fucking years. You're not reservists by the looks of you, so where have you come from?'

Bryn was learning to keep their story short. 'We volunteered last year, Sergeant. We did our training in Salisbury and we've been sent out to join the battalion.'

They were the first volunteers that the sergeant had come across and he stood shaking his head for a while. 'Well, I've been to Salisbury Plain a few times for training and it's a pretty grim place when the wind and the rain set in, but if I was you I would have stayed there. You boys seem far too keen to get to the front for my liking. I take it that there will be more of you coming in due course, will there?' The boys nodded. 'Well God help us,' was all he could say. The sergeant pointed to the corner of the yard. 'Put your packs over there and you can help pack the wagons for tonight.'

'But we're supposed to go to the front, Sergeant,' Huan said.

The sergeant stared at him. 'Not in broad fucking daylight you're not, you cloth head. Didn't they teach you anything? You wouldn't make it to the reserve trenches, let alone the front line. You will go up tonight with the supply run.'

*

It was mid-afternoon when a soldier came across to them as they were loading the last of the supplies onto the wagon.

'Do you boys want to go over to Armentières to help get some stuff?'

'I dunno,' John said. 'Do we?'

'The sergeant says you're goin' up the line tonight. Might be worth taking a few bits and pieces with you to help settle in, so to speak.'

'Sounds like a good idea,' Huan said, looking to the others for agreement.

The boys grabbed their kit and climbed into the rickety old cart that was harnessed to a docile-looking nag.

'Where did you pick up this old thing from?' Rhys asked as he climbed up alongside the driver.

'Hey, don't you knock this old thing unless you want to walk. This thing will still be going when you're dead and buried, which might not be too far away. As it happens, we managed to liberate it from the owner of the farm for a small price, when we first moved in. Her name is Maggie, or at least it is now, and she hasn't let us down yet, which is more than can be said for the motorised wagons that they gave us, and Maggie is as docile as they come. Steady as a rock under fire and never conks out at the wrong time. No, give me a horse and cart any day.'

The journey to Armentières took the boys through a maze of small villages, some scarred by the shellfire; others remarkably untouched. As they drove along the narrow roads the driver gave them a potted history of the battalion's war. 'We started in Mons. I presume that you've heard of it. Pretty bloomin' miserable that was, I can tell you. We had to walk down to Le Cateau and then down to the Marne and the Aisne. It was bloomin' miles. My feet were in tatters. I tell you, boys, it was the hardest soldiering I've ever done. Or at least it was until we got sent up to Wipers. My God that's a miserable bloody place. You want to avoid that place if you can. We lost far too many good blokes up there. Then we ended up down here. It's not bad and quiet most of the time.'

The more he told them the more intently they listened, eager to grab a snippet of advice. They asked about the companies, the sergeant majors and the trenches. Rhys asked about the food and was delighted to hear that he wasn't about to go hungry.

'Is it true that the Germans are all massive? Bryn asked.

The driver smiled. 'No, they're just like you and me; ordinary blokes getting on with life as best we can.'

The cart bounced its way slowly over the cobbled road through the ranks of men who were silently marching in the opposite direction towards the front lines with their weapons shouldered and tin hats, or 'steel bowlers' as the officers referred to them, strapped to their packs.

'*Duw*, they're a queer bunch if ever I saw one. Not one of them smiled,' Huan said.

'What did you expect, a brass band at the front and the men singing loudly? They're on their way to the front. I don't suppose they're too cheerful about it,' the driver replied.

'We always sang in training. The officers said that it was good for our morale,' John said.

'Well this ain't training and it ain't Salisbury bloody Plain. The only thing that keeps morale up round here is a ticket home and I ain't seen too many of those.'

The boys sat in silence.

*

As they got towards the town centre they passed a bedraggled bunch of soldiers who were sitting in clumps along the roadside. Their uniforms were indiscernible through the mud. They were unshaven and filthy; many had not even bothered to remove the tin lids that they had been wearing constantly for days. A few were dozing, others were smoking or scraping the mud from their uniforms. None of the boys spoke. A few minutes later the driver pulled up outside the divisional supply depot.

'You lads hang on here and mind the wagon. I'll go and see what's what.'

The boys sat in silence.

Rhys was the first to speak. 'Well this is not what I was expecting. It's a bit depressing.'

'You could say that,' Bryn replied.

'Did you see those blokes back there?' John asked. 'They looked a right shower.'

'I've never seen such a gloomy-looking lot,' Huan added. 'Do you reckon that they had just come from the front?'

'I reckon so,' John said.

'Looks like they've been up there for months by the state of them,' Rhys said. 'What do you reckon, Bryn?'

'I dunno, looked pretty shabby if you're asking me. They've probably been there a fair while,' Bryn replied, shrugging his shoulders.

'I can't believe that they were allowed to wander around like that in that state.'

'Perhaps they lost their sergeant major?' John suggested.

'Maybe, but what about the officers? Where are they?'

'Who do you reckon they were?' Rhys asked.

'I dunno, probably an English regiment,' John replied. 'I can't imagine a Welsh regiment looking like that.' The others nodded in agreement.

The corporal was walking back to the cart with a smile on his face. 'We're in luck, boys. A friend of mine is on duty so we should be able to pick up a bit of *bacshee* kit, which should keep the quartermaster happy when we arrive back late.' The boys looked at him blankly. He sighed. '*Duw*, you boys have got a lot to learn. *Bacshee* means extra kit. It's an old Indian word.' The boys looked back at him with blank expressions. 'Don't you lot know anything? If we pick up a load of extra kit then the quartermaster won't mind us getting back late, which gives us time to have a plate of egg and chips and a few beers.'

They loaded up the cart with everything they needed and a few extra bits and pieces to appease the quartermaster. The driver stabled the horse and led the boys out into the town.

Armentières had been occupied by the Germans for a short time at the start of the war until the Allies stopped them on the River Aisne and drove them back to the River Marne. As trench warfare brought the armies to a standstill there had been a race northwards towards to the coast to try and outflank each other. By the end of 1914 the Germans had retreated from the town, leaving it to the French and then the British. The boys marvelled at the tall, elegant buildings as they wandered about the town square. The highly decorative facades were a far cry from the tiny miners' cottages that they had been brought up in.

'How many families live in these houses do you think?' Huan asked as he craned his head to take in the panorama.

The square was alive with soldiers and a few civilians who had decided to remain in the town. There were accents from everywhere imaginable: London, Scotland, Birmingham and Liverpool. Commonwealth troops added a splash of colour and excitement. The boys had never seen a coloured man before and stared intently as a group of Sikhs passed them by. There were men staggering from too many beers, while others were playing cards at small round tables outside bars and estaminets. Their guide explained that when the battalion had first arrived the lads were allowed to go into any bar or restaurant but after a while the officers and soldiers found their own places so that they didn't have to mix. Not that he cared; he didn't mind drinking with any toff as long as he paid!

They found a table in a small café just off the main square. Private Davies, their driver, explained that they always came to the same place because the owner had a very pretty daughter, so they were disappointed when an old man shuffled towards their table with a collection of various glasses and a bottle of *vin blanc*. His hands were shaking and he chatted animatedly to the lads, who couldn't understand a word he was saying. They looked at Davies, who just shrugged and poured the wine.

'Good health,' he said, raising his glass to the lads. They cautiously sniffed it. 'I wouldn't if I was you, it doesn't help. It's best just to drink it and get used to it. It's cheaper than beer and occasionally it's alright. I prefer the white as the red tastes like vinegar.'

The boys took a sip and agreed that it was going to be a long war if this was the best on offer!

France
March 1915

My Dearest Cerys,

I hope this letter finds you as well as you should be. I'm fine and so are the others. We have made it to the battalion who went up to the line last night. We arrived not long after they had gone so we are helping out around the rear area at the moment and expect to go up to the line tonight. I'm pretty excited, I have to say. I can't imagine what it's like but the blokes that we have met are all pretty cheery so it can't be all bad.

We have seen a fair bit of France now on our travels and it is nothing like home. The areas that we have been through are pretty flat and mainly fields without walls or hedges. I'm not too sure why but it must be hard to keep the sheep in. Most places are pretty green but the roads are full of wagons, motorised trucks and even London buses. It's a funny sight alright!

We went into a large town today not far from where we are based. You can't imagine it. It was full of soldiers from all over the place – it was madness. Believe it or not we got egg and chips and a beer for a couple of francs. I'm not sure how much it is in proper money but Davies, the driver who took us, said it was very reasonable. We shan't starve at any rate. Anyway, must go as we are off in few minutes when it gets dark.

Take care of yourself.
Best wishes,
Bryn

CHAPTER NINETEEN

The boys waited in silence, listening for signs of the men returning from the front line. The boys had been expecting the front to be noisy and busy; they had expected men to be shouting, guns to be firing. Away in the distance there was the occasional chatter of a machine gun but other than that it was eerily quiet. It was unnerving the boys.

'This isn't what I was expecting,' John said quietly into the dark. There was no moon and the night was as black as the mine. He wasn't used to the isolation of the dark.

'Me neither,' Huan replied. 'Bloody quiet isn't it?'

'Do you reckon we're about to attack?' Rhys asked.

'Or we're about to be attacked,' Bryn offered.

'I think you four should shut up or piss off. This is normal so calm down and be patient,' Thomas said.

The boys returned to their isolation and thoughts. Bryn shivered. He wasn't sure if it was from the cold or the apprehension.

There was a shuffling sound from the entrance of the trench. A floorboard creaked. Men appeared like ghosts from the entrance of the trench. They said nothing as they passed Thomas the Thief; some nodded, one or two shook hands. As they moved away from the trench the soldiers started to relax. They stood together in tight groups, chatting quietly to each other. Most of them had a smoke cupped into their hands to shield the glow from the enemy.

When the lance corporal was sure that he had soldiers from each of the companies, he patted each of the groups as he passed them and they followed on behind him in silence as they made their way back to the regimental transport. They had only gone a few yards along the track when a couple of shells landed a hundred yards to their left. The shells split the silence like a meat cleaver through butter. The boys instinctively flung themselves into the drainage ditch that ran alongside the road and covered their heads with their hands. As the shelling subsided they raised their heads to see the lance corporal looking down at them. He was shaking his head and gave a little chuckle.

'Get up you soft bastards; you're embarrassing yourselves. And what's more, you're embarrassing the regiment.'

They clambered to their feet and looked at the other men, who gave them a bored, unconcerned look.

'Come on,' Thomas said as he turned back to the road. 'If you four are going to survive you'll need to understand the difference between a shell that's coming your way and one that's going somewhere else.'

'How do we work that out, then?' Bryn asked.

Thomas stopped and sniffed. 'If you make it to the end of the week you'll know the difference right enough.'

They remained silent as they passed back through the battery of guns that had been dug into the ground and concealed. A line of guns stretched to the left and the right of the road as far as the boys could see, which wasn't very far in the late dusk. The gunners were scuttling about in the darkness preparing the guns for their nightly exchange of tit for tat.

The transport wasn't far beyond the guns. The ground made it easy to get stores fairly close to the trenches, which pleased the men who were going to have to carry everything they needed back along the trenches.

One of the soldiers sidled up to Rhys. He was unshaven and scruffy he had a smoke in his hand. 'Any of you boys got a smoke?'

Rhys fumbled in his tunic pocket, glad of the opportunity to offer up one of his fags. Thomas had made sure that they were each carrying at least one pack in their tunic, 'to help settle in'. The soldier took the fag and pushed it through the side of his balaclava and behind his ear. He coughed, a rasping, guttural cough. 'Ta.'

'No problem.'

The soldier looked at Rhys for a moment as if he was trying to size him up. 'Who are you boys, then?'

'We've been posted in.'

'First time to the front, is it?'

'Yes.'

'Thought so.'

As the fatigue parties arrived at the transport, everyone visibly relaxed and greeted each other with the usual abuse and banter.

As the parties waited for their allocation of stores the banter increased to a low murmur and they stood around smoking cigarettes and asking after mates they hadn't seen for a day or two.

'There's some stew here lads, if you want some. You might as well get it whilst it's hot. Just make sure there's enough to take back for the rest of them,' one of the soldiers said. There was an orderly clamour for the stew. Thomas had told the boys that getting the stew before it was taken forward was one of the main perks being in the fatigue party.

'Do we get stew every day? Rhys asked.

'When we can,' he replied. 'The colonel's pretty keen to get a hot meal forward at least once a day. It doesn't always happen but we're pretty good most of the time.'

The men ate as quickly as they could as the transport platoon sorted out the loads. The corporals detailed off their men and let them sort themselves out.

'Right you lot, let's be having you,' the quartermaster said. 'You've had your rest. Let's get back to it. Otherwise your officers might start to worry that you've got lost and we wouldn't want them to fret, would we?'

They sorted out their loads and sorted themselves out for the return trip.

'Corporal Jones?' the quartermaster called in slightly hushed tone.

'Yes, sir,' came the response in the dark and in the next instant a thin-looking man in his late thirties appeared next the quartermaster, who almost jumped at the suddenness of his appearance.

'The good news for you is that you've got some hired help to take your stuff forward. There are four fine young men from the battalion's hometown who want to go and help you up at the front. God only knows why, but they do. Anyway, I'm relying on you to make sure that they get there in one piece. The adjutant wants them to go to B Company so call in at the company dugout on the way and I'm sure that the sergeant major will relieve you of them.'

'I didn't know we was getting any reinforcements tonight, sir.'

'Nor did I, but don't look a gift horse in the mouth. And make sure you go via the company HQ; I don't want you nicking 'em so that you can pad out the sentry roster.' He turned to the boys. 'Right, you lot – stay with Corporal Jones here and do exactly what he says.' He paused a moment. 'You'll be fine. Just do what you're told.'

Corporal Jones peered closely at the four young lads. *They're only boys,* he thought. He sighed. 'Right, who've we got then?'

'Privates Jones, Taylor, Roberts and Tallent, Corporal,' Bryn said on behalf of his friends.

'First time up, is it?'

'Yes Corporal.'

'Just what I fucking need,' he said. 'Right, grab what you can carry from the others, stay behind me, and I mean *right* behind me, understand? You do nothing other than what I say and say nothing unless I tell you to. Do you understand?' He didn't wait for a response.

'Barney,' he called to another man, 'come in behind these four, will you, and make sure they stay closed up. Swampy. Bring up the rear.' The corporal checked his lads off and turned to Huan, who was stood directly behind him. 'Right, let's get going. The sooner we get back the sooner we can get a few hours' shut-eye.'

*

173

Corporal Jones paused when they reached the entrance to the communications trench. The section of men closed in around him.

'Right, we'll stay in the trench all the way so that these blokes get to know it.' There was an audible groan from the other six men. 'Stop moaning, at least it will be solid underfoot. I'm going via the company HQ, so when we get to the junction of Castle Street and High Street, Barney, you take the stuff off these blokes and carry on to the front. I'll see you up there later and make sure there's some hot grub left for me.' He looked at the four boys. 'Welcome to our little bit of Wales, boys. This is the back door so make sure you wipe your feet.' He chuckled and moved towards the opening. 'You'll be fine. Fritz is probably tucked up in bed with a hot schnapps, if he's got any sense.'

The communication trench was firm underfoot. The duckboards had frozen into the mud, which made walking in the dark fairly easy. The entrance sloped down as they entered the trench system and within a few paces they were hemmed in on both sides. The walls of the trench quickly rose above them, blotting out the surrounding view and taking away all sense of direction. They went straight for a while but then began turning left and right around the traverses.

There was no noise except for the occasional grunt and swearing as they caught their loads on the corner of the traverse or stumbled on the duckboards. They moved silently along the narrow earthen corridors for what seemed like miles but what was in reality only a few hundred yards as the crow flies. Every now and again word was passed along the line so that every man knew where he was, not that it was necessary with these men; Corporal Jones was doing it for the benefit of the boys. Huan was the fifth man in the chain and duly passed it on to Barney who was following on behind. 'Rightho,' was all he kept saying in response, and didn't bother to pass it on any further. The only orders that he did pass along were 'wires underfoot' or 'break in the boards'.

The silence was smashed by the sound of explosions just to their front, and the ground shook, showering the carrying party with small bits of earth. Up ahead whistles were being blown and they could hear men shouting. Machine guns spluttered into life.

'Bugger!' Corporal Jones said as he crouched down further into the depths of the trench. 'Someone's upset Fritz. Minenwerfers by the sounds of it. It's not like him to let off a few rounds without some reason, unless of course he's planning a little stroll over the top. What do you reckon Barney?'

'I'd give it a few minutes if I were you. See what he's doing. We should be alright here for a few minutes.'

'Good idea. If he is coming over we'll dump the kit here and go straight up. We can come back later if it's still here.' As the shelling increased the corporal nudged Huan, who had crouched down next to him. 'You alright?'

Huan managed to force out a slight grunt from under his helmet. He was pressing himself as hard as he could into the recess of the trench with his hands clasped over his helmet. Next to him, John had his hands over his ears to block out the thunderous roar. He was suddenly conscious that he was shaking and muttering to himself over and over again. 'Breathe,' he kept saying to himself.

Bryn was crouched next to him, his heart pounding almost as hard as the walls were reverberating. He looked up slightly to see Corporal Jones squatting with his back to the wall, looking up at the parapet as if he had no cares in the world. The sky had turned red with the flickering tongues of flame. Behind him Rhys was crouched in a ball at the bottom of the trench with his hands clasped over his head.

Almost as quickly as it started, the explosions stopped. Darkness enveloped the trench again but their night vision had been ruined by the flash of the flames, making it difficult to see more than a few inches in front of their eyes.

'Just stay where you are for a few minutes,' Corporal Jones whispered. 'Just let it settle.'

Up ahead someone was screaming for a medic and then it went quiet.

'Sounds like someone's copped it,' Corporal Jones said. 'Seeing as no one's screaming here I take it that we're all alright? Good – right, let's get on then.'

They picked up their loads without a word and moved forward as if nothing had happened. They had only gone twenty yards when Corporal Jones shouted, 'Bearers coming through.' He turned to Huan and pressed him back against the wall as two stretcher-bearers skilfully negotiated the traverse with a full stretcher.

'Who is it, boys?' Corporal Jones asked as the carrying party brushed past.

'I dunno, but he'll be fine once we get him back.'

'Where's he from?

'Two Platoon. There's another couple who bought it. A shell landed square on their dugout. Bit of bad luck really as there's no other damage to speak of. And if you've got the rations, make sure you save us some!'

'Right you are.'

The stretcher-bearers melted into the darkness and the fatigue party stood in silence for a moment, lost in their own thoughts. The old hands knew full well that it could have been any of them.

'Oh shit,' Huan said, louder than he had intended.

'Don't worry about it lad. If it's going to happen it will happen. The best you can hope for is a Blighty wound,' a voice said from behind him. 'A bullet is what you want. A clean shot that hopefully goes straight through and misses anything important. You don't want artillery unless it's a direct hit. That way you are just vaporised.'

'What happens if not a direct hit?'

'You'll probably be sliced open by searing hot metal fragments like a leg of ham on a butcher's table and you'll be left with horrible injuries and a slow death.'

'I wish I hadn't asked now,' Huan said quietly as the line started to shuffle forward.

'Don't worry, you'll be fine,' the soldier said.

*

'Right, well here we are. Drop your stuff and we will go on to the company HQ. That wasn't too bad was it?'

None of the boys could speak. John was still gasping uncontrollably as if he had just sprinted the length of the Arms Park. Huan leaned to his side and retched. Rhys and Bryn just squatted down. It was bitterly cold and they were dripping with sweat, from fear rather than from the physical exertion of carrying the stores.

Corporal Jones seemed to be feeling the wall for something, and then his hand grabbed at a piece of cloth. He pulled back the gas curtain and stepped down into a dimly lit bunker. The boys followed on behind and moved inside.

The bunker was little bigger than the parlour in the cottages back in Gwersyllt. A lantern hung from the ceiling, which cast an eerie light across the desk. The walls and the ceiling had been reinforced with wooden beams and a couple of shelves had been built to hold a few home comforts. Along the far wall there were a couple of improvised bunk beds which were occupied by two officers, both of whom were fully clothed but soundly asleep as if nothing in the world could have disturbed them. In the middle of the room was a small wooden table.

The sergeant major was sitting at the table writing a note. He didn't even bother to look up. 'What do you lot want?' His tin hat was still on his head and a rifle lay across the table. In his left hand he held a set of identification disks. As he looked up the boys stood to attention. His gaze moved along the line until it arrived at Corporal Jones.

'What have you got here, Corporal Jones?'

'Reinforcements, sir. I brought them up with the stores. Compliments of the quartermaster, who said that they were for B Company, sir.'

'Did he now? Well that's jolly decent of him. I take it he doesn't want anything in return for them?'

'Not a farthing, sir. He said we could have them on a free trial. No obligation to keep them but if they go back then they are to be in full working order.'

'Fat chance of that.' He smirked.-'Right. Give me the run down. Names and where you've previously served.'

The boys looked at each other and then at Corporal Jones, who replied. 'No service, sir, they're new. Very shiny, with the wrapping still on.'

'Oh my sainted aunt. What is this army coming to?'

'At least they are from Gwersyllt, sir, so they shouldn't be too bad.'

'Right, give 'em to Number Two Platoon seeing as they are now three men short.' He raised his left hand and let a couple of identification disks dangle down. 'I'll be round to see you lads in the morning. Dismissed.'

France
March 1915

My Dearest Cerys,

We have finally made it to the front line. I'm afraid that I cannot tell you where we are but suffice to say that we are all safe and well. There are a few blokes here from our neck of the woods, which is great. We have been filling them in on all the news from home. A lot of them have been out here since the start but they are all in good spirits, as you would expect.

We moved up a few hours ago with the rations and other stores – carrying them, that is! It was quite hard work moving through the trenches with a load of kit but it wasn't too heavy, just awkward. We have been assigned to Number Two Platoon in B Company, which you can put on the address – you know the rest. Any mail should find me easily enough.

It's a bit chilly at the moment but I'm wrapped up pretty warmly so it's not too bad. We had a few shells land close to us but not so close as to cause us any concern. It was a bit different to training. Everyone here seems pretty relaxed so it should be fine. I hope you are going on alright. It seems an age since we left but it's only been a few days really.

Anyway I must go and get my head down (to sleep) for a few hours.

Take care of yourself.
Best wishes,
Bryn

CHAPTER TWENTY

Someone shook Bryn's shoulder.

'Stand to.'

The voice was quiet but firm, and gone in an instant. Bryn's eyes shot open at the order. It was pitch dark, as if his eyes had failed to open. The darkness enveloped his whole being. Bryn's hand gripped the rifle that he had lain on all night and he sat upright on the fire step. He looked about at his unfamiliar surroundings. People seemed to be moving all around him, silently rising from the ground and through openings in the side of the trench wall that were barely big enough to sleep in. They were like corpses rising from the dead. The only distinction between them and the dead was the warm breath coming from their mouths into the crisp early morning air. There were men who he hadn't seen last night putting on their helmet or folding up blankets.

'Stand to.'

There it was again. *Oh Christ*, he thought, *here we go*. He tore at the blanket to free himself as he struggled to his feet and shook the others firmly on either side of him.

' Get up, they're coming!' he said in a rather hoarse whisper.

The others were on their feet in an instant, grabbing at their rifles and helmets. They stood shoulder-to-shoulder on the fire step and peered over the lip of the trench, pointing their rifles in anticipation towards the unseen enemy.

'Where are they?' John asked as his eyes searched through the dark.

'I dunno,' Bryn replied.

'Just keep calm,' Huan replied as he pulled back his rifle bolt and slid forward a .303 round into the chamber.

'We haven't been told to make ready yet!' Rhys said.

'I don't give a damn. I'm not waiting to be told.'

The light was breaking away to the east. Red streaks were appearing above the horizon. To their front a thick layer of white mist was hovering above the frozen ground. The mist swirled slowly as if it was dancing a waltz around the pockmarked landscape.

'Christ, there's nothing out there,' John said.

'It's quite pretty really, with all the frost,' Huan replied.

'Really?' Bryn said. 'All I can see is barbed wire, and if I'm not mistaken there are a few bodies over there.' He pointed across to his right where mounds of rags did little to keep the frost from the bundle of bones.

'Do you reckon this is it then?' Rhys asked. No one replied. They were all looking to their front as they had practised doing on many occasions back in training.

'What are you doing up there lads?' Rhys looked down to the soldier who had tugged at his trouser leg. 'Why don't you and your pals here get down from there before you get your heads shot off? I'm quite sure that you don't want to die on your first day.' Rhys hesitated, but the soldier was wagging his finger at him. Rhys stepped off the fire step. 'There's a good lad.' The shadowy figure turned away and sat on the fire step a few yards away. Rhys tugged on Bryn's trousers. One by one they sheepishly stepped off the fire step.

The boys looked along the line at men who were taking their place at the bottom of the trench. A few men coughed as the cold air filtered into their lungs; a few others stamped frozen and partially numb toes. Mostly they sat in silence clutching their rifles between their hands whilst trying to coax some warmth in their fingers.

'New are you?' the old soldier said as he cupped his hands to his mouth to light a cigarette.

'Is it that obvious?' Rhys asked.

'Just a little bit,' he replied as he took a long drag on the cigarette that was cupped in his hand. 'My advice to you is that if you want to stay alive to have a bit of breakfast then watch and learn rather than do and die.' He paused for a moment to take another long drag on his roll-up. 'Of course, if you were to die then there might be more breakfast for the rest of us.' His chuckle turned into a splutter and then a rasping cough.

'Stand ready, Two Platoon,' the platoon commander said as he moved slowly but deliberately along the line, keeping his body half-bent but his head upright. It became a natural position after a few weeks in the line. 'Something's up; I haven't heard them squealing for their frankfurters this morning.'

The old soldier looked across at Rhys and winked. 'Well perhaps you were right after all; not a druid are you, by any chance?'

'No,' Rhys managed to reply before the first volley hit the lip of the trench.

'Stand up and face the trench wall,' the old soldier shouted. 'Hug it as hard as you can is my advice and don't stick your blooming head up until I tell you to.'

The boys didn't need telling twice as earth showered down on top of them. The Germans were spraying the lip of the trench with everything they had to hand. As more and more hell rained upon them the boys sank lower and lower in the trench. They covered their ears but kept their eyes fixed on the trench wall that was reverberating in front of them.

'When's this going to stop?' John shouted.

Bryn looked to his left and right to see the other men pressed against the wall of the trench. His left hand was on his helmet and his right hand was wrapped around his rifle as bullets whizzed overhead. 'I dunno but I hope it's pretty soon. I think my teeth are going to fall out if it goes on much longer.'

'When do we get to shoot?' Rhys yelled.

'Don't worry,' the old soldier yelled back, 'it will be our turn soon.' He chuckled to himself as he drew on his cigarette.

Lieutenant George was moving slowly along the line, offering support to his men.

'Make sure that you keep your weapons pointed in the right direction; we don't want any accidents, do we Private Murray?'

Private Murray laughed as the platoon commander passed him.

'What's so funny about that?' Bryn asked the old soldier.

'A few weeks ago he had an accident. He was cleaning his weapon and let off a round, which ricocheted off a spade and hit him on the arm, causing a graze. If we weren't all watching at the time he could have ended up being charged. He wouldn't have been the first bloke to give himself a Blighty. Anyway Lieutenant George didn't report the incident, which was very good of him. Murray was lucky and he knew it.'

'Which one of you has upset Fritz? Come on, own up. Then you can go over there and apologise and we can all have some breakfast in peace. What's the matter with you Perkins, lumbago bothering you again? Private Smith, keep your head down or you will have a permanent parting in your hair.'

He could have been walking along the pier in Brighton for all he seemed to care. He drew level with the boys.

'Aha, our new boys. Well I can only assume that you are responsible for this little affair; it's too much of a coincidence that you arrive and the Hun get haughty in the morning. Oh, and try not to get shot on your first day, it would be darn bad luck. Corporal Jones, make sure they know what they are doing.' Corporal Jones nodded to the platoon commander as he continued on to Three Section.

'He's a cool one isn't he?' John said as soon as the lieutenant had gone around the traverse into the next fire bay.

'As a cucumber I'd say,' Bryn replied as he pressed his back further into the trench wall.

'He's a young fella but a good officer so don't you lot start thinking that you can get one over on him. Never seems to sleep. As hard as they come if you ask me. Let's just hope that he lasts longer than the last officer that we had,' Corporal Jones said. 'Speaks fluent German as well, which is why he spends so much time out there listening to Fritz.' He nodded towards no-man's land.

It was a further five minutes before the firing suddenly stopped. 'Stand to.' The order could be heard coming along the line.

'Shit, here we go,' Rhys shouted as he scrambled to his feet.

The old soldier looked across at them and smiled. 'Well that stirred things up a bit, didn't it? Keep your heads down but have your weapons ready to poke over the top if Lieutenant George gives the signal and then just start firing. Don't bother to look, just keep firing. If they're coming you'll hit something alright.'

Rhys nodded and looked at the others.

Huan could hear his heart thumping and a bead of sweat started to trickle from under his helmet. His right hand was gripping the butt of his Lee Enfield rifle but he could feel it shaking as his left hand was on the stock, closing and opening in rapid movements as if the stock was too hot to touch. 'What are we waiting for?' he whispered.

'I dunno,' John replied.

'I need a shit.'

'Well you will need to put a cork in it. I don't reckon that this is the time to go looking for the shit house.'

'Maybe not but I'm going to have to go. Here, hold my rifle.' He passed his rifle to John and grappled for the buttons on his trousers. Squatting where he stood he let his bowels open and gave a satisfied sigh.

Bryn and Rhys looked across at where he was squatting and started to laugh. The rest of the section peered across and joined in the laughter. The old soldier smiled as Huan pulled his trousers up and sheepishly retook his place on the step.

'Well I hope that you are going to move that afterwards,' John said as the smell started to rise.

Men were starting to shiver with the cold as they waited patiently on the fire step. One by one rifles were propped against the wall and the men started to rub their hands to keep warm. Still no one left the step.

'How long is this going to be?' Rhys said, looking across the bay for an answer.

One of the old soldiers looked at his watch. 'Not long now, lad. It's usually about half an hour.'

The boys were almost numb by the time the word to stand down was passed quietly along the line. Men relaxed and started chatting and lighting up their smokes. Most of them got a brew on.

'What the heck was all that about?' Rhys asked Corporal Jones as he passed by.

'Lieutenant George thinks we upset them last night. They're probably just reminding us that they are still there. As if we hadn't already worked that one out. Anyway, welcome to Dragon's Alley, the finest trench this side of the one next to us. Or at least it was until someone shat in it,' Corporal Jones said, looking at Huan. 'Just get it cleaned up lad.' He turned to walk away and then turned back. 'And by the way, I don't want you lads sticking your noses over the top for a look-see. Curiosity killed the cat and it will just as easily kill you. There's a Fritz over there who fancies himself as a bit of a shot. He'll have your eye out before you can finish scanning the horizon!'

The boys sat on the fire step staring at the opposite wall of the trench less than two yards away. Above them the sky was turning bright blue. It was going to be a lovely day. Bryn pushed his helmet up onto the back of his head and leaned back and gave a big sigh. 'So much for a warm welcome to Wales!' he said as he grinned at his friends.

*

It was mid-morning when Corporal Jones found the boys dozing on the fire step. They were huddled together, each wrapped in a blanket. Unlike the rest of the men who had squirrelled themselves away into saps built into the trench wall, the boys had nowhere to go but the fire step.

'Listen, I couldn't care less if you were fucking related, you are not staying together. There is no discussion. Lieutenant George doesn't want you all in the same section and that's all there is to it. So you two can go to one section and you two have got the pleasure of staying with me. Now sort yourselves out.'

Bryn and Huan grabbed their kit and went round the fire bay to report to Corporal Hughes.

'Right boys, this is your place,' Corporal Hughes said, pointing to pile of debris. 'I know it doesn't look like much but by the time you've dug it out and shored it up it will be your bed, table and chair. If you're not working then I want you on the step.' Bryn was looking around the trench. *Surely*, he thought, *there must be somewhere better to lie.* Corporal Hughes read his mind. 'And before you say anything, you are not to lie on the trench floor. It hampers the stretcher-bearers. Come on, I'll introduce you to the rest of the section and then you can get cracking.'

They set to work shifting the chalky earth. It was easy work; after digging coal down the mine this was like digging in a sandpit. The other two members of the section looked on as the boys happily cracked on with the job, grateful for something to do at last. Bryn jabbed his shovel into the soft earth and threw the spoil onto the pile. He gasped as he did so. 'What the heck is…' The words died on his lips as they looked at the hand he had just thrown onto the spoil.

The men stopped what they were doing and stared at the severed hand and then back to where the remains of an arm was sticking out of the chalky white earth.

'Oh my God no,' Huan cried. He staggered back and fell on the earth.

Corporal Hughes came across and looked at the mess as one of the other men vomited. He stared at the arm and crossed himself. 'Well I guess that must be Simpkins or Jones, hard to tell now, poor bastards. Fill it in and shore it up. Whoever it is doesn't need to see daylight again.'

Bryn looked at his section commander. 'What about his hand, Corporal?'

'Give it him back and cover it up.'

*

Bryn and Huan asked for permission to go into the next bay to see Rhys and John. Corporal Hughes made it clear that if anything happened they were to be back round sharpish.

'Do you reckon we'll end up like that?' John said at length.

'We'll be fine,' Bryn said. 'And if we're not, well, so be it.'

'I'm not sure this is how I imagined it to be.'

'Hey come on, boys, it's not that bad. At least it's not raining,' Huan said.

Rhys looked up at the sky that had started to cloud over. 'Maybe not just yet but I wouldn't bet my house on it.'

'You don't have a house to bet,' Huan replied.

'Shut up, you idiot.'

'We have to look at the positives,' Bryn said. 'We've had plenty of food, it's not raining and we're all still alive. That's got to be something, hasn't it?'

'Well it's better than being down the mine,' John suggested.

'You don't go down the mine,' Huan replied.

'That's true, that is. I don't like it. Never have done. That's why I'm happier in the fresh air.'

'Working in a furnace is hardly fresh air is it?'

'It's fresher here though, so it must be better, see!'

Huan looked at Rhys. 'And you called me stupid? What does that make him then?'

187

The boys drifted into their own thoughts as they looked around the trench. One man was cleaning his rifle as another one stood against the sloping wall looking across no-man's land through a tiny hole that had been made in a sandbag screen. Two other men had wrapped themselves up in their coats and tucked themselves into shallow holes cut into the trench wall.

'Do you think it's different back home now?' Rhys asked no one in particular.

'What do you mean, different? I don't suppose anything has changed. My da and Huan's da will be down the mine. Your da has probably got a couple of new apprentices and will be giving them a hard time. John, your da will be smacking hell out of a lump of metal, Mr Hulbert will still be wondering how he's going to manage without us and—'

'That's the point, see,' Rhys said, cutting Bryn off. 'It hasn't changed; we've changed. The war's changed all that. We've moved on.'

'Well for now maybe, but we'll be going back won't we, once this is over?' Huan said.

'I dunno, will we? After that little lot this morning I don't know whether we will or not.'

'Bloody hell, if you lot are going to be so gloomy I'm going to find the privy. It can't be any worse than sitting here,' John said.

'Oh believe me, it is,' Bryn said. 'I've been there already; it's not a pleasant experience.'

'Nor was watching Huan drop his trousers.' Rhys laughed.

'I'm never going to live this one down am I?'

They were still laughing as Corporal Jones came round the traverse into the firing bay.

'Don't you two have a home to go to?' Corporal Jones asked, looking at Bryn and Huan.

'No,' said Huan. 'We've been evicted by a giant man-eating rat. You should have seen the size of it, Corporal. Massive, it was.' The others laughed but stopped when they saw that the corporal wasn't laughing.

'Why do you think it's so big, you fucking idiots? What do you think it's eating?'

Huan gagged as he thought of the arm that they had reburied earlier in the day.

'And if you lot don't sort yourselves out you will find yourselves being his main course.'

Bryn fought back the bile that was rising in his throat. 'Sorry, Corporal.'

'Sorry you might be, but try thinking before opening your gobs next time. The platoon commander is going out again tonight and wants a volunteer or two. I volunteered two of you. It will do you good to get a look over the top. It might stop your curiosity. I suppose you all want to go, do you?'

'Blooming right we do, Corporal,' Bryn replied first.

'Thought so. Well you can't all go so sort it out among yourselves and no fighting. There's enough fighting already without you four starting. One from each section. Got it?'

*

It had been dark for well over an hour before the platoon commander made his way to the foot of the ladder that had been propped against the trench wall. He had blackened his face and carried a rifle, the same as Bryn and John. He was wearing a thick leather jerkin over his tunic, and leather gloves. A woollen cap had replaced his tin helmet.

Rhys and Huan were still smarting from losing the toss as to who was going to go over the top. They had helped their friends blacken up and checked that none of their kit rattled. A couple of the old boys had sorted them out. They had dropped off most of their kit; they were only taking what they would need. 'No point in taking stuff that will slow you down when you are legging it back,' one of the old boys had said, chuckling to himself as he helped to blacken their bayonets and belt buckles.

The platoon commander had briefed Bryn and John an hour before the evening. 'Stand to.' They were going to cross the one hundred and fifty yard strip of no-man's land to the edge of the Germans' low wire entanglement. The platoon commander had a favourite spot that he liked to use, as it was about twenty yards from the sentry position and was in a slight dip in the ground. They were going to go out via the company machine gun position and return via the same route. They were briefed on what to do if they came under fire or if they encountered an enemy patrol.

'Are you two ready?' the platoon commander asked, as if it was the most natural thing in the world to be doing.

'Yes sir,' Bryn replied.

'Alright, well stay close.' Lieutenant George nodded to the platoon sergeant, grabbed the ladder and heaved himself up.

'See you later then boys,' Rhys said.

'Good luck,' Huan added.

Bryn went up the ladder behind Lieutenant George and moved forward about five yards before dropping to the ground to the left of the platoon commander. John arrived within seconds on the right-hand side. Lieutenant George allowed the lads a few moments to get their bearings.

He tapped Bryn and John on the shoulder. They both scrambled in their rush to move forward but Lieutenant George placed a hand on each of them to slow them down. The last thing they needed now was any sudden movement, or worse still, a noise.

Despite the cold Bryn found himself sweating freely. The tension was almost unbearable. He just wanted to drop the safety catch and let fly with a few rounds and charge forward at the enemy, screaming at the top of his voice as they had been taught to do in training. This was something new.

The progress was painfully slow as they moved silently from shell hole to shell hole. At each one Lieutenant George would make them crouch down and listen for signs of the enemy. They faced in different directions to ensure that they were not surprised by a

German patrol. The tap on the shoulder started the process again and the little group set off for the next hole.

Bryn counted that they had stopped fifteen times before Lieutenant George gave them a soft pat on the shoulder that meant that they had arrived. They lay down in a shell hole with their rifles down by their sides. They lay in opposite directions with Lieutenant George facing the trench that ran from his left to his right about twenty yards in front of him in his twelve o'clock position. Bryn and John faced outwards at twenty past and twenty to the hour, their feet touching so that they could alert each other without moving.

Bryn could hear murmurings from the direction of the trench but it meant nothing to him although he still tried to make out the words. 'Concentrate, watch your front,' he kept saying to himself as he kept his eyes strained to his sector. This was what he had trained for; he knew what he was doing. *Shit, what was that? It moved!* He realised that he had stopped breathing; his heart was pounding as a bead of sweat stung his eyes. He tried to clear it by blinking his eyes rapidly but it only blurred his focus. He moved his hand as slowly and as quietly as he could to wipe his eyes. He turned his head to try to move it away from the slight breeze that was blowing so that he could hear better, but there was nothing.

It took about half an hour before he realised that he had no idea if John and the lieutenant were still there. He daren't move for fear of alerting them. *They wouldn't have left me, would they?* Had the platoon commander tapped him and moved off without him? He fought to control his emotions as the panic start to rise. He started to shake and realised quite suddenly how cold he had become. *What am I doing in this hole in the middle of nowhere? This isn't fighting; this is just a waste of time.* He realised that his hands had gone numb and he tried to pull them into the ends of his tunic arms and put them under his armpits to warm them up. It was so cold he thought that he might freeze and not be able to move. *Perhaps they will find me in the morning as a solid corpse.*

Movement. His senses were alert. *There it is again.* Bryn came out of his trance. There was a tap on his foot. His body froze, only his eyes were raised and straining.

He looked from his left to his right but couldn't see anything. He daren't look around. 'Trust each other,' the platoon commander had said. He could hear shuffling less than a few feet away to his right. Someone was walking past John's field of view. Bryn lowered his head as far as he dared without losing sight of the ground in front of him. *Keep breathing,* he told himself; *be calm.* They lay in silence for about another fifteen minutes before Bryn felt a tap on his shoulder. He turned slowly to see Lieutenant George smiling at him with his hand pointing towards their own lines. Bryn tried to stand but the cold had numbed his feet and thighs. He stumbled as he stood up into a half-crouched position. It felt good to be on the move again. His fingers closed round the grip on his rifle, although he was sure that he had no control over his fingers.

'The journey back is the most dangerous,' Lieutenant George had told them before they set out earlier in the evening. 'It's when you are tired and cold that you make mistakes. A good soldier is one who stays alert right to the end.' The words echoed in Bryn's head as they moved silently back through a maze of shell holes. He had no idea where he was going or how far they had gone. He was grateful that his job was to provide cover for the platoon commander and not to lead them back.

The silence erupted with a *rat-tat-tat-tat.* Bryn and John were down on the floor in an instant. Lieutenant George slowly turned and came down to their level. 'It's alright, it's not meant for us,' he said in a low whisper. 'It's coming from over in the A Companies area. We'll make a break for it whilst someone else is taking the heat off us. Come on.' As he stood up flares shrieked into the air. They froze. Lieutenant George was in a half-crouch with Bryn and John still lying on the ground.

'Stay still. Don't move,' the platoon commander hissed. Bryn and John looked at each other. Neither of them had any intention of moving. Bryn looked up at the flare as it fell from the sky like a fairy lantern. It seemed to light up the whole battlefield. The flare hung in the air for what seemed like an eternity before it eventually fell to the earth and darkness enveloped them.

With their night vision ruined by the light of the flare they sank back down into the shell hole and waited until they could see again.

'Alright, let's get back and get ourselves a nice cup of tea,' Lieutenant George said as he clawed his way to the rim of the hole that they had been sheltering in. He rolled over the top and lay still for a minute before rising to a slight crouch. They only had to move a few short bounds before they found their own wire and traced the lengths along until they found the gap that they had come through several hours earlier. They moved a few more yards before lying down.

'Two Platoon, Two Platoon, patrol coming in.'

'Who's there? Identify yourself.'

'Two Platoon patrol, Lieutenant George and two others.'

'Advance slowly and be recognised.'

The platoon commander stood and moved forward to the sentry position whilst Bryn and John remained on the ground. Satisfied that they were who they said they were, the sentry beckoned Bryn and John to come in. As Bryn slid over the parapet of the trench, there was a single crack from a high velocity bullet. John's body fell over the parapet and landed on top of Bryn, pinning him to the ground.

France
March 1915

My Dearest Cerys,

Just a quick note to let you know that John and I are going out tonight on our first patrol. The platoon commander asked for volunteers and not surprisingly we all rushed at the chance, so we drew straws and John and I won. Rhys and Huan are a little miffed but we agreed that they could go next time.

Obviously I can't say anything about the patrol but we are very excited to be doing something after spending the whole day digging in the trench. I can't complain, it's easier than being down the mine and we get to see the sun all day. The weather is very pleasant at the moment although I expect it will get cold at night. I think there will be a frost. It's a good job that I have plenty of woollens to put on.

The food seems pretty good and we will have a good meal before we go out, which will keep us going. Anyway, much to do so I will say cheerio. I will write to let you know how we get on.

Best wishes,
Bryn

CHAPTER TWENTY-ONE

The snow obliterated the brown morass that lay to the front and rear of the trench. One barren landscape was exchanged for another. The sentries who remained at their posts along the platoon frontage relaxed a bit. There was no way the Germans would be patrolling tonight. Even without any moon the brightness of the snow highlighted every ridge and furrow of the ground that lay between the trenches. Any movement across the void would be suicidal.

As the men dismounted from the fire step music floated across the darkness. It was a foreign noise. The sentries looked up and about rather carelessly to see where the music was coming from. At any other time they would have been drilled through the head by a patiently waiting sniper, but the symphony created a sense of calm and the driving snow created a curtain between the trenches.

The boys gathered in small groups in their section fire bays. Wrapped in their poncho capes, they huddled together for warmth. They talked in animated whispers, cigarettes cupped tightly in their hands for warmth and concealment. The few hours before the relief arrived were always tense; no one was willing to take a risk at this stage. All that mattered was that they were leaving the trenches. If the Germans got wind that a relief was in progress the air would be filled with burning shards of metal from every trench weapon or artillery shell that was registered on their trench. The chance of a double target was too good an opportunity to miss. Nothing would be gained, there would be no attack, no ground would be made, no tactical advantage would be gained; it was just an opportunity to cause indiscriminate death or injury. The gramophone record had changed.

'I reckon I know this one,' Corporal Jones said as he tilted his head slightly to hear the music. 'We used to sing to this in chapel. I didn't know it was a German song.'

'Actually it's *Das Rhiengold* from Wagner's *Der Ring des Nibelungen*,' came a voice from the back of the huddle.

'Well aren't you a smartarse... oh shit. Hello, sir. Didn't see you there, sir. I do apologise. Make room for the officer, boys.'

Lieutenant George looked into the faces of his men as they moved apart. They were weary, wet and unshaven but there was still a glint of mischief in their eyes. They might be covered in mud and the snow was starting to mount on their helmets, but he only had to look into their eyes to see how they really felt.

'Are we off then, sir?' an eager young lad asked.

The young lieutenant looked at the young lad. 'Taylor, isn't it?'

Rhys pulled his shoulders back and raised his chin. 'Yes, sir,' he said with a smile.

'One thing that you will learn very quickly, Taylor, is that there are only two certainties in this war. Firstly, we will win and secondly, no relief will ever turn up on time. Isn't that right Corporal Jones?'

'Very true, sir.'

'Good. Well instead of standing around making a pretty target of yourselves why don't you make a start on the repairs?'

'Oh, right you are, sir. Come on boys. Let's make the place welcoming for the English. Grab your shovels and we'll make a start on the drainage.' His orders trailed off as Lieutenant George rounded the traverse into the next fire bay. 'Right then Taylor, seeing as you're such a smartarse you can make the brew. The rest of you just spread along and keep your shovels handy in case the platoon commander comes back.'

*

It was way past midnight before the first shadowy figures emerged from the mouth of the communication trench. The Welshmen had long given up the pretence of working and gone from grumbling to swearing and eventually resignation as the hours had ticked by. Surviving the cold became their overriding concern. They could cope with being cold but being cold and wet was more than just unpleasant, it was a trial of strength and fortitude. There was no respite from the squelching mud that seeped into their boots or the trickle of freezing water that dripped down the backs of their collars. Keeping dry was an impossibility that became a preoccupation.

'Look now boys,' the sentry said as a bedraggled file of men passed him, 'the cavalry has arrived.'

'Why don't you shout it to the rest of the world as well the Germans, you stupid Taffy idiot?'

'Don't you worry about them boyo, they've been very well behaved these last few days. There's no chance of them being up at this time of night. They've been having a dinner dance for most of the night, so they have. I expect that they're all tucked up in bed, snug and warm like.'

The first of the Middlesex men stopped next to Corporal Jones who was already grabbing his webbing that lay on the fire step.

'Not so bloody fast mate, we're only the advance party. The rest will be a while yet.'

Corporal Jones stopped with one arm through his webbing shoulder strap. '*Duw*. How much longer are they going to be?'

'Hard to say really, but long enough for us to nab the driest holes if there is such a thing.'

'Well, unless you're the platoon commander you've got no chance. There's only shit and sludge along here.'

'Nothing's changed then? I thought that you might have built a cosy little cottage along here by now. I thought you lot were all meant to be miners?'

'Even Welsh miners can't build a cottage in a sewer,' Corporal Jones replied.

The man gave a heavy sigh of resignation as he moved along the line towards to the platoon commander's dugout. The five-man advance party filed past the Welshmen, dutifully following their leader. They had been in and out of this part of the line for a couple of months and knew instinctively where to go. Corporal Jones dropped his webbing back onto the floor and pulled up the collar of his jacket.

'Another cup of tea then, Corporal? Rhys asked.

'Go on then lad, we might as well.'

*

Corporal Jones counted his men out of the communication trench that led onto the main road into Bois-Grenier, a small commune on the outskirts of Armentières. They were several hundred yards from the front line. It wasn't quite far enough to be safe but far enough away to avoid most rifle fire. Rhys had stuck to the section commander like glue, fearful that he might lose his way. As they waited for the rest of the section to arrive he squatted down to stretch his knees and to take a bit of pressure off his feet for a moment while the rest of the section filed out. He sighed when Swampy Moore emerged from the communication trench.

'Blimey, I was beginning to think that we were going to end up staying on for another day.'

'Not a rat in hell's chance of that, boyo.' Swampy said as he offered his hand to Rhys and hauled him to his feet

Rhys laughed. 'It's cat in hell, not rat.'

'Believe me, the rats are so big in there that they have eaten all the cats and it is Hell. So it's definitely a rat in hell's chance!'

'Come on you two – less chat, more action. I don't want to be hanging about here,' Corporal Jones said in a harsh whisper. 'I want to get settled while it's still dark and quiet.'

*

It was less of a march and more of an amble as a string of Welshmen made their way towards the shattered remnants of Bois-Grenier. Although the cobbled road was covered in mud and a layer of snow Rhys thought that there was something reassuringly civilised about having something solid underfoot. Like so many front line villages very little remained unscathed. It was another eight hundred yards to the village and the fear and anxiety receded with every step that they took.

The early morning darkness was slow in lifting as the sections shambled their way towards the village. Rhys walked backwards for a few yards to see if he could see Bryn and Huan anywhere, but it was too dark and the snow was coming down in a barrier of swirling white. As he turned again towards the village he could just about make out a body of men coming towards them. They were bent forward against the driving snow. The section moved to the side of the road to allow them through. They were Middlesex men, and they were late. At this rate they would end up moving into the trenches as daylight broke. The Welshmen knew it and so too did the Middlesex men. With any luck the snow would keep the Germans down for a while longer.

'Good luck boys,' someone mumbled as they passed.

The road on which the men were walking ran directly from the front line and past the village cemetery where they had laid to rest several of their own company, a stark reminder of their fate every time they went to and from the trenches. A line of terraced houses had once started a few hundred yards from the crossroads that marked the centre of the village. Now they were nothing but rubble. It was the same on all four roads than ran through the village. Even the church on the crossroads had been pulverised. Only three houses remained and the German gunners had made it their mission to remove all traces of the village one at a time.

The billeting officer and his runners met the company as they arrived at the crossroads. The old hands knew the area. Straight on meant proper billets, maybe a bath with hot water, clean clothes and perhaps, maybe perhaps, a day or two to visit a few mademoiselles in Armentières. Right turn meant they would stay in reserve for a few days, ready to reinforce the Middlesex in the event of a German attack and turning left meant… well, they had never turned left since they had been there but it could only mean a march to a new place in the line. The men stopped opposite the debris of the church that had once dominated the crossroads. It had been the focal point of the village but now it was reduced to rubble just like most buildings in the village.

'What do you think, Corporal?' Rhys asked his section commander.

'Don't ask me boy, I'm not a mind reader but judging by the way that officer is pointing I reckon we'll be staying in this shitty little place again.'

'It doesn't look that bad.'

'You haven't seen it in the daylight. The only decent thing here was that brewery,' Corporal Jones said, pointing to the remnants of a large red brick building on the opposite side of the road to the church, 'and even the fumes have left that place.'

'Does anyone live here, other than us?'

'Not that I've seen. As soon as the brewery and the church were hit most of the locals legged it as well. Never seen anyone since.'

The company sergeant major detailed off the runners to each platoon and the men turned right.

'Well there you go,' Corporal Hughes said to no one in particular. 'It's not Paris this time, boys.' A few men laughed but most just shambled on, heads bent against the falling snow.

Number Two Section looked at the barn that was to be their home for the next few days. There was a stone archway that seemed to be held up by thin air, and rather dubiously they walked beneath it into a cobbled courtyard. The buildings on the right-hand side had been almost entirely blown away but the other three sides remained, and they were now nomadic homes for passing troops. The snow had started to cover a multitude of sins but even so it was obvious that the previous occupants had left in a hurry. Empty boxes of ammunition, coils of wire, broken duckboards, broken shovels, bits of rags and a pile of wine bottles littered the square.

'Lazy bastards,' Corporal Jones said. 'There's no excuse for leaving this shit for someone else to clear up. Dump your kit and we'll clear away what we can before the company sergeant major comes round, otherwise he'll only dig us out of our pits to do it.'

Above the door a shell had struck the whitewashed brick leaving a gaping hole in the upper floor, but the tiled roof was still largely intact. There was a small mound of rubble in front of the doorway, which no one had bothered to remove and probably never would.

'Well, I've never been to the Ritz but I reckon that it's probably better than this,' Rhys said to no one in particular as he looked around the courtyard. 'Still, it's better than freezing our bollocks off up at the front and it might be a bit more comfortable than a muddy hole.' As they crossed the threshold the smell of rotting hay hit them.

'*Duw*, it reeks in here,' Rhys cried.

'Might well do but it's almost dry and no one's lobbing metal shit at us are they? So I would be grateful for small mercies if I was you,' one of the more senior members of the section said as he pushed past.

'Hardly the best accommodation if you're in it.' Rhys turned to the familiar voice that had crept up from behind them. Huan slapped Rhys on the shoulder. 'Hey boyo, how you doing?'

'All the better for seeing you. I thought we had left you behind.'

'Not flipping likely, is it? We were about to follow you out but Lieutenant George nabbed us as we was about to make a dash for it and he made us hang on for a while until the English boys had sorted themselves out.'

Rhys looked behind Huan. 'Where's the big lad?'

'He's being a martyr as usual. Helping one of the lads with his kit, he is.'

The rest of Number One Section filed through the doorway. Bryn brought up the rear.

'Not exactly the Wynnstay is it?' Bryn said.

'Have you ever been in Wynnstay?' Rhys replied.

'Er, no.'

'Well then you can assume that this is far better than Wynnstay other than the room service, which I'm told is no longer provided.'

'That's a shame. Who's going to plump my pillow?'

'If you can find a pillow I'll plump it for you, how's that?'

'Fair enough. Where are we going then?'

'Anywhere you like but if we don't find a spot soon we might end up outside. It's going to be cosy if the rest of the platoon arrive.'

They found a spot next to a small hole in the wall, for a bit of 'ventilation' as Huan put it, and laid out their kit to mark their patch. Rhys propped himself up on one shoulder as they lay down for the first time in what seemed like weeks.

'Where do you reckon John is, then?'

'Judging by the bloody fuss he was making he must be in Blighty by now,' Bryn suggested.

'Sergeant Price reckons he'll be back in a day or so,' Huan said.

Rhys rolled back onto his back, looking up at the roof. 'You know I still can't believe we missed it. What a laugh!'

'Oh yes, bloody hilarious,' Bryn said. 'But then he didn't land on you, did he? Nearly broke my bloody neck, he did. One moment I was stood next to Lieutenant George and the next minute there was a great lump falling on my head. I couldn't believe it. There he was on the ground writhing in agony. I was a bit winded myself, like, but I grabbed his tunic and turned him over. "I've been hit," he said, and I put his head in my hands. "Don't talk, boyo," I said, "I'll get a dressing on it. It'll be fine." Just stay with me, or something like that. Anyway Lieutenant George comes round the other side, we put our hands under his arms and propped him up against the side. Screamed, he did, as we dragged him into a sitting position. Lieutenant George was marvellous. Sorted him out pretty good. Turned him over, quick as you like, no messing about. Then he took his knife and slashed his trousers open. You should have seen his arse shining, like a bright moon. And there it was, his wound, a red streak stretched across his buttocks as if he had been whipped with a cane. I couldn't believe it – a grazed arse, for goodness' sake. I've had worse at school and there he is blabbing like a baby. Anyway we slapped a bandage on it, pretty hard mind, and off he went to the Regimental Aid Post.'

Rhys was lying back on his blanket, his head on his large pack. There were tears of laughter streaming down his face as Bryn finished relaying the story. Bryn looked at him and then at Huan, whose shoulders were bobbing up and down as he laughed. Their laughter had always been contagious and finally Bryn cracked a smile and joined in.

*

It was late afternoon when Bryn woke up. The light outside was starting to fade, which made the barn slightly eerie. He propped himself up on his elbow and looked around.

To his left Huan was in a deep sleep, and Rhys was snoring loud enough to wake the dead. They were surrounded by the rest of the sections, almost all of them cocooned in their blankets like moths waiting to hatch out. Sleep was a precious commodity that wasn't to be wasted.

Bryn shivered. He had changed out of his wet uniform last night and had wrapped it between the layers of his blankets to dry with his body heat, but there hadn't been very much of that. He felt his tunic, which was still damp but at least it wasn't frozen, he thought. He picked his way carefully through the prostrate bodies to the entrance of the barn and looked out onto a white blanket.

It had stopped snowing but the sky betrayed future intentions. There would be more later, he was sure of it.

His thoughts momentarily flashed to the Middlesex men in the trenches that they had left behind. He shivered and pulled up the collar of his greatcoat around his ears. As he thrust his hands deep into his pockets he brushed a small packet. He hesitated a moment as if unsure of what he had touched and then his hands gripped round the packet and he brought out some cigarettes.

He remembered the first time that he had smoked one. John had stolen one from his da and he, Rhys and Huan had climbed Caergwrle Hill. He smiled when he remembered that they had forgotten to steal a match to light it with. It was a few days later behind the school that they finally shared the tab. He remembered feeling sick and coughing a lot. He hadn't had another since then, not until yesterday. A voice startled him.

'You're up early, Tallent.' Bryn span around to see Lieutenant George standing behind him. He hadn't heard him approach.

'Sorry, sir. Couldn't sleep, sir.'

The young platoon commander smiled. 'Don't worry, you will when you need to. By the sounds of it there are a few sleeping champions in there,' he said. 'You did well the other night, on the patrol.'

'Thank you, sir.'

'I wouldn't thank me, Tallent. It means that you'll end up doing a lot more.'

'I don't mind, sir.'

Lieutenant George smiled. 'Give it a few weeks and you'll be able to sleep anywhere.' He raised his leather cane to his cap and turned towards the farmhouse. He stopped a few yards away and turned back. 'And by the way, Tallent, your friend Roberts – he'll be back tonight. No permanent damage done.'

'Thank you, sir,' Bryn called back. A genuine smile crossed his face.

France
March 1915

Dearest Cerys,

We have just returned from our first stint at the front. I have so many stories to tell you. As you know John and I volunteered to go out on patrol with the platoon commander (who is a very fine officer). To cut a long story short, John got shot in his bottom, which has given him a deep graze across both cheeks. Pardon my description. He is fine but needless to say he has been the butt of many a joke since it happened. We are currently enjoying a few days' rest (I hope). We are in a barn that has seen better days and it smells but it is pretty warm. It snowed here yesterday so we are grateful to be undercover.

I am with Rhys and Huan at the moment as the platoon is all together and we are expecting John back later on today. The blokes are a pretty good lot – most of them are career soldiers and quite a few have been here since the start. There are also a lot of reservists who have been recalled to the battalion. Most of them seem pretty pleased to be here. Quite a few of the blokes are from our way but equally there are blokes from all over the place.

I don't know what the next few days will bring but I don't suppose they will let us have too much time off. I haven't had any letters from you yet – not that I'm complaining or anything, I just thought I would let you know so that you can work out how long it takes. I am looking forward to hearing your news.

I must go. Look after yourself.
Yours as ever,
Bryn

CHAPTER TWENTY-TWO

May 1915

Bryn stood with the rest of the platoon in the middle of the main road that ran through the village. There was a nip in the early evening air and the dark clouds threatened rain. They were stood in loose lines waiting for the order to move back to the trenches. Most of the men had placed their packs on the floor with their rifles on top. They were not in a hurry to move.

They had been in and out of the trenches in front of Bois-Grenier for the past month, usually for three or four days at a time. The general had given orders that the troops were to be rotated fairly frequently due to the cold. They had been pretty lucky with the weather up until now. It had been cold but there had been very little rain. The last time that it had rained the landscape changed from a pockmarked, frozen, crusted desert into a sea of murky slime. The trench had been ankle-deep in brown sludge that seeped into their boots and through thick woollen socks. The mud penetrated every fibre of cloth until it reached their pasty white skin. The only consolation was that it drowned the lice for a while. Fortunately it had been on their last day in the trench so they had spent most of their time standing in their poncho capes around the trench brazier to keep warm until the relief arrived.

'How long have we been here now?' John asked.

Bryn looked at his watch. 'Best part of a couple of hours.'

'I really don't know why we rush so much. This is what... our fourth or fifth time in the trenches and every time it's the same: hurry up and wait.'

'It wouldn't be so bad if they didn't start yelling halfway through dinner... it gives me indigestion,' Rhys said.

'No it doesn't. Your tummy hurts because it wobbles when you have to run around,' Huan said. 'You need to do a bit of training, boyo. You'll not make the team when we get back.'

The boys looked at each other for a moment.

'When are you expecting to get back, eh? We're going to be here for a long time yet,' Bryn said.

'That's where your wrong, see, Bryn. Positive thinking, that's what you need. Think positive and we'll be home before you know it.'

'Jones,' Corporal Hughes shouted.

'Yes, Corporal?' he replied as he scrambled to his feet.

'SHUT UP!

'Oh, right you are Corporal.'

The boys were still laughing as Bryn looked up and the first spots of rain hit his face. He sighed. They had had a good run but it had to rain at some point.

'I'll give you a penny for 'em?' Rhys asked as he poked a finger into Bryn's ribs.

'Oi!' Bryn replied, snapping out of his thoughts. 'You can keep your penny. I'm not thinking of anything that's worth a penny.'

'I bet it's Cerys. Tell me I'm right.'

'No, you're wrong, as usual and if I was thinking of Cerys it would be worth more than a penny.'

'Well what are you worrying about then?'

'I'm not worried.'

'It's alright, you know, to be worried about going to the trenches. We're not going to go for a few hours yet, not during daylight. I'm sure everyone else is a bit nervous.'

'I'm not nervous and I'm not worried, alright?' Bryn said, raising his voice more than he had intended. He stared at his friend and gave him one of his reproachful looks. Rhys raised his eyebrows. Bryn shook his head. 'Why would I be worried? We've been in the trench enough times.'

'I suppose so,' Rhys said. 'How many times have we been there now, do you think?'

'I dunno. Nine or ten I suppose, I haven't actually been counting.'

'Do you reckon the more we go in the less the chance we have of being hit, or more?'

'I've no idea. Why?'

'Well if it's less then you've nothing to be worried about, have you?

'I'm not worried.'

'You look worried.'

'You'll need to be bloody worried in a minute if you don't shut up.'

Rhys was quiet for a moment. Huan was stood on his left, fiddling with his rifle sling. Rhys nudged him and nodded his head towards Bryn and winked. 'I suppose you never really know do you?'

'Know what?' Huan asked.

'Well it's just that Bryn's just a bit worried about going back.'

'No I'm not!' Bryn said, giving his friend a punch on the arm.

'What's up?' John said as he came to join the conversation.

'Bryn's worried,' Huan said.

'No I'm not. Nothing's up. I'm fine!' Bryn protested.

'He's a little nervous,' Huan added.

'I'll give you fucking nervous in a minute,' Bryn shouted as he prodded Huan in the chest.'

'No need to be nervous boyo,' John said. 'Take it from me, you know, having been shot and all that.'

Bryn took off his headdress and smashed it on John's head. 'You weren't shot, you were scratched and you cried like a girl. It's a shame the fucking useless German missed your head when he shot you. It might have knocked some sense into it.'

Rhys, John and Huan looked at each other and chuckled. The men standing around them shook their heads. They had grown accustomed to seeing the boys winding each other up.

John was saved from further violence by the dulcet tones of Sergeant Price. 'Attention!' he cried as Lieutenant George approached the platoon. 'Number Two Platoon ready for duty, sir.'

'Thank you, Sergeant Price. Stand the men easy.'

'Yes sir.'

Sergeant Price turned to face the platoon. 'Stand easy.'

'Good evening men,' Lieutenant George began. He looked tired and drawn. His uniform was as polished as ever, his batman made sure of that, but it didn't disguise the lines that had appeared on his face. 'It's back to work I'm afraid. We can't have the Middlesex enjoying the hospitality of our trenches too much, can we?' There was a wry bit of heckling but it was good-natured, which showed the strength of the platoon and the respect that they had for their commander. 'All of you have been there before, unless there have been any new additions that I am not aware of?' Lieutenant George looked at Sergeant Price.

'No, sir,' came the response. 'Same old useless bastards as last time, sir!'

'Good. Then you know the drill. I want to be in and settled and the Middlesex out by midnight. And it goes without saying that we don't want the Hun to know anything has changed until we want him to know. Is that clear?'

The response was emphatic. '*Yes sir.*'

Lieutenant George smiled. 'Remember, our trenches are not the front line, which is…?' He cupped his hand to his ear, waiting for the response.

'The German trenches!' the men shouted back.

'Exactly. There is no no-man's land, it is our land and the front line is the German trench. Just remember where we are from. We are Welsh and that bit of land in front of our trenches is part of God's land. We will not let a Hun trespass on our land. We will dominate our land and ensure that any action by the enemy is met with a level of force and violence that he will never forget.' The men cheered. Lieutenant George looked at his sergeant. 'Right then, Sergeant Price, you know where you're going. It's up to you when you need to leave but it should be dark enough by seven thirty to make a start. Make sure that you take over in good order and make sure the Middlesex take their rubbish with them.'

'Yes, sir.'

*

The trench was wet and the water was lying two inches deep below the duckboards. Before the war a complex network of ditches had irrigated the land until the constant shelling had destroyed every channel and ditch. The water now lay in whatever ditch or hollow that it trickled into. The only irrigation was the trench, which quickly turned into a stream.

Above the trench the land was waterlogged with pools of sludge that would swallow up a man should he be unfortunate enough to slip into its lair. Digging down more than a couple of feet was impossible due to the high water table, so the men had learned to build the trench up into a breastwork of sandbags, wood and iron. Running repairs were a nightly activity, which kept the men busy carrying trench stores forward or repairing a section that had been blown in by a shell.

'Good evening gentlemen,' the adjutant said as he announced his arrival into the dimly lit dugout. He blinked several times as the smell of paraffin stung his eyes. 'Smells a bit down here.'

Captain Simon Smithfield, the company commander, looked up from his hand of cards. 'Andrew. How lovely to see you. What on earth brings you out here on a night like this? Not lost again are you?'

'Always a friendly welcome in B Company,' Captain Pierson replied as he took off his helmet. For all the banter the adjutant was a frequent and welcome visitor. He tried to keep the company commanders informed of what was going on and invariably returned to the Regimental Headquarters with useful intelligence for the commanding officer. 'Actually, I have brought you a present.' He stood aside and ushered in a rather new-looking second lieutenant. 'Gentlemen, I would like you to meet Second Lieutenant Charles Symonds, newly posted in on attachment to your fine parish.' He held his arm outstretched as if to introduce a new celebrity.

Captain Smithfield laid his cards on the table and rose to greet the new arrival. 'Well, this is a nice surprise. Good to meet you old chap, and welcome to our humble abode. You will have to excuse the mess, we weren't expecting visitors.'

As his eyes adjusted to the candlelight Symonds took in his new surroundings. It was a ramshackle place. Two other officers were sat at a wooden table in the centre of the room. The corrugated roof was shored up with wooden beams and there were two bunks along the far wall. There was a coat stand next to him by the entrance. It seemed illogically out of place. On the opposite side of the dugout was another small table with a broken mirror above it. There was a washbasin and jug on the table. There was kit hanging on the ends of the bunks and on the chairs. Four rifles were stacked one above the other on hooks in the wood-panelled walls. It smelt stuffy, sweaty and damp.

'Thank you, sir. It's very good to meet you too.'

'Good, good. Let me introduce you. On the top bunk and snoring loudly we have Lieutenant James Wilkinson. This is Lieutenant Peter Stuart,' he said, pointing to the officer sat on his right, 'and last but by no means least Second Lieutenant Stephen George.'

Peter and Stephen rose as they were introduced and shook hands with their new arrival. Symonds looked at them, nodding curtly as each of them shook his hand. *They're filthy*, Symonds thought.

'And this is Private Jones 298. Who will, in due course, stop gawping and take your bag from you. Won't you, Jones?'

'Sorry sir, of course I will, sir. Here we go, sir, let me take that from you. Oh now, feels pretty heavy, sir. A few home comforts no doubt? I'll put it over here so you don't forget it when you leave.'

Jones took the pack from Symonds, who seemed unsure as to whether his personal possessions would be safe with such a grubby little man. Jones was old for a private. He had been promoted several times and demoted several more. There wasn't a lot that you could tell him about being a soldier, other than how to keep his stripes.

Captain Smithfield pulled up a spare chair and offered a seat around the small wooden table to Symonds. 'Anyone with a bit of news from Blighty is always a welcome distraction from our normal busy lives. Jones, have we got any of that malt left?'

'Indeed we have, sir.' Jones opened a small locker that stood at the end of a small washing table and produced a bottle of fourteen-year-old single malt and a glass. 'I'm afraid it's a glass for the new officer only, sir. We seem to have lost another couple.' He laid the glass on the table in front of Symonds. If nothing else Jones was a good judge of character. He had a bad feeling in his stomach about Mr Symonds. Most new officers were respectful, cheerful and excited. *Not this fellow*, he thought. He could sense the resentment in the way he stood and looked around, almost as if he was disgusted by what he saw. *Well, if he thinks this is bad wait till he gets into the lines,* Jones thought to himself and placed the bottle in front of Captain Smithfield.

'Not to worry, it all goes down the same way. Andrew, are you going to stay for one or are you in a desperate rush away to sharpen your pencils?'

'Well, as you don't offer the whisky around very often it would be rude to say no.'

Andrew placed his cap on a peg sticking out of the wall and took his coat off. Jones gathered the mugs from around the small dugout that still held the dregs of a coffee that he had made earlier. 'I'll just give these a clean, sir,' he said as he made for the entrance.

'Don't forget mine, Jonesy!' came a voice from the top bunk.

'Perish the thought, sir,' Jones replied over his shoulder.

'I might have known that you would wake up at the mention of Scotch!' Smithfield said, looking up at the bunk. 'We have a visitor James, are you going to join us?'

James rolled over on his bunk and looked at their new guest. 'Good evening, or is it morning? Never can tell in this place. James Wilkinson at your service.' He gave Symonds a mock salute and rolled back onto his side.

'You must forgive James, he's off out in a while and needs his beauty sleep,' Simon explained. 'Anyway, how long are you staying with us? Captain Pierson mentioned something about an attachment.'

'Charles is only with us for a short time. He's come to see if he likes it and then he's off back to Blighty, lucky blighter. So do try to look after him,' Andrew said.

'Really?' Smithfield asked, raising his eyebrows in surprise. 'What's so pressing in Blighty that drags you back so soon rather than staying here with us and having some fun?'

Symonds looked at the company commander for a moment. 'Training, sir. I am one of Kitchener's volunteers and like many of the other officers I have been posted out here for a few weeks to experience life at the front, so to speak. So that we can prepare the soldiers more thoroughly for their eventual deployment. It means that we can add a small degree of experience and context to their training.'

'Excellent idea. I'm sure that you will have experienced quite enough by the time you get back.'

'So what is happening back in Blighty?' Stephen asked. 'I hear the War Office has got half the population running around Salisbury Plain and the other half knitting socks.'

Jones placed the clean cups on the table. 'Should I pour?' Smithfield nodded and the conversation paused as the peat-coloured water splashed into their mugs. Symonds took the glass that was offered to him and swallowed the whisky as if he hadn't had a drink in months.

'Good health,' he offered as he put the glass on the table, as if expecting a refill. The other officers stared at him and raised their mugs in response before taking a small sip.

'Well to answer your question,' he said at length, looking at Stephen, 'Salisbury is awash with soldiers. Of course it's not just Salisbury; they have set up camps all over the country. There's nowhere to go for a bit of piece and quiet. The whole country has gone war-mad. Everywhere you look there are soldiers marching around, digging trenches or charging at bags filled with straw. All rather dull really.'

'You sound like you're not enjoying your training,' Captain Smithfield said.

'I wasn't aware that it was meant to be enjoyable,' Symonds replied.

Smithfield scoffed. 'Ah, keen to get out here eh? Well I don't think any training is wasted but it would be good to have some new men out here sooner rather than later.'

'Indeed, sir,' Symonds replied.

'Well,' Simon said, swilling his Scotch around in his mug, 'I hope that you find our little corner of Wales more to your satisfaction. We have some entertaining moments from time to time.' As if on cue a shell landed near the dugout, sending loose pieces of earth showering over the table. The officers barely noticed. All they saw was their visitor flinching in his seat. 'I thought it had been too quiet. Don't worry about that, old chap. You'll get used to it,' Smithfield said as he swallowed the last of his Scotch.

The curtain covering the dugout entrance was pulled back and the burly form of the sergeant major ducked through the small opening. He was a hard man, short on words, big on courage. If there was trouble he would be there to sort it out.

'Good evening, sir,' he said, addressing the company commander whilst taking in the visitors. 'If I'd known you had company, sir, I wouldn't have bothered you.'

214

'Not at all, Sergeant Major. You are most welcome. You know the adjutant of course.'

'Indeed I do, sir, How are you, sir?' he said as he grasped the outstretched hand of his old platoon commander.

'I'm very well, Sergeant Major Russell, thank you for asking. How are things at the sharp end?'

'Can't complain, sir. It never does any good anyway so I don't bother,' he said with a grin across his face.

'Never a truer word, Sergeant Major. Can I introduce you to Second Lieutenant Symonds who will be joining B Company for a while?'

The sergeant major nodded to the newcomer. 'You're very welcome I'm sure, sir.' Symonds nodded back without making any comment. 'Always good to see a new face, sir,' the sergeant major added.

'Lieutenant Symonds was just telling us about the endless battalions who are training in Blighty,' Lieutenant Stuart said to the sergeant major. 'It seems we are to be inundated with reinforcements. Lots of new men for you to shout at, Sergeant Major.'

'That's made my day, sir. Just what I need, a sore throat to add to my woes!' the sergeant major replied with a thin smile. He looked at the new officer. 'It's a sergeant major-type joke, sir, no offence meant. It will be good to see some new men out here. We've had a few recently, good lads. If they are as good as the four we've had recently then they will be very welcome.'

Symonds looked down at his glass and twirled it in his hand. 'I'm not sure where they came from but it seems that you have been lucky. Most of the men can't distinguish one end of the rifle from the other. Don't get me wrong; they are not idle, just slow to learn. Although hardly to be unexpected when they are recruiting anyone who can stand still long enough to state their name and cough.' A shell fell close to the dugout but its dull thud was ignored. The officers were looking at Symonds with slight disbelief.

The sergeant major broke the silence. 'If you will excuse me, sir, I think it's probably time that I took a wander along the line. I hate to think of the men getting too idle.'

Captain Smithfield gave him a curt nod. 'Thank you, Sergeant Major. I will catch up with you later.'

The sergeant major replaced his helmet. 'Excuse me, sir. Good to see you again Captain Pierson. You take care.' He gave a brief nod to the other officers. 'Gentlemen.' The officers mumbled and nodded back.

The adjutant reached for his coat and hat. 'Well, I suppose that I had better be getting back. I'm sure the commanding officer will be missing me by now.'

'I'm sure that he's forgotten your name already. Come on, I'll see you out old chap,' Captain Smithfield replied.

Outside the night was clear and the cold hit them immediately. Away in the distance a machine gun was spluttering away but it was quiet in B Company's trenches. Simon took hold of Andrew's arm and pulled him away from the entrance. 'What do think of our new recruit, Andrew?'

'I think he's an arrogant arse who is likely to be shot by his own men before the Hun get their chance.'

'Well thanks very much for bringing him here. I thought we were friends?'

'We are, that's why I brought him to you. I know that you will sort him out.'

'Ha, flattery will get you nowhere!'

'I know, I'm sorry, but if anyone can sort him out I'm sure that you will. He's already upset the old man, which is why I was despatched *tout suite*. He's meant to be with us for a couple of weeks. I'm sure he'll settle down after a few days. A bit of mud and bother will knock a bit of arrogance out of him.'

'Well I shall try to make sure that you get him back in one piece. Just promise me one thing. If he does come back to the battalion you make sure that he is posted to another company.'

216

The adjutant laughed. 'I think that I can probably sort that one out. Thank you.'

'Don't thank me just yet. I said *if* he comes back in one piece.'

They both laughed and shook hands. 'Go on then, get yourself back and don't get lost. The colonel will be starting to worry about you being out so late.' As Smithfield watched the adjutant disappear into the maze of the communication trench he looked along the line. The nearest sentry shuffled slightly to assure the company commander that he was awake. Further along the line he could hear one of the platoons bedding in the new sandbags to strengthen the trench wall. He reminded himself that he should take a wander down the line in an hour or two. He was still thinking what he should do with his officer when a low voice pierced his space.

'Is that you, sir?' The sergeant major's baritone voice was unmistakable.

'Yes it's me, Sergeant Major. How are the men?'

'They're fine, sir. Normal grumbling, which is always a good thing. It always worries me if they aren't moaning about something.' He gave a short laugh and then looked along the trench line. 'It's a bit too quiet for my liking though. I can't help thinking that something's brewing?'

'Maybe, or perhaps they are just as cold as we are and are trying to keep warm?'

'There is that I suppose,' he replied. 'What are you going to do with our new officer, sir?'

Andrew sucked through his teeth for a moment. 'I thought that we would put Mr Symonds with Lieutenant George for a couple of days, see how he settles in. I'm sure that he will be fine once he knows the routine and gets to know the men. Having been here for so long we tend to forget what a God-awful place this is for those who are experiencing it for the first time. Perhaps you would be good enough to give him a tour of the company lines in the morning after stand to. I'm sure that he will appreciate your experience.'

'My pleasure, sir.'

'In fact, why don't you organise a "hate" for him at stand to? We haven't done one for a while and it will wake out neighbours up. It might also stop the men worrying about it being too quiet.'

*

Bryn poked his head out from under his blanket. It was still pitch black. He had only been asleep for an hour. They had spent most of the night repairing the breastwork and then he had been unfortunate to draw a two-hour sentry stag. There was movement everywhere. Boxes of ammunition were being broken open and men were grabbing packets of bullets. Huan's head appeared from the hole next to him. 'What's all the commotion?'

'I dunno, but it looks like we are meant to be up,' Bryn replied. He stuffed his blanket to the back of his hole rather than folding it away. He was pulling on his coat as John brushed past him. 'Hey, boyo, what's going on?' Bryn asked.

'Blimey, where have you been? There's a hate on, that's what. Got to go. See you later.'

Bryn grabbed John's arm. 'Oi hang on. What's a "hate"?'

'Well, I dunno really but it I think it's pretty big. See you later.' And with that John was cloaked by the night.

Bryn found Corporal Hughes dishing out ammunition. 'What's going on Corporal?'

'Ah, there you are, twinkle-toes. Right, grab what ammunition you can and make sure that you have got it to hand. You'll need it. In fact, take these two boxes and put them in the section bay.'

Bryn did as he was told and told Huan to do the same when he finally arrived, but neither of them were any the wiser as to what was going on. They filled their pouches and grabbed a box each. The other members of the section were already in the section bay.

'Anybody know what's going on?' Huan asked.

'A hate, lad, that's what,' one of the old regulars replied. 'We haven't done one of these for a long time. Basically, when the order is given to fire, every weapon we have, including the artillery, if they can be bothered, will open up on the Hun. It just wakes them up a bit. Captain Smithfield probably wants to stir things up a bit because it's been so quiet. Why he can't leave things well alone I don't know. It will only piss them off.'

'What happens when we have finished firing?' he asked.

'Depends. Fritz will probably be pretty upset and do the same back to us and then, God willing, we will all still be here and we'll have some breakfast. And if I was you I would put some cotton in your ears!'

'You mean we don't go over the top?'

'Certainly not,' the old boy replied. 'Do you want to get yourself killed or something?'

*

The battery of guns boomed and a couple of seconds later shells screamed over the heads of the Royal Welsh.

'Fire!' Corporal Hughes screamed and the section fired at will across the void to their front.

All along the company position everyone was firing at the lip of the German trench. The company machine guns cackled as they spewed their pieces of death and then the crump of the trench mortars started a rhythmic beat. Two hundred yards to their front, the lip of the German trench disintegrated under the impact of the rifle fire. Earth, sandbags, wire and wood were thrown into the air by the artillery and mortar shells. It was indistinguishable from any human form that might have been caught in the maelstrom.

Lights filled the sky; white and then red flares shot up from the German lines. They were signals to their own artillery to counter-fire on the British batteries. Within a minute shells were crossing in mid-air, the British ones aimed at the trenches and the Germans ones aimed at the British guns. Within the section bay men were grabbing more ammunition. Nobody cared if they weren't hitting anything; most men weren't even aiming at anything specific. But they were smiling as weeks of tension was slowly released.

Further along the trench Lieutenant George was making sure that the platoon was keeping up a steady rate of fire and keeping half an eye on his watch. Five minutes was all that the company commander wanted, no more, no less. Symonds stood next to him, his fingers pushed firmly into his ears. Lieutenant George had invited him to take up a rifle and join the section on the fire step, which he had declined, saying that it was his belief that the men should see their officers in command rather than behaving like one of their own. At five minutes on the dot Lieutenant George put his whistle to his lips and blew as hard as he could. Within seconds the thunder stopped and along the trench line rifles and machine guns were silenced. For a moment or two no one moved. Bryn gave Huan another gleeful look. 'Wow, that was something.'

'Sentries in position... but keep down. The rest of you take cover,' Lieutenant George managed to shout before the first response came from the German lines. The lip of their own trench spewed earth on the men, who had now flattened themselves along the front face of the trench.

'Sir,' shouted one of the sentries. 'The flares have changed colour.'

'Right, standby, incoming.' It was all he was able to shout before both sides of the trench erupted.

The ground shook and the men pressed themselves as hard as they could into the side of the trench wall. The earth lifted and fell; vibrations ran along the length of the trench.

*

Lieutenant George was finishing his report to the company commander on the morning's activities as Symonds stood in the background smoking a cigarette. Two men had been wounded in the fire but the hate had gone better than expected. The German response had been pretty paltry with very little small arms fire, which might suggest that they had been pretty badly shaken up. Even the artillery response had lacked intensity.

Captain Smithfield looked across at Symonds. 'Lieutenant Symonds, how did you find your first morning?'

Symonds looked at the company commander. 'Most entertaining, sir, as you suggested.'

'Well I can't offer you quite so much entertainment but after breakfast I suggest that you go and find the sergeant major. He will take you on a tour of our estate. Familiarise yourself with our neighbourhood, so to speak.'

Symonds stubbed out his cigarette and nodded. 'As you wish, sir.'

Symonds ducked inside the dugout to ferret out a cup of tea. Captain Smithfield looked at Stephen. 'So, how did he get on?'

Stephen coughed. 'I'm sure that given a period of adjustment, sir, and some real experience he will be fine.'

'That's rather diplomatic Stephen, even for you.'

'Yes, sir, but sometimes it is easy to forget that we have been out here a while.'

'He doesn't have a while, and more importantly neither will his men. Make sure you give him the full experience, will you? Get him over the top with a few men; it might take some of that polish off his buttons.'

'Of course, sir. I'll get him out tonight. It will be useful anyway to know how Fritz responds to this morning's fireworks.'

*

Rhys and John were already sat on the fire step scoffing some bacon and chunks of bread with mugs of lukewarm tea when Bryn and Huan found them.

221

'Where have you two been?' Rhys tried to say through a mouthful of bread.

'Never mind that,' Bryn replied, 'we're in trouble. You'll never guess who we've just seen.'

Rhys and John looked at each other and shrugged.

'I dunno, er... the King?' John suggested.

Huan leaned forward and lowered his voice. 'Symonds.'

'Who?' John asked.

'Symonds,' Bryn added. 'You know, Lieutenant Symonds from training.'

'Symonds,' John blurted out.

'Shh!'

'What's he doing here?' Rhys asked.

'I dunno,' Bryn said, 'but he's been hanging around with Lieutenant George all night.'

'Oh bloody hell,' John said. 'I hope he's not taking over or we're dead meat. We might as well stand on the parapet and shout, "Oi Fritz – over here!"'

France
May 1915

My Dearest Cerys,

Well, we are back at work, as I like to call it, just as we were the other week. Same place, same routine. It's not too bad – the rain has stopped and the trenches are drying up a bit. Thanks very much for the parcel that you sent, just what the doctor ordered. You can never have enough socks and the fruit cake was just the best. Needless to say I shared it with the lads. We share most things so that we are never short of anything. Rhys got a massive parcel from his mam the other day. How excited was he until he opened it to find a bunch of leeks from their garden, which she had wrapped in sacking. We had to laugh but nothing was wasted. We gave the leeks to the company cook and he let us have an extra-large portion come dinner time. We managed to get into our mademoiselle's just before we came back into the trenches. I've told you about the place that we go to. It is a bit run-down as most places are now, but she still manages to make the most fantastic chips with ham and fresh eggs – just what we needed to see us through the next few days. We washed it all down with a couple of glasses of vin blanc – how posh are we?

Well it is time for me to do some work. All very quiet so nothing to worry about. Take care of yourself.

With all my affection,
Bryn

CHAPTER TWENTY-THREE

It had been a damp morning, never quite raining but wet all the same. It was the kind of rain that never seems to fall; it just hangs in the air and seeps slowly into every fibre of clothing. The duckboards on the floor of the trench were covered in a thick brown slime like congealed gravy, making movement hazardous. Men were sitting on pieces of board and sacking along the fire step. Most of them were smoking or chatting quietly as they cleaned their rifles. Every other man in the section was cleaning his rifle under the supervision of the section commanders, while the other half of the section stood to and watched their front for any sign of enemy action.

'Do you know what? I reckon I have spent more time cleaning this ruddy thing than I have firing it,' Rhys said as he looked around for somewhere dry to put the breech block. 'Pass that empty sandbag over will you?'

'Well at least if you ever hit anything it will be a clean kill,' Huan replied and chuckled at his own joke. The others looked at him and shook their heads. 'Clean kill... get it?' Huan said again. 'I don't know why I bother.'

'Nor do we,' John replied.

'Well there's bugger all else to do, is there, and if Fritz does decide to show his face over the top at least you've got a chance to hit him,' Bryn added as he blew smoke into the air, his head tilted back against the trench wall.

Corporal Jones appeared from around the traverse. 'There you are. I've been looking everywhere for you.'

'Sorry Corporal,' Rhys said. 'We just popped down to the shops.'

'Shut up Taylor. You're not funny. Never have been and never will be. Got it?'

'Yes, Corporal.'

The boys laughed as Corporal Jones smacked Rhys on his helmet with the bundle of letters that he was carrying.

'Lieutenant George has asked for volunteers to do a short reconnaissance tonight of the ground that lies due east of our little trench. By that I mean the rest of Wales, as Lieutenant George puts it.' Corporal Jones laughed at his own joke and the boys humoured him by joining in. 'Right, who's in?' They just looked at each other and shook their heads.

'Not tonight Corporal, thanks very much for asking though,' Bryn responded for his friends.

'What do you mean, no? You always volunteer.' Corporal Jones looked confused. 'Oh I see. My mistake, I'm sorry, did I say volunteers? What I meant to say is which two of you are going over the top tonight?'

'Well as you put it like that, Corporal, I'll go,' John said.

'I suppose I had better go and look after him,' Huan leapt in.

'Me too,' Bryn chimed in.

'Well you can't go without me,' Rhys said.

'Hang on, you can't all go. Lieutenant George only wants two volunteers,' Corporal Jones started to say.

'Well I said it first,' John replied.

'No you didn't, you liar,' Huan retorted.

'Right, shut the fuck up all of you. What is it with you four?' Corporal Jones asked as he took stock. 'Right, who's going? And don't start again. I'm a busy man.'

*

It was late afternoon when Bryn and John made their way along the fire bays and round the traverses that formed their stretch of the line. The rain had eased and lighter streaks of cloud were stretching across the sky. The platoon commander had a 'day' dugout, as he called it, at the end of the platoon position. It was at the head of the communication trench so that everyone knew where to find him. Turn left for Number Two Platoon and right for Number Three Platoon. As the boys rounded the last traverse they saw Lieutenant George stood in front of his dugout talking to Sergeant Price. Lieutenant Symonds was stood to one side, smoking a cigarette.

'Oh shit,' Bryn said under his breath. John looked at Symonds.

'Ah, there you are. Well done. Tallent and Roberts; I might have guessed it would be you two,' Lieutenant George said in his normal good-natured tone. 'Right, well let's get on shall we? Tallent, Roberts, this is Second Lieutenant Symonds. You will be going out with him tonight.'

The exchange of glances between the boys and Symonds was lost on Lieutenant George. The boys just nodded.

'Lieutenant Symonds is only with us for a few days so make sure you keep him safe. Sergeant Price will be coming with you as well just to make sure you don't get lost.' Stephen turned to Symonds. 'These are good men, almost the best I would say. For some reason they seem to enjoy going over the top. You will be fine with them.'

'I'm sure I will be,' Symonds replied.

*

Lieutenant George was more thorough than normal in the briefing, pausing to explain some of the normal procedures that the platoon had adopted more for Symonds' benefit than the others. It was going to be a fairly simple patrol. They would go out at twenty-one hundred hours from the sentry position where they were currently standing. Sergeant Price would lead the way towards the German wire, followed by Symonds. Bryn and John would bring up the rear. They were to watch and listen from a position in front of the German wire.

Lieutenant George explained that there was no point in trying to probe the wire or getting too close unless they were intending to capture a German or raid the trench. He just wanted them to watch and report on whether the enemy were capable of carrying out routine work following the hate earlier that morning. They were to stay for two hours and then move to a new position for another hour before making their way back in through the same sentry position. As there were no questions they synchronised their watches and agreed to meet back at the same spot later that night. Bryn and John were dismissed.

'Are you happy with all that, Charles?' Stephen asked once the boys were out of earshot.

'Perfectly, old chap. Not exactly complicated is it?' Symonds replied as he pulled another cigarette out of his cigarette holder. 'Want one?' he asked, holding the case out towards Stephen.

'No thanks.'

'I notice that your men don't bother to salute you.'

Lieutenant George was startled by the comment. He turned slowly to look at Symonds. 'Not if you value your own life. It's easy enough for a sniper to pick out an officer as it is. I don't see any merit in making it any easier for him.'

'Even so, the men can get above themselves sometimes can't they?'

'Not from my experience,' Stephen said with a note of irritation in his voice.

*

Symonds didn't have to go far to find who he was looking for. The platoon position was only a hundred yards long. He found the boys in the third bay. They were sitting on the fire step as he came around the traverse. They were talking quietly.

'Not interrupting you, am I?' Symonds said, looking around to see if anyone else was listening. The boys looked at him. 'It seems that it is a small world after all. You didn't think that I had forgotten you, did you?'

Bryn spoke first. 'No, sir. It's nice to see you again, sir.'

'Is it? I seem to remember that you and your chums disappeared fairly quickly after the last time we met. Bit of a coincidence perhaps.'

'I'm not sure what you mean, sir. We were posted at short notice.'

Symonds took a step closer and lowered his voice. 'Don't mess with me, you cretin. You know exactly what I'm talking about. You cost me a lot of money. You and your friends.' Bryn didn't bother to answer. 'Thought so. Well let me assure you that I will get my money back, with interest. Do I make myself clear?' The boys looked at each other but stayed silent. 'Well?'

'Quite clear,' Bryn replied.

'Private, I think you mean quite clear, *sir*.'

'Quite clear, sir.'

France
May 1915

My Dearest Cerys,

I spoke too soon about the rain. It's not too bad but it has been damp since we arrived back in the trenches. It's warm enough but everything gets covered in mud. It's a bit like being down the mine except we are all brown instead of black. You wouldn't recognise us at the moment. Still, it's nothing that a good bath won't sort out. We had a bit of fun this morning but everything has quietened down again – it lets me catch up on a bit of sleep (if Huan would only stop snoring!).

I had a letter from Billy Jones the other day – do you remember him? He was with us down the mine. He sometimes played on the wing. Nice chap. Anyway he is still in Salisbury. I think the others are getting a bit fed up with training. I'm glad that we managed to get out here so soon. I forgot to ask how the play was the other night. I do hope it was funny. We could do with a show out here although we often make up our own entertainment. It's surprising how talented some of the other blokes are. I'm not sure that I have the nerve to stand on the stage.

Anyway, I must close and get on with some work. Take care of yourself and pass on my regards to your mother and father.

With all my affection,
Bryn

CHAPTER TWENTY-FOUR

Bryn woke with his feet in a puddle. The water had started to seep through his socks and was chilling his toes. The aches in his body were telling him that he had fallen asleep in an unnatural position, half-in and half-out of his funk hole; his legs dangling over the fire step into the trench. He knew that he needed to move, but movement brought pain.

He tilted his head forward and could see that the light was fading. He closed his eyes and Cerys appeared in his mind. His thoughts lingered on her face. She was so beautiful, he could see her as if she was standing in front of him. Oh how he wished that he were back at the top of Caergwrle Hill where they first met. A smile appeared on his lips.

'Stand to,' someone muttered along the line.

Corporal Jones was cajoling his men to ready themselves for stand to. He gave Bryn a kick to wake him but got no response. 'Come on Bryn, lad – Fritz is coming. I know you don't want to miss him.'

'Tell him I'm out.'

'You'll be out in a minute alright – out on your ear, so come on, shift your arse and get on the step.'

'Corporal?'

'What?'

'Is there any chance of a cup of tea to go with my early evening call?'

'No there isn't but you can swap your patrol for donkey duties if you want?'

'I don't mind doing the donkey trail if someone else wants to go out on patrol,' Bryn said. Corporal Jones almost slipped on the mud.

'What? What's the matter with you? Not going soft on me are you?'

'No, Corporal. It's just that I'd rather not go out with that Lieutenant Symonds, that's all.'

'Getting choosy now, are you? Well you're going and that's that. You'll be fine. Sergeant Price will lead it out. The lieutenant is just going along for the ride. He'll be fine.'

'You don't know him, Corporal. He's a bad 'un.'

'No, I don't but I do know a rude and insubordinate soldier when I see one. Now get your arse out of that pit and get on the step. I'll not have you disrespecting an officer. Do you hear me?'

*

Bryn was rolling up the kit that he was going to leave in the trench. The last thing he wanted was to come back to a soggy blanket and wet pair of spare socks. He stuffed the kit into a hole he had made in the side of the trench wall.

'What do you think Bryn?' came a voice.

Bryn turned and was faced with a shadow. 'Shit,' he said, almost jumping out of his skin. Staring back was a black statue of John, who had blackened himself up from head to foot. 'What the heck are you doing? You nearly gave me a heart attack, you idiot.'

'Some use you'll be tonight then, hey?'

'You look like a right idiot.'

'I might do but at least Fritz won't see me.'

'Just as long as you keep your mouth shut and your eyes closed I guess. Please tell me you're not going to wear that balaclava.'

'Why not? It's the height of fashion.'

'Well to start with you will be patrolling on your own as the rest of us wouldn't be seen dead with you, although that could be the case if we're not careful, and secondly you won't be able to hear anything.'

'I'm not going to wear it, am I; it's just keeping me warm for now. Are we ready to go or what?'

'As ready as we're ever going to be. What do you reckon about Symonds?'

'There's not a lot he can do is there? Sergeant Price will be with us the whole time and then he'll be gone. The best that we can hope for is that he cops a stray bullet.'

'Hush up. You can't go round saying that, not here.'

'Yeah well, I wouldn't be so quick to drag him in. He can stay out there and rot as far as I'm concerned.'

*

Bryn blew on his fingers and bounced up and down on his toes as he and John waited in the dark for Symonds to appear.

They had been stood outside the dugout for about fifteen minutes, their faces blackened and their bayonets covered in thin pieces of sacking to prevent them shining or banging against the wire pickets. It was a quiet evening although away in the distance there was plenty of activity, which would mask a bit of noise. It was a shame that it was not a bit closer as it would distract the German sentries. At least it was cloudy, which kept the temperature up a little and blocked out the moon. It was as dark as it was ever going to get and the boys were eager to be off. Sergeant Price appeared at their side. For a short, stocky man he could move around the trench with such stealth that the boys were never sure where he was, which made him invaluable on patrols.

'Still no sign of the officer then?'

'Not yet Sergeant,' John replied.

'Oh well, perhaps Lieutenant George is giving him a final briefing.'

'Or maybe he's having second thoughts,' Bryn said.

'Any change to the plan, Sergeant?' John asked.

'No, it should be straightforward. Lieutenant George told me to take him to the wire and sit for a while to see what's occurring. We'll go out the same way we did last time. Out of here and head right. We'll pick up the ditch and follow it along to the willow tree and then head due north until we hit the wire. There was that big hole we dropped into last time. Hopefully it might still be there, or it may not. I reckon about an hour and a half will do it. I want to be back before this cloud cover breaks.'

*

'Good luck old chap,' Lieutenant George said, patting Symonds on the back as they made for the entrance of the dugout.

'I was hoping that there was more in my favour than just luck,' Symonds replied.

'Of course, it's just a figure of speech. You're in safe hands with Sergeant Price. I'll keep a tot of rum and piece of cake for when you get back. My sister's own. The cake that is, not the tot!'

'An incentive if ever I needed one.'

They were plunged into darkness as they stepped into the trench. Symonds stopped and put his hand on the trench wall to steady himself. Stephen stood behind him. 'Just take a moment or two to get your bearings and let your eyes adjust to the light. There's no rush.'

Symonds took a few deep breaths and moved cautiously along the trench, taking care not to fall on the slippery boards. Sergeant Price and the boys were only a few yards away.

'Evening, sir,' Sergeant Price said in a low, hoarse whisper. 'A cracking evening for it.'

Symonds looked up at the sky. 'Marvellous,' he replied.

'Right then, sir, if you're ready, I'll lead off.'

'As ready as I ever will be, Sergeant.'

Sergeant Price patted the sentry to make sure he knew that

they were going out. The sentry checked his watch. As Sergeant Price slid over the lip of the trench John started up the ladder, paused at the top to see where the sergeant had gone and similarly moved onto his belly, paused and then pushed himself up into a crouch and moved forward.

Symonds took his pistol from his holster and turned to the ladder. He took a couple of deep breaths and hauled himself up until his head appeared above the parapet. His eyes widened as he took in the scene. He looked across to see John crouched in front of their own wire. His hands were locked on the ladder. *Move*, he told himself. His hands were trembling as he forced them onto the sandbags that lined the top of the trench. He pulled himself over the top and lay prone for a few moments to steady his breathing. He could just see Sergeant Price and Roberts in front of him, lying down in the mud. They were just lying there. He ran a few paces at a crouch and stopped next to the sergeant.

As Bryn moved to the ladder Lieutenant George grabbed his arm. 'Just keep your eyes and ears open, Tallent. This is not a night for fireworks.'

'Yes sir,' Bryn replied and slid over the top like a lizard hunting its prey.

Bryn loved the feeling of sliding over the top. It was like moving into a parallel world. All of a sudden there was space and he could see around him, as opposed to looking upwards at the sky. It was still quiet apart from a few flares whooshing skyward and falling like failing stars some way off in the distance. He gained his composure and slid forward to the right of John. He tapped him on the ankle three times to let him know that they were all clear of the trench. John passed on the signal to Sergeant Price, who rose and led the party forward at a cautious pace into no-man's land.

They reached the ditch at exactly the spot that Sergeant Price had intended. He was good at his job. He could recognise almost every crater across the hundred and fifty yards that separated them from the Germans. They stopped and lowered themselves to the ground and listened. Sergeant Price was a patient man; he was never rushed into moving before he was ready. They were all lying prone on the ground except Symonds, who had dropped to one knee and was beginning to shift his weight around. He was anxious to get going. Sergeant Price touched Symonds' arm and bent forward to speak to him. 'Might be wise, sir, if you got down; less of a target.'

Symonds turned so that he could whisper back. 'If I had wanted your advice, Sergeant, I would have asked for it. Now let's get moving.'

'It's too soon, sir. We need to listen first.'

'There is nothing there so get moving.'

Sergeant Price turned to look at Bryn and John, who were facing away from him. He paused for a moment and then raised himself. Once he was on one knee he tapped Bryn and John who turned and saw that they were about to move off. They followed the ditch for about fifty yards until they came to the stump of a willow tree, one of many that had lined an irrigation ditch. The trees had been blown away and the ditch had all but been blown in. It was a good reference point for the patrol to know where they were and which way they would be going next. Sergeant Price also knew that it was an obvious landmark and approached it with caution before lying down again to listen. Bryn and John did likewise. Symonds rested against the tree. He closed his eyes and sighed. 'What the fuck am I doing out here?' he said to himself. 'I've had enough of this.' He leaned across to Sergeant Price. 'Get a move on. Now.'

Sergeant Price jumped at the loudness of Symonds' voice, which seemed to boom across the dead space in front of them. 'What are you doing?' he whispered back to Symonds. 'You'll be heard; noise carries at night.'

'I'm well aware of that, Sergeant. Now get a move on so we can get out of this place.'

'We need to wait and listen. It's normal–'

'Listen to me. I don't give a damn what you normally do. I'm the officer here, not you, in case you hadn't noticed, Sergeant. Now get a move on.'

Sergeant Price looked around at Bryn and John, who had turned to listen to the commotion.

'Now, Sergeant!'

Sergeant Price sighed but rolled back onto his stomach; then pushed himself onto his side and then onto one knee. He tapped Bryn and John, who were surprised to be moving so quickly. Sergeant Price had taken about four paces before a hail of bullets ripped through the air. He was too late to react. The first bullet smashed through his shoulder, spinning him around and exposing his back to more bullets that slammed into his side and tore through his left thigh. As he fell his head levelled with the trajectory of the bullets that were screaming through the air and a bullet grazed his head. Bryn and John were just rising as the carnage exploded around them. They immediately dropped and hugged the earth before the horizontal storm of steel traversed across them.

'Shit,' Bryn screamed as his hands clasped his helmet to his head.

Sustained fire was coming from their right as a phosphorous flare shot into the sky, fracturing the cloak of darkness. Bryn instinctively closed one eye to save his night vision. He glanced at John, who was next to him with his head equally close to the ground. As they looked forward they could see Sergeant Price lying in front of them, bullets dancing around him. Mud flailed over their heads but the bullets remained trained on Sergeant Price. John looked to his left and could make out the dip in the ground around the willow tree and the ditch that they had walked along.

'Bryn,' he screamed, 'get in the ditch.'

Bryn looked across and could see where they needed to be. 'Wait. They'll take us out if we move now. Wait until the flares have dropped.'

'If we wait any longer we might not be alive to move.'

'Just hang on a minute.' The silvery flares fell slowly from the blackened sky as a machine gun spluttered from C Company's position. They now had bullets flying from both sides. 'When I shout, start rolling that way.'

As the flares floated to the ground Bryn heard the rush of another shooting upward. 'Now!' he shouted. They had a couple of seconds to spare before the flare reached its height and burst, bathing them in white light again. Without their kit on they were able to roll quickly and managed to get into a dip before the flare burst overhead. A second later bullets bit into the mud a yard to their front. The willow tree started to take the full force of the volley. They slid backwards further into the dip until they could feel the bullets passing over the top of them.

Bryn exhaled and looked across at John, who was smiling from ear to ear. 'How bad was that, boyo?' John laughed.

Bryn looked to his left and saw Symonds cowering in a hollow a yard or two from where Sergeant Price lay motionless. 'What's that bastard doing now? Why is he just lying there?' Bryn said. 'We need to get Sergeant Price into cover. Bloody hell. Here, you take my rifle and I'll make a dash for Sergeant Price when the flares come down. Alright John… John?' Bryn turned to look at his friend. John had stopped smiling. He was starring back at Bryn; his mouth was moving but no sound was coming out. Bryn grabbed his tunic and dragged him close. 'Sorry Bryn,' he managed to say.

'Oh no, no, no! Don't be daft, boyo, you'll be fine. Where have they got you?'

'I guess they got me properly this time.'

'Rubbish. Just hang on.' Bryn felt a warm sticky patch on John's left side. He slid his hand round John's back to find an exit wound. 'It's okay; it's not too bad. The bullet's gone straight through.' Bryn ripped open a field dressing and pressed it hard against the wound as he cradled John in his arms. 'Looks like you've copped a Blighty, you lucky bugger.'

John looked at his friend and smiled. 'At least my feet are warm now.'

Bryn looked down at John's feet. His left ankle had been shot clean through. His foot was grotesquely bent. '*Shit*.'

'Let me guess, they got my feet as well?'

'Only a scratch,' Bryn lied, 'a bit like your arse the last time you were wounded.'

John managed a laugh, which turned into a cough. Bryn laid him on his side whilst he put a dressing on his ankle. 'Right as rain by the morning, you'll see.'

'Don't mention rain, it's bad enough already!' John managed to say as he laid his head back on the sodden earth.

The air was suddenly filled with explosions as the artillery laid a protective barrage between them and the German ambush. Symonds raised his head and looked at Bryn. 'We need to get out of here,' he screamed.

'Yes, sir. You grab Sergeant Price and I'll bring John,' Bryn screamed back.

'They're dead. Just leave them.'

'Hang on,' Bryn screamed back as he dashed the few yards to where Sergeant Price lay. Bryn lay down next to Sergeant Price and turned him over. There was a faint groan. 'He's alive. Give me a hand to get him back into the ditch.'

Bryn heard the click and looked up. Symonds had his pistol pointed at Bryn. '"He's dead", I said.'

Bryn took a moment to make sense of what was happening. 'We can't leave them,' he screamed above the roar. The ground was shaking violently 'We have to get them back.' He glanced at the rounds falling on the German positions. It was too close for comfort. 'If the artillery drops any further it will get us. Just give me a hand.' Bryn went to raise Sergeant Price. 'Come on, sir. They'll both be fine. Let's just get them back. We can sort this out later.'

'I said put him down,' Symonds screamed. His pistol wavered in his hand. Bryn could see that Symonds was losing control. His eyes were bulging as he started to shake. 'We're sorting it out alright, only you won't be there to spoil it this time.'

'What? What are you talking about? Put the gun down and let's get out of here. We don't have to say anything to anyone. Let's just get out of here before we get killed.'

'You're right,' Symonds screamed, 'we don't have to say anything. You won't be there to say anything.' Spittle was flying from Symonds' mouth, as he stood upright in the middle of the killing field. He was oblivious to the shrapnel that was slicing through the air. 'Not this time. You and your bastard friend cost me dear. Not this time, you pathetic idiot. This time it will cost you far more.'

Bryn was on his knees, panting with the effort of getting Sergeant Price into the sitting position. 'You bastard,' he cried. 'You got us into this and now you want to run away and leave them. You won't get away with this. No one is going to listen to you, not when Lieutenant George finds out.'

'Oh God, you are as stupid as you look. You won't be telling Lieutenant George anything, you idiot. I will be happy to report how you panicked when your friend got hit and ran off leaving me and Sergeant Price to get ourselves out, and how Price was shot trying to stop you. They won't miss a cowardly private.'

'It will be my word against yours when I get back, and John's. You can't kill us all,' Bryn screamed.

'You really are stupid, aren't you? No one will be saying anything except me. These two won't be going back and neither will you. You won't be saying anything.' A thin smile spread across Symonds' face as he pointed his pistol at Bryn's chest. 'This will teach you to play rough with me.'

A shot rang out and Symonds' arm was thrown upwards. He was still standing but his expression had changed from rage to uncertainty. He wavered slightly and his pistol fell from his hand. Bryn sprang up to tackle the officer as the world exploded in a blinding flash and heat. Bryn felt himself lifted from the ground and thrown back down with such force that the breath was forced from his body. It was the hardest tackle he had ever experienced. He turned his face in the mud and groaned. Instinctively he tried to stand, but stumbled and fell to his knees. On all fours, he tried to clear his head. He could see John a few yards to his left. He lurched forward and he slid and scrambled into the ditch next to John. He clutched John's head into his chest and dipped his head as earth showered over the pair of them. Bryn spluttered and coughed to clear his mouth of dirt.

As quickly as the first shell had landed and turned no-man's land into an inferno, the last shell brought back the silence and isolation. Everything was quiet except Bryn's frantic breathing. Bryn tried to steady it. 'Are you still with me, boyo?' he whispered. John nodded slightly, his eyes closed and his body limp. 'Shit, what the fuck was all that about? I thought he was going to kill me.'

'I know.'

'He's a bloody lunatic he is. Christ, we need to get out of here.'

'Symonds?'

'I dunno. Still out there somewhere. Chances are the artillery got him – God willing.' Bryn looked over the rim of the ditch but there was no movement. 'Stay here while I sort the sergeant out.'

Bryn checked the sergeant's wounds and put a dressing on his head. There were no signs of life. He dragged the sergeant's body back to the willow tree stump.

'How is he?' John asked.

'I'm not sure,' Bryn said. 'Come on, let's get you back first. I'll come back for him later.'

Bryn managed to get John over his shoulder and he set off along the ditch, following the path they had taken earlier in the night. He rested after what he thought was fifty yards and set John down. Bryn was breathing hard. John's breathing was getting shallower.

'It's not far now. I reckon we are about twenty yards from the wire. We'll do another bound and then I'll find a way in, alright?'

John nodded. 'Water?'

Bryn put his water bottle to John's lips. 'Here you go boyo, not too much, we need to keep moving.'

They set off again at a slightly faster pace. Despite the cold Bryn was sweating and he was struggling for breath. He set John down again and tried to make sense of the ground. He was starting to panic that he might be going around in circles. John's breathing was beginning to labour. 'John! John, listen. I need to go and find a way in, alright? I'm going to leave you for a few minutes but I'll be back as soon as I can. Don't move okay?'

John squeezed Bryn's hand. 'Wait.'

'It's okay, I'll be as quick as I can.'

'No, no. Symonds.'

'It's alright, we'll sort it out.'

'No. Just listen,' John said, gasping for breath. 'I shot him.'

Bryn grasped his friend's hand and smiled. 'At least you hit something for once.'

John laughed and tried to stifle a cough.

'I've got to go. Our secret, eh?' Bryn gave his friend a pat on the shoulder and was gone. He tried to retrace their movements in his head and then worked it out backwards. He kept telling himself to stay calm as he counted out the steps that he was taking. He darted off to his right until he came to the wire. He heaved a small sigh of relief; then turned around and walked back out into no-man's land the way he had just come, counting out the paces as he went. It had been thirty-five paces from the ditch. On the thirty-fourth step he slid forwards into the ditch and worked his way to his left until he found John.

'Hey, it's me. Told you I'd be back. One more push and we'll be back. Hang on in there boyo.'

With John on his back Bryn found his way to the wire again and moved along it until he found a break. He walked forward. He stopped and put John down as they got to the end of the break. Bryn lay down and paused to get his breath. 'B Company,' he called in a low whisper. 'B Company!'

'Who's there?' came the response.

'Two Platoon patrol.' There was silence for a minute.

'That you, Bryn?' came the response.

Bryn almost laughed at the sound of his friend's voice. 'Yes it's me, you lardy arse.'

'Bloody hell boyo, you'd better get in here pretty quick. All kind of shit's gone up.'

'I need a stretcher for John.'

'Shit. Bryn, come on in now. There is a stretcher crew here waiting to go out for John. It'll be quicker.'

'Just send them out now. I'll help them.'

'Bryn! You need to come in now. The platoon commander said so.'

Bryn thought for a moment and tapped John on the shoulder. 'It's alright, boyo – the stretcher boys are coming now. I've got to go in. They'll only be a moment. Hang on in there.'

Bryn dashed the last few yards to the lip of the trench. As he rolled over the lip of the trench the stretcher-bearers were waiting to clamber up the ladder. Bryn sat on the fire step and grabbed the tunic of the first medic. 'Ten yards straight ahead,' he said to them.

'What happened?' Rhys asked. 'Symonds has been in for ages. Shouting about you and John running off.'

'He's alive?'

'Of course he's alive. A bit wounded but very much alive and ranting.'

'That lying bastard is the one that tried to run off. He's trying to stitch us up good and proper.'

There was movement above the trench and one of the stretcher-bearers rolled over the edge. 'Give us a hand lads,' he said as he slid the stretcher over the lip. Hands grabbed the stretcher and lowered it into the relative safety of the trench.

Huan, Rhys and Bryn crowded round the stretcher-bearer. 'How is he?' Huan asked.

'Difficult to tell in this light. We'll get him to the Aid Post and let the doc have a look at him. Looks like he lost a lot of blood though.'

'Just look after him,' Rhys added.

'Move out the way,' Corporal Jones cried as he pushed his way through the group of men who had gathered at the sentry post. 'Right you lot, fuck off if you're gawping. Taylor, get up on sentry. Tallent, get here.'

Lieutenant George came up behind Corporal Jones. 'What happened, Tallent?'

'We were ambushed, sir. I think there was a German patrol the other side of the willow tree. It looked as if they were waiting for us.'

'What happened to Sergeant Price? Where is he?'

'He was leading, sir, and was hit in the first volley and then Roberts was hit. I managed to get Sergeant Price back to the tree but he didn't look good, sir. I'll go back and get him, I know where he is.'

'No you won't. Corporal Jones, get a few men and get out to the willow tree and see if you can find Sergeant Price.'

'Yes, sir!'

'And while you're at it, get me a couple of men to escort Tallent.'

'Sir?'

'You heard me, Corporal. Private Tallent is under arrest.'

Wrexham
May 1915

My Dearest Bryn,

Your letters of the 3rd, 4th and 5th all arrived today.
Imagine my delight to get three letters all on the same day,
although it is horrible to think of you in the trenches again.
It has been raining here and when it does I think of you
even more. Hopefully you have managed to avoid the worst
of the weather. It's wonderful to think that you receive my
letters so soon after I have written them. Hopefully it brings
us closer together, even if it is only in our hearts rather
than miles.

I'm sure that you are not in the least bit interested
in what's going on here; it is nowhere near as exciting as
being in France. I met up with Mary and Bron last
Sunday and we took a stroll out towards Gresford and
then round to Gwersyllt. The village is very quiet without
you and the other men being there. I passed your cottage
but daren't look in case your mam saw me. I know it's silly
as she doesn't know me yet but it felt odd walking past
your house in case she did know. I know I'm being silly.
Hopefully I shall meet her and your da when you come
home. I so long for you to come home. Not too long now I
hope?

Things are bit more difficult at work as ladies are not
buying so many hats. Mrs Evans hasn't said anything but
I know that the business is struggling. I think that she might
have to let one or two of us go. I shan't be sad if it is me. I
have been speaking to some of the girls who are working at

the Infirmary. Some young men are being brought there now so there might be some useful work that I can do - at least it will be helping the war.

Stay safe and well my dear. I will write again tonight.
Yours affectionately,
Cerys

CHAPTER TWENTY-FIVE

The regiment had taken over a small manor on the outskirts of Bois-Grenier. It had once belonged to a wealthy landowner but he and his family, along with their possessions, had departed at the end of 1914. The regiment had maintained the manor as their Regimental Headquarters since they had arrived in the area. The adjutant's office was in the main reception room next to the commanding officer's office, which had once been a small anteroom.

Andrew sat at the head of the room where he could oversee the small headquarters staff as they planned regimental operations. The room was currently empty and slightly eerie. The windows had been blown in many months ago and boarded up with planks of wood. Cloth screens covered the boarded windows to block out the light. On his desk a candle burned low. It had been a long night.

Bryn was stood in between two fusiliers. All three stood to attention, staring ahead. The sound of boots striding along the corridor broke the silence. The doors to the adjutant's office were flung open and the commanding officer strode in. He was a tall and serious-looking man but well respected. He had a reputation for looking after his men. Even at four o'clock in the morning he was immaculately dressed. The adjutant sprang to attention. The commanding officer glanced around the room, taking in the guards and Bryn.

'My office,' he said quietly to the adjutant, who picked up his papers and followed the commanding officer into the anteroom and shut the door. Bryn could hear the murmurs coming through the door. His head hurt. The explosion had given him a slight concussion but he knew he had had worse on the rugby field. He looked down at his uniform. He was covered in mud and his face was still blackened. He pulled the cuff of his sleeve over his hand and started to wipe his face.

'Stand still lad,' his escort said through the side of his mouth.

Bryn could feel his heart starting to race. *I've done nothing wrong,* he said to himself. The commanding officer's doors flew open. The adjutant stared directly at Bryn. 'March the prisoner in.'

Bryn's heart started to pound as he came to attention in front of the commanding officer's desk. The commanding officer looked at him intently. 'Private Tallent, look at me. I want you to tell me what happened on the patrol last night.'

Bryn took a deep breath. 'It was a routine patrol, sir. Sergeant Price was leading, Lieutenant Symonds went second, then Roberts and I was bringing up the rear. We went firm at the first rendezvous but Lieutenant Symonds seemed keen to push on quickly to the second.'

'Why?'

'Sir?'

'Why do you think he was keen to push on to the second rendezvous?'

'I don't know, sir.'

The commanding officer made a note on his pad. Bryn's mind was racing. 'Carry on.'

'Yes, sir. We stopped at the willow tree for a few minutes and as we moved off we were engaged from close range. The Germans had been waiting for us, sir. Sergeant Price was hit and then–'

'How do you know that the Germans had been waiting?'

Bryn thought for a moment, but he was getting flustered. 'Erm... I... I don't know, sir. They were just there.'

'But you don't know that they had deliberately set an ambush.'

'No, sir but–'

'Carry on.'

'Sergeant Price was hit and then Roberts. I managed to get

Roberts into a dip in the ground but Sergeant Price was already down and the artillery started.'

'So you left him?'

'No sir, but the artillery made it impossible to get to him.'

'And where was Lieutenant Symonds at this stage?'

'I'm not sure, sir.'

'And then what?'

Bryn hesitated. 'I'm not really sure, sir. It all got very confusing.'

The commanding officer removed his glasses and placed them carefully on the desk. He leaned back in his chair and looked at Bryn. 'War is confusing, Tallent, but I want you to think very hard and tell me what happened next.'

Bryn's mind was racing. He could feel a trickle of sweat running down his back. 'There were shells coming down all around us. I went forward to see if Sergeant Price was alive. Lieutenant Symonds was there.' Bryn paused to steady his breathing. 'There was an explosion and I didn't see the lieutenant again. I managed to get Sergeant Price back to the willow tree. I'm not sure if he was still alive. Then I carried Roberts back to our own lines. Sir.'

The commanding officer leaned forward in his chair. He looked intently at Bryn, weighing him up. 'How long have you been in my battalion, Tallent?'

'Since March, sir.'

'And before that?'

'Training, sir. I volunteered, sir. Last September, sir.'

'How many patrols have you been on?'

'I don't know, sir. Quite a few.'

The commanding officer glanced at a piece of paper that he was holding in his hand. 'It seems to me that you have been doing quite a few. Why's that, I wonder?'

'I just enjoy going out on patrol, sir.'

'A regular volunteer I see.'

'Yes, sir.'

'But not tonight. Why's that?' Bryn looked at the commanding officer. 'Well? Corporal Jones tells me that you seemed reluctant tonight. Why were you so reluctant?'

'I don't know, sir. I normally go out with Lieutenant George or Sergeant Price. I just didn't want to go out with Lieutenant Symonds, sir.'

'Damn it, man!' the commanding officer shouted. 'Lieutenant Symonds isn't here, Tallent. He is on his way back home with wounds that will probably delay his deployment for some months, so don't you dare stand there and say you don't know. Well?'

'I… I don't know… I think—'

'No, you didn't think, did you Tallent? Well you had better start thinking, and start thinking very carefully. You need to start with the truth because it will come out, Tallent. I have never heard such a pathetic tale. I've got a wounded officer, a soldier who is probably dead by now and a bloody good sergeant still missing, presumed dead, so I am going to ask you again, Tallent: what happened out there?'

Bryn could feel his legs starting to tremble. Beads of sweat were forming on his hairline. 'That's how I remembered it, sir,' he heard himself mumble.' Bryn lowered his head.

'Look at me Tallent,' the commanding officer barked. 'Don't you dare lower your head to the floor when you are concocting the biggest lie I have ever heard.'

Bryn's head snapped up.

'How dare you suggest that an officer would run away just to cover your mistakes? Have you no shame, no self-respect? You stand there and tell me a load of nonsense and expect me to believe it? Well, I've got news for you, Tallent. I already have Lieutenant Symonds' account of what happened, which differs wildly from your account. He suggests that you were jumpy from the start and had to be restrained by Sergeant Price. He suggests that during this commotion the enemy were alerted by your indiscipline, which is what caused them to open fire, probably killing Sergeant Price and wounding Roberts.'

'That's not true,' Bryn pleaded.

'Be quiet, I haven't finished,' the commanding officer shouted. 'In a brave effort to control you, Lieutenant Symonds states that he threatened to shoot you. Is that true?

'Yes sir… but–'

'And then you were both blown apart by the artillery. Is that bit true?'

'Yes, sir.'

'Lieutenant Symonds was wounded during that attack. Did you try to help him?'

'No, sir. I couldn't find him, sir.'

'Lieutenant Symonds then took what I believe to have been the most sensible course of action, considering your outburst, and made his way back to his own lines to report the incident and to get help. What do you make of that, Tallent?'

'It's not true, sir.'

'Something is definitely not true, Tallent. Unless Sergeant Price or Roberts are able to corroborate your story, which seems pretty unlikely, then you are in a great deal of bother. It seems to me that you were jumpy before you even left the trench and I have no reason to doubt Lieutenant Symonds.'

The commanding officer paused and looked at the file in front of him and shook his head.

'It seems that we took quite a chance on you, Tallent. You came to the battalion with excellent references and recommendations. It seems to me that they were misplaced. I thought that it might have worked but clearly I was wrong. You can't turn a civilian into soldier overnight and I take responsibility for accepting you in the first place. However, your actions last night were unbelievable and deplorable and I will not have this kind of ill discipline in my battalion. There is only option: you will be court-martialled and I should warn you to expect the severest of sentences.' The commanding officer slammed the file shut. 'Get him out of my sight.'

Wrexham
May 1915

My Dearest Bryn,

We have had another very quiet day. We only had five customers and only one of those bought anything. Mrs Evans spent most of the afternoon sighing. I don't think it will be long now before she says something. I spoke to Martha about it on the way home and she is very worried as she was the last one that Mrs Evans took on. Obviously she thinks that she will be the first to go. I told here that things would work out for the best - what else could I say?

I am sat at home now with my mam, who is sat by the fire knitting. I hope you don't mind but I told her about us. She is looking forward to meeting you. Da has gone out to a meeting at the town hall. No doubt he will stop by the Prince of Wales on the way home - just to catch up on the news, as he says. So I have you in my thoughts, all to myself. It is difficult to think of what you are doing this evening. It makes me shudder to think what you might be doing but I know that you will be careful. I spoke to Mary the other day who said that Rhys was looking after you. I'm sure that will make you laugh. I'm sure that you are all looking after each other. I will send this note with an ounce of Mr Parmenster's special mints. I don't know where he gets them from but they should keep you warm.

I think about you everyday. I hope my letters mean as much to you as yours do to me. I have not received one from you for the past five days – I'm sure you are busy. I hope there will be a letter tomorrow.

Yours affectionately,
Cerys

CHAPTER TWENTY-SIX

Bryn's head snapped up the moment he heard the key turn in the lock. His neck was stiff and he felt a bit of saliva at the corner of his mouth. He wasn't sure how long he had been dozing on the window ledge. He swung his legs down and stood to attention as the military police corporal set a tray of food on the table. There were two chairs, not that Bryn was expecting any company. His bed, unused, was on the far wall. Three blankets, more than he had ever had in the trenches, were still neatly folded on the end of the bed.

'Is there any news yet, Corporal?' Bryn asked.

'No.'

'Is anyone coming to see me?'

'Dunno.'

'Do you know how long they are going to keep me here?

'No.'

'Do you know anything?' Bryn hadn't meant it to sound sarcastic but his exasperation made his voice lift slightly. The corporal took a couple of paces forward and stood in front of him, so close that Bryn could smell his breath.

'Yes, I do,' the corporal said. 'I know that you are a filthy piece of shit.' Spittle rasped from his mouth. 'A lazy slithering coward who didn't give a shit about his mates, a selfish coward who left his mate to die, a worthless maggot who very shortly will be following the other lying bastards who tried to run away. You will be a pathetic, crying baby who we will have to drag to a post, blindfold and shoot like a common criminal. That's what I fucking know, so I suggest that you eat your lunch because you won't be getting many more.'

Bryn's head almost exploded. He had never run and never left his mates. 'Well then, you're wrong. I never ran and I never left my mates. That officer has set me up and I'll prove it,' Bryn said.

'Really, you reckon, do you? Well I reckon you'll be in a grave before the week's out. So I suggest that you shut the fuck up if you know what's best for you.' As he turned towards the door he flipped the plate on the table, showering Bryn's lunch onto the floor. 'And that had better be eaten by the time I come back.'

*

Bryn didn't even bother to look up when the door opened. He was staring out of the window, still lost in his thoughts. He would be branded a coward. What would his mam and da think? They would be mortified. The village would shun them. What would Cerys think? He couldn't even bear to think about that. Tears pricked the corners of his eyes.

'Alright Bryn?' came a voice that he knew. A Welsh voice, a friendly voice. Bryn looked up to see Rhys standing in the doorway. A smile returned to Bryn's face. 'Are you going to invite us in or do we have to stand here all afternoon?'

'Us?'

Huan's head appeared around the door. 'Hello, boyo. Still here then?'

'What do you think, you idiot? Get in here.'

'How the heck did you get here?'

'Lieutenant George let us have a pass and sorted out a ride for us. Done his best for us, he did. He's a good officer, you know.'

'He's not that good otherwise I wouldn't be in here, would I?'

'You can't blame him for that Bryn, it wasn't his fault,' Rhys said. 'That bastard Symonds had it in for us, simple as that.'

'What about John? Have you heard anything?'

Rhys and Huan looked at each other and shook their heads. 'I spoke to one of the bearers who took him down the line,' Huan said, 'and he said that he was still alive when they got him to the clearing station but that he had some pretty serious wounds. We haven't heard anything since then so there is still hope.'

'Sergeant Price?'

'Corporal Jones brought him in about an hour after you were taken away. He didn't look good at all. He was unconscious when they took him down the line. I don't think he was going to make it,' Huan replied.

'Listen Bryn,' Rhys said, 'there are a lot of stories going about at the moment about what happened. We need to put them straight you know.'

Bryn nodded and sighed. 'It's quite simple really. From the moment we went out he was jumpy. Sergeant Price tried to keep him calm but he was just losing it. We got to the willow tree and all hell opened up. Sergeant Price got hit and then John. Next minute the guns opened up and well, you know how that is.' Rhys and Huan just nodded. 'I sorted out John and then went to get Sergeant Price. As I turned around Symonds had his revolver on me and was ranting about how we had screwed him over back in Salisbury and that he was going kill me.'

'What was he going to do about Sergeant Price and John?' Huan asked.

'They weren't going to make it back either.'

'What a bastard,' Rhys said.

'Anyway, next minute we're flung in opposite directions and I didn't see him again. And I guess you know the rest.'

'Unfortunately,' Huan said, 'Symonds got back before you – mind you he was lucky not to get shot. I had just come on stag so that we would both be there when you were due back in and he came stumbling through the wire shouting the odds. I wish I had shot him now.'

'John shot him,' Bryn said.

Huan and Rhys looked at him. 'What?'

'John shot him just before we were hit by the guns. That's why he didn't shoot me. John saved my life.'

'Bloody hell,' Rhys said.

'He missed!' Huan said. Bryn couldn't help but laugh.

'Have you told anyone this?' Rhys asked.

Bryn shook his head. 'Can't really, can I? There's point in us both being damned. Anyway, what happened when Symonds got back?'

Huan thought for a moment. 'Oh, he dropped into the trench clutching his arm, shouting that he had been shot. Within a couple of minutes the rest of the section was up and then Lieutenant George turned up, by which time Smithy had got a bandage on his arm. He told me that it was only a scratch. Symonds then gets himself up and tells Lieutenant George that he was going back for Sergeant Price. He was calling for volunteers until Lieutenant George stopped him.'

Huan paused for a moment and looked at Bryn.

'And then he said that you had started gobbing off that they were lost and tried to make your own way back, but that Sergeant Price grabbed you. Then all hell opened up and Price was killed and John was hit, and you and Symonds were in a shell hole together but you lost it and tried to run. Sorry!'

They sat in silence for a few minutes. 'Well I reckon that's me well and truly buried then,' Bryn said as he put his head in his hands.

Rhys broke the silence. 'What's going to happen now?'

'They're going to court-martial me, that's what. An officer came to see me earlier. He said the general would be convening a court martial. Apparently it won't take long, he said, if that was meant to make me feel better. He was a nice enough officer but he made it quite clear that it was pretty serious.'

'It might not be so bad,' Huan suggested. 'The truth will come out and then Symonds will be well and truly for it.'

'I'm not so sure. Without John and Sergeant Price to give their account it's Symonds' word against mine.'

'Once you tell them about what happened in training they'll have to believe you.'

'What, you think I haven't thought about it? Nothing was ever proved, was it? We never told anyone who it was we saw that night, and he wasn't caught doing anything. As far as anyone is concerned it never happened. It will just look like a pretty desperate excuse.'

'You're buggered then,' Huan said before he realised what he had said.

'Well thank you very much for that.'

'You're such an idiot,' Rhys chided.

'I didn't mean it like that. I'm sure it will be fine.'

'Do you have good news?' Bryn asked.

Rhys looked at Huan, who shrugged. 'Corporal Jones has taken over as the platoon sergeant.'

'Brilliant,' Bryn said. 'I was thinking more along the lines of any letters?'

Rhys and Huan stayed for about another hour but eventually, and rather reluctantly, they had to leave. They promised to tell Lieutenant George what Bryn had told them and they promised to find out what they could about John and Sergeant Price. It seemed to Bryn that they were the only ones now who could support his story. Without them it was his word against Symonds' and he was starting to realise that the truth didn't really seem to matter. Rhys and Huan said they would visit as soon as they could but they didn't know when as they were going back into the trenches. Bryn wished with all his heart that he could be going with them. Despite the mud and the cold and the incessant noise there was nowhere he would rather be.

The door opened again a few minutes after his friends had left. Bryn looked up, hoping they had come back, but the corporal was standing in the doorway with a huge smug grin on his face.

'Friends of yours were they?'

Bryn stood up. 'Yes, Corporal.'

'Just come from the trenches by the look of them. I thought I had better check their passes, just in case they were deserters as well.'

Bryn looked at the corporal. 'What would you know about the trenches? Judging by your fat belly and smart uniform this is as far forward as you've ever been. I bet that tunic has never seen a speck of mud, let alone the blood or brains of your mates splattered all over your face. Why don't you try doing something useful—'

The corporal's fist smashed into Bryn's face, sending him sprawling across the floor. As he turned over Bryn felt blood beginning to trickle down his lip. Bryn smiled at the corporal, who was frothing and snorting like a rampant bull.

'Thought so,' was all Bryn said before a rain of kicks caught him in the belly, legs and chest. The corporal was quickly out of breath and resorted to throwing a plate of bully beef and hard biscuits over him before stamping out of the room and slamming the door so hard that the windows rattled in their frames.

France
May 1915

My Dearest Cerys,

It is difficult to know where to begin without worrying you too much. As you know, John was badly wounded while we were out on patrol some days ago. I say 'we' because I was with him when he was hit. Do you remember that 'officer' that we encountered in Salisbury that night that we went out with Rhys and Mary – the bad one? He turned up here a few days ago and recognised us. He confronted us and said that he was going to sort us out. Well, we were right about him: he is a coward but unfortunately he has got me into a bit of bother. John and I went out on patrol with him and Sergeant Price and he bodged it. Because of him we were seen by the Hun and Sergeant Price was killed and John was hit. I tried to get the officer to help me get John and the sergeant back to our lines but he threatened to shoot me and ran away. By the time I got back with John he had already concocted a story that has dropped me right in it.

I regret to tell you that I am about to be court-martialled for cowardice and disobeying an officer (him!). I must tell you that nothing could be further from then truth and I am confident that the trial will vindicate me. As soon as John gives his evidence it will be the officer's word against ours and our officer (the one that I have told you about) is going to defend me so it should all be fine.

I don't want you to worry. If you do want to worry then give a thought for John. He wasn't too bad when I got him back to the trench. The medic said that he would have a

Blighty, the lucky chap. He'll be back home in no time, you'll see. You will be able to visit him and he can tell you all about what we are doing. I wish I could tell you myself but at least you will get it from the horse's mouth.

I'm fine so need to worry about me. In fact I am under arrest so I am quite some miles from the front. They are treating me well and I get three meals a day, which I can't complain about, and at least I don't get wet! My trial is tomorrow so I should be back with the boys by tomorrow night. I will write and tell you what happened as soon as I can but please don't worry.

With all my love,
Bryn

CHAPTER TWENTY-SEVEN

Two officers stood in a small anteroom on the ground floor of the chateau that had been Bryn's prison for the past week. Three officers had been 'invited' by the divisional commander to form a court martial board to try Private Tallent, 2nd Battalion, the Royal Welsh Fusiliers.

On any other occasion they would have welcomed a few days away from the front line; a few days to wander around the cobbled streets taking in the sights and smells of normality. Time to have a decent dinner and a bottle of wine, time to sit with a coffee and a smoke, time to lie on a feather bed. This was not one of those times. It was not a duty that any of them relished; all three of them would rather have remained at the front than try a soldier for capital offences.

'Have you been brought back up to strength yet, Colonel?' asked the younger officer, who didn't take his eyes off the coffee that he was stirring. He was relishing the simple pleasure of drinking coffee out of a proper cup and that didn't taste of petrol. The soft chairs and century-old paintings were easily overshadowed by a hot cup of coffee.

'We should be so lucky,' Lieutenant Colonel Thackeray replied. 'We lost a lot of boys at Gheluvelt last year and replacing that amount of experience has been difficult but we are getting there. The new boys are eager; thankfully most of them are ex-regulars although they seem to have forgotten more than they've remembered. Still, they're better than nothing.'

'I heard that this fellow was one of the new army. Seems a bit odd to have them here so soon. I thought that we weren't going to see these chaps until the end of the year.'

'Yes, well,' the colonel replied, 'that's really why I'm here. They wanted a president who was a bit more senior so to speak; to make sure that matters are conducted properly. Just my luck I suppose. There is a lot of interest in this case for the very reason that he is one of the new breed. The high command want to make sure that justice is done properly and if necessary, the right example is sent out to all the other would-be volunteer soldiers. Not that any of that presupposes his guilt, you understand.'

There was a sharp knock on the door and a clerk entered. 'Lieutenant Gooding, sir.'

'Ah, good. Then we are gathered.'

A young lieutenant almost fell through the door and came to attention. 'Good morning, sir. Lieutenant Anthony Gooding, sir.' He swung up a salute that any self-respecting regimental sergeant major would have been proud of.

Lieutenant Colonel Thackeray extended his hand. 'Marvellous. Julian Thackeray; thank you for coming. And this is Captain Samuel Gordon.' The formalities over, Thackeray suggested that they take full advantage of the coffee that they had been offered along with real milk and sugar.

'Milk and sugar, a real treat. You know, I think that they are trying to butter us up a bit,' Thackeray said as he reached for a second biscuit. 'Now, before we get started let me just give you a bit of background to make sure that we know what we are doing, or at least give the poor blighter some confidence that we know what we are doing.' He gave a rather forced laugh. It wasn't that he thought the proceedings to be a laughing matter. Thackeray's smile faded. 'Let me rephrase that. It's not enough to look right, it has to *be* right. Right for him, right for us, right for the soldiers in his unit and for the army as a whole. It's got to be right for everyone concerned. So you will need to concentrate as much today as you would if you were leading your troops towards the Hun. If you don't understand something then it is beholden upon you to ask. As well as judging this fellow on the evidence and deciding upon his guilt, my job is also to see that justice is carried out fairly and correctly. And I mean to do just that. The lad has been given a defending officer who will provide him with advice, so he will get a fair crack at the whip.'

'Will he be shot, sir?' Gooding asked as he stared into his cup of coffee.

'Whether he is shot or not, is not our concern. Someone else will decide his eventual fate. Our job is to ascertain his guilt or innocence and make a recommendation on sentence, that's all. I want you to put any thoughts of his execution out of your minds and concentrate on the here and now.'

He looked in turn to Gooding, who nodded slowly, and then to Gordon, whom he was relieved to see looking a lot less nervous than his junior colleague.

*

The tick of the clock that hung above the president's chair at the end of the room was the only audible sound that resonated around the room. The large dials moved seamlessly from one minute to the next in perpetual motion. Bryn had been seated at the wooden table for the best part of half an hour. In front of him were a piece of paper and a pencil. His only companion was a royal military policeman who was stood in front of the door through which they had entered.

Bryn guessed that the court martial had been set up in what had been the main dining room of the chateau. The walls were panelled in dark brown wood from floor to ceiling. Bryn imagined that this was where the owner would have hosted parties, with ladies and gentlemen dancing in their fine clothes. Funny, he thought, that a place where there had been such pleasure was now being used for a far more serious matter.

There was an empty chair next to Bryn. Adjacent to his table but separated by a yard was another identical table with a single chair. The table was piled with red manuals and a couple of blue folders. At the front of the room was a large bench with three chairs behind it. The bench was bare except for a few books and a bit of stationery, not unlike his own table. The full-length windows to his left had been sandbagged halfway up so he couldn't see out into the gardens. The only view was the bright blue sky.

Footsteps echoed on the tiled floor outside the door to the dining room. The door opened abruptly, hitting the policeman in the back and knocking him forward.

'Ruddy stupid place to stand,' a captain said as he pushed open the door.

'Sorry, sir,' replied the military policeman as he braced up to salute the captain. 'I was guarding the door, sir. Just in case the accused made a run for it, sir.'

The officer had his arms full of red manuals and a couple of folders. He looked at Bryn, who quickly span around and faced his front. 'I take it that you are Tallent?' the officer said as he placed his books on the table.

'Yes, sir,' Bryn replied.

'Well perhaps you had better start by standing up when an officer addresses you, or do they not have any standards in your regiment?'

Bryn scrambled to his feet, almost knocking over his chair. He loomed high over the officer, who was short with a pinched-out face and a severely manicured moustache that most officers maintained in accordance with King's regulations. The officer drew out his chair and sat down next to Bryn. The captain laid his cap on the desk and picked up a brown file. He made a deliberate show of carefully untying the documents, as if they were some sort of precious gift, and began reading the contents. He skimmed the pages, snorting every now and again, and shook his head.

'Sit down, Tallent. I am Captain Burgess and I have been appointed as your defending officer, although I'm not entirely sure what I am meant to defend. Not exactly convincing evidence is it?'

'Where's Lieutenant George, sir? I thought he was going to defend me?'

'He was, Tallent, but he has been called as a witness for the prosecution, which is why they have appointed me to assist you. I think it goes without saying that you are up against it, Tallent. You are aware, I take it, that these are very serious charges. Disobeying a lawful command by an officer in the face of the enemy, threatening an officer, striking an officer, cowardice... no need to go on, I suppose?'

He paused and threw the papers back onto the table. He took a handkerchief from his pocket and cleaned the lenses of his glasses, holding them up to the light to check for smears.

'The evidence is quite damning; Lieutenant Symonds' statement is clear and unless you have any evidence to the contrary or witnesses who can testify on your behalf then it is your word against his. My advice is to plead guilty. The best that I can do for you, although goodness knows why, is to try to put together some form of mitigation.'

'But I am not guilty, sir.'

'I'm quite sure that you think you're not, Tallent, but the fact remains that you do not have a case. You need to understand that the board could impose a death sentence in this case. Your only hope is to plead for mercy.'

'Sir, I can't admit to something that I didn't do. My mam always told me—'

The captain snorted. 'Yes, but your mother's not here, is she, and I don't suppose she would be particularly proud of you at this moment, would she? So why don't you listen to me and save your sanctimonious speeches for the board?'

The door opened and another captain entered the courtroom. He looked at Captain Burgess and strode across the room towards him, his hand extended.

'Good morning. Hargreaves, Peter Hargreaves, prosecuting counsel,' he said, introducing himself to Burgess.

'Bertie Burgess, defending, for what it's worth, or at least he's worth,' he added, nodding to Bryn.

'Well, good luck old chap.'

'Thanks, same to you.'

The door at the front of the room opened and a clerk appeared, which was the signal for those present to rise. As the members of the board filed through the door the corporal who had been standing at the rear of the court bellowed at the accused. 'Accused! Accused 'shun!'

Bryn stood to attention, his eyes fixed on the clock. It was ten o'clock. The president stood behind his chair. Captain Gordon moved behind him so that he sat on the president's right-hand side. Lieutenant Gooding was last to take his seat on the left.

Lieutenant Colonel Thackeray looked around the courtroom to satisfy himself that everything was at it should be. 'Please sit down,' he said.

The members and the officers were seated. Bryn stared at each of the members in turn as if he was trying to read their thoughts. 'Private Tallent, my name is Lieutenant Colonel Julian Thackeray. I am the president of this court martial board, which has been convened on the direction of Major General Kier, General Officer Commanding 6th Division. On my right is Captain Samuel Gordon, he is the senior member, and on my left is Lieutenant Simon Gooding, the junior member. Do you have any objection to being tried by myself or either of the other two officers whom I have just introduced?'

Captain Burgess leaned towards Bryn. 'No you don't,' he whispered.

Bryn stood up. 'No, sir.'

'Thank you. There is no need for you to stand up every time you speak. Remain seated unless you are otherwise instructed.'

Bryn sat down and chanced a glance at his defending officer, who responded with an exasperated sigh.

'Thank you Captain Hargreaves,' the president said, looking towards the prosecuting officer.

Peter Hargreaves stood up, pulled down on the tails of his service dress and adjusted his Sam Browne belt. His uniform had fitted him perfectly when he had bought it but as a staff officer in the Divisional Headquarters he had never experienced the deprivations that came from serving at the front. His buttons were under a serious amount of pressure.

'Thank you, sir,' he replied. 'Five-One-Six-Zero, Private Bryn William Tallent, Second Battalion, the Welsh Fusiliers, you are charged with three offences under the Army Act 1881 in that you did on 11th May 1915 at Bois-Grenier strike or use or offer violence to Lieutenant Charles Symonds, an officer of the same regiment, whilst he was in the execution of his office, and secondly under Section 4 (7) at the same time and date misbehaved before the enemy in such a manner as to show cowardice, such that on conviction by court martial be liable to suffer death, or such less punishment as is in this Act mentioned. And thirdly under Section 9 (1) disobeyed, in such a manner as to show a wilful defiance of authority, a lawful command given personally by Lieutenant Symonds, a superior officer, in the execution of his office.'

Captain Hargreaves looked across at Captain Burgess with the smugness of a petulant child.

'Thank you, Captain Hargreaves. Private Tallent,' Thackeray said, addressing Bryn directly, 'given the seriousness of these accusations I will explain these charges to you again in a slightly less formal manner. I will then ask you if you understand the charges. If you don't understand the charges then you must say so.'

Lieutenant Colonel Thackeray summarised each of the charges, adding where applicable that if found guilty the accused could be sentenced to death. He was thorough and took his time, trying as best he could to see a reaction in Bryn's manner that might reflect his attitude. Finally he looked directly at Bryn and asked him if he understood the charges.

'Yes sir,' Bryn replied. Thackeray was looking intently at Bryn.

Satisfied that the accused understood the charges he made a note on the paperwork that lay on the desk in front of him.

'Private Tallent, as these charges carry the death penalty I am required to enter a plea of not guilty. Do you understand?'

'Yes sir.' Bryn looked at the clock. It was eight minutes past ten o'clock.

'Thank you, Captain Hargreaves. Your evidence if you please.'

Peter Hargreaves rose and readjusted his Sam Browne belt again. He made a mental note to have his batman adjust the buttons on his tunic and the belt. 'Sir, gentlemen,' he said, addressing himself to the board members. 'I will submit that this case is straightforward and indeed a poor reflection on the decision to deploy volunteer soldiers who have, perhaps, not had the time and benefit of an established career to–'.

'Captain Hargreaves,' Lieutenant Colonel Thackeray said, 'whatever your motives are for voicing your opinions I will not tolerate them in my court, is that clear? I have asked you for the evidence and that is what I expect. Do you wish to proceed?'

'My apologies, sir. The evidence will prove that Private Tallent was detailed to conduct a patrol in an area between the front of his own company lines and the front line of the enemy–'

'I take it that you are referring to no-man's land?' Thackeray asked.

'Yes, sir.'

'Well then say so, Captain Hargreaves. We do not all have the luxury of your staff training. We are simple soldiers that sit before you and so is the accused. I would prefer it if you would use language that we all understand.'

'As you say, sir. Private Tallent was ordered to accompany Lieutenant Symonds on a patrol so that the aforementioned officer, who was on an attachment to the Second Battalion, the Royal Welsh Fusiliers, could gain some experience of patrolling in front of the enemy. Also in the patrol were Sergeant Price and Private Roberts, also of the same battalion.

'The evidence will conclude that when the patrol came under enemy fire, Sergeant Price received wounds to which he would eventually succumb. As the firefight continued Private Roberts was also seriously wounded. At that point Lieutenant Symonds ordered Private Tallent to assist him in recovering Private Roberts back to their own lines. Private Tallent refused to obey the order and threatened to shoot Lieutenant Symonds.

'Fearing for the safety of Private Roberts, who by this point was delirious and crying out uncontrollably, thereby drawing fire to their position, Lieutenant Symonds aimed his pistol at Private Tallent and ordered him to help. It was at this point that both men were blown over by an artillery shell. When Lieutenant Symonds regained his composure he saw Private Tallent running away from his position, towards the German lines. Lieutenant Symonds tried, as he might, to lift Private Roberts but was unable to do so due to his own wounds so he made his way back to his own lines to get help.'

Captain Hargreaves closed the blue folder and laid it on the desk.

'Thank you, Captain Hargreaves. Call your first witness.'

Hargreaves turned and nodded to the military policeman who had been stood motionless at the back of the courtroom throughout the proceedings. He sprang to attention and went outside.

The witness marched in and came silently to attention in between in the prosecution and defence tables. Bryn clenched his fists on the table.

'State your name please?' Captain Gordon asked.

'Second Lieutenant Charles Symonds, sir,' he replied with a sly smile and a note of arrogance. Bryn turned and looked directly at the witness. His fists were so tightly clenched that his knuckles were white. Symonds remained focussed on the president of the board. Captain Gordon asked Symonds to take the oath, which Bryn thought laughable.

'Lieutenant Symonds,' Lieutenant Colonel Thackeray said, 'it is customary in this court that witnesses stand during their evidence but given your recent wounds you may sit down if you wish.'

'Thank you, sir. That would be very welcome.' Symonds glanced across at Bryn as he took his seat. Bryn was sure that a smile had creased his lips.

'Captain Hargreaves. When you are ready please.'

'Thank you, sir. Lieutenant Symonds, on the 11th May 1915 were you ordered to lead a patrol into the area known as no-man's land?'

'Actually sir, I would have very much liked to have led the patrol; indeed, looking back on events it would have been better had I done so. However, Lieutenant George was the platoon commander to whom I was attached and it was his decision that his sergeant should lead the patrol.'

'Did Lieutenant George explain to you why he made that decision?' Captain Hargreaves prompted.

'I can only assume that he made this decision for the best of reasons. Sergeant Price was, I believe, very experienced and knew the area well. As you will be aware it was my first patrol in the area.'

'Thank you, Lieutenant Symonds. Please continue.'

'I would have been only too pleased to relieve Sergeant Price of the burden of command for a short while at least. I know that he had been in the thick of things for some months. However, I was unfamiliar with the ground and the procedures so I admit that I did not challenge Lieutenant George's decision. With hindsight, perhaps I should have done.'

'Indeed, Lieutenant, how very courageous of you. Perhaps you would tell the court, in your own words, what happened on that night.'

'Certainly, sir. Lieutenant George briefed the patrol – that is to say, myself, Sergeant Price, Private Roberts and the accused, in the afternoon of the day in question. The briefing was very thorough and I was confident that I would be able to lead the patrol safely. However, after the briefing Lieutenant George suggested that I should take my lead from Sergeant Price. I was of course delighted to have someone of his experience to show me the ropes. It was after all my first patrol. I also got the impression that he wanted someone who knew Private Roberts and the accused who were to accompany us, as a sort of... mentor. I understand that they were, themselves, quite inexperienced.'

'Did you know either of the two privates when you met them?'

'No, but I have since learned that they were under training in the same camp as myself, which surprised me somewhat as most if, not all, of their cohort are still in training. I can't quite understand why they were allowed to deploy to France having received only the rudiments of training.' Symonds held his bandaged arm as he shuffled in his seat and gave a slight wince.

'Please continue, if you are able.'

'Of course, sir. Sergeant Price and I briefed the patrol and we set off about an hour after stand to. I regret that I cannot remember the exact time. I confess to being slightly nervous and rather excited. Anyway, we left the trench via the extreme left-hand sentry position and moved into no-man's land. It was only about one hundred and fifty yards between the two front lines and it was my intention to leave from the right of the platoon position and to make our way into the centre of the location, watch and learn for a couple of hours and then return via the same sentry position.

'The patrol was going very well and we settled into a shell hole next to the stump of a willow tree. My intention was that we should watch and wait for a little while before moving into the centre of no-man's land. We hadn't been there for more than a few minutes when I started to get the impression that Private Tallent was becoming agitated. He kept fidgeting, moving position, and he was moving his rifle in his hands. I believe Sergeant Price spoke to him and then he settled for a little while. Sergeant Price then suggested to me that we should move forward on account of Tallent's unease. I did recommend that we stayed for a few more minutes but I'm ashamed to say that I bowed to the sergeant's experience.

'You say "ashamed", Lieutenant. Why so?'

'Whilst we were in the holding position I thought that I had heard something but I wasn't sure, which is why I suggested that we wait for a few minutes. Were it not for my lack of experience I am sure that I would have been more insistent with the sergeant. As I said at the beginning of my evidence, this is why I had wished that I had been leading the patrol; I would almost certainly have waited.'

'Please continue,' Hargreaves urged as he swept a glance across the members of the board to ensure that the point had been registered.

'As we stood up I immediately saw exactly what I thought I had seen. A German patrol were less than fifteen yards away and we were immediately engaged.'

Symonds paused and poured a glass of water from the carafe on the table.

'Lieutenant Symonds, I appreciate that this is difficult. Would you like a moment or two or are you happy to continue?' Thackeray asked.

'Indeed I will continue, sir. Merely a dry throat, sir, I do apologise.'

'No need to apologise. In your own time.'

Symonds gave the president another of his wry smiles and glanced towards Bryn who was staring directly ahead. He followed Bryn's gaze, which seemed to end at the clock above the president's head. It was twenty minutes past ten o'clock.

'As I was saying, sir, the patrol was moving from our left to our right as I was looking at them.'

'In your opinion, would they have seen you before you moved off?' Hargreaves asked. Symonds looked at the prosecutor and considered his response.

'I don't believe that they had seen us and if we had been more patient, we could have watched them pass without incident. From my limited experience, of course.'

272

'And how many enemy were in the patrol, Lieutenant Symonds?'

'It is difficult to be sure but I would say about four or five men.'

'So a reconnaissance patrol, not unlike your own patrol?'

'Yes, I would say so.'

'So there was no need or intention of engaging with the enemy that evening?'

'No, we were not equipped for a major engagement. The brief was quite clear: watch, listen and report. Had it not been for Tallent's unease we would have remained in that position for several minutes longer and completed what was an important reconnaissance patrol. Anyway, I was facing the enemy, Sergeant Price was on my right, Tallent to my rear and Roberts on my left.'

Lieutenant Colonel Thackeray nodded as if to acknowledge that the procedure was correct.

'As soon as the enemy saw us and opened fire we immediately went to ground and returned fire. I realised almost immediately that Sergeant Price had been hit very badly. We managed to get back into the hollow by the tree stump, all except Sergeant Price who had fallen a few yards away from the hollow. He wasn't moving and appeared to be dead. Tallent and Roberts were to my left. Unfortunately, we were not in the most defendable of locations. But Roberts and I returned fire.'

'What was Tallent doing?'

'Nothing. Absolutely nothing I regret to say. He seemed to be squirming further down into the hollow. I looked across at Roberts and told him that on the count of three that he was to fire on the enemy, give them everything that we had so that I could grab Sergeant Price. I gave Roberts a count of three and I hurled myself over the ridge and made a grab for Sergeant Price but he was dead as far as I could make out.

'Then Roberts cried out, having been wounded. I rolled back into the hollow and quickly checked him. It was clear that he was badly wounded but maybe not life-threatening, if we could get him out fairly quickly. I screamed at Tallent to help but he wouldn't. I regret to say that I had to aim my pistol at him. It is not something I had ever imagined having to do. After that my recollection is slightly hazy. There was a huge explosion and I must have been knocked unconscious. When I came to, Tallent was running away. The enemy patrol had retreated so I tried to lift Roberts but he was heavy. I managed to drag him as far as I could but when I got to our wire I didn't have the strength to lift him; I had to leave him there. I can assure you, sir, that I tried my best. I'm only sorry that it wasn't good enough. Who knows whether he would be alive today if I had managed to carry him a little quicker?'

'There is no need for self-recrimination here, Lieutenant Symonds. I have no doubt that you did what you thought best at the time. We are not here to judge your actions.'

'Thank you, sir.'

'I think that we have heard quite enough, Captain Hargreaves, unless you have any other evidence from this witness?'

'No, sir. Thank you, Lieutenant Symonds. That will be all for now but please remain seated for the moment.'

Lieutenant Colonel Thackeray addressed Bryn. 'Private Tallent, do you wish to ask Lieutenant Symonds any questions regarding the evidence that he has just given?'

Bryn's looked at his defending officer, who shook his head. 'No thank you, sir.'

'Private Tallent, are you quite sure? This is your opportunity to ask him any questions that might show your actions or the sequence of events of that night in a different light. Something, perhaps, that Lieutenant Symonds might have misinterpreted. You will of course have an opportunity to put forward your side of the story in due course.'

Bryn looked to his defending officer again. 'Sir?'

Burgess leaned across and whispered to Bryn. 'Not in your best interests. You can't challenge him directly, you can only ask questions of fact. Do you have any questions of fact that you would like to ask?

'I don't know, sir.'

'Well then.'

Bryn looked back to the president. 'No thank you, sir.'

Thackeray conferred with his members, asking each of them in turn if they wished to pose any questions of their own.

Captain Gordon shook his head.

'No, sir,' Lieutenant Gooding replied.

'Very well. Thank you Lieutenant Symonds. If your account is to be believed you acted selflessly and bravely under some very difficult circumstances, for which you should be commended. I am sure that you will be a credit to your regiment when you have recovered.'

'Thank you, sir.' Symonds saluted and glanced at Tallent as he turned to leave the room.

'Captain Hargreaves, I believe that you have another witness, is that correct?'

'Yes, sir. Lieutenant George, sir.'

'And what is the relevance of this witness?'

'Lieutenant George, sir, is the platoon commander of Number Two Platoon to whom Lieutenant Symonds referred, sir. He was the officer who was responsible for ordering Sergeant Price to lead the patrol and was present when Private Tallent returned.'

'I will allow this witness but I would remind you to constrain your questions to areas of relevance.'

'I am grateful for your guidance, sir,' Hargreaves managed to utter through a thinly disguised smile. He turned and once again nodded to the military policeman. Moments later Lieutenant George stood in the centre of the courtroom. Bryn glanced at his platoon commander. He looked younger than normal, freshly washed and shaved, and his batman had evidently made a special effort to clean and press his uniform for the occasion. His buttons gleamed. Gone was the mud and blood that normally adorned his uniform.

'Lieutenant George, could you please confirm your name, unit and position to the court?'

'Yes, sir. I am Lieutenant Stephen George, Second Battalion, the Royal Welsh Fusiliers. I am the platoon commander of Number Two Platoon, sir.'

'How long have you been in that position?'

'Since February of this year, sir.'

'During which time you have been rotated in and out of the trenches almost continually, is that right?

'Yes, sir.'

'It must be quite exhausting.'

'It is tiring for everyone, sir.'

'Of course, but in your position there is additional responsibility is there not?'

Stephen looked at the prosecuting officer. *Where is this going?*

'Lieutenant George? An answer if you please.'

'I'm sorry, sir. Erm… yes it does, of course it does.'

'Then I assume that you must have been delighted when Lieutenant Symonds offered to lead the patrol to give you a rest.'

'Well it wasn't quite like—'

Hargreaves cut him short. 'Oh come now, Lieutenant, there is no blame here. If Lieutenant Symonds had not gone on the patrol I am sure that you would have done so.'

'Well, yes, sir, but—'

'And I am sure that you thought he was capable of going on the patrol, otherwise I am sure that given your experience, you would not have allowed him to go.'

'No, sir.'

'You selected Sergeant Price. A good man, I believe?'

'Yes, sir. One of the best.'

'And Privates Tallent and Roberts. Equally good I suppose? Two of your best men?'

'Yes, sir. They are both experienced soldiers, sir.'

'How long had they been in your platoon?'

'About six or seven weeks, sir. I'm not quite sure.'

'Six or seven weeks? Lieutenant, that doesn't suggest to me

that they are very experienced. They weren't with the battalion during the long retreat, so can the court assume that they are regular reserves?'

'No, sir; they are New Army men, sir.'

'I'm sorry; I'm not quite following this. Perhaps for the members of the court you could explain what you mean by "New Army".'

Stephen looked quizzically at the prosecutor. *Why does he need me to explain this?* 'Erm... At the outbreak of the war the government asked for volunteers to join the army—'

'Captain Hargreaves, this is all very well but I think you can safely accept my assurance that the members of the court understand what the witness meant by "New Army". We might be humble soldiers but we are not imbeciles. Kindly move on.'

'Of course, sir. I was merely trying to highlight the distinction between a regular soldier, a regular reserve and the background of the accused, he being a New Army soldier, sir.'

'I can assure you, Captain Hargreaves, that we appreciate your thoroughness but please move on.'

'Lieutenant, could you tell the members of the court when did the soldiers of the New Army start to deploy?'

Stephen shrugged. 'I don't know, sir.'

'I presume that they have started to deploy in large numbers?'

'No, sir. I believe that Private Tallent is one of only a handful of New Army soldiers to have deployed so far.'

'How very unusual. Perhaps the few who have been deployed are a trial, so to speak, to see how they get on?'

'I don't know, sir.'

'No you don't, Lieutenant, but you must have known how much training they had received. One month, two months?'

'I can't recall how much training they have received, sir.'

'Can't recall? Surely, Lieutenant, you know how much training your soldiers have had and how experienced they are? After all, the safety of your platoon depends upon their collective experience and training. Are you seriously asking the members of the court to believe that you allowed not one but two partially trained soldiers to accompany Lieutenant Symonds without any regard for his safety or the safety of your men?'

'No, sir.'

'Perhaps you were expecting Sergeant Price to mentor them as well as Lieutenant Symonds? That must have placed an enormous burden on Sergeant Price.'

'Sir, you have to understand—'

'What I understand, Lieutenant, is that you have been in and out of the front line for the past four months. That's tiring for any man.'

'Yes sir.' Stephen's head dropped slightly. He knew he was tired but no more so than his men. He was confident that it wasn't effecting his decisions.

'When Lieutenant Symonds went out on patrol what did you do?'

'I'm not sure, sir.'

'Lieutenant. You sent out a young, inexperienced officer on patrol under the command of a sergeant with two barely trained soldiers and the officer returns having been shot by one of your men are you expecting the court to believe that you can't remember what you did that night? Did you inspect the sentries, order men to go and collect some stores, supervise some trench repairs perhaps?'

'I believe that I spoke to some of the men, sir.'

'You *believe* that you spoke to some of the men? Lieutenant, your patrol was out for nearly three hours. Surely you didn't speak to your men for all that time?'

'No, sir.'

'No? So please tell the court what you did.'

Stephen hesitated. 'I was asleep, sir.'

Hargreaves let the comment hang in the air and looked towards the members. He was pleased to see all three of them scribbling notes on the paper in front of them.

'Asleep? Indeed. And why not? I'm quite sure it's important to get as much sleep as you can and I'm sure that Lieutenant Symonds will be glad to know that his actions allowed you to take a few hours of well-earned sleep.' Hargreaves paused. 'So you were not present when the firing started in front of your platoon?'

'No, sir. We have exchanges most nights and the sentry didn't think the situation warranted waking me.'

'Perhaps he didn't know that Lieutenant Symonds and three of your men were out in no-man's land?

'They did, sir.'

'They did but they didn't think it necessary to wake you? I am sure they were experienced enough to make that decision, unlike Private Roberts and the accused. Can you assure the members that these were experienced men?'

'N-no, sir. Privates Jones and Taylor arrived with Roberts and Tallent seven weeks ago.'

Captain Hargreaves glanced at the members, who were writing furiously.

'And you were still sleeping when Lieutenant Symonds arrived back in the trench?'

'Yes, sir.'

'So you were eventually aroused from your slumber and made your way out of your dugout to be confronted by what exactly?'

'It was rather confusing, sir.'

'I have no doubt that it was confusing given that you had just woken up but I'm sure that you have had many confusing moments before. So please indulge us in what happened, Lieutenant.'

Stephen chanced a glance across at Bryn, who was sat rigid, looking ahead at the clock.

'It was pitch black and the machine guns were firing intermittently. Lieutenant Symonds was in the trench, he was holding his arm and there was blood coming from his head. His revolver was hanging from his lanyard. He was sitting on the step of the parapet whilst Corporal Phelin was dressing his wound. I asked Lieutenant Symonds what had happened. He said that Sergeant Price was dead, Roberts had been hit and Tallent had run off.'

'And was Private Tallent there?'

'No, he wasn't.'

'When did Private Tallent come back in?'

'I'm not too sure, sir. About half an hour later I would say.'

'Was Private Roberts with him?'

'No sir, he had left Private Roberts by the wire, sir.'

'Is that what he told you, Lieutenant?'

'Yes, sir.'

'But you didn't see him bring Private Roberts to the wire, did you?'

Stephen paused. 'No, sir.'

'Thank you, Lieutenant, that's all I have. Please remain where you are.'

Thackeray looked at his fellow members on his right and left. They both shook their heads to confirm that they did not have any questions. 'Private Tallent, do you have any questions that you would like to ask Lieutenant George?'

Bryn looked at Lieutenant George. 'No thank you, sir.'

The court was silent as Lieutenant George left the room and the heavy wooden doors were closed. Thackeray finished writing a brief note on his paper and cleared his throat. Do you have any other evidence Captain Hargreaves?'

'Yes sir. It is a written statement from Private Roberts. I have provided copies of this statement. If it would help the court, sir, might I suggest that instead of reading the statement out verbatim I paraphrase the contents? It might speed things up a little.'

Lieutenant Colonel Thackeray glared at the prosecutor.

'Captain Hargreaves, might I remind you that we are trying a soldier here today who could very well lose his life? I think that he has got all the time in the world. In full, if you please.'

Captain Gordon leaned across to the president and said a few words. The president listened and nodded and then sat back to include Lieutenant Gooding. When the members had finished the president addressed Captain Hargreaves.

'Captain Hargreaves, during his evidence Lieutenant Symonds inferred that Private Roberts had died. Is this the case or not, and if it is the case then how and when was this statement obtained?'

'Indeed, sir. Private Roberts made this statement some days ago, sir, whilst he was still receiving medical attention. I am unable to tell the court for certain if he is still alive but my understanding is that he has subsequently died of his wounds.' Hargreaves was unaware that the staff officer had done his best to elicit a coherent statement as John lapsed in and out of consciousness. The young officer had been told the gist of what had happened and did his best to piece together the occasional lucid word into a coherent statement that fitted what he had been told by the prosecuting officer.

Bryn looked at the prosecutor. He felt sick.

Captain Hargreaves continued with the evidence. *'I am 5162 Private John Roberts of the Second Battalion, the Royal Welsh Fusiliers. On 11th May 1915 myself and Private Tallent volunteered to go out on patrol in front of Number Two Platoon's location. We were told that we would be escorting Lieutenant Symonds and Sergeant Price. During the afternoon of the same day we met Lieutenant Symonds and Sergeant Price to discuss the patrol and to ensure that we were familiar with the battle procedures. Later the same day Private Tallent asked if he could be removed from the patrol. I do not know why he didn't want to go; he was usually a very willing volunteer. Sergeant Price led the patrol out, I went next, then Lieutenant Symonds. Private Tallent brought up the rear. We made it to the willow tree and I remember Sergeant Price and Lieutenant Symonds talking. As we moved off we came under fire from a German patrol. Sergeant Price was hit. We were in a slight hollow so we stayed where we were. Private Tallent was on my right and Lieutenant Symonds was to his right. I saw Lieutenant Symonds shouting at me and then he leapt out of the hollow, presumably to help Sergeant Price. I was then wounded. I am not able to recall the rest of the incident.*

'As you will note, sir, the statement has been signed on behalf of Private Roberts by the officer who wrote his words on account that Roberts was too weak to sign the statement himself, but you can be assured that these are a true and accurate record of his account.'

'I have no doubt, Captain Hargreaves. It certainly appears consistent with the evidence that we have previously heard.'

The president looked at Tallent, who he noticed seemed to be staring directly above his head.

'Private Tallent. Do you have any questions with regards to the evidence that you have just heard, bearing in mind that Private Roberts is not here to answer them directly?'

Bryn lowered his gaze so that their eyes locked on each other. He didn't bother to consult his defending officer. 'No sir.'

'Captain Hargreaves. Does that conclude your evidence?'

'Yes, sir.'

'Are we to assume then that Sergeant Price died as Lieutenant Symonds supposed?

'I believe so, sir. I have no information to the contrary.'

Colonel Thackeray shuffled the papers on his desk into a tidy pile and checked his pocket watch. It was quarter to eleven. He glanced at his two board members. 'I think, gentlemen, that this would be a good time to adjourn. Are we agreed?' The members nodded their agreement. 'We shall reconvene at one o'clock.'

Wrexham
May 1915

My Dearest Bryn,

At last, a letter, which was so very welcome, regardless of your terrible news. Let there be no doubt in your mind: I do NOT believe for one minute that you are a coward. I cannot believe that you are to be tried for something that you haven't done. I know that they will vindicate you. As soon as they hear John's story they will see what a cad this officer is. Your officer sounds like a very nice man and I am sure that he will sort things out for you. John is still in France and seems to be reasonably well. Mrs Roberts told me that he was in a General Hospital but I'm not too sure which one. I will write to you again later after work but I want to get this into the post without delay.

Please let me know that you are well and back with Rhys and Huan. I can't bear to think of you locked up for no reason.

Yours affectionately,
Cerys

CHAPTER TWENTY-EIGHT

Rhys was looking to the sky. It was a beautiful clear day although the sun hadn't risen high enough for the rays to reach into the trench to provide a little warmth.

The deep blue sky reminded Rhys of Mary's eyes. He had been thinking of her all morning but try as he might he couldn't picture her face. He closed his eyes and imagined her standing in front of him, but all he kept seeing was Bryn, John and Huan. He couldn't imagine life without his friends. There had been no news of John since he had been transferred to the General Hospital. He'd be fine, he kept telling himself, and then he would wonder what Mary would feel if it had been him. The more he thought about it, the more he realised that he loved her. He told himself over and over again to imagine her long auburn hair flowing across her slender shoulders; her smile that made her cheeks dimple on both sides, but time and again the image faded as soon as it started to form.

He searched in his tunic pocket for a picture that he kept in a leather folder. Mary had sent it to him not long after they had first arrived in France. He sat down on the fire step and caressed the photo with his forefinger. A shell landed so close to the trench that the parapet blew dirt over his head. He didn't flinch, but his hand covered the photo so that nothing landed on his love. He quickly pushed the photo into the folder and replaced it carefully in his pocket next to his heart. He sighed and stood up. He grabbed a shovel and started to scoop up the earth that had been blown over the top of the trench.

The aeroplanes had been circling all morning, registering the front line and dropping the coordinates in tin cans to the guns a few miles to the rear. The shots were fired and the aeroplanes registered the fall of shot and then relayed the information back to the guns until they were spot on. Then nothing. Rhys didn't know if they were preparing for an attack or just bored. No one seemed particularly bothered.

'Alright, boyo?'

Rhys looked at his friend. 'I guess so. You?'

'Alright I guess.'

Another shell smacked into the ground about a hundred yards to their left just in front of the next platoon. It was too far away to make either of them flinch.

'Give it a rest!' Huan yelled over the trench towards the Germans. 'I thought that they had finished. They must have the whole line registered by now.'

'You'd think so.' Rhys sighed as he drove the shovel into the earth and put his hands on the handle. 'You heard anything?'

'No. You?'

'No.' They both stared at the muddy floor of the trench.

'I bet he's packing his kit now and coming back with Lieutenant George.'

'Probably.'

'Lieutenant George will sort it out. He knows what happened.' Another shell exploded a little closer. 'Shit, I reckon that one hit Four Section. I reckon that they're coming back along the front just to make sure that they have got it all sorted. Bryn will be wishing he was back inside if he comes back to this little lot.'

'Well we won't be bloody well here if they keeping dropping them in the trench.' The telltale whine of another shell was coming their way. 'Get in here,' Rhys shouted as he grabbed his friend's webbing strap and pulled him into a funk hole that they had dug into the wall of the parapet. The shell smashed into the traverse that separated them from the next section.

'Bugger me, that was close.'

'That one might have just got us home with a nice Blighty.'

285

'Well why the blazes did you drag me in here then?'

'Dunno really.'

There was a call for stretcher-bearers from further along the trench.

'Shit,' Huan shouted, 'that's Dickie's voice. Come on, let's give him a hand.'

As they ran round the traverse Lance Corporal Dickie Parson had his hands over Corporal Hughes's arm, or the stump that was left. The front of the trench had taken a direct hit, forcing earth, wood and metal into the trench. The gaping hole was a magnet for German snipers.

'Watch the hole,' Dickie cried as he tried to drag Corporal Hughes towards Rhys and Huan. Blood was seeping through his fingers. A splinter of searing hot metal had sliced through his upper arm like a butcher would slice through a piece of fillet steak.

'Grab that strap and wrap it round his arm above where my hands are,' Lance Corporal Parson shouted at the boys. Huan grabbed a webbing strap off the fire step and looped it round his section commander's arm.

'Good lad, now get it as tight as you can and keep it tight.'

Lance Corporal Parson kept his hands where they were until he could feel the flow of blood easing.

'Taylor, grab a bandage from the medical kit and get ready to slap it on here as soon as I let go.'

Rhys unwrapped the bandage and splayed it out so he was ready to put it on the arm.

'Here we go, good lad, press it on.'

Corporal Hughes groaned and Rhys released his grip slightly.

'No, keep the pressure on. Don't worry about his moaning, if he's moaning he's alive and that's where we want him to stay. Keep that tourniquet tight while I get this bandage on.'

He worked quickly but not hastily. Speed wasn't going to stop the blood. He knew from experience that if he stayed calm and managed to get a good tourniquet on the limb and a clean bandage on the wound that his friend would survive. All the while he kept talking slowly and calmly to his section commander, a man who had survived eighteen years in the ranks without a scratch.

'You holding that tight Jonesy?' the corporal asked as he looked away from his wound.

'Yes Corporal.'

'Good lad. I wouldn't want to lose any more than I have to. Mrs Hughes wouldn't be very happy with that now would she?'

'No, I don't suppose she would, Corporal.'

Lance Corporal Parson finished tying the bandage and secured the tourniquet.

'There you go Sid. You won't even notice that it's not there.'

'Thanks, Dickie. You're a good friend. Make sure you look after this lot won't you?'

'Course I will,' Dickie laughed. 'How much trouble can they be?'

'Well these two can be a right pain by themselves,' Corporal Hughes smiled as he nodded to Rhys and Huan. 'Isn't that right lads?'

'We'll try our best, Corporal,' Rhys said.

'I know you will lad, but just for now try a little bit harder and get me a fucking stretcher before I die of fucking boredom!'

Rhys scrambled round the traverse shouting for a stretcher-bearer as Corporal Hughes leaned back against the trench wall and took a drag of his cigarette.

*

Corporal Hughes was not a small man and the stretcher-bearers strained every muscle to lift him. The whole of Number Two Platoon lined the side of the trench to wish him luck as he passed each of them. As he reached the end of the line he signalled the bearers to stop. He looked up at Rhys and Huan.

'Listen lads, your friend Bryn will be fine. You'll see. And keep your heads down.'

'Thanks Corporal.'

'Ah, there you are.'

The padre emerged panting from the communication trench. He wore the same officers' regimental dress but with a white collar instead of a tie. The men were not surprised to see him; he was always in the thick of things. The men liked having him around as he led a charmed life, 'God's protection' as he called it. He wasn't naive enough to believe that all of his flock were devout believers but he knew that even the most unbelieving soul needed comfort every now and again.

'Oh Lord, that's all I need,' Corporal Hughes said when he saw the padre.

'No it's not the Lord, it's just me but by the look of things you could be meeting the Lord if you don't get that scratch sorted out.'

'Thank you for those kind and reassuring words, Padre. I don't know what I would have done without them.'

'Well, I've seen worse so I reckon that you will live.'

'Well that's some comfort.'

'Come on, I'll walk with you down to the RAP. If you behave yourself I'll get you seen first. The doctor owes me a favour.'

The platoon murmured a few good wishes as the stretcher-bearers began the toil of negotiating the mile of narrow trench towards the rear of the battalion position. The men stood looking at each other.

Acting Sergeant Jones broke the silence. 'Come on then, let's be having you. Let's not all hang around in the same place or there might be more than just one of you making the same trip.' The men started to shuffle along the trench. Huan looked at their sergeant.

'Not yet, son. I'll let you know when they get back.'

'Thanks Sergeant.'

'Go and get yourselves a brew and a bit of shut-eye. It might be long night if they keep this little lot up.'

*

Huan had made a stew of bully beef and a few leftover bits of vegetables that he had brought with him when they had returned to the trenches a couple of days ago. He'd managed to mix it up with a bit of beef stock into a reasonable meal. His mam wouldn't have been too impressed; she made a fantastic mutton stew with suet dumplings. He and Rhys had hardly spoken since they had sat down on the fire step. Rhys had pulled out his picture of Mary while Huan made the lunch. Rhys had just sat and stared at the picture.

Huan divided the stew between the two of them and handed a mess tin to Rhys, who muttered his thanks. Up above them the sky had cleared of enemy aeroplanes. The front line was scarily quiet.

'I'm on stag in a minute,' Huan said as he pushed his food around the plate. 'Can you sort this mess out?'

'No problem.'

Huan grabbed his webbing and put his helmet on. 'It'll be alright you know.'

'I know it will.'

'Ah well, I had better get up to the sap otherwise Jim will be after me. See you later then.' As he turned to leave, Dickie Parson the new section commander stuck his head round the traverse.

'Platoon commander's back.'

'Shit, come on let's go,' Huan shouted at Rhys, who was already on his feet and grabbing his rifle.

'I'll stag on for bit while you bugger off then, shall I?' Dickie called as they disappeared round the corner.

The dugout was thirty yards away at the end of the platoon line. Lieutenant George was speaking to Sergeant Jones as Rhys and Huan bounded round the last traverse and halted a few yards away. Stephen George looked at them. His face was drawn. He saw the anticipation drain from their faces. They looked back at him quizzically.

'Where is he, sir? Where's Bryn?'

'He won't be along just yet. They are still hearing the evidence.'

'What do you mean? I thought you were defending him?' Rhys blurted out.

Sergeant Jones thrust his rifle at Rhys' stomach. 'Oi! Just you remember who you are speaking to, boy, otherwise we'll be having a little chat down the trench there.'

'It's alright, Sergeant Jones. Thank you. I was not able to assist Private Tallent as I was called as a prosecution witness.'

'Who is defending him, sir?' Huan said.

'A captain from the divisional staff.'

'What does he know about what happened?'

'Probably nothing but he is more experienced than I am in these matters, so Tallent is in good hands. I'm hopeful that we shall see him again soon.'

'*STAND TO!*' a sentry yelled as the first shells screamed through the air, just seconds before the earth erupted.

France
May 15

My Dearest Cerys,

It hasn't been the best of mornings. As you know the trial started today but my lieutenant was not able to help me as he was called as a witness for the prosecution. Unfortunately they tied him up in knots and I think he has managed to get himself into trouble. The other officer was there and managed to turn the whole story around. I am beginning to think that I may be in a whole heap of trouble. Never mind, the truth will come out I'm sure but I would like to get it sorted sooner rather than later as I wouldn't want my mam and da to hear what's been going on; I don't want to worry them. They said in the court that John was dead. I thought he was going to be fine – I don't know what to believe!

I am back in court after lunch so I should be able to let you know how it goes later on. I hope you are keeping well and the shop is keeping you busy.

Bye for now,
Bryn

CHAPTER TWENTY-NINE

The officers ate in relative silence despite the mess steward withdrawing discreetly to allow them to discuss the trial. There was little appetite for small talk after their morning's work. Having mopped the last of the gravy from his plate with a piece of bread Lieutenant Colonel Thackeray laid his knife and fork on the plate and pushed it aside.

'Well, gentlemen, I'm afraid that we do need to make a decision.'

He sighed and wiped the corners of his mouth with the starched napkin before laying it on the table. 'I know that this is a most difficult position and I, like you, would rather not have been selected to sit on this trial, but we were and so we must dispense justice fairly, appropriately and above all, as it relates to the evidence.' He let the last sentence hang in the air for a moment. 'I suggest that you put aside any emotion and constrain your thoughts to what you have heard this morning.'

Captain Gordon and Lieutenant Gooding nodded.

'You will recall that we heard a very clear account of the events from Lieutenant Symonds. He is a new officer, one of Kitchener's men, so to speak, and therefore relatively inexperienced but his evidence, and indeed his conviction of what took place, were unequivocal. As you heard me ask at the end of each witness testimony, Tallent did not wish to question the witness, or indeed provide any contrary evidence.

'However, his reluctance to question or counter the evidence should not be taken as an indication of guilt. We have to be sure in our own minds as to whether this young man, who not so many months ago was, I believe, a miner in North Wales, did or did not fail in his duty. The fact that he was not a professional soldier may be a point of mitigation but it does not have any relevance to the events that occurred.'

Thackeray paused to allow the officers a moment to consider what he had said.

'In a moment I will ask each of you in turn for a decision: guilty or not guilty. I will start with you, Anthony, so that you cannot be influenced by Captain Gordon or myself. Take a moment to think about it.'

*

Thackeray rose from the table and readied himself for the court. The large oak door that led to the members' room opened abruptly.

'Accused, Accused, 'shun!' the military policeman barked from the rear of the room.

Bryn shot to attention as he watched Captain Gordon lead out the members. Captain Gordon and the president took their seats without looking towards the court, but Lieutenant Gooding couldn't help but steal a glance towards him. Bryn stood ramrod-straight, his eyes fixed above the president's head.

'Sit down please. Captain Burgess, do you have any evidence of the accused's character?'

Burgess was taken aback by the directness of the question. He glanced sideways at Bryn, who sat as dispassionately as he had all morning.

'I have his conduct sheet here sir, which has no entries at all.' For the first time there was some genuine respect in his voice. 'And if it should please the court I have a written statement from Lieutenant George, who you may recall gave evidence earlier this morning.'

'Thank you, Captain Burgess. Perhaps you will be good enough to pass the conduct sheet to Captain Gordon so that it can be included in the court's proceedings?'

Captain Gordon took the conduct sheet and checked that it was indeed blank. He held it so that his two co-members could satisfy themselves that it was as described, to which they nodded their agreement. Gordon took a pencil and added the letter *F* to the top right-hand corner and laid it on top of the pile of other evidence.

'Please proceed, Captain,' Thackeray instructed.

Burgess began as he read from a prepared statement. '*I am Lieutenant Stephen George of the 2nd Battalion, the Royal Welsh Fusiliers. Private Tallent was posted to my platoon on 2nd March 1915. It was evident from the moment that he arrived that he was a very high-quality soldier. Despite this relatively short period of training he can be compared against the very best of my men. He has a passion for taking the fight to the enemy and quickly established himself as a skirmisher and a regular volunteer for patrolling duties. He has natural soldierly abilities. I regard him highly and believe that he will become a first class junior non-commissioned officer. I cannot explain his actions on the incident in question, which I believe are completely out of character. I have the honour to be, sir, your obedient servant, Lieutenant S. George.*'

Captain Burgess handed the testament to Captain Gordon, who admitted it into the court's proceedings. Gordon took the statement and inserted a large letter *G* in the top right-hand corner before placing it on top of the empty conduct sheet.

Thackeray addressed Bryn. 'Private Tallent, do you have anything else that you would like to say to this court?'

Bryn looked directly at the president and then slowly at Captain Gordon and Lieutenant Gooding. 'I'm not sure what you want me to say, sir.'

Thackeray sighed. 'Anything you like, Private Tallent. Anything that you think we should know that will have some bearing on this case.'

'Sir, I was brought up in a small village in North Wales. I attend chapel every week and I believe in God. I know the difference between right and wrong and I know for certain that I have done nothing wrong. I cannot explain why Lieutenant Symonds has said the things that he did; he... he is mistaken, sir.'

Thackeray looked at his members in turn as if to offer them a chance to speak. Neither spoke, but nodded in acknowledgement. 'In which case, this court is now concluded. Tallent, you will be taken from here to a place where you will be held in confinement until the verdict and sentence are confirmed.'

The court rose as the members filed out without a backwards glance.

Captain Burgess turned to Bryn. 'Tallent, do you understand what just happened?'

'No, sir, not really.'

'I didn't think so.' He sighed. 'Sit down.' Burgess took a deep breath. 'You have been found guilty of the charges for which there is only one punishment – death. The proceedings will need to be confirmed but unless there is a recommendation for mercy the sentence is likely to be carried out within the next week. Now do you understand?'

Bryn stared at the officer. 'Yes sir.'

France
May 1915

My Dearest Cerys,

I don't know what to say. I don't understand what has happened. Everything that I told you in my last letter is true, but no one believed me. I only hope that you do; you are the only one that matters. If you believe me then I will accept my punishment with courage. I have been found guilty of the charges. This was not supposed to happen; I was doing my duty, I faced the enemy and I did not run, unlike that officer. But they didn't believe me. I don't know what to believe anymore. Your letter said that John was alive but the officer in the court said that he was dead. I pray to God that you are right and he was wrong. If only he was alive, he would back my story. I don't know what will happen but you should know that it will probably not be good. Whatever happens you must know that I will never flinch or give that ~~basta~~ officer any satisfaction.

With all my love,
Bryn

CHAPTER THIRTY

Huan and Rhys were crouched at the bottom of the trench as a wall of noise reverberated around them, smashing their ears and making their heads vibrate. Shells were falling faster than a spring rainfall.

They had their backs pressed hard into the trembling wall of the trench. The vibrations shuddered through their bodies, making them shake as if they were chattering with cold. All the while sweat trickled from under their helmets. They kept their mouths open to allow the compression out of their bodies. All around them the air was rent with scorching hot fragments of shrapnel. Splinters splattered the opposite face of the trench. The oxygen seemed to have been sucked out of the atmosphere and replaced with sulphur-laden earth.

Above the trench the earth was being ploughed and ploughed again, showering clods of earth on top of them.

'This can't be happening,' Huan yelled. 'It's got to stop soon or they'll run out of shells.'

'Hang on in there, boyo,' Rhys screamed back. 'They're not getting us this easy. If they want us they'll have to come and get us. Right?'

'Bloody right, they will. But I wish they would hurry up about it. I'm getting cramp in my leg.'

Rhys looked aside at his friend and smiled. 'You are such an idiot.' They both started to laugh. The other members of the section looked at them and shrugged.

Huan stopped laughing and breathed in deeply. 'At least Bryn's out of this shit. Do you reckon the trial's finished yet?'

'I reckon so. They should have that bastard Symonds in the dock by now.'

There was a shrill whistle as a shell reached the peak of its parabolic curve and gravity took over. It hurtled towards the ground at terrifying speed, seeking out something solid to detonate the fuse. The shell hit the front glacis of the trench and buried itself deep into the mud. The men waited for the explosion. Like so many shells, it failed to explode. One by one they looked up. One of the young lads in the section started to scream. His friends grabbed him, looking for an injury but there wasn't anything to be seen. As he screamed, his friend put his arm around him and hugged him tight until the screaming stopped and the crying started.

'Thank God,' one of the older men said as he peered heavenwards. 'Someone up there is looking after us today.'

Rhys looked at Huan, who was still crouched with his hands clasped around his rifle. The grip was so tight that his knuckles had turned white. His head was still down; his body was shaking noticeably. Rhys grabbed his arm.

'Hey. You alright?'

Huan nodded his head.

'That was lucky, that one, wasn't it?'

Again he nodded his head and breathed out deeply. He raised his head and looked at his friend. 'Are you scared, Rhys?'

'Scared? I'm fucking terrified.'

Huan laughed. 'Me too. I haven't been this scared since we went down to Llanelli that spring and ended up playing their Colts team when we were nippers. Remember that?' Rhys smiled and nodded. '*Duw*, they were hard bastards.'

'We still stuffed 'em in the end though, didn't we?'

'That we did. But we had John and Bryn with us then.'

'True, and we'll have them back again soon, you mark my words.'

They both fell quiet for a few moments and looked around the trench. Huan caught Corporal Parson's eye and he nodded back and mouthed something that he couldn't hear. The thumbs-up gave him some reassurance.

Rhys broke the silence. 'Do you reckon we'll beat this lot then?' 'Bloody right we will, boyo. We'll sort them out. That's if they ever stop lobbing bloody shells over.' They both started to laugh. Corporal Parson looked across at them and shook his head. *Try as I might I will never understand those two idiots!* he thought.

Huan rubbed his leg and then stood up to relieve the pressure. Rhys grabbed his tunic and pulled him down as several clumps of debris and earth showered them. Huan fell back down, rubbed his leg again and then brought his knees up towards his chin and rested the rim of his helmet against his rifle. There was nothing to do other than endure the pounding and hope that the German gunners were as bad as their own. With a bit of luck they would drop a few short on their own men.

Rhys looked along the trench bay at the rest of the section. Each man was locked in his own thoughts. They all looked grey and weary. Johnson had collapsed in a heap at the bottom of the trench and had curled into the foetal position. He was still crying but no one moved to help him. Rhys wondered if he looked as drained as the rest of men did.

What would Mary think of me looking like an old man? he thought. Rhys tried to picture her in his mind but the shelling kept rattling his head and he struggled to form an image of her. He fumbled in his top pocket for his picture of Mary. He opened the slim brown wallet and stroked the photo as his eyes lingered on her face. *She is beautiful,* he thought. *I wonder what she's doing now? Perhaps she's working, or it might be the weekend in which case she's probably having a wander around Wrexham.*

There was a sudden lull in the firing that was barely noticeable but enough for the men who had spent hours enduring such conditions to know what was coming. Corporal Parson looked across at his men. 'They're switching fire,' he screamed. 'Get ready to shoot the bastards off our fucking front lawn.'

Rhys snapped the wallet shut and stuffed it back into his pocket, making sure that the button was done up securely. 'Looks like this is it,' Rhys said, looking his friend in the face.

'Well, bring it on then,' Huan screamed as he struggled to his feet. They looked at each other for a moment and Huan extended his hand. Rhys looked at his friend's hand and shook his head. He hugged his friend for a moment and then screamed in his ear. 'Let's give them one for John, eh?'

Lieutenant George rounded the traverse. His pistol was already in his hand. 'Corporal Parson, get your men ready.'

There was no need. Number Two Section had already turned around to face the front, still bent against the trench wall waiting for the order. Pieces of flannelette that had been stuffed into the muzzles of rifles to keep them clean were being pulled free and men were cocking their weapons. The lip of the trench was still being smashed by shells, but a smaller calibre than the previous ones. The big shells were dropping behind them on the support trenches. Within seconds there was silence along the line.

'This is it,' Corporal Parson screamed. 'Make every shot count. Let's ruin their fucking day.'

The whole company rose. Rifles were lifted across the lip of the trench; the men positioned themselves and waited. It was rare to see across no-man's land during daylight. Most men had never seen the ground in front of their location. Men stared at the desolation and destruction. Gases rose from the craters to their front like a thick fog swirling in the late autumn morning. The air was full of particles that were falling slowly to earth like raindrops. The Welshmen waited. Shells continued to scream as they flew overhead into the rear area. Men panted like dogs in anticipation but nothing stirred across the divide.

'What's going on, Corporal?' one of the lads shouted.

'How the heck should I know? Just wait a minute, they'll be over in a second or two.'

Lieutenant George jumped up onto the fire step next to

Corporal Parson and stared across the abyss. He scanned the horizon for any movement.

'Where are they, sir?'

'I don't know, Corporal. Having tea maybe?'

'Well it must be better than ours, sir, otherwise they would have been over five minutes ago.'

Lieutenant George raised his binoculars to his eyes and scoured the enemy trenches for movement. There was nothing. He lowered his glasses and thought for a moment. 'Get the men down, Corporal.'

'Sorry, sir?'

'I said get them down now!' he screamed as he jumped down from the parapet and started to run along the line, zigzagging round the traverses screaming for the men to take cover.

Corporal Parson looked across at his men, who were staring back at him. 'You heard the officer. Get down.'

The men got to the bottom of the trench as the lip of it erupted in flames. The earth rocked and bucked as shrapnel whizzed across the gap. The ferocity of the roar made the last few hours seem like a picnic.

A shell hit the traverse between Number Two Section and Number One Section. The wall exploded, sending two men at the far end of the bay crashing into the opposite wall of the trench. They were buried under a ton of earth, which smouldered with escaping gases. The third man along clutched the side of his head. As he withdrew his hand blood gushed from a hole where his ear had been. He rolled towards Rhys, who grabbed him and pulled him back towards the front edge of the trench.

'Jim, you're hit!' Rhys screamed.

He pushed him onto the parapet and pulled his hand away from his ear. Blood sprayed them both.

'Shit. Stick your hand back on there and press hard. You'll be fine.'

Huan grabbed a dressing from the box that had been placed

in the middle of the bay and tore off the outer covering. Rhys held Jim upright as Huan wrapped the bandage around his head.

'You'll be fine, Jim. There's not much damage although you might have a headache for a while.'

Corporal Parson and a couple of other men were frantically digging at the pile of earth that had been blown in. They found a leg, put down their shovels and started to dig with their hands.

'Keep digging lads, we're nearly there,' Corporal Parson shouted. 'Grab that leg and follow it down. One of the section pulled the leg. It came out unexpectedly without the rest of the body. The man holding the bloodied stump retched and threw the limb aside. The men just looked at each other and knew that Johnson wouldn't be crying anymore. The soldier continued to retch as a friend passed him a canteen of water.

Corporal Parson urged the rest of the men to keep digging. Rhys stayed with Jim as Huan clawed at the earth with his bare hands. He felt a tunic and then the body.

'I've got him,' he screamed.

Many hands clawed at the earth. It seemed like an eternity but it was only minutes before they dragged a body from the earth. Huan grabbed the man's face and cleared the earth from his mouth. He shook him frantically to urge him to breathe.

'Come on you bastard, breathe. Get me some water,' he screamed.

One of the section passed him a canteen and he slopped the water over the unconscious man's face. There was a splutter as the man sucked in some air. Huan slumped on the mound of earth, oblivious to the shells that continued to pound the earth around them as the others pulled the man from his premature grave and sat him on the fire step. Corporal Parson was still barking orders for the others to clear the earth that was blocking the traverse, and that still held the bodies of the other members of the section.

The bombardment lasted about ten minutes and then it stopped as suddenly as it started. The men looked at each other in anticipation. Corporal Parson grabbed one of his men.

'Get up there and have a look. Shout if you see anything move. The rest of you sort this mess out.' He pointed to what used to be their trench, which was now just a series of random holes. 'Let's get this lot connected again.'

It was dark by the time they had finished shoring up the trench wall and recovered Johnson's body. The stretcher-bearers had taken the body, or what was left of it, back down the communication trench. Jim shared his cigarettes with the rest of the section, as well as his cake that his wife had sent him. A stretcher-bearer had assured him that he wouldn't die without his ear but it was definitely a Blighty wound, particularly if he couldn't hear properly, if he understood his meaning as he tapped his nose. Jim knew exactly what he meant and promptly became deaf. He was pretty cheery as he left the front line with his Blighty wound. He knew that he was well out of it.

Sergeant Jones had been along the line a few times to give the boys a bit of encouragement and confidence – not that they really needed either but it showed his leadership. He looked every part the platoon sergeant now. To a man, the platoon hoped that he would keep his acting rank. Lieutenant George had doubled the sentries at first but reverted back to the normal stag roster once it was evident that the Germans were not coming after all. Most of the men were resting when Sergeant Jones shock Corporal Parson awake. It was still quite early and a small wiring party had gone out an hour or two earlier to repair the damage caused by the shelling. Number Two Section were three men short and had been spared wiring duties. After a brief chat Sergeant Jones went to move on to the next section. Rhys grabbed at the sergeant's arm as he moved along the trench. 'Sergeant. Any news yet?

Sergeant Jones bent forward so that he could talk quietly. 'Not yet lad, but hang on in there. We're going out tonight so we will find out when we get back to the battalion lines.'

'Thanks Sergeant.'

Wrexham
May 1915

My Darling Bryn,

I'm not sure that I have the words to say everything that I want to say. This cannot be happening. What have they said? What are they going to do? Surely they won't punish you? They need you, they need all of you. Of course I believe you. I don't know any man in the world who wouldn't. I spoke to Mrs Roberts on my way home and explained what has happened. I'm sorry but I started to tell her before I realised that you might not have told your mam and da – please tell me that you have. I couldn't bear it if they found out another way. That would be awful and they would think me an awful gossip – which of course I am not. Mrs Roberts still hasn't heard from John although she had a card that said that he had been wounded and that he was alright so he must be there somewhere – you have to find him. He has to tell them what happened. I will go and see Mrs Roberts every day until she has some more news. Please tell me that you are well. I will pray for your safe and swift return, if not to me, then to Rhys and Huan.

With all my love,
Cerys

CHAPTER THIRTY-ONE

Bryn rubbed the window with his hand. He guessed that it hadn't been opened for a few years, let alone cleaned. The windows had been barred – not recently, some years ago. He guessed that it was to stop young children falling from the window onto the cobbled courtyard below. Outside the window a spider had spun a large web and now lay in wait, in the corner of the eaves of the protruding wall and the overhang of the slated roof, for its prey. Although it was a sheltered spot, out of the wind and the rain, he wondered how the spider had known that it would be a good spot to trap flies.

He had been moved into the new room as soon as he had left the court. The guard had almost doubled him up the stairs, making him mark time on each landing, and had screamed at him all the way up the stairs until he caught him up. The fat jailer, a military policeman, looked as if he had never been far enough forward to dirty his boots or feel the tingle of a bullet as it whizzed past your ear, but Bryn was in no mood for a fight that he wouldn't win. It was easier to let him think he had won. If it made the fat bastard feel like a real soldier then so be it.

As soon as he had stepped into the room the door slammed shut behind him. There was a bed on the right with a blanket and a pillow. There was a bedpan under the bed and pile of old newspapers. In the centre of the room were a small wooden desk and a couple of chairs. His belongings were already there.

He stood still for a few minutes before walking across to the window. As he gazed down his stomach lurched with the sudden realisation of what had happened. He gripped the bars to steady himself. His knuckles went white as his grip tightened on the bars before he started to pull them back and forth. Tears started to pour down his cheeks.

Bryn didn't hear the door open. His head was on his hands, which still gripped the bars. His shoulders were heaving up and down as the sobs came readily. There was a cough behind him. Bryn turned to see an officer standing in the doorway. It took him a moment to understand that the officer was a padre. The door had already closed behind him. Bryn wiped his face with his hands and stood staring at the visitor.

'I'm sorry.'

'It's alright my son, you have every right to cry.'

The padre looked uncomfortable as he fiddled with his hat as if it were a string of rosary beads. The padre looked at the big man in front of him. 'Why don't we sit down?' the padre suggested, gesturing to the table.

Bryn nodded and moved awkwardly across the small space and almost crashed through the chair, as his legs seemed unable to hold his body weight. He put his elbows on the table and his head fell into his hands. There was silence for a minute or two before Bryn's shoulders began to shake again. It was a few minutes before Bryn seemed to pause for breath. He looked up from his hands and wiped his eyes with the backs of them. He rummaged in his trouser pockets and pulled out a handkerchief that had seen better days. He held the filthy rag up and laughed before blowing his nose.

'I don't suppose it will kill me!' Bryn said.

The padre smiled. 'No, I don't suppose it will.' He reached inside his tunic pocket and produced a flask. 'It's Bryn isn't it?'

Bryn nodded. 'Yes, sir.'

'Sir! Oh, I'm not a sir, my son; I have a proper job.' They both laughed. 'Fancy a drop?' he said, holding up the flask.

Bryn looked at the flask and then at the door.

'It's just you and me, Bryn, and the Lord of course, let's not forget him. And I know that he wouldn't mind you taking a drop of this stuff. Go on, have a drop or two. It's medicinal.'

Bryn nodded and muttered his thanks as the padre poured him a large measure into a metal beaker that he produced from his other pocket. Bryn took a small sip and let the liquid trickle down his throat. He had always been a beer-drinker; never one for the spirits. He gave a slight gasp as the single malt burnt the back of his throat. The padre urged him to have another, which he did willingly, this time savouring the sensation rather than fighting the invasion of his taste buds.

'I'm sorry about that, Padre,' Bryn said. 'You know, the crying and stuff. It's not for me you understand. I don't think I have ever cried. Perhaps when I was a baby but not since. I won't cry for myself. I just feel like I have failed everyone. Mam, Da, my girl… everyone really.' Bryn paused and gave a deep sigh. A moment of silence passed between them as they both drank the amber nectar. Bryn rolled the metal beaker round his fingers. 'They're going to shoot me aren't they?'

'From what I understand, the verdict wasn't the best result that you could have hoped for. And, yes, the sentence is death but the verdict and the sentence will have to go through the chain of command before it is confirmed. So there is still hope, Bryn.'

'Do you know how long I have?' Bryn asked. The padre looked at Bryn and shrugged. Bryn rubbed his temples. They were pounding. 'Well I guess it will be soon. I'm sure that they won't waste too much time keeping me here.'

'I'm sure that it will be a little while yet,' the padre replied. 'Enough time to… to sort your affairs out and make your peace with the Lord if you would like?'

Silence descended between them. Bryn looked at the padre. He was a young man with a kindly face. He had the look of a man who had seen a bit of action. Bryn was used to the Reverend Morris, a senile old vicar who would preach fire and brimstone from the pulpit every Sunday to his congregation of sinners. Bryn smiled at the thought. He often used to wonder why the vicar bothered to do a sermon; no one listened to a word he said.

'I don't mean to sound insincere or anything, like, but I don't need to make my peace with God, Padre. I'm not afraid to die. I would die for my country tomorrow but I don't want to die for something that I haven't done. God knows what happened and I know that he will look after me.'

'Of course God will look after you and keep you at peace but from what I hear you didn't do much to help yourself in court. If you were wronged then you should have said something.'

'The officer... the one who was meant to help me... *duw*, he just... he just told me to keep quiet. I trusted him.' Bryn's eyes were starting to sting as tears pricked their corners. 'But then I trusted Lieutenant George as well, but he let me down too.'

'Do you want to tell me what really happened?

'Will it make any difference?

'Not to the decision and the sentence, I suppose, but I could put a good word in for you upstairs if you would like?' the padre replied with a smile.

Bryn was warming to his visitor and returned his smile. 'There is probably no point. Nobody seems to have listened so far; it's my word against an officer and that's all there is to it really.'

'Perhaps, but it might make you feel better to know that you have told someone else what happened. If nothing else, your family and friends need to know your side of the story and I might be able to help you with that.'

Bryn leaned back on his chair. The whisky was starting to have the effect that the padre had intended. Bryn's thoughts drifted back to Gwersyllt. He could picture his mam and da in the cottage sitting across from each other next to the fire. His da had a pipe. His mam was darning. Darning! That's all she ever seemed to do. He had humiliated them. There would be no compassion or understanding from anyone. It would destroy them. It would destroy Cerys in time when everyone else found out and shunned his family and friends.

'You know, when I walked in I couldn't help overhearing you say that, "He can't get away with it." Who can't get away with what, Bryn?'

Bryn hadn't realised that he had been speaking aloud. 'Lieutenant Symonds.'

'Was he the officer in the court? The one who you allegedly disobeyed?'

'Yes.'

'What is it that he shouldn't get away with?'

'He lied.'

The padre checked himself briefly. 'Why do you think he would do that, Bryn?'

Bryn looked away towards the window. It was starting to get dark. In the distance he could see flashes of light, and felt the rumble of the guns, like a thousand feet marching across the floor in the church hall, back in the village. He felt his tears as they started to well up again and took a deep breath. He could see his mam standing at the sink peeling potatoes for dinner. His da was sitting in the parlour in his favourite chair smoking his pipe and reading the paper. He turned to the padre. 'I need to write to my mam and da. Explain to them what happened. They need to know the truth.'

'I can certainly pass a letter on for you and I can make sure that it doesn't go through the censors.'

Bryn turned back towards the window.

'You said he lied,' the padre said.

Bryn looked at him intently for a moment or two. 'Yes he did. It was all lies.' Bryn shuffled in his chair. 'We had met before, Lieutenant Symonds and me and my friends.'

It was dark outside by the time Bryn had finished his story. He sat back and sighed. He thought he felt better, as if a weight had been lifted from his shoulders. The padre had sat silently at the table with his hands clasped together. He hadn't needed to encourage Bryn to talk. He finally moved them and spread them flat on the tabletop. He had been expecting a fanciful story. He had expected Bryn to say that none of it was his fault; that he was a victim, but he hadn't. His story was credible; he couldn't have made it up.

'Why didn't you say any of this at your trial?'

Bryn shrugged in the growing gloom. 'We don't have any proof that it was him who was going to steal the money, and there is no one to back up my side of the story from the patrol. I thought it would be alright,' he whispered, 'but it wasn't, was it?'

'No it wasn't,' the padre replied. 'I think your mother and father would appreciate you telling them the truth. I'll make sure that they get it.' He pushed his chair back, scraping the wooden legs across the rough floorboards. Bryn was drained. 'Try to get some sleep. I will make sure that you get some paper and a pen tomorrow. I'll come back and see you if you like?'

Bryn stood up. 'Thank you,' he said. 'I would like that.'

The padre turned and banged on the door for the guard to let him out. 'Keep your spirits up. It's not over just yet. There is always hope.' The key turned in the door and the corporal held the door open for the padre. 'Till tomorrow then?'

'Padre!' Bryn called as his visitor left the room.'

'Yes Bryn?'

'I don't know your name?'

'Hughes. David Hughes. Cheerio Bryn.' The corporal slammed the door shut, leaving Bryn alone in the dark with nothing but his thoughts.

France
May 1915

My Dearest Cerys,

There is no easy way for me to say this so I will tell you straight: they intend to shoot me for what they say I did. I knew that this war would kill me one way or another but I hadn't banked on this. I want you to know that you are the best thing that has ever happened in my life and I am thankful for the little time that we had together. I just wish that it could have been longer. People will say some dreadful things about me when they find out what has happened but that doesn't matter. All that matters is that you know the truth. It will be difficult for my mam and da to understand what has happened although I have written to them. A very nice padre has helped me let them know the truth. They will not be able to escape the shame that I have brought on them but you can. You need to forget about me. Only a few people know that we are together and they will know the truth. I want you to ignore what people say and just move on. Please promise me that you will do that for me, I cannot bear to think of people looking at you and sneering – no one must know about you and I; you must not let on. I know that it is a lot to ask but time will pass and I will be just another casualty of this war – forgotten in time. Please promise me that you will do as I ask.

With all my love,
Bryn

CHAPTER THIRTY-TWO

Padre Hughes stood in the entrance of the court martial building and placed his service dress hat on his head. The rain was coming down in vertical rods. There wasn't a breath of wind. He looked to the heavens – *God, isn't it bad enough without the rain?* he asked. The clouds lay across the sky in a continuous blanket. The rain was in for a while. He checked his watch: half past six. He stepped out from under the porch and strode off in the direction of the headquarters on the other side of the town square.

The square was empty aside from a few soldiers dashing in and out of the doorways trying to keep dry. The rain was starting to collect in the many holes that had appeared in the cobbled square. He tried to avoid the obvious ones but slipped on the wet cobbles and his left foot ended up submerged just long enough to soak his foot. He shook it and rushed on.

The headquarters had been set up in a large town house that looked onto the square. The Marie was an imposing building with a double stone staircase with wrought iron railings that led up to large wooden double doors. A sentry stood outside of the door to check the passes of the staff going in and out. He jumped to attention and saluted as the padre approached. Hughes returned the salute, more out of politeness than duty. He paused momentarily as he passed the soldier, who had scrunched his shoulders up to his ears and had his chin on his chest trying to stop the rain dripping down his tunic. 'Hello Jenkins,' he said.

The soldier looked up. 'Hello Padre. How are you, sir?'

'I'm fine thank you. What brings you out on a filthy night like this?'

The soldier thought for a moment. 'Just lucky I suppose, sir.'

'Well if you don't drown I'll see you on Sunday.'

'You certainly will, sir,' he shot back with a smile.

The sentry opened the door to allow the padre to enter. 'Have a good night, sir.'

'Thank you,' the padre replied as he looked to the heavens again and took a faceful of rain. 'You too!'

The interior had changed little since the Franco-Prussian War of 1870. The entrance and the hallway were fairly businesslike: polished marble floors and eggshell walls that had become brown-tinged with age. There were lighter patches on the walls where paintings had been removed. A clerk looked up from the desk, and seeing the padre he stood up smartly.

'It's alright, Lance Corporal Pritchard, sit down. It's only me.'

'Good evening, sir. Bit damp out there?'

The padre removed his cap and shook it. He looked down at his trousers, which were sticking to his legs, and shook his feet. Water squelched from his shoes. 'You could say that. Have they all gone in to dinner?'

'Yes they have, sir, but only just. They probably haven't sat down yet. You could just squeeze the Grace in, sir, if you hurry.'

'Heaven help me if I'm late.'

The mess sergeant was closing the dining room door as the padre rounded the corner. 'Gor blimey, sir. That's a sharp one. Through you go, sir.'

'Bless you, Sergeant.' The padre slipped through the door as the general looked around the dining room. He followed the line of officers, fifteen of whom stretched out before him on his left, around the bottom of the table and up the right-hand side. The light was considerably dimmer than in the anteroom and the general was taking a moment to adjust to the candlelight.

'Padre?' he called. 'Ah, there you are. Must have missed you. Would you care to say Grace?'

The padre clasped his hands and bowed his head. 'May God

bless this food and all who sourced it, stole it, scorched it and serve it. Amen.' He couldn't help but stifle a smile along with several other of the junior officers. The general gave him a raised eyebrow, and the mess was seated.

'Padre, that was quite possibly the worst one yet. You know he's going to get upset sooner or later. He'll have you back up the front quicker than your last sermon.'

'A lot can be said in a few words. You could recommend it to the general.'

The padre had sat himself down next to Captain Hilary Richardson, one of the few staff officers that he liked. Hilary had been out with the Old Contemptibles since the start of the war but had copped a Blighty wound early on at Mons. It had taken him almost nine months to get himself back out but the powers that be refused to let him near the front. The general had taken a liking to him and made him his personal staff officer; nothing happened that Hilary didn't know about.

'Anyway, I thought the old chap had a good sense of humour?'

Hilary laughed. 'You must be joking. Between you and me, he prefers his own company. He only dines in the mess on the odd occasion to remind the officers that he is still here.'

'I thought it was because he was keeping all the best wine for himself.'

'Padre! You'll be heading in the opposite direction from heaven with that one!'

'I'm sorry Hilary, that was uncalled for. Still, I bet he has a few decent bottles of claret stuffed away upstairs?'

'I couldn't possibly comment Padre,' Hilary said, raising his eyebrows. 'However, I believe that the 1900 Chateau Margaux was a particularly good year.' The two officers stifled a laugh. 'If you don't behave yourself I'll make sure that you get an invite to dine with him one evening – just the two of you.'

'You wouldn't be that cruel would you?'

Hilary laughed. 'Probably not.'

The mess orderly placed a bowl of brown liquid in front of Hilary. He looked inquisitively at the soldier and raised an eyebrow. 'Brown soup, sir.'

'Well, that's original. Thank you.' He turned back to the padre. 'Anyway, how have you been amusing yourself today? You're jolly wet you know!'

'Yes, sorry about that. I got caught in the rain on my way back from the Court Martial Building. If it keeps on all night I might have to build an ark.'

'It won't need to be very big. I think the chef has killed most of the animals round here, although there is no evidence of anything having made it into this soup,' Hilary joked as he swirled his spoon around the brown liquid.

'I was having a chat with the young fellow who was in court today. He's a very pleasant young man. He's from North Wales; you might know him.'

'Padre, you think the best of everyone. However, I'm not sure that I know everyone from North Wales and I definitely don't wish to get to know him.' Hilary took a slurp of his soup and grimaced. 'I hear that he was sent down. Rum business. Very unsettling for the regiment.'

'Yes, I imagine it is. Still, I don't suppose that he's too happy at the prospect of being shot, do you?'

'That's a bit of a cheap shot. I say, that was a rather amusing pun?' Hilary said with the look of a cheeky schoolboy. The padre furrowed his brow and gave his friend a disapproving look.

'Oh, I'm sorry, that was rather distasteful.'

'Wine, sir?' the orderly asked.

'Erm… yes, thank you.'

Both the officers took a glass of fine red wine from the cellars of the Marie. The mayor certainly knew how to look after his council colleagues. Town business was seldom concluded quickly and never without refreshments. The soup was cleared away to make way for steak and kidney pudding, a weekly treat for the general.

'I'm sorry about the pun; it was rather childish and crass. I think this job has made me insensitive.'

'Well, perhaps I will see you at Mass this Sunday to make up for it?'

'I'm not that sorry! You can't bribe people into going to church you know; it's unethical.'

'What, and this war isn't?'

'Shh… If the old man hears you he'll have you in the court and order himself to sit as the president. You'll be joining your young friend again quicker than you might have planned,' Hilary said as he stirred a little sugar into his coffee.

'Which young friend might that be?' the padre teased.

Hilary raised his eyebrows. 'The one who was in court today. The one you are dying to tell me about.'

'Oh yes, him. Erm, in reasonable spirits considering his position. You know, I'm not altogether sure he really understands what's going on.'

'Poor fellow. He had an officer to assist him didn't he?'

'Yes, I believe so.'

'Who was it, do you know?'

The padre leaned towards his friend and glanced around. 'Simon Burgess.'

'Oh my lord, sorry, Padre. Not the best option I grant you.'

'I'm sure that he did his best.'

'I heard that your young fellow didn't say a word. Very bizarre if you ask me.'

'He's not my young fellow, Hilary, he's *our* young fellow.'

'Even so, you would have thought that he would have come up with some excuse.'

'We didn't really get around to talking about what happened, although he briefly mentioned being on a patrol with a young lieutenant. Do you know whom he was referring to? I can't imagine that it is anyone I might know,' the padre said with his fingers crossed behind his back.

'There's no reason why you would have done. He was one of Kitchener's men. He was only over here to complete his training. He got a bit more than he bargained for, that's for sure.' Hilary moved a little closer to the padre and said in hushed tone, 'Not that I would wish anyone ill, but he got what he deserved if you ask me.'

'You met him?'

'Yes, I had that unfortunate pleasure. The old man asked to see him before the trial. Wanted to make sure that he understood what was what. You know, give him a bit of grilling to make sure that he wouldn't fall apart in the court and make a fool of himself. It wouldn't do for a new officer to undermine the morale of the troops at this stage. Not with so many new troops arriving. We need them to integrate as seamlessly as possible.'

'But I thought the general was the confirming officer. Isn't his job to review the evidence before confirming or rejecting the court's decision? He can't be involved with the witnesses!'

'Padre, it's bad enough trying to keep him amused and out of the way of the staff all day so they can get on with managing the war without trying to dissuade him from seeing one of the witnesses. To be honest it wasn't a very long interview. Symonds was a rather odd fellow; very sharp, far too much misplaced confidence for my liking. Actually, between you and I, the old man took an instant dislike to him. Almost threw him out.' Hilary laughed at the recollection. 'He then barked at me for allowing "the scoundrel", as he described him, into his office. I can't win sometimes.'

The padre sipped his coffee. 'And was he a scoundrel?'

'There was definitely something shifty about him. Let me put it this way: were it not for the war he would not have been considered suitable for a commission into my regiment! In fact, I have written to the Regimental Headquarters to express my concerns about him.'

'Hilary, according to you no one is good enough for your

regiment. I'm surprised that you have any officers at all. So where is he now, this lieutenant who isn't good enough for your regiment?'

'Gone, I believe. Sent back down the line. He wasn't particularly badly hurt so I think he's going back to complete his training, and no doubt boast about his war wound.'

Wrexham
May 1915

My Darling Bryn,

Please tell me that this can't be true. They cannot do this to you. They must know that you are innocent! You must tell them, they must believe you. I will tell everyone who will listen what really happened. I am not ashamed of you and never will be. People can say what they like - as long as I know the truth I will put them right. No one will speak badly of you - not now, not ever. You must do everything you can to make them see sense - can you tell them about John, tell them that he is alive somewhere and he will tell them exactly what happened? Please, please come home to me. I love you so very much that you are always in my heart and always will be. You will never leave me - I won't let you, so please do not tell me to do so. Your news has left me numb. I need to think how I can help. I will write again later. I will pray for your safe return. Have no fear, I will be with you.

With all my love,
Cerys.

CHAPTER THIRTY-THREE

The rain finally stopped in the early hours of the morning as the bedraggled Welshmen dragged themselves into their adopted home on the outskirts of Bois-Grenier. It was a far cry from the comforts of their real homes but after a few days in the trenches anything that wasn't covered in mud, had a roof and was relatively dry was home.

The bombardment had created chaos in the trenches. Whole lengths of the parapet had been blown to smithereens. The trench line was barely visible; instead there was a series of loosely connected craters. As the barrage had lifted from the front line, much to the relief of the Welshmen, it pounded the communication trenches, which prevented the wounded being evacuated or reinforcements coming forward. The Welshmen had done what they could to dig a route out but it was badly exposed in places and flooded in others.

The relieving battalion finally gave up trying to claw their way through the mounds of earth and walked across the top in full view of the enemy. Either the darkness and the mist or the exertions of the afternoon kept the Bosch from engaging them as they came forward to relieve the weary and wounded Welshmen. Lieutenant George followed the example of their relief and ordered his men over the top facing towards home. The landscape was a desert of rapidly filling shell holes as the water table re-established equilibrium. The men kept in single file to avoid falling into the swampy pits, more fearful of drowning than a German bullet.

Outside the barn Huan leant back against the wall and took a long drag from his cigarette. He kept it tightly cupped in his hand more out of habit than necessity; there was no way that the enemy could see the faint glow of his smoke. Rhys was squatting on his haunches next to him as he stared through the darkness towards the front line.

News of Bryn's conviction had filtered down the line as they moved towards the village. No one had to explain what it meant. As the news spread around the battalion it was received with a mixture of indifference by those who just wanted to get their heads down for a few hours, rage by men who thought that the battalion would be tarred with collective shame and incredulity by those who knew the truth.

'I don't believe that this is happening. This isn't what we joined up for,' Huan said as he stamped on his fag end and slid down the wall next to his friend.

'He didn't do it, did he?' Rhys asked as he looked across at his friend.

Huan stared at his friend. 'How can you ask that? Course he didn't do it you stupid sod. What kind of a question is that? Don't you dare doubt him. We know that bastard Symonds did it for him.'

Silence remained between them for a few minutes.

'Sorry.'

'There's no good saying sorry to me. It's Bryn that we've got to feel sorry for.'

'What are we going to do?'

Huan thought for a minute, staring into the darkness. 'I dunno. I just don't know.'

They were still sat with their backs against the wall as brighter streaks started to split the inky black sky. Huan looked to the sky and wondered how many more dawns Bryn would see. He shivered in the cold and shifted his position to stave off the cramp. He thought of the bombardment the previous day and wondered how many more he would make.

Rhys sniffed and rubbed his nose with his sleeve. Huan

looked across at his friend and realised that there were tears streaming down his face. He put his arm around him for the first time since they last played rugby. They sat in silence for a while, lost in their thoughts. Nothing needed to be said. Behind them in the ramshackle house they could hear the rest of the platoon snoring.

'Christ alive, how do we normally sleep though that racket?' Huan said as he stood up to stretch his legs.

'You can sleep through anything,' Rhys said as he sniffed and wiped his eyes with his sleeve. 'It's the rest of us that have to suffer.'

'We can't just sit here moping. We need to see if Lieutenant George can tell us anything.'

'Do you think he will?'

'I dunno but it's better than listening to this racket.'

*

Padre Hughes was dozing in an old Louis VI chair next to Hilary's desk when his friend arrived at the office. The padre had cajoled the duty clerk to allow him to wait in the general's outer office, where he would catch Hilary first thing. He knew that the duty clerk was also responsible for maintaining the fires in the headquarters during the night so he had pulled the chair up to the fire and wrapped himself in Hilary's greatcoat.

Hilary gave a loud cough. Padre Hughes gave a startled jerk and looked about, as if he was unsure as to where he was. He looked at Hilary and smiled.

'Ah! Good morning, Hilary. You're here, well done. I thought perhaps you were taking the day off.'

'The thought of a day off, Padre, is not something that I have given a great deal of thought to recently. However, as to why you are still wet, in fact wet and now covered in mud, and you appear to have been asleep in my office is something that I am giving considerably more thought to.'

'Yes, well I can probably explain that.'

He then sat in silence for a moment.

'Well?'

'Perhaps a cup of tea first?'

Captain Richardson sighed and turned towards the door. 'Private Soames,' he called.

The duty clerk appeared at the door. 'Sir?'

'Could I have a pot of tea please?'

'Two cups, sir?'

'Yes, and sugar if we have any. I have a feeling I might need it.'

Two steaming cups of tea arrived as the two officers were chatting about nothing in particular. The clerk closed the door as he left the office.

'Right. Now are you going to tell me why you look like you've been in the trenches all night or do I have to guess?'

'Guessing won't be necessary. I just took a trip out to see one of our regiments to see how they were getting on.'

'Really? And how was this regiment getting on?'

'Marvellous. They had a bit of rum day of it yesterday. They lost a couple of lads but on the whole they are pretty resilient. Mind you, aren't they all?'

'And which particularly resilient regiment did you visit, or do I have to guess that as well?'

'I went up to see your regiment if you must know. A fine bunch of fusiliers, albeit a bit wet. I managed to catch them just as they moved back into Bois-Grenier.'

Hilary couldn't hide his surprise. 'You've been to Bois-Grenier? Last night... on your own?'

'Yes, it wasn't too far and I managed to get a ride back.'

Hillary looked at the padre, sighed and shook his head. 'This is to do with that court martial isn't it?'

'Well, yes as it happens, it is.'

'"As it happens" be damned, Padre. I think that perhaps you are straying a little too far from your vocation.'

'Actually Hilary I don't think I have. In fact, I think I am doing exactly what God would expect me to do.'

'I'm sorry, David. That probably came out a little more terse than I meant it to sound. What is it, exactly, that you think God has asked you to do?' Hilary asked.

Hughes thought for a moment, trying to find the right words. 'I'm not sure what he wants me to do at the moment other than speak to you. As you know I have always welcomed your counsel and–'

'My dear friend, stop it. Flattery will get you nowhere. Just tell me what you've been up to because by the state of you, you could do with a hot bath, a shave and a few hours' sleep!'

'If you would prefer me to be blunt, then I will. I'm not so sure that the whole truth came out at the trial and I just thought–'

'And you just thought that you know better than the three officers who sat and listened to the evidence and made, from what I've read, a very sound judgement.'

'Exactly. The difference, however, is that they didn't speak to him did they? He didn't speak at all. They didn't hear his side of the story, Hilary. Don't you think that's odd?'

'Not really. I'm sure that he was given every chance to say his piece and he refused. If the chap didn't agree with the evidence then he should have said so.' The padre sat stony-faced, looking at his friend before pursing his lips and lifting his eyebrow. 'Let me guess, he told you all about it when you went to see him. How perhaps it was all a mistake; that it wasn't his fault, blah, blah, blah. I can't believe that you fell for it.'

The padre scowled. 'I think, Hilary, that you would agree that I am a good judge of character and I'm not wrong about this. If I thought for one minute that he was guilty of this crime I would administer to his needs without judgment or interference and I would prepare him for his punishment to the best of my ability. Preparing a man for his death is not a pleasant duty at any time but preparing a man for death at the hands of his own colleagues knowing that he has been wrongfully judged is an intolerable task.'

Hilary sagged and massaged his temples. 'I'm sorry but what would you have me do, reconvene the court on your request? You know full well that isn't going to happen. If the man didn't provide any evidence, what choice did the members have? There are innocent men dying out there on the front line every day. They don't have any choice in the matter; they are doing their job, which is what your friend should have been doing.'

'Yes, they die because they are soldiers but that doesn't make this right for this chap, does it? It doesn't mean that we can lead a man, who I believe to be innocent, out to a stake, tie him up, blindfold him and get ten of his own sort to shoot him. That's not justice, that's indifference.'

Hilary sat and looked at the padre. 'Oh God! Sorry, that's not what I meant to say. Why can't you be a normal Padre like the rest of them?' Hilary sighed and slumped back into his chair. 'What do want me to do?'

'Sit on his file. Just for a day or two. I need to speak to a couple of people.'

'I can't just sit on the file. The general will want it as soon as it's ready.'

'Of course you can Hilary, don't be so stuffy. You are his trusted staff officer; you can do anything. All I'm asking for is two days. Then if nothing comes of it I will administer to the young man's needs to the best of my ability.'

Hilary sighed. 'I can give you twenty-four hours and then I will have to give it to the general or I will have some explaining to do. However, if he asks for it I will have no option but to give it to him.'

The padre smiled. 'Done. Bless you Hilary. You won't regret this.'

'I very much doubt it. Now please get out of my office before the general gets here and wonders why his padre is covered in mud and stinking of... well, of goodness knows what.'

*

Stephen George had been awake since the platoon had returned from the front line. He had been awake all night. He had heard the commotion downstairs but was still startled by the knock on the door when it came. Stephen opened the door.

'Tell them I will be down in a minute,' he said without waiting for the orderly to speak, and shut the door. The orderly returned to the front door, took a deep breath and informed the boys that the lieutenant would be down when he was good and ready. He let them know that they were free to stand in the gutter until he arrived, and with that he shut the door.

Although he had managed to remove his boots Stephen still lay in his uniform. The mud and goodness knows what else had dried to a hard crust and cracked as he stood up. He buttoned his tunic and looked in the mirror. He didn't recognise the man who was staring back at him. His skin was pale and eyes were bloodshot. The uniform that he had had made in Savile Row barely fitted his shrunken frame. He turned towards the door and paused as his hands gripped the handle. He let his head fall against the door and sighed. 'What went wrong?' he whispered to himself. He steadied his breathing and stepped onto the landing. The other officers were still asleep and the house was quiet. He trod carefully on the wooden boards, but footsteps echoed around the derelict building.

The boys sprang to attention and saluted when Stephen opened the kitchen door 'Sir. We are terribly sorry to disturb you but might we have a word please, sir?' Rhys blurted out.

'It's about Private Tallent sir,' Huan added.

Stephen sighed. 'I think I could have guessed that.' He looked behind himself and closed the door. 'Come on, let's take a walk, there is no need to wake everyone else.'

They walked across the courtyard and past the platoon barn. The archway led onto the main road that ran through the village.

Stephen stopped and took out a packet of cigarettes. He took one and offered one to Rhys and Huan. 'Listen, I know that you are upset, we all are. The platoon has taken it very badly but he has been convicted of a very serious crime... and I'm not sure that I can help.'

'But he didn't do it. He wouldn't do it. We all know what happened,' Rhys said.

'He has never let anyone down, sir,' Huan persisted.

'The point is, we don't know do we? We weren't there. Tallent has been tried by a court martial and all of the evidence was presented. If he hadn't done it then he wouldn't have been convicted. That's all there is to it.'

'You don't believe that he did it, do you, sir?'

'It doesn't matter what I think, Jones.'

'It's that bastard Symonds' fault, sir. If you'll pardon the language,' Rhys added.

Lieutenant George sighed. 'Can I remind you, Private, that as Lieutenant Symonds is not here to defend himself I would caution you against your language and such accusations and insubordination?'

'Yes, sir. Sorry, sir but he's had it in for us ever since we were in training, see.'

Lieutenant George's eyes narrowed. 'I'm not sure that I do... see. I thought that he had never met you before?'

'Oh he's met us alright, sir.'

Lieutenant George looked across the courtyard but no one was stirring. The officers, like most of the battalion, were sound asleep. Lieutenant George looked around and then at the boys. 'Well perhaps you had better start at the beginning.'

Rhys started the story outside the hotel that evening in Salisbury. 'He was in trouble with some local sharks and we overheard him planning to steal the soldiers' fund in the camp to pay off his debts. So we told the regimental sergeant major, without mentioning what we had heard or who it was, and they sorted it so the money wasn't pinched. Only it was pinched, but there was no money; it was just paper.'

'Stop,' Stephen said, trying his best to follow the story. 'How could the money have been pinched but not pinched?'

'I dunno really. I think they changed the money somehow. Anyway, the money wasn't pinched but Lieutenant Symonds found out that it was us that blew the whistle.'

'That's why we were posted out so quickly I think,' Huan said, taking up the story. 'He said he was going to sort us out so the sergeant major, who is a good friend of Sergeant Major Rolland, our coach, got us posted. We never thought we would see him again.'

'So why wasn't Lieutenant Symonds arrested?

'Well nobody knew except us and him, obviously.'

'So when he came to the trench that day he arrived, he collared us and said that he hadn't forgotten,' Rhys said.

'And then he sorted out Bryn good and proper,' Huan added.

'And he probably would have shot John if he hadn't shot him first,' Rhys blurted.

Lieutenant George couldn't understand a word that they were saying, let alone keep up. 'Shut up! Speak slowly and one at a time,' he cried in exasperation. There was silence. Lieutenant George sighed. 'I'm sorry. It's been a long night. What do you mean, John shot him?'

Huan starred at Rhys.

'Well?'

'Who said anything about that?' Rhys asked.

'You did. Look, you might as well tell me. It's hardly going to make any difference is it?'

Rhys sighed. 'Bryn, Private Tallent, told us that Roberts shot Lieutenant Symonds as he was about to shoot Bryn.'

Stephen thought for a moment. 'Well that's quite a story.'

'But it's true,' Huan blurted out.

Stephen stared at the soldier.

'Sorry, sir, but IT IS TRUE.'

'Perhaps it is and perhaps it isn't,' Stephen said at last. The boys looked at him and then at each other. 'The question we have to ask ourselves is what are we going to do about it?'

France
May 1915

My Dearest Cerys,

Your letter cheered me so much. The past few days have been very confusing and so very lonely, although the padre I told you about has been round a few times. He is a decent sort and has promised to keep me informed of how the appeal process is going. He said that it might take a few days yet. I told him that John might still be alive and he said that he would look into it – I'm sure that he will; he seems that sort. I haven't seen Rhys or Huan for a few days but I expect that they are busy at the moment. There has been some pretty heavy shelling going on. With a bit of luck they will keep their heads down. At least I am safe in here! I told you that I wrote to my mam and da and explained as best I can what has happened. I haven't heard from them yet. Hopefully I will very soon.

There is so much that I want to say to you and at the same time so little to say. I sit here all day and night looking at the four walls. It could be worse I suppose, at least it is warm and dry and I get three meals. I dream of looking back on this when we are together and laughing about it, although it is difficult to laugh about it at the moment. Please don't worry, I have every faith that it will be alright. We just need to stay strong and pray.

With all my love,
Bryn

CHAPTER THIRTY-FOUR

'What do you mean you're off? Off where?' Corporal Parson demanded. He was irritated at being woken up, and even more so to find two of his section packing their kit, intent on disappearing without anyone telling him.

'I dunno Corporal. Honest we don't. We just got told by Lieutenant George to grab our kit and get ourselves back to Battalion Headquarters.'

It was almost true; they really didn't know where they were going but they knew why they were going. Lieutenant George had made it quite clear that they were not to tell anyone what they were up to.

Corporal Parson huffed, but he was too tired to argue and rolled over in his blanket. He turned his head sideways to look at Rhys. 'Well just make sure that you get back sharpish when you're done. And remember, you're one of us, not one of them,' he said. 'If you get the chance to get your hands on a few bits and bobs that the quartermaster won't miss then you know where to bring them. Right?' he called after them as they ducked through a large hole in the wall.

The quartermaster's wagon was already hitched up and waiting for Rhys and Huan by the time they reached the battalion's rear echelon. Lieutenant George had pulled in a favour with the quartermaster, not that a young platoon commander carried much sway with the wily old major. The quartermaster liked young Stephen; the battalion was full of good officers but some were more noticeable than others.

'Where are *we* off to then boys?' the driver asked. Rhys and Huan looked at each other and shrugged.

'I dunno really,' Rhys said.

'I got dragged out of bed half an hour after I got in it to drive you two somewhere, so I suggest you come up with an answer pretty quick or I'm going to get back to bed!'

'We need to get to the Field Hospital,' Huan said. 'The one where our blokes go.'

The driver threw the reins down. 'Well that could be just about anywhere, couldn't it? You ever heard of a needle in a haystack? Listen, the QM told me not to ask too many questions but I'll need more than this. Right, I reckon that you're looking for someone. Am I right?'

Huan looked at Rhys, who raised his eyebrows and shrugged.

'For goodness' sake, I am sworn to silence; the quartermaster threatened to rip my limbs off one by one, disembowel me and stick my head on a pole and then for good measure he would wave it above the trench until the Hun blasts it to kingdom come. And that's only because he likes me.' He gave a short chuckle. 'I reckon that three heads are better than one and as you two clearly have no idea what you are doing, I think you should just spill the beans.'

Huan sighed. 'We're looking for the place where they would have taken John Roberts.'

'He was wounded the last time we were at the front,' Rhys added.

The driver sat and thought for a moment. 'A couple of days back?'

'Well, a few before that. Maybe five or six days ago?'

'Blimey, you're not after much, are you? I see a lot of blokes going to and fro. I'll need more of a clue than that.'

'He was with Sergeant Price,' Huan suggested.

'Oh right, now we're getting somewhere. I don't know your boy but Sergeant Price and I joined together. Blimey, must have been sixteen years ago. Good lad he was. I was sorry to hear that he'd taken one for the King. They always seem to get the best ones. Mind you they seem to get their fair share of the bad ones as well. Not that your friend was a bad one, mind. I didn't mean that.' He paused and puffed his cheeks and rubbed his stubbly chin. 'Right you are then,' he said suddenly, 'we'll try Hazebrouck. Most of the blokes start there and work their way back.' The boys just looked back at him blankly and shrugged. 'Cor blimey, don't you two know anything? They go to the Field Hospital and then they get moved back as far as they need to. You know, to sort themselves out and then hopefully they get better and then they come forward again. Course, if they're really lucky they get a Blighty and get off home.'

'How long do they normally stay in each place?' Huan asked as the horse and wagon lurched forward.

'Well, that depends. I've known blokes who have been hit at breakfast and been back in Blighty by teatime. Others spend a couple of days at the Field Hospital and then a few weeks at the General Hospital and then months at a convalescent camp. Lovely places they are, by all accounts. Not the hospital you understand; they're pretty grim I expect. People dying and all that. No, I mean the convalescent camp; they are meant to be fantastic, white sheets, pretty nurses, proper mattresses, good food and no duties. One bloke I know was in a place by the sea. They went swimming every day, by order of the camp commander no less. Imagine being ordered to have a good time. Beggars belief if you ask me.'

'Did your friend come back again?'

'Oh yes, fighting fit he was when he got back. Killed the next day though.'

They sat in silence for a while as the horse-drawn wagon trundled over the cobbles. The sky was uniformly grey but at least the rain had eased. They hadn't got far before Rhys almost toppled from the driver's bench. Sleep was a luxury that neither of the boys had been able to indulge in for almost two days.

'Why don't you get your heads down for a while?' he said.

*

'Hey boys!' the driver called for the third time. The tarpaulin moved. 'Look lively now, we're here.'

Rhys and Huan popped up from a dreamless sleep that was so deep they would have happily been there for a week. They looked around at buildings that were largely intact. Normal people, in civilian clothes, were walking along the street. There were soldiers everywhere. Shops were open and had goods in the windows. The boys sat up and stared.

The driver laughed. 'You two look as if you've never seen a town before.'

'Not for a while,' Huan said.

'Well my advice is to make the most of it while you're here. I can show you a few places if you like. We've got a couple of hours before we need to be going back.'

Rhys looked at him quizzically. 'What time is it?'

'Almost ten minutes to eleven.'

'How long have we been asleep?'

'About three hours I suppose.'

'*Duw* blimey, I didn't realise that it was this far,' Rhys said as he scrambled up onto the driver's bench. 'How far is it now?'

'Just up the road here. Only a couple of minutes.'

Huan plonked himself on the bench next to his friend. 'I've got to say, that was the best sleep I've had in weeks.'

The hospital had been set up on the western side of the town in the grounds of a small chateau. As they entered the gates, a gravel path led to a large turning area in front of a stone stairway that fanned out from the front doors. In front of the house a field kitchen had been set up. The cooks were busy chopping and boiling. The smell of stew wafted over them as they drove past. A rather large and irate sergeant was bellowing at his men to get a move on as they needed to get the food out now before they had to move again.

Away to the right of the house was an ambulance station where casualties were transferred to motorised ambulances that would take the most serious casualties to the nearest railhead and hopefully England, or anywhere other than the front line. To the left, a number of army medical corps men were busy pulling down tents.

'Looks like they're on the move,' the driver said. 'I'm not sure that you'll find your pal here, you know, but it's a pretty good place to start.'

The boys looked around in wonder at the sheer scale of the hospital. The wagon had barely stopped outside the front steps before a medical corps man came running down them.

'More business lads?' he said, jumping up to the side of the wagon to see in the back.

'No, mate,' the driver replied. 'Just dropping these two off and there's bugger all wrong with them that a week of sleep wouldn't cure.'

'Oh,' the medical orderly said, somewhat disgruntled. 'I needn't have bothered running down the steps.'

'Well I'm sorry to disappoint you. I'll try harder next time,' the driver said, shaking his head in disbelief. He looked at Rhys and Huan. 'What you boys waiting for? Get in there and have a poke about. I'll wait over there by the ambulance station.'

The boys jumped down and looked up at the double doors. 'What do we do now?' Rhys asked.

'I suppose we ought to go in and ask if he's here.'

'Do you reckon they'll tell us?

'I dunno, but if we don't go in we'll never know, will we? Come on.'

They walked up the steps into a cavernous reception area. Ahead of them were men seated on benches running along the corridor. They all had crimson-soaked bandages wrapped around some part of their body or another. Some were smoking; others just sat staring into space.

A nurse in white uniform walked towards them and smiled. She pointed to the desk on the right. 'Just book in over there and you'll been seen as soon as the doctor can get to you.'

The boys looked at each and Rhys said in a whisper, 'Oh no. We're not ill or anything like that. We're here to find a friend.'

The nurse smiled. 'Then I suggest that you go and speak to Lance Corporal Weaks. He'll be able to help you,' she said in a whisper.

'Thank you very much miss… nurse,' Rhys said.

'It's my pleasure but why are we whispering?'

The boys looked at each other blankly and shrugged.

The nurse laughed. 'I'm sorry, I'm teasing you. Go on over there. I'm sure Lance Corporal Weaks will be far more help than I have been.' She winked and walked on past them.

'Blimey, she can tease me anytime,' Huan said.

'Oi! We're not here for that. Come on.'

The boys walked across the reception to the table where the lance corporal was sitting. 'Right then,' he said, 'if there's nothing wrong with you then you obviously want something or someone. What's it to be?'

Huan cleared his throat. 'We think a friend of ours was brought in here a few days ago and we were wondering if we could see him?'

'A few days ago?' the lance corporal said. 'I'll be very surprised if he's still here.' He grabbed a record book from his tray. 'What regiment are you?'

'Royal Welsh, Second Battalion,' Huan replied.

'We had a few of your lot in yesterday. Was he with that lot?'

'No, I don't think so. It was a bit before that.'

'Well how long ago? Roughly?'

'Maybe six days or so.'

'You're joking aren't you?' the lance corporal said, slamming the report book shut. 'We don't keep blokes here that long. We patch 'em up and move them out sharpish. And we're about to move again so unless you know how to find a needle in a haystack I suggest you write him a letter. It will get to him before you will.'

'But we haven't got that much time,' Rhys blurted out.

The lance corporal looked at him and shrugged. 'Neither have I, mate, so I suggest that you look somewhere else.'

The boys walked to the front door and walked slowly down the steps. They stopped at the bottom and sat down on the step.

'What do we do now then?' Rhys asked as he looked across the front lawn that was strewn with tents.

There were men moving everywhere. Stretcher-bearers were moving in and out of tents with men who only hours earlier had been fighting alongside their comrades on the front lines. The stretchers were placed in groups. Some groups were chatting amongst themselves; some men were even sitting up and smoking. In another group, nurses moved among the prostrate bodies, occasionally kneeling and offering a few words of encouragement or adjusting bandages or giving a sip of water. Another smaller group was forming over towards the rhododendron bushes. The lifeless bodies were lifted from the stretchers and laid on the ground. A padre stood among the lifeless forms.

'*Duw*, this place is depressing,' Rhys said.

'Pity the poor bastards over there,' Huan said, nodding towards the growing group of dead.

'It's probably the biggest congregation he gets,' Rhys said, referring to the padre who was threading his way through a group of wounded men. 'Fat lot of good he'll do them now.'

'Don't be like that. He's doing his best, I'm sure.'

'Really? Then why doesn't he place a word upstairs and get this mess stopped?'

'It doesn't work like that does it?'

'It would if he could be bothered to come up the front and see what's going on. I bet he'd pray a bit harder then.'

'What's got your beef? I'm sure he's doing his best. A few prayers aren't going to stop this little show and that's a fact.'

'Who are you all of a sudden, Lloyd bloody George?'

'No, I'm just saying that... well... it's not his fault is it?'

'No I suppose not, and it's not mine and it's not yours and not

John's but he's not here is he, so it's got to be someone's fault that he's not here, hasn't it?'

Rhys got up and strode off towards the kitchen.

'Hey, where you going, boyo?' Huan called after him, but Rhys was in no mood to sit about. Huan sat back down on the steps and sighed.

'That was a heavy sigh,' came a voice from behind him. Huan looked around and saw the nurse who they had met earlier staring down at him. He scrambled to his feet. 'I take it from your friend's reaction that you didn't find what you were looking for?'

'No. He's a bit upset I think. You know, seeing all these men and that.'

'I suppose it is a bit of a shock seeing so many wounded men in one place, but at least it shows that he still cares. You will be surprised how many men stop caring after a while.'

'I guess so.'

'I'm Nurse Williams by the way, Elizabeth Williams,' she said, offering her hand.

Huan went to shake her hand, but stopped when he saw how clean and pale it was. He glanced at his own hand, which was almost black with ingrained dirt. 'I'm sorry,' he said, showing her his hands, 'they're a bit grubby.'

Elizabeth laughed and kept her hand outstretched. 'Don't worry, I'll make sure that I wash them afterwards.' Huan took her hand and shook it gently. It seemed so small and soft. He had forgotten what it was like to touch something delicate and clean.

'It's nice to meet you.'

'Do you have a name or should I guess?'

'Oh sorry. Huan… Huan Jones.'

'And what are you doing here, Huan Jones, if I might be so bold as to ask?'

Huan looked at Elizabeth. She was wearing a crisp white uniform with a pinafore apron. Her hair had been pinned back under a white hat but it was her smile that caught his eyes; it radiated happiness and warmth. He hadn't seen anyone smile so beautifully since he had been in France.

'We-we're looking for a friend who was injured,' he stammered. 'We were wondering how he is.'

'And you didn't find him?'

'No. It was stupid really. We didn't think that there would be this many people coming through here,' he said. 'We thought someone might remember him.'

Elizabeth looked at Huan. 'Was he a good friend?'

'Yes, we grew up together. He was our hooker, see. Rhys, my friend over there, and I used to prop him up. In rugby you know?'

Elizabeth laughed. 'I might be a girl, but even a Llanelli girl knows what a hooker and prop are,' she teased. 'Where are you from then?'

'Gwersyllt, near Wrexham.'

'I should have guessed from the cap badge,' she said, pointing to the hackle in his headdress. 'I can't say that I've ever been up there.'

Huan smiled as he thought of home. 'Unless you like slag heaps there's not much to see, but it's home. And there's some really pretty areas thereabouts.'

'I didn't realise that they played rugby up there.'

'Steady on now, that's fighting talk where I come from,' Huan said as he laughed.

'How long have you been in the regiment?'

'Believe it or not, only three months.'

'What were you doing before that?'

'We're miners. Born and bred, we are. My da is a miner and so was his da before him.'

'So how did you end up here?'

'We all joined up together. Me, Rhys, John and Bryn. We thought it would be a bit of a laugh really. But John got hit a week or so ago, so we're trying to find out how he is.'

'So that's Rhys over by the cookhouse?'

'Oh, that's a surprise! Yes, that's Rhys. He props on the other side of me.'

'So that leaves… Bryn? I presume that he is manning the trench while you two do the visiting?' she teased. Huan's smile suddenly faded. 'Oh, I'm sorry, I didn't mean to–'

'No, it's alright. It's just that Bryn has got himself into a bit of bother. It wasn't his fault, mind, but it is pretty serious trouble and we need to find John to sort it out.'

Elizabeth looked at Huan thoughtfully. 'Then I had better see what I can do to help. We can't have a Welshman getting himself into trouble, can we? I take it that Lance Corporal Weaks wasn't much help?'

The smile returned to Huan's face. 'No, but it's not his fault, he was a bit busy I think.'

'Why don't I go and get the admissions book and we can see what we can find?'

Huan's smile got even wider. 'That would be smashing if we could.'

'You wait here and stay out of mischief. I'll be back in a moment.'

She turned and skipped up the stairs, closely followed by Huan's eyes. He was watching an angel in flight. True to her word she was back in a moment and told Huan to sit on the step next to her.

'Right, let's start with his name shall we?'

Huan was staring at her. She paused and smiled. 'Name?'

'Oh, er, Roberts, John Roberts.'

'And when do you think he was wounded?'

'Six days ago I think. Give or take a day, I lose track of the days sometimes.' He laughed and shrugged.

Elizabeth started to thumb through the pages. She paused and looked at Huan. 'Look, I don't want to get your hopes up. He will have gone to another hospital, in which case all I can do is send you there. You really are on a wild goose chase you know.'

'I know but we could still have a look couldn't we?'

'Of course we can. We'll start about eight days ago just to be sure.' She found the right date and started to run her finger down the page. She turned the page and continued to check each name, running down column after column. Huan went to lean towards her to see the pages himself, but withdrew slightly when he realised how much he must smell. 'Well, it's not the thirteenth,' she said as she turned another page and saw a new date at the top. 'Let's see if it was the fourteenth.' She continued down and over the page into the fifteenth and sixteenth. 'Are you sure it was about six days ago?'

'I think so. Only because we had been in the line and then out of it for a few days and then back in for three days and then it happened and then we came out and then back in and then out. So how many is that?'

Elizabeth looked at him and laughed. 'I've absolutely no idea.' She shook her head and sighed. 'Why don't we just keep checking?' Her fingers started to run down the page and then suddenly stopped. 'John Roberts, Second Battalion, the Royal Welsh Fusiliers. Here he is.' She passed the book to Huan. 'See here,' she said as she pointed to John's name. 'Came in on the seventeenth and left again on the eighteenth; that's only three days ago. You've got a very bad memory. The good news is that he must have been alive when he left.' She continued to read across the page. 'It says here that he had a bullet wound to the left side – clean through, that's good – a slight graze to the right side and…' She paused and looked a Huan.

'What?' he demanded

'It says that he had several bullet wounds to his lower leg, which had shattered his left ankle.' She paused again and shut the book. 'It says that he should have his leg amputated below the knee. I presume that he was stabilised here before being taken back to the General Hospital. I'm sorry.'

Huan looked at her, slightly bemused. 'But he is alive isn't he?'

'I don't know, but if he made it to the General Hospital they would have amputated his leg and then sent him straight back to England. Either way he will not be there now and I can't say with any certainty whether he is alive or not. I'm sorry, I think you have had a wasted journey.'

Huan stared out across the garden. Men were lining up at the field kitchen for their evening meal while others were still tearing down the tented hospital wards. He felt a sudden sensation of despair. Salty tears grew in the corner of his eyes. As Elizabeth touched his arm Huan shivered as if suddenly conscious of her presence. Instinctively he ran his sleeve across his face. 'Sorry,' he mumbled.

'Don't be sorry,' she said, 'he is very lucky to have you as a friend. I'm sure he will be alright.'

'You're right, tough as nails he is,' Huan said as he tried to compose himself. 'He'll be playing for Wales, he will be, even with one leg. Daft bastard that he is... Sorry, I didn't mean to swear.'

Elizabeth smiled. 'With you and your friend to support him on either side I have no doubt that he will.'

Huan looked across to where Rhys was still wandering about with a mug of tea in his hand. 'Thank you. I'm sure Rhys will be thankful too, if he wasn't too busy drinking tea.' They both laughed. Huan sighed. He looked across at Elizabeth. 'Would he have been in a lot of pain do you think?'

'I expect that he would have lost quite a lot of blood and he would probably have been in and out of consciousness. They would have given him plenty of morphine, so probably not too much pain. He wouldn't have known a lot about it to be honest.'

'Well, let's just hope he's alright. Better out of it now I suppose.'

'If he has your determination, I'm sure that he will be fine. You know, if he had died, they would have let the regiment know by now, so there is every chance that he is still alive.'

Huan smiled. He sat for a moment and then stood up abruptly, making Elizabeth jump. 'I'm sorry. I didn't mean to make you

jump.' He put his hand out to help her up. 'I'd better be off and…
er… well, get back to it I suppose. Lovely to meet you, and thanks
for your help. If you're ever lost in Wrexham I would be very glad
to show you around.'

Elizabeth smiled. 'If you are going, you will have to let go of
my hand.'

Huan looked at his hand, which was still grasping Elizabeth's
as if they were stuck together. He let her hand go. 'Sorry again.
Bye then.'

'Good luck and stay safe,' Elizabeth replied as Huan turned
towards the garden.

She was about to go through the doors when there was a shout
behind her.

'Hang on a minute,' Huan called as he ran back towards the
steps. 'Did a sergeant come in at the same time? Sergeant Price?'
Elizabeth opened the book and found the right page. 'Yes. Yes, he
did. According to this he came in and went out the same day.
Unconscious, trauma to the left-hand side of the skull – fractured,
probably – and a couple of minor splinter wounds. He was
certainly alive when he left here and the description of the wounds
suggests that he might have been lucky. If the skull heals and there
is no permanent damage he could be alive.'

Huan's eyes lit up. 'That's brilliant, that is. And if he'd died then
they would have let the regiment know wouldn't they?'

'Yes, I suppose they would but please don't take my word for
it.'

He reached across and kissed Elizabeth on the cheek. 'Thank
you, thank you so much. That's absolutely brilliant, that is. You're
brilliant and beautiful and wonderful and I have to go!'

Elizabeth put her hand to her face where he had kissed her
and watched him running across the garden to where Rhys was
talking to a group of walking wounded. She smiled and then
started to laugh. 'You're very welcome Huan Jones!'

Wrexham
May 1915

My Darling Bryn,

It is difficult to stay strong when I think of you locked in a cell but I am praying as hard as I can for your safe release. You did the right thing telling the padre about John. I hope that he is able to do something to help. I spoke to Mrs Roberts and she said that she had a telegram saying that he was being moved to a hospital in England. We just need to make sure that they do not make any decisions until they talk to John. Nobody has said anything back here but it is becoming increasingly difficult to keep it to myself. Would you like me to go and see your parents? I could talk to them about it. It might help them understand. I know that it would help me but I won't do it without your permission.

I know in my heart that we will be together again so please believe that. We will fight this to the bitter end until they let you go. Stay strong, my darling. I have to go to work (although I can barely concentrate) but will write again later.

With all my love,
Cerys

CHAPTER THIRTY-FIVE

Huan was struggling to contain his impatience. Despite his persistent encouragement and the driver's best efforts the wagon couldn't go any faster. If the badly rutted road wasn't bad enough they were stuck in a mile-long convoy of similar wagons heading towards to the front.

'Don't even open your mouth, boy, or I swear I will wrap these reins around your neck and get Doris here to pull hard until your eyes pop. Do you get it?' the driver said through gritted teeth as Huan was about to open his mouth.

'I just wondered if you wanted a mint imperial? My mam sent them last week.'

'Oh, in that case, ta.'

'However–'

'Shut it.'

Much to the bemusement of the other soldiers Huan had dragged the driver out of the food queue at the hospital. As soon as they were hitched and on their way Huan explained what the nurse had told him.

'I still don't see how that helps?' Rhys said.

'Look, John was clearly in no fit state to give a statement when he was here, the nurse said so, and Sergeant Price can't be dead otherwise we would have been told. So assuming that he is still alive, he might be able to say what happened, see?'

'No, not really, I don't. If John isn't here and Sergeant Price isn't here they can't help can they?'

'Listen, you idiot. Lieutenant George said that John had given a statement saying that Bryn was off his head and went a bit barmy, like. He would never have said that even if it was true. Would he?'

'Probably not, but he must have said something otherwise he couldn't have written a statement.'

Huan was getting exasperated. 'I'm going to hit you in a minute if you don't listen. And it will hurt.'

'It's not my fault I don't get it. You're the one trying to explain it.'

'We don't have time for this now. We need to get back. At least Lieutenant George will understand.'

*

The road from Hazebrouck was packed with troops moving up towards the front line. A convoy of London buses were carrying a group of men from a Lancashire regiment. Most of the men were dozing or waving at everyone they passed. Wagons were lined up nose to tail, ferrying stores and ammunition trucks were stacked with artillery shells.

'Bugger, bugger, bugger,' the driver said as the wagon in front of them stopped again.

'What is it?' Huan asked.

'I dunno but it looks as if we are all going that way,' he said, nodding his head to the left. 'It looks as if they've shut the road off.'

As they approached a junction the driver could see that the road ahead was empty. The traffic was all turning left. A bored-looking military policeman was stood in the middle of the road. The driver drew in the reins so the wagon stopped next to the policeman, who swore and started to wave them to the left.

'Keep moving,' the policeman screamed.

'What's up?' the driver shouted down.

'None of your business. Just go left.'

'Well how do we get back down there, then?'

'Dunno, don't care. Just follow the rest. Just keep moving.'

'Some help he is,' the driver said to the boys. 'I guess we'll be going this way then.'

'Where does this go, then?' Rhys asked.

'Erm… Poperinge I think, and then we will have to go via Wipers and back down that way. It will add a couple of hours I'm afraid.'

Huan was giving Rhys one of his quizzical looks.

'What now?' Rhys asked.

'Bryn's in Poperinge, isn't he? So, we could stop and see him.'

'Great idea,' Rhys said. 'The only problem is that we don't have a pass for Poperinge, which means that we are quite likely to get ourselves locked up. Hadn't thought of that, had you? Not so bloody clever now, are you?'

'I really am going to land you one in a minute. We've been diverted, haven't we, by a policeman, so it's not our fault if we end up there.'

'If it would help,' the driver said, 'one of the horses could go lame for a bit. It might give you an hour, particularly if we have to go looking for a blacksmith in the town square. If you get my drift?'

Huan smiled at Rhys. 'See, stupid, that's the kind of thinking we need.'

'Aha! If we are looking for a blacksmith we could pass the place where Bryn is and pop in to see him. See, not so stupid now am I?' Rhys said.

Huan looked across at the driver, who had his chin on his chest trying to stifle a laugh. Then he looked at his friend. 'Well, thanks be to God. I hadn't thought of that.'

'Just as well I'm here then. We could have driven right past and missed an opportunity,' Rhys replied.

*

It was early evening by the time the driver brought the wagon to a halt in the centre of the town. Soldiers were everywhere. The cafés and estaminets were crowded. They had stopped behind a squadron of horses. Their riders were milling about, shouting across to a group of soldiers sitting outside a bar drinking beer. A rather large French lady was busy arguing with another group over the payment.

'Are you sure this is a good place to stop?' Huan asked.

'Couldn't be better,' the driver replied. 'More open the better, and no better place than behind a squadron of cavalry. Where else would you find a supply wagon?'

The driver busied himself with the horses.

The town centre was fairly small and they set off towards the far side where the court martial centre stood on the edge of the cobbled square. They passed the YMCA and a cinema that was showing a Charlie Chaplin film. Soldiers were queuing up for about fifty yards. Every building seemed to be occupied for one reason or another. There were signs outside every building: Headquarters, Officers' Mess, Transportation Office and the Provost Marshall's Office, which they gave a wide berth. They had worked their way around the outskirts of the town centre and now found themselves on the other side of the square. They stopped outside a tall, imposing building, which might once have been a rather grand town house.

Rhys looked up at the window. 'Come on, let's see if he's in.'

'Well he's hardly likely to be out here, is he?'

The corporal on the desk looked up at Huan and Rhys as if they had just crept out of a hole like rats coming from the sewer. Their clothes were still caked in mud, they were unshaven and they smelt as if they hadn't washed in a week, which they hadn't. The corporal brushed his hand under his nose as the stench reached him. Before they could even reach the desk he put up his hand.

'Stop right there,' he said, pointing to the line on the floor. He looked them up and down. 'What have we got here then? Lost are we?'

They looked at each other and Rhys nodded his head at Huan.

'No Corporal, we're not lost. We're in the right place I think,' Huan said.

'Really, and what makes you think that then?' he said, reclining back in his chair with a slight air of interest and amusement.

'We've come to see Private Tallent, Corporal.'

'He's been court-martialled, you know,' Rhys added. Huan shot him a glance.

'I know he was court-martialled,' the corporal replied, trying to stifle a smile. 'But what has that got to do with you?'

'Oh, well it's like this, see,' Rhys said, taking over from Huan, who could only sigh. He could see their chances of getting to see their friend rapidly evaporating. 'We were on our way to Hazebrouck to see another friend in the hospital and we got diverted by one of your chums at the crossroads – you probably know him, short lad... er...' Rhys thought a moment. 'He was wearing the same armband as you. Anyway, he told us to come this way and now our horse has got lame and the driver said we had to stop so that he can get it fixed. So here we are.'

The corporal couldn't work out if the creature standing in front him was making fun of him or not, but on balance he decided that no one could keep a straight face and still be that stupid. He leaned forward in his seat. 'And I take it that you thought that you would visit your friend, is that it?'

'Yes Corporal, if you don't mind. We have come a long way after all.'

The corporal leaned back in his chair and thought for a moment. 'I take it you have got some travel papers?'

'Yes Corporal, but obviously they're not for here,' Huan said. 'We aren't meant to be here but for the confusion on the road and the horse being lame. But obviously we didn't want to go into the bars or restaurants while we were waiting, because that wouldn't be proper, so we thought if you wouldn't mind we would like to see our friend instead.'

He took a pace forward and handed the papers over. The

corporal took the papers and looked Huan in the eye before raising his eyebrows. Huan stepped back and the corporal opened the scrunched-up ball of paper in his hand. He read the document carefully.

'So your horse is lame, is it?

'Yes Corporal.'

'And where is it now?'

'In the centre of the town square Corporal, with the driver.'

'And how long will it take for this lameness to go?'

Rhys jumped in before Huan could even think. 'It will be fine as soon as we've seen Bryn, Corporal.' The corporal nearly choked. He coughed and sat upright. He tried to compose a serious face.

'And then, I take it, you will be going back to your unit won't you?'

'Yes Corporal,' they said in unison.

The corporal folded the travel papers and creased the sides so they became a neatly folded square, and held out his hand. Huan stepped forward and took the paper and stepped back smartly. The corporal sat back in his chair and looked at the two vagabonds in front of him. After a few seconds he snatched up the keys from his desk and stood up.

'You won't be able to see him tomorrow, so you might as well see him now. You can have ten minutes. After that I will give you five minutes to get your wagon hitched and out of town and if I ever see you two again I will personally jail you and throw away the key. Is that clear?'

'Yes Corporal,' Huan replied.

'Sounds fair enough to me, Corporal. Thank you very much,' Rhys added.

*

Bryn heard the boots on the marbled staircase and then the wood-panelled floor long before the door opened. As the keys rattled in the lock he sat up and swung himself off the bed. He was expected to stand to attention whenever the warder came in but had decided that there was nothing else they could do to him so they could stuff their discipline. It was the only defiance he had left in him. A corporal opened the door and looked across at him.

'Visitors, Tallent,' the corporal said. 'Ten minutes only.'

He pushed the door aside and two figures blocked out the light as they both tried to push through the door at the same time. Bryn was on his feet; he grabbed Huan then Rhys and stood back to stare at them.

'Wow, you two stink!' Bryn said as he laughed.

'Thanks for that. Hello to you too!' Rhys replied in a fake hurt tone.

'What are you two doing here?'

'Well we were passing and our horse got lame and we were trying to think of anyone we might know in the area and your name sprang to mind. We thought you would probably be in so we stopped.'

Bryn looked at Huan and raised his eyebrows. Huan looked back with a smile, shook his head and just shrugged.

They sat at the rickety wooden table in the centre of the room. Bryn perched on the side of his bed. They looked at each other for a moment.

'Actually we've been to Hazebrouck, to find John,' Huan said.

'But he wasn't there, Rhys said, butting in. 'But we did find out that he has probably had his leg amputated and is probably in England.'

Huan sighed and gave Rhys one of his looks.

'What?'

'Lieutenant George sent us to find John. He reckons that if we can find him and Sergeant Price we might be able to sort this mess out.'

Bryn was starring quizzically at his friends. 'But Sergeant Price is dead isn't he?'

'Maybe not,' Huan said. 'I met this nurse who said that if he had been killed the regiment would have been informed... and they haven't, see.' He looked at Bryn, who was quiet. 'Well, aren't you pleased? We've got a way to get you out here. You'll be marching back into the trenches with the rest of us tomorrow.'

Bryn put his head in his hands and sighed. 'I don't think so. It's a bit late for all that.'

'Of course it's not. Lieutenant George will get it sorted as soon as we get back.'

'For all the help he's been, he had better be quick.'

'What do you mean by that?'

Bryn took a deep breath and blew out his cheeks. He lifted his head and looked at his friends. 'They confirmed the findings this morning.'

'What do you mean?' Rhys asked. 'What have they said?'

'Oh no, they haven't. Tell me they haven't,' Huan said.

Bryn just nodded his head and started to shudder. Within seconds his whole body was rocking as he cried silently to himself.

'No, no, no,' Rhys shouted. 'That's not bloody right!'

'Come here, boyo,' Huan said as he put his arm around his friend. Rhys moved around the other side and gripped his arm.

'They won't do this. They can't do this. It's not going to happen. Do you hear me?' Huan said.

For a few minutes no one said anything. Bryn finally lifted his head and breathed in and out quickly to regain control of his senses. Tears were flowing silently down Rhys' cheeks. He didn't know what to say. Bryn gripped his arm.

'Dry it up, boyo. There's no sense in you crying as well. I would have died out there anyway. At least this way it will be over pretty quickly.'

'Don't say that. Don't you dare say that. There's not a man in the regiment who believes that you're guilty,' Rhys said as he gripped Bryn's arm.

'When?' Huan asked.

'Tomorrow morning unless there is a reprieve, and that doesn't look likely does it?'

'We need to get to Lieutenant George, he'll sort it out.'

'This is beyond even Lieutenant George. Nothing is going to change their minds now. They are hardly going to admit they got it wrong are they?'

They sat in silence for a few minutes. None of them knew what to say. Bryn stared through the window at the fading light.

'I need you to do something for me,' Bryn said at last. 'I have written a couple of letters to Mam and Da and Cerys. I need them to get back somehow without going through the censor. The padre has been helping me but I'm not even sure that I trust him with these. It doesn't matter when they get there as long as they get there. Can you do that for me?' He handed the letters to Huan, who took them from his friend.

'They'll get there, I swear it.'

The sound of hobnailed boots on the stairs broke the silence. The boys looked at each other. There was a loud cough outside the door. The three men grasped each other, reluctant to let each other go.

'We'll sort it. Don't you bloody well give up, you hear me?' Rhys said at last.

'We'll see you in a couple of days, you'll see,' Huan added without looking Bryn in the eyes. Bryn just nodded his head. The keys turned in the door.

'Come on then lads, let's be having you.'

France
May 1915

My Dearest Cerys,

It seems that I am beaten. This is one game that I am not going to win. The findings of the court have been confirmed: I am to be shot. I know that it is not just but I am not sure how else I could have played it. I feel sad, not for myself but for you, my family and the lads, and especially for John who knows nothing of this. I beg you to tell him what happened and that he is no way to blame for any of it. There is no sense in more people being hurt than necessary. Huan and Rhys came to see me earlier. They were pretty upset but they have a job to do and God willing they will return home, which will be a great comfort to me and hopefully to you.

I have no regrets in my life other than not being able to spend more time with you. I cannot tell you what to do but I implore you to move on with your life and enjoy it to the full. This would make me very happy. There is no point in crying over what cannot be undone, you can only look forward and change injustices and above all make a difference. That is what I thought I was doing and I still believe that we were right to do our duty. If only the circumstances had been different.

There is little else for me to say. I will do my final duty with as much dignity as I can and with you in my thoughts and prayers. With God's help I will be free from this madness and in a better place along with some good men.

You will always be in my prayers, my love.
Bryn

CHAPTER THIRTY-SIX

It was getting late when the driver finally reined in the horses and brought the wagon to a halt outside the battalion stores. The weather was on the change; the temperature had dropped and clouds lay flat across the greying sky. Rain was definitely on the way.

'Hang on there. I won't be a minute,' he said and was off in a flash into the quartermaster's office.

The battalion store was always easy to spot; other than the officers' mess building it was always the best building available. There were a few men loading another wagon with wire and stakes, more detritus for the front line.

A burly old man with a large moustache came out of the office. The boys had never met the quartermaster. He had been brought up in the regiment from a boy soldier and was said to have been a formidable soldier and a very fair quartermaster. The boys stood to attention.

'Stand at ease boys,' he said. He looked them up and down and then glanced around him to see who was listening. He patted one of the horses and rubbed its nose. 'I hear that it's not been the best of days for you lads?' The boys just nodded. 'When you get back to your platoon just you remember who you are. You are Welsh Fusiliers, the finest soldiers in the British Army. All of us, every single one of us has a duty to do and this war will have need of good men for a long time yet. This isn't the time for despair and regrets. This is a time when you need to be strong for your friends. Understand?'

'Yes sir,' the boys replied.

'Here.' The quartermaster gave Rhys a bag of tea and sugar.

'Give it to your section commander. If he thinks you've been working for me all day he will have expected you to have nicked something. Now go on, bugger off.' The boys saluted and marched off towards the company location. The quartermaster watched them go. He turned and almost bumped into the driver, who was stood smiling at him. 'What are you looking at? And what have you done to my horses?' the quartermaster roared.

'Nothing, sir.'

'Exactly. You've been here ten minutes. Get 'em sorted out.'

'Yes, sir,' the driver replied as he turned away, still smiling to himself.

'And wipe that stupid smirk off your face!

*

Two Platoon was a scene of frenzied activity when the boys arrived back. Large packs were lined up outside the barn and boxes of ammunition were strewn across the pavement. One man was handing out two bandoliers of ammunition for each man to carry. Another soldier was handing out two grenades per man. Sergeant Jones was barking at the men to sort themselves out. As the boys approached the banter died away. The men stopped what they were doing. Sergeant Jones sensed the mood change and turned as the boys approached. He looked back at the platoon.

'Corporal Parson,' he cried. 'Get over here. The rest of you crack on, we need to be gone in half an hour.' He turned and walked towards the boys so that he was out of earshot from the rest of the platoon. 'Alright lads?'

'Yes, Sergeant.'

Sergeant Jones nodded back as he searched for the right words. Corporal Parson appeared from the house and strode across.

'You boys okay?' he asked. Rhys and Huan just nodded.

'Why don't you take these lads away, Corporal, and get them sorted?'

'Yes, Sergeant. Come on lads. We've got a lot to do.'

Huan went to move but stopped suddenly. 'Sergeant–'

'It's alright lad, we've heard. There's nothing to be done now. We just need to get on.'

The boys threaded their way through the rest of the platoon behind Corporal Parson. Silence followed them. They went into the platoon house and up the wooden stairs into a large room that had been cleared of furniture. Their large packs had been placed in the corner.

'They asked for volunteers,' Corporal Parson said. 'They said the firing party had to come from the battalion.' He looked at the boys to ensure that they understood. Huan just nodded and looked at Rhys, who gave a slow nod. 'Not a single man volunteered, you understand. Not a single one. They drew lots in the end. A section of men went up this afternoon. It's not their fault.'

'I know, Corporal,' Rhys said as he bent down to pick up his kit.

'Where are we going?' Huan asked.

'Back to the front, where else? At least it will take your mind off things for a bit.'

Rhys handed the bag of tea and sugar that the quartermaster had given him to his section commander. 'This is for the boys.'

'Thanks lads,' he said. 'I'll see you outside in five minutes. I'm really sorry, you know.' Corporal Parson made his way down the stairs. Before his footsteps had reached the bottom Rhys had slid to the floor and started to sob quietly. Huan dropped his pack and sat down next to him. They sat in silence for the five minutes.

Outside the shouting got louder. The men were finishing off their preparations. Huan slid his arm round Rhys' shoulder and gave a tight squeeze. 'That's enough now. We're fusiliers, remember. Let's not let him down just yet. But I promise you this: we will have our revenge. We will survive this madness and we will have our revenge on that bastard. Right?'

Rhys rubbed his sleeve across his eyes and nodded. He took a deep breath and blew out hard. 'Too bloody right we will.'

As they shuffled down the stairs Lieutenant George stepped through the hole in the wall that was used as a door. The boys stopped on the stairs and looked at their platoon commander.

'A moment of your time?'

Lieutenant George looked tired. He looked at Rhys and Huan as they stood in front of him. 'There was, it seems, nothing to be done,' he started. 'The general read the evidence and found the case to be overwhelmingly compelling. I'm sorry, but there it is. We need to put this affair behind us and move on. We need to rebuild the regiment's reputation. I understand your suffering and–'

'And what of Bryn's reputation, sir?' Rhys said.

Stephen caught his breath and swallowed hard. 'I understand how you must be feeling now, Private, but I would remind you that we have a job to do and we will do it to the very best of our ability. Is that perfectly clear?'

Rhys looked at the young officer, not much older than himself, and held his tongue just for a moment. 'Yes sir.'

'Good. Pick up your kit and fall in with the others.' He turned to leave.

'Sir,' Huan said. 'He wasn't there, sir. Roberts, sir. We went to the Field Hospital and he wasn't there. He has probably had his leg amputated. The nurse said that he had lost a lot of blood and would have been unconscious for most of the time. She said that he would have been moved quickly to the General Hospital, had his leg removed and then sent back to England.'

'I'm sorry to hear that but hopefully he will be fine. I think you should–'

'That's not the point, sir. The nurse said that he would not have been in any fit state to have given evidence.'

Stephen swallowed hard. 'You might be right, but his account was accepted by the court.'

'Yes, sir. The same court that accepted that Sergeant Price was dead. But he's not dead, is he, sir, or the regiment would have been informed. We haven't heard have we, sir?'

Stephen felt his stomach lurch. He thought for a moment and then cleared his throat.

'Thank you, Private. Now I think you had better fall in.'

He stepped aside as they shuffled past him through the hole in the wall.

*

The platoon was assembling in three ranks as the boys left the house. Most of the men were chatting quietly or smoking. The men were heavily laden with extra ammunition, coils of wire, shovels, picks and piles of sandbags. Carry parties would follow them in later with sheets of wriggly tin and wooden supports. Another group would hopefully bring some food and tea, if they were lucky. As Huan and Rhys joined the end of the front and middle rank the chatter died. A man on Huan's right put his hand on his shoulder and squeezed slightly. Huan just nodded.

As the platoon commander approached, Sergeant Jones brought the platoon to attention. He turned smartly to his left and took three paces forward, halted and saluted Lieutenant George.

Stephen coughed to clear his throat. 'Stand the men at ease, Sergeant Jones.'

'Yes, sir. Stand at ease,' he barked at the assembled platoon. There was a scrunch of feet in unison. Lieutenant George stepped forward.

'Stand easy.'

The men visibly relaxed and one or two shuffled their feet, which were already getting cold as the remnants of the watery sun had dropped over the horizon.

'You have all heard that the sentence that has been pronounced on Private Tallent. I won't try to pretend that this is anything other than a difficult day for the battalion, and particularly for Number Two Platoon,' he paused as he cleared his throat, 'and for his friends.'

A few heads glanced along the line.

'There is no point in dwelling on the tragic events of the past few days. What's done is done and it cannot be undone. It is up to those of us remaining to ensure that the fine name of the battalion is restored. Every one of you is responsible for what happens on the battlefield. We are honourable soldiers; we will do our duty. We didn't start this war; we were forced to leave our homes and families to defeat a wicked enemy and we will defeat him. We will triumph because we are better than him. We will fight not just to win, but to avenge our fallen comrades, no matter how they have fallen. We are fighting a war of survival, for our very way of life, but most of all I want you to fight for each other because that is what is important right now. Fight for the man next to you, fight for your section and fight for your platoon. If we fight for each other I guarantee that our King and country, our loved ones, our regiment and most of all our friends will be proud of what we achieve.'

He let the words hang in the air a moment before chancing a look across to the end of the line. Huan was looking straight ahead, unflinching. 'Sergeant.'

'Yes, sir.'

'Get them away.'

'Yes, sir.'

Lieutenant George watched as Sergeant Jones marched his men towards the front line. He had one last call to make before he joined his men back at the front.

*

'Lieutenant George. What can I do for you?'

'Begging your pardon, sir. Might I have a minute of your time?'

'A minute I have, but I'm not sure that you do. Shouldn't you be making your way towards the front with your men?

'Yes sir. Sergeant Jones is—'

'Sergeant Jones is not their platoon commander, Lieutenant. I hope I have no need to remind you of that.'

No, sir. I assure you, sir, that I will catch up with them before they reach the communication trench.'

'Then you had better be quick.'

Stephen took a deep breath. He knew the commanding officer's patience would only last so long. He had rehearsed what he had wanted to say and spoke quickly but concisely. 'Sir, during the trial a statement by Private Roberts was read out. Roberts supposedly dictated it to an officer. Sir, when the statement was taken Roberts had just had his leg amputated. It is most unlikely that he would have been coherent enough to remember the events or dictate a statement due to the morphine. Either way it is highly unlikely that he would have said the words that he supposedly did. He is a common miner, sir, he would not have said the words that were read out.' Stephen could see the commanding officer starting to bristle. 'Secondly, sir, it was stated in court that Sergeant Price was dead. I am not aware, sir, that we have been informed of his death and therefore there is a possibly that he is still alive.'

'Enough,' the commanding officer said sharply. 'The members of the court martial were good and experienced officers, Stephen. I am quite certain that they considered Tallent's case on the evidence that was presented. They cannot rule on speculation or evidence that is not presented. Tallent had his moment in court and an experienced captain represented him. I understand your concern. It is admirable but misguided. The general has made his decision and that decision is final. You need to put this behind you quickly and move on. You have more pressing concerns now; your men need strong leadership to get them through this unpleasant business and to get them through the next few days. God knows they'll need it. You are a good officer, Stephen, and I understand your concern for one of your men but it must stop here and now. You did your best for Tallent but you have other men who need you just as badly. I attach no blame to you for what happened and neither should you blame yourself. You need to draw a line under this episode. I do not wish to hear any more on this issue, is that clearly understood?'

'Yes sir.'

'Good. Dismissed.'

CHAPTER THIRTY-SEVEN

Padre Hughes trotted down the marbled staircase that wound down two floors in a wide spiral and hurried towards the door. The duty clerk saw him approaching and stood up as he would for every officer who passed his position. He checked his watch.

'Nineteen thirty-five, sir. It'll be a close one.'

'Thanks, Perkins. Just what I needed to hear.' Perkins smiled back.

'And it's raining, sir!' Perkins was right; it was coming down in ramrods.

Hughes trotted across the road as quickly as his dignity and position would allow. The mess was only a couple of hundred yards away. He could see that the main entrance doors were still open. Thank goodness. With fifty yards to go the door started to close.

'Hang on there,' he called. The mess sergeant stuck his head around the door to see who had shouted and smiled at the padre as he sprinted the last few yards.

'Thank you, my son.'

'One of these days, sir...' the mess sergeant said with a smile and a chuckle. The padre smiled back.

'Maybe, but where would be the fun if I was always on time?'

'True, sir. The other gentlemen are about to go through but I can give you a couple of minutes to get your breath back if you like.'

'That would be very much appreciated, Sergeant.'

'Wait there a moment, sir. When I go through to announce dinner I will leave this door slightly ajar and then as the other

363

gentlemen go through to the dining room you can slip through and join the back of the group, sir.'

*

'Ah, there you are Padre,' the general called across the anteroom as the officers took coffee. 'And don't think I didn't notice you skulking in at the back of the dinner queue. I didn't get where I am without knowing what's going on around me. Eyes in the back of my head, you know.' He chuckled and raised his glass to the padre and took a sip of port. 'How's morale? Not yours of course – the men's?'

'Actually, General, I was wondering if I might have a quick word about that very thing?'

'Were you? Well of course you can, Padre. Just have a chat with Richardson; he'll find a slot for you in the morning. He's a good lad although I do wish he would desist from all that nonsense of going up to the front. I don't think he realises that wars are won through good staff work and planning. Still, I can't help but admire his courage. I'm sure that we would all rather be at the front than stuck back here.' The other officers who had gathered around gave lighthearted laughs.

'Unfortunately, General, tomorrow would be a bit too late. I was hoping we could do this sooner rather than later.'

The general's smile faded. 'Hmm… I take it that it's this confounded Welsh fellow? Well let me tell you, Padre, I am not of a mood to discuss it in the mess. I know that you are only trying to do your job but then so are hundreds of thousands of other men out there and they manage to do their duty. Confound it; this is not a matter that I take lightly. Without rules and regulations there would be anarchy and where would we be then, eh? I'll tell you where: nowhere, that's where! Discipline has to be maintained and as much as it disappoints me that I have to make these decisions it was not one that I found difficult in this case.'

The mess had grown silent as the general's voice got louder and louder. The other officers in the general's circle were looking down at the floor and noticeably stepping back so as not to be caught in the crossfire. Only the padre stood his ground.

'If you want to do something useful then I suggest that you go and pray for his soul because that's all he's got left.'

The general excused himself and strode for the door. The mess steward held the door open as he left the silent anteroom. Captain Richardson placed his glass on the steward's tray and walked off after his general. As the door closed there was an audible sigh of relief and a low murmur started. The padre stared after the closed door.

One of the officers smiled at him. 'Don't worry Padre; we all catch his wrath at some point. It was just your turn tonight.' He patted his shoulder. 'Anyway, the fellow deserves everything he gets.'

The padre rounded on the officer, his eyes blazing. 'Really? You think he deserves to be stood up against a wall, alone, blindfolded and shot by his own friends, all of whom will probably fire to miss and then to have a young officer, his own hands shaking with fear, fire a fatal shot into his head? Oh, I'm sure he deserves that.'

'I say, I didn't think—'

'No, you probably didn't. Now if you'll excuse me I have a job to do.' The padre pushed through the group of officers and strode purposefully from the room.

The officer looked at his colleagues. 'What did I say?'

*

The mess sergeant was ready with the padre's hat as he strode towards the front door.

'Thank you, Sergeant.'

'Not at all, sir,' he replied in a low whisper. 'Goodnight sir.'

The padre crossed the square. His stride was measured and purposeful. The sergeant sighed. He had heard the general's rant, as had most of the mess staff. He would have to speak to them all later to remind them that what went on in the mess stayed in the mess. It wouldn't do to spread gossip, even if he agreed with the padre. He didn't wish to be in his shoes tonight.

'Sergeant,' an officer called from down the hallway.

'Yes, sir? Ah, good evening Captain Richardson.'

'Where's the padre?'

'Just left, sir. Would you like me to call him back, sir?'

'Yes. Tell him to meet me in the anteroom as soon as he can.'

'Is that wise, sir?'

'What do you mean?'

'Well, sir, there are still other officers in the anteroom and after—'

'Perhaps you're right.'

'Can I suggest the morning room, sir? It's quiet in there, sir. You won't be disturbed. I can see to that.'

'Good thinking, Sergeant. Find him as quick as you can, will you?'

'Right away, sir.'

The sergeant ran down the steps and looked across the square. The square was still well lit by the lights of the bars that surrounded the cobbled square, and he caught a glimpse of the padre towards the far end, heading towards the court martial centre. He raced across the square, dodging small groups of men who were meandering after one too many *vin blancs*. He was a few yards away when the padre reached the few steps that led up to the administration building.

'Begging your pardon, sir,' he said. The padre turned in surprise to see the sergeant standing with his hands on his hips, breathing deeply. 'Sir. Captain…' he sucked in the air. The padre smiled.

'Take your time, Sergeant.

'Thank you, sir.' He paused again to control his breath. 'Blimey, I'm a bit out of shape, sir.'

'So I can see. What brings you over here at such a trot?'

'Captain Richardson, sir. He would very much like to see you, urgently, sir, in the morning room.' The padre thought for a second and looked across at the mess on the far side of the square.

'Did he say what it was about?

'No, sir. Just that it was quite urgent, sir.'

'Thank you, Sergeant.' He skipped down the steps. 'I'll leave you to make your own way back, shall I?' He smiled at the sergeant, who was now holding onto the metal railing.

'Very kind of you, sir.'

*

The morning room was in darkness, save for a candle that Captain Richardson had lit on the far side of the room. The padre poked his head around the door. Hilary was seated in one of the tall-backed chairs and leaned forward when he heard the door.

'Come in, Padre. Best shut the door.' The padre closed the door and sat down next to his friend. 'You're very wet. Seems to be becoming a habit.'

'Yes, but at least I am still alive.'

'Oh stop it. Let's not start that again. You caught the old man at the wrong time and you were hardly tactful. The mess was full, for goodness' sake, what was he meant to say? This has not been easy for him.'

'What, and you think it's easy for the young man over there?' he said, pointing in the direction of the administrative building.

'Look, nobody is saying it's easy for anyone but shouting at me won't help.'

The padre sighed and sank back into the chair. 'I'm sorry Hilary, it's just that... well, this is not right.'

'I know it's not right but we will need more than emotion and gut feeling if we are going to win the old man over. If he thinks that there is good enough reason to change his mind then he is not an unreasonable soul.'

'Really? I got the impression that he definitely wasn't in the mood to change his mind.'

'Oh come on, he changes his mind as often as the wind blows.' He paused a moment as if to think. 'We just need to make sure that there is a breeze blowing in the right direction.'

'As it happens I might have some information that will cause more than just a breeze, but we are running out of time.'

CHAPTER THIRTY-EIGHT

The rain started to fall as soon as they reached the entrance to the communication trench. It was only a light drizzle but it soon soaked through the heavy wool tunic to the cotton vest undershirt where it met the sweat that was trying to escape in the other direction. Some men thought that it was a bad omen. With very little faith left to cling to superstition gave them hope, and if they had hope there was always a chance of getting out of the madness. Huan and Rhys barely noticed as the rain started to beat harder on their helmets. They automatically bent slightly forward and trudged on in silence towards the labyrinth of trenches that had become their life.

One of the section commanders stopped at the entrance to count the men through as Sergeant Jones led the way accompanied by a soldier from the incumbent battalion. The section commander would bring up the rear and confer with Sergeant Jones when they arrived to ensure that they still had the right amount of men. It was not unknown for men to disappear underfoot during a relief in place without anyone noticing.

'Keep it quiet now lads,' the section commander said in a hoarse whisper as they moved past him in single file. 'Watch your footing and keep up.'

The grumbling stopped as soon as the platoon entered the communication trench. As they descended into the high-sided trench any vestige of normality was lost. Each man held on to the man in front for stability and so that they didn't get lost. Although they had been in this particular communication trench many times there were always changes caused by a bombardment or a flood repair or just an officer's good idea to keep the men busy. Most of them could do the route blindfolded but they still slipped on the mud that was rapidly being churned up underfoot. Silently they crashed into the trench walls, unable to steady themselves as they fought to balance under the extra weight of the stores they were carrying. Dropping their load meant stopping to pick it up and the risk of the chain breaking. No man would thank you for delaying the changeover. The platoon shuffled along in fits and starts as messages were whispered from front to rear: *speed up, slow down, watch the blast netting, passing the aid post.* Finally, the order came down to rest as Sergeant Jones reached the head of the trench and reported to the outgoing platoon commander.

*

The platoon dugout was a poor affair, barely big enough for a couple of men but at least it was reinforced with wooden struts that supported a corrugated iron ceiling.

'Hello, sir,' Sergeant Jones said to the young officer who was just getting into his kit.

'You're early, Sergeant. You almost caught me with my trousers down,' the officer replied.

'Heaven forbid, sir. We made good time, but we can always come back tomorrow, sir, if you would prefer?'

'Not blooming likely Sergeant. Where's Lieutenant George? I thought he was taking over this little bit of England. Hasn't worked out a decent excuse has he?'

'No sir, he has been momentarily delayed by the commanding officer. He'll be along shortly to take over this little bit of Wales, as you say, sir.'

Both men laughed. They had been swapping about in the front line for some months. The entrance sign changed from *Croeso I Cymru* to *Welcome to England* each time they changed over.

'I've left some coffee in the pot, should still be warm if you'd like it. I shan't tell Lieutenant George you had it. Serves him right for being late.'

'Very kind of you, sir. Don't mind if I do.'

'Are you happy to take over or would you prefer to wait until your errant platoon commander arrives? Of course if you do wait, you will have to share the coffee!'

Sergeant Jones laughed. 'I think I can probably manage for a while, sir. I'll just get my lads settled. I'll let you know when the last of your lads are moving, sir. You might as well stay here, in the dry, for a few minutes.'

'That's jolly decent of you, Sergeant. I might just leave you a biscuit to go with your coffee in that case.'

*

As each section commander arrived Jones gave them their final instructions and sent them along the trench. The men meandered around buttresses until they found their allotted fire bay to be welcomed by the friendly banter of the Middlesex men who were already kitted and ready to leave. The usual banter started, but it was kept at a low whisper. Sergeant Jones eventually made his way along the trench, sending back the Middlesex men as he passed each section until he got to the end of the line.

'Corporal Parson,' he said when he finally found the section commander, who was busy allocating funk holes to his boys. 'You're the end of B Company and you've got C Company on your left, then D and then A on the far end, alright? Make sure that you link up with them as soon as you can and then let me know where they are putting their sentry.'

'Right you are, Sergeant.'

'And another thing,' he said, quietly pulling the corporal to one side. 'Make sure that Jones and Taylor are kept busy at first light and if you have to put them on stag tonight make sure it is sooner rather than later. The less time they have to think about tomorrow the better for all of us. Got it?'

'They're going to be gutted tomorrow. It's not right you know, Sergeant. Tallent was a good lad; I'm pretty sure I believe his story, you know.'

'It doesn't matter what you, I or anyone else thinks for, that matter,' Jones said, giving his old colleague a knowing look. 'Just keep your thoughts to yourself or you will find yourself on the wrong side of the commanding officer's desk. The best thing that we can do now is to make sure that they are in a fit state to fight. Keep 'em busy. They'll be fine in a few days.'

'I suppose you are right, Sergeant. Don't worry about Jones and Taylor; the rest of the boys will keep them going.'

*

The rain had mostly eased, but a fine drizzle persisted in keeping everything damp. It was deathly silent over no-man's land. Rhys chanced a peek over the parapet. He had copped the first sentry stag while the rest of the section sorted out their kit in the vain hope of keeping it dry. There was a belt of fresh wire that the Middlesex had lain over the old wire. They had obviously been busy for the past few days. Beyond the wire there was only desolate blackness.

He peered into the void – it was still, the wind had died and the rain had stopped. It was very quiet, unusually quiet. There was usually a flare or two arcing into the sky from both sides to catch patrols unawares. There were no shadows and no movement. All around him the platoon was starting to fix broken parapets and repair the revetting that held the trench walls in place.

Every night in the trench was the same routine; trench repairs, wiring, fatigues or stag duty. Each man had his favourite. Rhys liked the solitude of the sentry duty so that he could at least put his head above the parapet and see across no-man's land; it was a luxury that no one could afford during the day if they wanted to live.

'Hey Taylor, are you still awake up there?' Corporal Parson said in a hoarse whisper.

'No, Corporal.'

'Thought as much. What's happening?'

Rhys looked down. 'Nothing, Corporal.'

'I know there's nothing happening. The question is, why not?'

'Dunno, Corporal. Would you like me to go and ask them?'

'No, don't bother, they're probably busy having a sausage party or something. Just keep an eye out. They're up to something, I can tell.'

'Right you are, Corporal.'

*

Lieutenant George opened the curtain of the platoon dugout and bent slightly to get inside. He sighed as he looked around. He was back in familiar territory. There was a faint glow from a candle in the far corner, but enough to see Sergeant Jones busy around the Primus stove.

'Welcome home, sir. Just brewing up. Tea?'

'Thanks, Sergeant Jones. That would be very welcome. How are the men?'

'They're fine, sir.'

'You made good time getting here. I thought that I would catch you up.'

'You know how they are, sir. Always eager to get here.'

They both smiled. Stephen laid his kit on the bottom bunk as he always did – a perk of his rank, he always told Sergeant Jones. He sat on the bunk and gratefully accepted the steaming mug of tea.

'How did it go, sir?'

'How did what go. Sergeant Jones?

Your interview with the colonel, sir. I presume that it was about Tallent, sir?'

'You seem to know an awful lot.'

'I'm your platoon sergeant, sir. I know everything.'

'In which case you'll know how it went! I don't suppose Lieutenant Farrington left any sugar did he?'

'Er... no sir, but I do have a little stash that came my way just recently, sir.'

Stephen smiled. It never ceased to amaze him how his sergeant always had a little something of everything that 'just came his way'. Sergeant Jones dug out a small bag of sugar from his satchel that he always carried into the trenches. It was like a bottomless pit, Stephen thought absently, as he stirred the sugar into the tea.

Sergeant Jones sat on the rickety chair at the table. 'I take it there's no hope then?'

'Not unless you believe in miracles.'

'I've been praying for one of those for months and it hasn't made any difference so far.'

'What's going on out there?' Stephen asked as he nodded towards the entrance.

'Just the normal, sir. The men are busy making the place look pretty. The sentries are posted and I've spoken to the companies on our left and Three Platoon on our right. It's pretty quiet actually. A bit too quiet if you get my meaning. It doesn't feel right.'

'Maybe Fritz is just having a night off. God knows we could all do with one.'

'You look about done in, sir. Perhaps you should get your head down for a few hours. I'll keep an eye on the blokes.'

Stephen was about to protest but one look at his sergeant told him that he wasn't about to concede. 'Thanks, Sergeant Jones.'

Stephen unbuckled his Sam Browne belt and draped it over the back of the chair and slumped back onto the bunk. He lay looking up at the bottom of the bunk above him. He was tired; his eyes ached so much that they stung when he closed them. As the stinging subsided he felt his body relaxing. It was so quiet. *Peace at last*, he thought. His eyes snapped open. *Peace – shit.*

'Sergeant Jones,' he screamed, just as the earth around him started to shudder. He felt himself being lifted towards the ceiling of the dugout and his world went out.

*

Rhys felt the vibrations through the ground as he stared out into no-man's land. The faint tremor suddenly grew into a deep growling rumble as if a runaway train was about to scream past him. Within a second or two the earth at the far end of the trench erupted into the air. Earth and bodies rose up as if they were riding at the head of a spewing volcano.

Rhys was flung from the parapet against the back wall of the trench. The force of hitting the wall knocked the breath from his chest, leaving him in a crumpled heap at the bottom of the trench. His head was numb and his body hurt. He tried to push himself up but could scarcely move. He looked along the trench at the rest of the section, who were lying flat on the floor. As he looked up the first clods of earth were striking the ground all around him. The sky was raining mud, wood, metal and pieces of bodies that had been ripped to shreds by the force of the explosion. He could see Huan a few yards away, screaming at him, but there was just silence. All around him men were clambering, grabbing at bodies and helping men up, but there was no noise.

Huan scrambled across the floor of the trench and grabbed his friend's arm. Through his daze Rhys could see Huan's mouth moving. He shook his head to clear the daze and then clasped his hands over his head as another shower of debris rained down on them, threatening to entomb them.

'Shit,' Huan repeated over and over again as each piece of earth hit him. Finally the earth stopped falling. Huan looked up and realised that he was still alive. He tried to turn onto his side to see where the rest of the section were. The brief respite was shattered as the earth started to churn again. Huan covered his head with his hands and groaned.

As the shells pummelled the ground Huan clawed at the earth that covered most of Rhys' body. 'Rhys!' he cried. 'Don't you go dying on me, you bugger.' He drove his hands into the soft clay and pulled up his friend's face. He brushed the dirt from his face and tried to pull him upright but Rhys' legs were pinned to the ground by the mound of earth that had half-buried him. 'Come on, you bugger. Speak to me.'

'Am I dead?' Rhys croaked.

'Not yet,' Huan screamed above the noise of the artillery furnace that was pounding their position. Rhys was struggling to open his eyes and his body flinched with every shell that landed around them.

'Come on, don't give up now,' Huan cried as he started to tear at the mud with his bare hands. Within seconds another pair of hands were clawing at the earth.

Corporal Parson nodded at Huan. 'You alright?' he screamed above the inferno. Huan just nodded as he clawed at the earth. 'Get him sat up and give him a drink,' the section commander yelled. 'He'll be okay. Just keep your head down until this lot stops.'

Huan cradled his friend and watched as the corporal lurched at a low crouch along the fire bay, checking the other men as more earth continued to crash down around them. The next bay had collapsed. What had been a trench was just a mound of earth. A leg was sticking out directly towards the sky. A couple of men were frantically digging but stopped as an arm came out without the rest of the body.

A shell landed within yards of them, blowing them back into the fire bay. One of the men just lay where he landed, unmoving. His mate looked as if he had been buried waist-deep until Huan realised that he had been blown in two. The man looked down, gasped and toppled forward. Huan gripped Rhys harder and cried. There was nothing else he could do.

The barrage lasted another ten minutes before the rate slackened and the enemy switched their aim to the rear trenches where they hoped to catch the reinforcements coming forward and the casualties going backwards.

Corporal Parson was moving more freely along his section. He looked around the bay and counted his men.

'Where's Billy?' he screamed.

One of the other men pointed to a patch of blood, charred clothing and bone fragments that were embedded in the rear wall.

'Gone,' was all he said before he started to shake uncontrollably and tears started to stream down his face.

The corporal put his hand on his shoulder. 'Alright boyo, just hang in there.' One of the men was detailed off to continue along the trench towards C Company to see how they were doing. The man came back in a few minutes.

'About as well as us Corporal, getting the shit kicked out of them!' he yelled. 'It looks as if there was a mine under us. I think we were just on the edge.'

'Alright, make sure you keep yourself down. They'll be over the crater in a few minutes. We'll need to be ready.' The man nodded and took his place at the bottom of the trench. Corporal Parson moved among his men to explain what was happening. He stopped and sat down next to Rhys. He put his mouth next to Rhys' ear. 'How you doing, lad?'

'I've been better, Corporal.'

'Not much of a lookout are you? You didn't see that one coming,' he said as he grinned like a Cheshire Cat. Rhys returned the grin and nodded.

Corporal Parsons leaned across towards Huan, who was still clutching his friend. 'You alright?' he yelled. Huan mouthed back that he was fine. 'Just hang on lads, it won't last forever.'

The bombardment lasted another hour, by which time the trench had ceased to exist. The front and the back had been blown in. All that remained was a series of deep shell holes that were barely connected. Despite the ferocity of the barrage the section were all still in one piece, bar a few cuts and grazes and Billy. Shortly before first light the barrage changed to a box bombardment. Fire was lifted from B Company completely and a wall of fire was placed on either side, smothering C and D Companies, and on the battalion on the right. A storm of steel continued to pulverise the support trenches, trapping B Company in the remnants of their trench.

*

'Get ready boys, they'll be coming over in a minute. Just wait till you hear the whistle before you stick your head up and then give 'em everything you have, and then give 'em a bit more. The bastards aren't having our trench,' Corporal Parson shouted at his men.

The men didn't needed telling. Bolts were being wrenched back in anticipation. Men were trembling from fear and excitement in equal measure; they needed to vent their anger and frustration. Huan wiped the sweat from his brow as rows of grey figures clambered over the lip from the safety of their trench. They quickly spread out, crouching and darting as they moved across the crater-strewn landscape. The Welshmen starred in wonder and tried to steady their breathing.

'Just give the bloody order to fire,' Rhys muttered to no one in particular. Huan looked across at his friend and smiled as a machine gun from A Company started chattering away to the left. The rush of Germans faltered for a moment as the machine guns scythed through the grey ranks. The line went to ground for a few minutes; then groups started to work their way forward from one shell hole to another.

'Don't let them get within bombing range,' Corporal Parson screamed.

He lifted his head to make sure that everyone had heard. A

bullet took him through his temple and his lifeless body toppled forward into the earth.

Bullets and shells rained all around, but in Number Two Section there was silence. Lance Corporal Smith drew back the bolt of his Lee Enfield rifle and took aim.

'You heard Corporal Parson – shoot like you mean it.' He snatched at the trigger and a grey-clad soldier fell backwards.

*

Number Two Section held the German advance for most of the morning with the aid of the neighbouring machine guns. The British guns had finally worked out the correct coordinates and were delivering their own storm of steel over the German trenches. The Germans were trapped between the crater and the British curtain of steel rain that was dancing over the German front line. Moving forward was their only option. They crept forward as individuals, darting from shell hole to shell hole. They regrouped where they could in twos and threes, paused and then scampered forward to the next hole.

'Can anyone see them?' Huan cried above the cannonade of fire that was raining down behind them, in front of them and on both sides. He looked across at two of the men on his right, who were hunkered down. 'Get up you bastards, you won't hit anything from down there,' he cried. The men looked at each other and then did as they were told. Huan gave them a knowing nod. As he looked to his left another man was busy firing potshots over the rim of his shell hole. 'I'm not sure I was expecting it to be like this,' Huan shouted across to him.'

'Nor me,' he shouted back, then smiled and looked across at the scene in front of him. Smoke obscured most of the battlefield. 'Christ, I can hardly breathe.'

'Hey,' Rhys said, grabbing his friend's sleeve. Huan peered at his friend from under his helmet. 'My head hurts!'

'Oh, you're awake then! Of course it hurts, you've been thinking too hard.'

'What's happening?'

'What do you think is happening? The Germans blew half the trench up and have been attacking for God knows how long!'

'Help me up, boyo,' Rhys said as he tried to steady himself on his feet.

'No. You stay down there. You're not fit to shoot straight. You'll probably do more damage than good.'

'I can't stay down here doing nothing while you're up there,' Rhys screamed.

'Then do something useful. Break open the ammo boxes and pass the ammo along to the other lads.'

Rhys grabbed a box and smashed it open with his bayonet. To the left the fire bay was blocked with earth, wood and metal. There was no way through unless he crawled over the top, so he did. He moved along the remnants of the trench, which had ceased to exist, passing boxes of ammunition to the other lads. A couple of lads were in a deep hole that had been blocked off by the explosion, so he threw some boxes over to them. He finally crawled back to Huan, who was steadily firing across the parapet.

'Here you go, boyo,' he called up to his friend.

Huan put his hand down and grabbed a couple of boxes and placed them on the parapet next to him. 'Ta. How you feeling?'

'Better, thanks.'

'Good, then best get your arse up here before Fritz comes down there!'

'Well why didn't you say?' Rhys replied, jumping up next to his friend.

He looked out across the desolation. Most of the scene was obscured by smoke; artillery was landing a hundred yards in front of him, which created rhythmic thuds that shuddered through his body. The noise was so intense that he could barely hear his own voice.

'Just watch the rims and as soon as someone makes a dash take him down,' Huan screamed, and they stood with their rifles in the alert position, looking over the sights like poachers waiting for a rabbit.

'Do you know what time it is, Huan?'

'Not a clue, but I guess it's nearly midday.' He looked at his friend and grinned. 'You can't be hungry at a time like this?'

'No, not today,' he said, looking at his friend. 'It's been and gone, hasn't it, and we never gave him a thought.'

'What are you on about?' The look on Rhys' face said it all. 'Bollocks!' Huan said. He let the rim of his helmet rest on the ground in front of his face and breathed softly. Gently, he slid down the face of the trench and rested on the fire step. He sat still for a moment and then his body started to shake gently. There were no tears. Rhys put his arm around his shoulders and they sat quietly in the mayhem for a few minutes as shrapnel rained all around them.

Huan looked at his friend. 'What do we do now?'

Rhys thought for a moment. 'We'll do exactly what Bryn would have done: fight these bastards and then we'll find Symonds and make sure that he gets exactly what he deserves.'

Huan looked up as another shower of earth rained down on them. 'Getting out of here might need a minor miracle but if it means that we get to see that bastard Symonds swing then best we get on with it.'

Rhys turned his head. 'At least if we die here, we'll be with friends. Who did Bryn die with, tell me that?'

'We might not have been there but he was with us in our hearts and minds. Even if we were a bit busy at the time. He'll understand that. The important thing is that we will never forget him and neither will anyone else. We'll make sure of that. So don't you go forgetting it, I know you've got a brain like a sieve.'

'Well in that case,' Rhys said, grabbing his rifle, 'we'd best get out of this mess and we won't do it skulking down here. He gave us a letter to deliver and one of us is going to get it home for him. Right?'

'Bloody right.' They scrambled to the parapet and peered into the furling smoke. They began firing rapidly in the general direction of the enemy. Huan suddenly laid his weapon down and looked across at Rhys.

'What are you doing?' Rhys screamed.

'Where is it?'

'Where's what?'

'The letter.'

Rhys looked blankly back at his friend. 'I thought you had it?'

'No, I thought you had it.'

'Shit! Well in that case we had better both survive!'

*

A cry from the right made them turn as four Germans were charging a shell hole ten yards away. A Welshman in the shell hole rose with his bayonet fixed. The first German was shot at point-blank range and the second was impaled as he ran into the bayonet. Huan and Rhys fired simultaneously along with several other men. Without waiting to see if their bullets had hit home, Huan and Rhys were on their feet and scrambling from their hole. They screamed as they covered the short yards towards the Germans, who wavered a moment too long. Huan took his target in the chest. The German was too stunned to scream and looked back at Huan with disbelief. His hand grasped the muzzle of the rifle as Huan thrust again. The German sank to his knees as Huan twisted his body and pushed down. To his right Rhys sliced his target in the left side of his stomach. The German gave a short gasp and lashed out with his own bayonet. The top of the bayonet sliced the air in front of Rhys' chin. Rhys rocked back on his rear leg and lunged forward again as the German was unbalanced. He jabbed his bayonet into the German's belly and pushed hard. The German's eyes bulged; his mouth moved but no sound came out. Rhys pushed hard and the German fell backwards, hissing as he hit the ground. Huan had dropped onto one knee and was panting hard, oblivious to the bullets that were pattering around his feet. Rhys looked down at his friend as he wiped the cold sweat away from his eyes.

'Oi! Get in here boys,' the Welshman cried. Rhys grabbed Huan by the collar and pulled him down into the slight hollow. They rolled over and crawled up next to the old soldier. 'Thanks lads. I thought that was me then,' he said.

'So did we,' Rhys said with a short laugh.

Huan looked around for support and saw a couple of men from the section a few yards away to his right. He tapped Rhys and the other soldier on the shoulder. 'Let's try and get across to the others,' he shouted as he pointed to where they lay. Rhys and the old hand nodded. 'On a count of three… three!' Huan screamed and threw himself across the lip and rolled into the next shell hole.

Rhys looked at the other man and shrugged. 'He was never very good at counting,' he yelled.

Huan and the others were already firing. The older soldier gave a deep sigh. 'Ready?'

'As I'll ever be,' Rhys replied.

The older soldier nodded and they rose, stumbled forward and crawled into the shell hole next to Huan.

'You daft bastard,' the older soldier shouted as he rolled into Huan, who was already lying on the lip of the shell hole firing like a man possessed.

The old soldier checked that Rhys was with him and lay on his back to take a look around. The reserve trenches were still being bombarded; a curtain of fire on all four sides boxed them in. To his left he couldn't see anyone and to his right were two other lads from the section who were getting as low in the shell hole as possible. A burst of machine gun fire brushed over the lip of their shell hole, spraying them with mud. The rest of the platoon was either dead, buried or keeping a very low profile. They were alone.

He chanced a look over the lip of his own hole. Away to their right at the end of the platoon position, where the mine had exploded, there were still a few Bosch desperately trying to get to the lip of the crater. A group of Cameron Highlanders were pushing them back with relentless machine gun fire towards the centre of the platoon position.

'How much ammo have you got left?' the old soldier shouted in Huan's ear. Huan rolled from side to side so that he didn't have to expose himself and checked his pouches.

'Bugger all,' Huan called back. 'A few rounds and one grenade.'

'What about you?' he shouted at Rhys.

'Much the same! What are we going to do?'

'I don't know. Where's Lance Corporal Smith?'

Huan shook his head. 'No idea. I haven't seen him for ages.'

The old soldier took another look over the lip of the hole. The air was thick with smoke and dust. Artillery shells were landing sporadically across his front, adding more earth and debris to obscure the view. There was a little movement at the far side of the no-man's land. A few Germans were scurrying forward from hole to hole. He could see an officer shouting and pointing towards his own position.

'Looks as if they are going to give it another try, lads, and as I see it, if the Germans get into that fucking great hole over there, we'll be sitting ducks.' He paused as he took another look over the rim. 'If we stay here we're done for and if we go that way or that way,' he said, pointing to his left and right, 'we're done for. So I reckon we should go that way,' he said, pointing towards the Germans. The boys groaned. 'It looks as if it's just us and then a whole heap of nothing until they reach the rear area, so I reckon we should stop them. What do you think?'

Rhys nodded to Huan, who nodded to the old soldier.

'Right we are then; five of us should be enough. He called over to the next shell hole. 'Oi, you two. Hold your fire until I shout "fire" and then give them everything you've got, lobb a few grenades and then charge at the far side of the crater – got it?' The two men nodded. Huan looked at Rhys and grinned. Rhys clasped his friend on the shoulder.

'It's just another game, boyo. Let's win this one for Bryn.'

'FIRE!'

CHAPTER THIRTY-NINE

'Grenades!'

Four grenades were hurled over the rims of small shell holes that the five soldiers occupied.

'Ready? Charge!'

The five Welshmen rose as one and scrambled over the slight inclines of the shell holes that they had been sheltering in. As they scrambled forward, bullets smashed into the earth around their feet and zipped through the air.

Rhys could feel the bullets whipping past his head but they seemed to part as he charged forward. They had barely taken ten paces when a shell burst behind them, sending them sprawling forward. Huan hit the earth head first before tumbling forward several times. Rhys landed with a thud on Huan's back and rolled to his side.

The old soldier was blown several feet in the air, enveloped in a ball of orange flame and landed back in the shell hole. Rhys shook his head and glanced back at the old soldier, willing him to get up but there was no movement and no screaming. Huan looked at Rhys, gritted his teeth and struggled onto his feet again.

To their right the other two members of the section were a few yards ahead. They were screaming at the top of their voices. Their weapons were lowered parallel to the ground as they ran into the flank of the Germans, who were consolidating on the far side of the crater.

Rhys and Huan screamed and thrust their bayonets into the Germans who were still crouched on the ground. The Germans had been focussed on their front and were surprised by the small band of men who appeared from their flank.

The boys stabbed and kicked the bodies away from the bayonets before their victims had even finished breathing their last. Thrust, twist, draw, step forward – it was textbook training. They didn't need to think; they just had to kill. The attack became frenzied; animal instincts to kill or be killed took over.

The ferocity of the attack tore through the German soldiers. One or two raised their hands but it was too late to stop the cold steel slicing through their chests. The rifle butt swept left, cracking skulls; then the blade swept right, gouging into flesh, slicing through bone and cartilage, leaving limbs dangling. As the Germans screamed, so too did the Welshmen. There was no plan, just a lust for life and the need to kill.

When there were no more Germans to stab or slash the boys fell to the earth, panting like the dogs they had become. Their lungs ached for air as sweat dripped from every pore of their bodies. Rhys looked at his friend, who had collapsed on all fours. Blood was dripping from his hands; it was smeared over his face and clothes.

'Yours or theirs?' Rhys asked between gasps.

Huan checked himself and grinned. 'Definitely theirs,' he said with a thin smile and sat down next to Rhys. 'I reckon we won that one.' Rhys nodded and leaned away as he retched several times. 'You need to work a bit harder in training.'

'Really? You were one having trouble keeping up.'

A burst of machine gun fire from the German lines sent them both scurrying over the inside lip of the crater. The other two Welshmen rolled over the top and slithered down the mud to get as far below the withering German fire as possible.

'What do we do now?' Rhys asked. All four soldiers looked at each other and shrugged. Sustained rifle and machine gun fire started to strafe the lip of the crater. Earth showered the boys as bullets brushed overhead.

'I'm getting really pissed off with this,' Rhys shouted.

Huan was still looking back through the swirling smoke towards what had been the British front line. He stared for a few moments, looking left to right and back again. 'You'd be even more pissed off if you knew it was our own boys – look!'

The boys looked in the direction that Huan was pointing and could see a row of rifles in front of them blazing away.

'Blimey, I think we've upset everyone. Get down in the crater,' Rhys cried as he started to shuffle down the crater.

They managed to squeeze down about another yard as bullets continued to zip overhead. At least they could no longer feel the bullets brushing their cheeks. Huan faced his front and could just about make out some grey figures charging from the right and being cut down by withering rifle fire.

'They're trying to stop another counter attack,' he screamed at the others. 'There's bugger all we can do now except hope that they don't come over the top. Anyone got any ammo left?' There were shaking heads all round. 'In that case, let's dig!'

*

Huan was lying on his back looking up at the sky. A stream of British aeroplanes had flown low over their position and dropped bombs on the German lines. They had left long trails of white cloud. The firing had died down about an hour earlier and the bombardment had all but stopped apart from an occasional thud. The relative silence was as unnerving as the cacophony of noise that they had endured all day.

Rhys and Huan crawled to the rim of the crater to sneak a quick look at their situation. Rhys put his shaving mirror on his bayonet and lifted it above the rim. Lying on his back with his head to the rim he was able to sweep the area in front of the crater. Nothing was moving. He could see the German line, or what was left of it. Nothing was moving. He angled the mirror so that he could see no-man's land. Grey figures carpeted the barren landscape; many were bent double as if they were kissing the earth. Arms and legs were detached from torsos. Bodies lay on the earth as if they had been sprinkled from above. Rhys stared in horror at the destruction.

A gasp close by made him flick the mirror so that he could see just over the ridge to the area that they had attacked. He had no idea what had happened. It had been frenetic, a blur; it could have been a ruck or maul – bodies were everywhere, but the ball was nowhere to be seen. He saw something move. It was a hand. It moved backwards and forwards like a stem of corn in the wind. He focussed the mirror so that he could see where the hand led. It belonged to a German soldier. Rhys looked at him through the mirror. He was a young man, no older than himself. He was gasping. He couldn't have been more than four yards away. Rhys could see tears in his eyes as he mumbled something that Rhys could not understand.

'One of them is still alive.'

'Well I'm not going over the top to finish him off,' Huan replied.

'He's hurt.'

'Good.'

'What do you mean, "good"?' Rhys said as he lowered the mirror. 'He's no older than you and me.'

'Well that's not our fault, is it? He chose to fight.'

'Yeah, but we can't leave him. What if that was you or me?'

'Well if it was you I'd leave you but if it was me, I'd want someone to help me.'

'Exactly. So we need to help him.'

Huan looked at the other two soldiers and sighed. 'We need to talk about this first. There are four of us, right? So if we stick together we might make it through. If we go over the top, who knows what might happen? We're pretty safe here. I vote that we stay put and Fritz will have to take his chances.'

'Well I can't leave him like that. His moaning will get on my nerves if nothing else. Look, he's the same as you and me and if I were wounded I would want someone to come to help me. I don't suppose he wants to be here any more than we do. We're all soldiers at the end of the day.'

Huan sighed and lay back to look at the sky. 'I suppose so.'

'Anyway, he might have some sausages on him.'

'Well why didn't you say?! Come on then.'

*

Rhys and Huan left their weapons with the other two soldiers and crawled back up to the lip of the crater. It was only a few yards but they were both breathing heavily by the time they were poised just below the lip. They could hear the German groaning on the other side.

'Do you think we should tell him we're coming?' Huan suggested.

Rhys looked at his friend. 'And say what? "Sorry we stabbed you but we'd like to help you now"?'

'We could at least let him know that we are here.'

Rhys thought for a moment and nodded.

Huan cleared his throat as if he was going to address a crowd in the Town Hall. 'Hello... hello, *mein* friend!' There was a low moan from the other side of the lip. 'We're coming to help... stay there!'

'Stay there? Where else is he going to go, you idiot?' Rhys chided. 'On the count of three we'll roll over the top, grab his tunic on either side and crawl back over. Okay?'

'One... two... three!'

They hurled themselves over the rim of the crater and slid down next to the young German, who gave a short gasp. Huan and Rhys grabbed his lapels and crawled back towards the rim of the crater. A bullet smacked close to the boys as they heaved themselves over the rim. More bullets smacked against the rim.

'Hang on in there, boyo,' Rhys screamed at the German as they heaved him over the rim. They tumbled down into the crater and lay panting. The German was moaning and grabbing at Rhys' jacket.

'It's alright boyo, calm down. Let's take a look at you.' With care Rhys took the German's hands and slowly pulled them off his jacket. 'Has anyone got any water?' Rhys asked. Huan passed him a canteen and Rhys offered it to the German, who nodded vigorously. Rhys put his hand behind the young lad's head and put the canteen to his lips. As the German drank greedily Rhys looked down at his grey tunic. It was so saturated with blood that it was difficult to see where he had been hit. The German coughed and spluttered.

'*Danke, danke.*'

'It's alright boyo, but we need to sort you out,' Rhys said as he pointed towards the young man's stomach. Rhys gently undid the first button. 'I'll just have a look.'

'*Ja, ja, danke.*'

Rhys moved more quickly and got the tunic open. There was a small hole in the side of the man's stomach. Rhys looked over the side of the man's body and could see a larger exit wound where the man's kidneys should have been. Rhys tried to keep his face neutral. He looked up at the German, who was panting rapidly. Rhys smiled. 'It's fine.' He gave the German a smile. 'Only a scratch, not bad,' Rhys said as he dressed the wounds.

The German turned his head towards Rhys. Tears were flowing freely down his cheeks.

'Hey, no need for all that,' Rhys said as he patted the man's hand. 'You'll be right as rain in the morning.'

'Thank you,' he replied weakly. 'Thank you.'

'Hey, hear that Huan – he speaks English.'

'What's your name?'

'Shultz... Martin Shultz.'

'Well it's good to meet you Martin, I'm Rhys and that's David and Evan,' Rhys said, pointing at the other two soldiers, 'and this is Huan.'

Huan was lying on his side, breathing heavily and holding his leg. Blood was seeping through his fingers.

CHAPTER FORTY

Huan blinked. It was dark; his mind raced as he tried to raise his head. He moved and pain surged through his body. He looked down at his leg, which was covered in a huge bandage.

'Oh God, am I dead?' Huan croaked.

Rhys was sitting next to him smoking a cigarette. 'Not yet boyo, but you've been doing a pretty good impression. You had me worried for a while.'

'What happened?'

'You've been hit in the thigh. It went in the back and came out near your manhood but I don't think it touched it. It would be a bit unlucky if it had hit something that small.' Huan groaned and shook his head. 'It's only a scratch,' Rhys said as he passed him across a cigarette. Huan shook his head.

'Water, I need some water,' he replied.

Rhys passed him a canteen and Huan drank greedily. He lay back. His breath was short and he coughed a few times.

'It's getting cold.'

Rhys took off his coat and wrapped it around his friend. 'Here you go, you'll be fine. We'll be out of here pretty soon. David and Evan have gone back to get some help. I didn't think we could manage you and Martin so they have gone to get a couple of stretchers.'

Huan leaned across to where the German boy was lying. 'How is he?'

'Not good. I'm not sure that he is going to make it. It's a shame; he's a nice lad when you get to know him. He's only seventeen.'

Huan shivered slightly and he could feel sweat on his forehead. 'I told you it was a stupid idea.'

Rhys looked across at Martin, who was quiet. His breathing was shallow. 'He probably doesn't think so. You know, he's not too dissimilar to you and I. He had told the *Hauptfeldwebel* that he was nineteen. That's a recruiting officer you know.'

'I'm not completely stupid!'

'Oh well, anyway. Apparently he had known that he wasn't old enough but merely shrugged and smiled and clasped him on the shoulder. Martin said his mother had been very angry with him but his father had taken him to his local *Bierstube* and bought him his first beer. He learnt English at school, and from his English mother who had met his father in Germany in 1894 when she was employed as a governess to a wealthy German family. He had even been to London in 1908 to meet his mother's family.'

'Is there anything you don't know about him? We're meant to be fighting them, remember, not swapping life stories.'

'I was just passing a bit of time with him. The poor lad's scared stiff.'

'What, and I'm not?' Huan said.

Rhys grabbed his arm. 'I'm sorry. It's my fault I know, but we couldn't have left him there.'

Huan sighed. 'I know.'

*

Huan woke up again. There was an eerie silence. The darkness enveloped him. He couldn't move; his body was stiff. His leg was cold.

'Rhys?'

'I'm here, boyo. You've been asleep. How are you feeling?'

'I need some water,' he croaked.

'Me too boyo, but we haven't got any.'

Huan looked around. 'Where are the others?'

'They went back to get some help, remember?'

Huan thought for a moment. 'What time did they go?'

Rhys blew out his cheeks. 'I dunno. A few hours, maybe longer.'

'And they're not back?'

'I guess not,' Rhys replied. 'You don't think they're lost do you? It wasn't far.'

'Who knows? I can't see sod all.' Huan looked across at Martin, who was breathing quietly but evenly. 'How's Fritz?'

'He's hanging on in there.'

Huan looked up at the moon. He shivered. 'Do you reckon he's up there? Bryn?'

Rhys looked up and thought for a moment. 'You know he is. He'll be laughing at us now. Asking himself how we managed to get ourselves in such a sorry situation.' Rhys smiled as he thought of his friend and sighed. 'You know that we have to get back to tell his mam and da what happened. I can't imagine how they are feeling.'

'What about Cerys?'

Rhys sighed. 'She'll be pretty cut up about it as well. But at least she will be able to move on.' His thoughts turned to Mary and he touched the picture that was in his pocket. 'I'm going to ask Mary to marry me when we get back.'

Huan laughed and patted his friend on the shoulder. 'As long as she doesn't stop you playing rugby you have my permission!'

Rhys smiled and thumped his friend lightly. 'I don't think that either of us will be playing much rugby when we get back. I think we've played our last game.'

'Hey, don't say that. We'll be back next season.'

'You've got a bloody great hole in your leg and will no doubt be off to Blighty, we don't know where John is but he's probably not going to be in a fit state to play and Bryn... well, there will never be another back row like him. I think our playing days are over.'

The friends lay on the earth, looking up at the stars in silence.

'What time is it?'

'That's the third time you've asked me and if you ask me that again, I'm going to put a bullet in your other leg just to shut you up.'

'Well if you told me the answer I might shut up.'

'I dunno but it's late.'

'Or early. We're going to need water before it gets light. How about going over the rim and seeing if the dead Germans have got any? They don't need it.'

'I don't think you should go anywhere at the moment.'

'Not me you idiot, you!'

Rhys looked up at the rim. It had been quiet as a grave for some hours. He could easily slide over the top and be back in a few minutes. He gripped his friend's arm and gave it a reassuring squeeze.

'You stay here then. I'll be back in a tick.'

He looked up and started to crawl up to the rim. He paused just below the rim and steadied his breathing. He could feel the fear rising, his heart was starting to pound. He willed himself to be calm and slowly raised his head above the rim.

It was deathly quiet. There were no flares to light the eerie landscape that had been, a few hours earlier, a field of carnage. There was no sign of life of any sort. Even the rats had retreated to somewhere safer. He slid over the top and took a few minutes to listen to the silence. He edged forward, feeling his way more than seeing. The moon had disappeared over the horizon as a prelude to another day in hell.

He edged forward to where several bodies lay. He reached the first body and turned it over. Rigor mortis had set in and the arms reached up as if they were trying to grab him round the throat. As the body rolled the air trapped in the lungs hissed from the mouth. Rhys gagged and let the body roll back over. As his eyes adjusted to the darkness he could make out bodies all around him. Some lay where they had been hit, doubled over from the knees, others were sprawled in grotesque positions clutching the earth or grasping at an invisible lover, or mother, while others were just pulp and body parts. Rhys sat on the ground staring at the bodies as tears welled up in his eyes and he sat quietly sobbing, surrounded by bodies that he had killed.

CHAPTER FORTY-ONE

Rhys gave a start at the sudden movement. He looked up to see shadows swarming over the rim of the trench. He wasn't afraid; it was the cold that made him shiver, he told himself. He was tired but couldn't sleep, although the night enveloped him. He had spent the last few hours wondering what it was all meant to be about. It was meant to have been a laugh, he thought, and here he was surrounded by death and mutilation. He had wept for his friends but he was now past weeping. He had never really felt anger but now he was enraged. He had never wanted to kill anyone, yet they had made him kill, he thought. He looked across at Martin, who had finally stopped muttering. He didn't hate him; he didn't even know him, yet he had tried to kill him.

'Taylor? Is that you?' the familiar voice of Sergeant Jones hissed through the gloom.

Rhys looked up, startled, from his inertia. 'Sergeant?'

Sergeant Jones looked across the small crater at a broken man hunched forward with his friend in his arms. 'Thank God!' Sergeant Jones cried as he scurried across the crater. Others followed him. He dropped down next to Rhys. 'You alright lad?'

Rhys looked at Sergeant Jones and nodded.

'Take it easy lad, we're here now. How's Jonesey? Do you want me to take a look at him?'

Rhys sniffed and wiped his eyes with his bloodied tunic sleeve. 'No,' he said quietly as his tears rolled down his cheeks. 'There's no need.' He hugged his friend closer to his chest.

Sergeant Jones sighed. 'I'm sorry lad, truly I am. He was one of the best. He deserved better. At least he had you to keep him company.' He coughed and cleared his throat. 'Do you want to give him to me lad, and we'll let him lie down, eh? We'll get him back in and give him a proper burial. You have my word on it.'

Rhys let the sergeant take Huan and one of the other men placed a coat over his body as Rhys sat and stared at his friend.

'Listen lad, I need to worry about the living now before it gets light, so you stay here for a minute okay?'

Rhys nodded.

'Good lad. I'll be back in a minute.'

Sergeant Jones started to issue orders to the section that had followed him in. They broke off to the right and started to dig. Another section dropped over the ridge and made their way across the hollow. Corporal Thomas headed for Sergeant Jones.

'Ted, can you take the left side and link up with C Company if you can? I don't know how far it is so get one of your lads over there and tell them to start digging towards us. Bob's got his lads just to the right here. We'll make a redoubt out of this hole until we can link up with the other two platoons.'

Corporal Thomas looked across at Rhys. 'How's he doing?

'Not particularly good at the moment but he'll be alright. He lost Jonesey and he's taken it quite badly. 'Where's that lad I gave you earlier?'

'He's just coming.'

'Good, I'll go and brief him.'

Corporal Thomas started issuing orders to his men. One man went to the rim of the crater as a sentry while the rest dropped their kit and started to dig.

Rhys sat with his head between his knees. A soldier sat down next to him.

'You alright?' he said.

Rhys looked up and stared. 'Bryn?'

Bryn nodded.

'Oh my God, it's you. It's really you!'

Bryn gave a faint smile. 'I'm afraid so.'

'Oh my God!' Rhys flung his arms around his friend. Bryn grasped his friend. As they hugged Bryn felt Rhys' body start to convulse. There was nothing to say; they just cried. Rhys finally drew breath and wiped his eyes. 'They got Huan. I'm so sorry. It was all my fault.'

'Hey, don't be stupid. It wasn't anyone's fault.'

Through the tears he looked at his friend to make sure that he wasn't dreaming. 'You… you're really here, you're alive.' Rhys looked quizzically at his friend 'Oh my God, you're really here! I don't understand. How did you get here? You haven't run away have you?'

Bryn laughed. 'If I was going to go on the run I would hardly have come this way would I, you idiot?'

'I don't get it.'

'Neither do I but I'm here now and that's what matters.'

'Well, that's great news I suppose,' Rhys said. His shoulders sagged as he looked at Huan's body.

Bryn put his hand on his friend's shoulder. 'I'm sorry I wasn't here with you.'

'We wanted to win, you know, for you. We didn't think we would ever see you again. He would have been so happy to know you are alive. I promised him that we would make it and in the end I let him down.'

'Hey, you haven't let anyone down. From what I heard you two took on the whole German army on your own. You're heroes, the pair of you.'

'I don't feel much like a hero.' Rhys sighed. He was thirsty so I popped over the rim to get some water and when I got back he was gone. I thought he was fine when I left. We were talking about next season and who would be hooking instead of John and who would take your place.'

'Who do you reckon was going to take my place?'

'Taff James.'

'That lightweight scrag? You've got to be joking.'

Rhys laughed. 'I guess so but he is quick,' he said, teasing his friend.

Bryn sat with his arm round Rhys' shoulders. 'I would love to have seen his face when I turned up. He would probably have thought I was a ghost and shit himself.'

'He'd have shit himself alright but that's because he sold all your stuff.'

'He never?'

'Talking of which, how come you're back? Really?'

'I don't know what happened. Really I don't. One minute I'm talking to the padre and getting myself ready to go out to meet my maker and the next thing there is a bit of a hoo-ha and the provost corporal comes into the cell and tells me to fuck off – I was free to go. It was that nasty bastard who smacked me in the gob. He looked really hacked off. Then this captain got the guard to give me my kit and he said that the general had overturned the court's decision. He took me outside to a wagon and told me to report back to the battalion. Next minute we're on our way here.'

'So does that mean you're back for good?'

'I guess so.'

Sergeant Jones crouched down next to the boys. 'You lads okay?'

Bryn nodded. 'As right as we'll ever be, Sergeant.'

'We've only got an hour at most. The others are digging a new position so we can defend this crater, which we still own thanks to you, Taylor. The others will be digging a new trench towards us but it will take a few hours yet so we need to hold this hole till they can get to us. Do you boys want to grab a stretcher and take Jonesey back to the battalion?'

Rhys looked at Bryn, who nodded.

'Sergeant, can you spare a couple of blokes to get the German back to the Aid Post as well? He's pretty badly hurt.'

'There's no point in wasting any time on him; he's dead.'

Rhys looked at the body, which had been quiet for some time. 'Can we take him anyway, Sergeant?'

CHAPTER FORTY-TWO

The sun was trying to burn through the steel grey mist that was intent on blocking out the warmth of a new day. The battalion had marched from their billets during the last of the night. They were weary but the spirit was still willing. Some of the men had minor wounds that had been bandaged at the Regimental Aid Post but they weren't going to miss the parade. Those who could took a bit of time to clean their kit. They marched along as if they were on parade at the barracks in Wrexham.

They had formed up in a hollow square; A Company formed the right guard, C Company the left guard and B Company the base. The battalion had lost so many men that D Company had been temporarily disbanded. There weren't enough officers and senior ranks to form a coherent fighting body of men. Those who were left were slotted into the other three companies. Opposite B Company and completing the square was a pyramid of drums. The battalion's drummers had marched on to a single drumbeat, halted and laid the drums on the ground in a small pyramid. One of the sergeant majors had laid the Union Flag on one side of the drums and *Y Ddraig Goch* on the other. The men were standing easy but there was none of the normal humour and banter. Many of them smoked quietly whilst others raised their faces to the heavens.

As the commanding officer approached, the regimental sergeant major brought the battalion to attention. A padre, dressed for business in his white surplice over his khaki, walked forward with the commanding officer but broke off to stand in front of the drums whilst the commanding officer stood in the centre of the square.

Bryn looked at the padre and smiled at the familiar face. Padre Hughes said a few words of introduction, most of which were carried away with the slight breeze. The wind was starting to whip the mist into menacing clouds that reminded the men of the acrid smoke of the battlefield. It mattered not a jot to the assembled men that they couldn't hear; they didn't need words to remind them of why they were there or what had passed; they only had to close their eyes to relive it all again. There was a sudden burst of sun as it finally broke through the mist just as the padre finished speaking. The men were not slow to notice.

The padre nodded to the regimental sergeant major, who was stood by the twelve men who had volunteered to carry the bodies of their fallen comrades. When he asked for volunteers the regimental sergeant major had not been surprised when the whole battalion had stepped forward. In the end he had left it to his company sergeant majors to select soldiers who had a personal reason to help bury the dead. Fifteen bodies had been wrapped in hessian sacking and placed on the ground under a tarpaulin. Their identification disks had been sewn into the material at the top end of each sack.

The previous afternoon volunteers had dug a trench six feet wide and twenty-seven feet long with a shallow slope at one end so that the bearer parties could walk in easily with the bodies. The regimental sergeant major had chosen a spot a little way from the village in an area that had been untouched by shells. He wondered, as he looked at it, whether it would still be untouched at the same time next week or month, and he could but hope that the bodies would lie undisturbed. It was a small meadow covered in little yellow flowers that he thought were buttercups or daisies – he didn't really know but they had reminded him of home. The soldiers had mostly worked in silence, and no one complained.

The regimental sergeant major nodded and the bodies were brought forward one by one, each draped in the Welsh flag. They were placed in the trench in no particular order. 'They fought together as officers and soldiers, they died together as men and will be buried as one,' the commanding officer had ordered.

Bryn and Rhys were at the front corners of the third body. Sergeant Jones and Corporal Thomas held the back two corners. As they approached the grave the padre read out the name of the deceased: 'Private Huan Jones, B Company, the Royal Welsh Fusiliers.' Tears trickled down Rhys' cheeks as they placed the body next to Corporal Parson. The four soldiers stood straight, saluted and returned to pick up another body.

*

The burial party and most of the battalion had gone. A few men remained to think about lost friends, others just wanted to remain where it was quiet. The commanding officer had stood the men down until mid-afternoon.

Bryn and Rhys stood at the head of the grave. It was silent but for the distant rumbling that could so easily have been thunder but for the clear blue sky.

'Hello Bryn,' Padre Hughes said as he sidled up to the boys.

Bryn saluted. 'Hello, sir, how are you?'

'I'm very well thank you. And you must be Taylor?' he said, looking at Rhys as he extended his hand. Rhys was momentarily confused, then he took it and shook it firmly.

'I certainly am, sir. Pleased to meet you.'

'The pleasure is mine I can assure you. I have heard a lot about you.'

Rhys looked at Bryn and smiled. 'All bad, no doubt?'

'Absolutely nothing else,' the padre said with a smile. They looked at the bodies lying neatly in the grave. 'It never gets any easier, no matter how many souls you see resting.' Rhys and Bryn nodded as they stared at the graves. 'I am very sorry for your loss, both of you. I know that Private Jones was one of your closest friends. If it is any consolation he is in a good place. It might not feel like it just now but he died a very brave man, fighting for good. There can be nothing more selfless than helping to save one's enemy. It was a very brave act of which you and his family can be rightly proud. And I know it will have been a great consolation to him to have had you with him, Taylor, to ease his passing.' Rhys nodded as tears started to prick the corners of his eyes again. He wiped his eyes with his sleeve.

Bryn put his arm around Rhys' shoulder. 'He was one of the best friends anyone could ever have. We were lucky that he was our friend.'

'Friendship like yours is rare and special. The best you can do now is to look after each other. I am sure that you will be able, in time, to offer his family some comfort too. I hope they will also take some comfort knowing that his bravery has been recognised.'

Rhys blew his nose and nodded.

'Talking of which, I heard that Private Jones wasn't the only one who has been commended for his bravery,' the padre said, nodding at Rhys with his eyebrows raised. 'I believe that you have also been awarded the military medal, Taylor?'

Rhys blushed. He had been paraded in front of the commanding officer the previous day. The regimental sergeant major had given nothing away; his normal scowl was etched onto his face. He had double-marched Rhys into the commanding officer's office with the same vigour as an accused man.

The commanding officer looked up and smiled as he explained why he had written a citation with a recommendation for a military medal. 'Selfless disregard for the safety of himself to save his comrades and an enemy soldier… courage in the face of the enemy… courageous leadership that prevented a breakthrough…'

Rhys had no idea what to say; he tried to explain to the commanding officer that it had been a mistake and that they had only charged because they didn't know what else to do. He explained that he had tried to help Huan and the German because he couldn't think of anything else to do. In the end the regimental sergeant major told him to shut up, turn about and fuck off… very quickly!

The padre and Bryn laughed.

'I think that there is a bit of fake modesty, Taylor,' the padre said. 'It doesn't matter why you did it; the point is that you did do it. Have you managed to locate your other friend… John?' he asked. Rhys and Bryn nodded and looked at each other.

'He lost a leg,' Bryn said. 'He'll mend though, in time.'

The padre looked at them both. 'Yes he will, particularly with good friends like you around him.'

'He'll not be playing rugby again though, will he? Who's going to hook now?' Rhys said.

'I am quite sure that you will find someone else, someone who you can train and nurture.'

'No, I think our playing days are over, Padre. It could never be the same, not after this.'

'Give it time,' the padre said. 'You might be surprised at how things turn out. There will be a whole generation of young men, not unlike yourselves, who will have the same youthful spirit. And they will need expert coaching. How else are you ever going to beat England?'

Bryn and Rhys looked at each other and laughed. 'The real enemy!' Bryn said.

The padre shared the joke and looked around as a group of soldiers started to fill in the grave. 'Anyway, I had better get on. It's good to see you in better circumstances, Private Tallent, and do try and stay out of trouble.'

Bryn smiled back. 'I will, sir… Thank you, sir, for everything that you did.'

'I'm not sure I did a great deal.'

Bryn looked at him and grinned. 'I think you did, sir.'

The padre shrugged. 'I did what I could but I certainly can't take all the credit, in fact I had very little to do with it. Much of the credit has to go to Lieutenant George, God rest his soul,' he said as he crossed himself. 'He certainly believed in you and believed in doing the right thing even if it meant putting his own reputation at risk.'

'I'm not sure what you mean,' Bryn said.

'As I understand it, Lieutenant George went to see the commanding officer just before the battalion left for the front line. He explained what Taylor and Jones had found out at the hospital about your friend John and Sergeant Price. He tried to convince the commanding officer that there was sufficient doubt to warrant a stay of execution, even for a day or two to verify the facts. He suggested to the commanding officer that it could save the reputation of the regiment.' He paused as he let this sink in, 'You know after the court martial his reputation had been damaged. Some of the other officers were blaming him for what had happened but despite this, he went to see the commanding officer with a very strong risk of being sacked.'

Bryn looked at the ground and shuffled his feet. 'It's a shame he's not here. I would like to have thanked him. He was a good officer.'

'He was, and I believe that his spirit is still with us, if not his body.'

'Blimey I can't believe that the commanding officer changed his mind. He seemed pretty cross when I last saw him.'

'Well it wasn't the commanding officer who stopped the execution, even he doesn't have that much power, but don't tell him that or he'll be court-martialling me. No, it turns out that he was sufficiently concerned about what Lieutenant George had said so he rang Headquarters and spoke to the general. Of course the general thought that he had gone mad and was losing his bottle. Told him that it was too late and to get on with it.'

Bryn raised his eyebrows and shook his head. 'I don't get it, who did stop it?' he asked.

The padre couldn't help looking to the heavens as he gave a wry smile. It was almost a smug grin.

'It was you! I knew it was.'

'Crikey, no. I can't claim the credit there either. The general doesn't listen to the padre on military matters. All I did was find the officer who had been sent to the hospital to take John's statement and I had a fatherly chat with him.' The padre balled his fist and smashed it into his other hand. The boys laughed. 'It's amazing what some people will do when a padre threatens to punch them on the nose! He is not a bad chap and I'm sure he thought he was doing the right thing but it turns out that the officer wrote the statement based on what he had been told by the prosecuting officer, rather than John. And that, as they say, is between you and I and no one else, you understand?' The boys nodded in agreement.

'But what about Sergeant Price? Is he still alive or not?' Rhys asked.

'Indeed he is. He is currently recuperating at one of those hospital camps near the sea. Some friends of mine helped me track him down and I spoke to him on the telephone and got him to send a telegram to Headquarters. He is doing very well. His telegram landed on the desk of another very good friend of mine, who was thankfully in an influential position to advise the general. He did the rest, so to speak.'

Bryn blew out his cheeks and shook his head. 'Duw, it's all a bit complicated, not that I'm complaining like. It was a close call, I have to say.'

'Far too close to be funny,' Rhys added.

'The important thing is that you are both still here and I have no doubt that you will manage to cause enough trouble for a whole battalion. Just don't get caught!' the padre said with a smile.

'What will happen to Lieutenant Symonds, sir?' Bryn asked.

'I hope they catch the bastard and put him up against the wall,' Rhys said and received an admonishing stare from the padre. 'Sorry, sir.'

'From what I hear, not a lot.'

'What?' Bryn gasped.

'I am reliably informed that Lieutenant Symonds has gone missing. It seems that he got on the ship to go back to Blighty and didn't get off. At least he didn't get off when the ship docked.'

Rhys looked puzzled. 'You mean he jumped overboard, killed himself?'

'Possibly. Perhaps the shame was too much for him to bear,' the padre suggested.

Bryn looked thoughtful. 'No, not that one; he's too bad a bloke to do something honourable.'

'Well that's all I know, I'm afraid. Now you must excuse me; I must get on. God bless you both,' he said with a smile.

They shook hands and the boys saluted. The padre gave them his best salute in response. Bryn mumbled a few words of thanks but nothing he could say seemed enough.

The boys watched the young padre wander away across the meadow as the breeze blew gently over the sea of little yellow flowers. The men were making swift work of covering the bodies, blotting out the sunshine for the last time. The padre stopped to talk to the burial party for a couple of minutes and then continued on his way. The commanding officer was chatting with another officer as the padre joined them. They all shook hands and chatted for a few minutes.

'Who's that talking to the colonel, then?' Rhys asked his friend.

'I dunno, his face is familiar though. I think that's the officer who got me out of jail. What was his name now? *Oh crikey*, it was all such a rush I can't remember. I wonder what he's doing here?'

'Perhaps he's come to take you back,' Rhys said without thinking.

'I bloody hope not.'

'Course he hasn't you idiot. The padre just said what had happened, didn't he? You are well and truly in the clear my friend.

'What are you two girls gossiping about now?' came the dulcet tones of Sergeant Jones.

'Sergeant, who's that talking to the commanding officer?' Bryn asked.

'Captain Richardson. He's our new company commander. He's just been transferred from Headquarters.'

'I bet he's at bit miffed at being sent to the front,' Rhys quipped. 'No doubt I shall have to break him in.'

Bryn punched his friend on the arm. 'Who do you think you are now, with your bloody medal?'

'What? I'm only saying he's probably never been to the front and will need my guidance.'

*

It was late afternoon when Rhys and Bryn returned to stand at the head of the grave. They stood in silence for a while as the sun warmed their backs and dried the freshly dug earth. The regimental sergeant major had chosen the spot well. The meadow was as untouched by the war as it was by the farmer. Where the crops had once been sown and reaped wild flowers now swayed gently in the breeze. A pair of swallows swooped overhead, which made Rhys look up. The cloudless sky went through a spectrum of light blue to dark blue. The sky seemed so deep that Rhys thought he could almost see the heavens.

'Do you think he's up there?'

Bryn looked up and thought for a moment. 'More likely down there.'

'Oh, you're not still moaning about your kit are you? He was going to send the money to your folks you know.'

'Well that's something I suppose… hang on, where's the money now?'

Rhys thought for a moment and looked down at the grave. 'In his tunic pocket.'

Rhys started laughing and then Bryn. 'Whoever said, "You can't take it with you" had never met Huan. He'll probably need the money to buy himself into the first team, wherever he is.'

'Do you reckon that if God had a team it would beat Wales?' Rhys asked.

'If God had a team it would be Wales.'

Rhys thought for a moment. 'In that case I hope he makes it into the first team.' He put his hand in his pocket and drew out the letters that Bryn had given him.

'Do you want these back or shall I keep them for next time?'

'I'm bloody sure there won't be a next time.'

'Well I dunno, you have a track record now boyo…'

Bryn grabbed the letters from his friend and looked at them for a moment.

'No, there won't ever be a next time,' he said as he stuffed the letters into his pocket.

ACKNOWLEDGEMENTS

With grateful thanks to Helen, Sharon, Karen and Jennie for their help, belief and support.

Front cover photograph – Corporal Thomas Evans.

AUTHOR'S NOTE

This book is a work of fiction; it's not true, it didn't happen... or at least not to the characters in the book who are figments of my imagination, and any resemblance, superficial or otherwise, to any soldier or officer of the Royal Welsh Fusiliers during the First World War is entirely coincidental.

However, the Second Battalion, His Majesty's Twenty-third of Foot, the Royal Welsh Fusiliers was a real battalion (recently amalgamated and now known as the Royal Welsh) and served during the war with great distinction. They have five battle honours on their Sovereign's Colour: Marne 1914, Somme 1916, Ypres 1917, Somme 1918 and the Hindenburg Line. The battalion took part in many more actions during the war; eighty-three officers were awarded medals, for gallantry or otherwise, and one hundred and seventy-eight other ranks. There are a number of excellent books that describe in detail the actions that the battalion took part in and which give a valuable insight into the daily life of the officers and soldiers. I have highlighted three books below, not as a bibliography, but to point you in the right direction should you wish to expand your knowledge of the Second Battalion, the Royal Welsh Fusiliers.

I have tried where possible to place the story in the right place at the right time. Bois-Grenier is a small village just to the south of Armentières. It can be seen today much as it was in 1915, albeit in a slightly better state. I have described the trenches as I believe them to have been and it is still possible to trace their location on the ground today.

The spelling of 'Welsh' may confuse readers. In its early history the regiment was known as King's Own Royal Regiment of Welch Fusiliers but this changed over time and by 1815 the regiment was referred to as the Royal Welsh Fusiliers. This continued throughout the First World War until it until it changed back to Welch in 1920.

FURTHER READING

The War the Infantry Knew 1914–1919, Captain J. C. Dunn. An outstanding collaborative narrative of the battalion's history during the war.

Old Soldiers Never Die, Private Frank Richards DCM, MM. Private Richards was one of the few soldiers to have served in the battalion throughout the war. His book provides a soldier's perspective of the life in and out of the trenches. A classic.

Duty Done, David Langly. The nuts, bolts, facts and figures that underpin the history of the Second Battalion. An invaluable source of reference.